The Courtier of Versailles

The Courtier of Versailles

Donna Russo Morin

Published 2021 by Next Chapter
Cover art by Cover Mint
Mass Market Paperback Edition

Praise for THE COURTIER OF VERSAILLES

(previously titled THE COURTIER'S SECRET)
Finalist: National Readers' Choice Award
Winner: Best First Book, RWI

"Russo Morin fills her tale with maidens, mistresses and musketeers mired in intrigue...supplying lots of action as Jeanne goes through quick costume changes, one minute a virgin about to be raped, another a daring do-gooder, rapier in hand."

-Publishers Weekly

"A novel as opulent and sparkling as Louis XIV's court and as filled with intrigue, passion and excitement as a novel by Dumas... a feast for the senses."

-RT Book Review

“Absolutely enchanting…refreshing and utterly exciting!”

-Front Street Reviews

“A wonderfully spun gem of a story.”

-Jenny Salyers, Armchair Reviews

"The author has a very good knowledge of the time period, as well as a gift for prose. I like her writing style and her vocabulary. I couldn’t put it down. There are several twists I wasn’t expecting and that is rare in books I read!”

-Historical-fiction.com

"Filled with vivid imagery, delightful dialogue, and highly spirited characters, this page turner kept me up long into the night. Ms. Russo Morin’s writing style is as smooth as fine cognac, while the story’s plot rolls along like thunder across the French countryside."

-Steven Manchester, Author, The Unexpected Storm and Pressed Pennies

"Exquisitely done… fabulous historical research… unforgettable characters!

-Kwips and Kritiques

"Magnifique!! Donna Russo Morin's debut novel is a delightful dance through the decadent Louis XIV era. The Courtier's Secret is intoxicating! Russo Morin has done her homework-the story moves quickly as the reader zips through this well researched time period."

-Robin Kall, host Reading With Robin 920 WHJJ

Other works by Donna Russo Morin

Gilded Summers
The Flâmes of Florence: Da Vinci's Disciples Book Three
The Competition: Da Vinci's Disciples Book Two
Portrait of a Conspiracy: Da Vinci's Disciples Book One
The King's Agent
To Serve a King
The Secret of the Glass

To my mother Barbara, my son Devon, my daughter-in-law Celia,
Erin, Megan, Billy, and Spencer…
We will always have Versailles

Dramatis Personae

*denotes historical character

JEANNE YVETTE MAS DU BOIS: Born in Paris on May 2, 1665. Daughter of Gaston Louis du Bois, the Comte de Moreuil and Adelaide Lomenie du Mas.

JULES HENRI DU MAS: Born 1643. Brother to Adelaide Lomenie du Mas, second son of the Comte de Clemont. Serves as one of the King's fencing masters. Married to Berthe de Grange. Father to two daughters.

*LOUIS XIV (1638-1715): The Sun King. Inherited the crown at the age of four from his father, Louis XIII, in 1643.

GASTON LOUIS DU BOIS: The Comte de Moreuil, born 1639. Serves as a minor member of the *Counseil d'État* as a finance minister.

ADELAIDE LOMENIE MAS DU BOIS: The Comtesse de Moreuil, born 1645. A member of the *Bas Bleu*, a society of intellectual, educated women.

RAOL LEON MAS DU BOIS: Born 1663. Former soldier and Musketeer. Overseer of the Du Bois estates and instructor at a regional academy.

LYNETTE LA MARECHAL: Born 1664. Daughter of the Duc du Vermorel. Best friend to Jeanne du Bois.

OLYMPE DE CINQUE-MARS: Born 1665. Daughter of the Marquis de Solignac. Best friend to Jeanne du Bois.

*FRANÇOIS-ATHÉNAÏS DE ROCHECHOUAART DEMORTEMART, MARQUISE DE MONTESPAN (1641-1707): Daughter of the great house of Mortemart. Educated at the Convent of St. Mary at Saintes. Married to Louis-Henri de Pardaillan de Gondrin, Marquis de Montespan, a minor Gascon noble with whom she bore two children. Became mistress of Louis XIV in 1667.

*FRANÇOIS SCARRON (1635-1719): Born in a jail, granddaughter to a Huguenot hero. Befriended by the Marquise de Montespan, she became the governess to the children of Louis XIV and Athénais.

*MONSIEUR PHILIPPE, DUC D'ORLEANS (1640-1701): Only brother to Louis XIV.

PERCY DE POLIGNAC: Born 1663. Son of the Baron L'Haire.

HENRI BOUCHER D'AUBIGNE: Born 1663. Son of the Baron d'Aubigne, former soldier, current Musketeer.

ANTOINE DE LA FERTE: Born 1662. Best friend to Henri d'Aubigne. Musketeer.

GERARD DE GRAMONT: Born 1661. Friend to Henri d'Aubigne. Musketeer.

LAURENT DE VENTADOUR: Born 1663. Friend to Henri d'Aubigne. Musketeer.

BERNADETTE FANTINE MAS DU BOIS: Born 1667. Jeanne's sister.

*FRANÇOIS MICHEL LE TELLIER, MARQUIS DE LOUVOIS (1639-1691): Minister of War under Louis XIV.

*MARIE-THÉRÈSE D'AUTRICHE (1668-1683): Daughter of Philip IV of Spain. Queen Consort of France. Married to Louis XIV in 1660.

~One~

"Are you ready, *mon cher*?" Uncle Jules asked, voice obscured by his protective headgear.

Jeanne nodded; her own helmet—nothing more than a tin plate with peepholes—wobbling precariously.

Jules raised his sword before his face, aiming it straight up like a finger pointing to the heavens, and bowed slightly but respectfully to his niece, the graceful move revealing a glimpse of the swordsman's prowess.

Jeanne mirrored her uncle's salute and waited, willing her lungs to do their job, to breathe deeply in and out, storing air for what was to come.

"*En garde*!" Jules barked.

Jeanne dropped into a crouch, half-extending her sword arm, protecting the waist with the elbow and the chest with the wrist. Her left arm hung high in the air behind her head, the forearm gracefully bent and the wrist curled, a counter-weight.

Quadricep muscles twitching with strain as they bore the brunt of her weight, biceps and triceps burning with rage at the repetition of the position for the tenth time that morning.

Her own breathing echoed back to her as it bounced against the crudely constructed helmet; the scent of the peach she'd eaten that morning still clinging to each vapor.

Jules moved. Left foot over right. Jeanne mirrored his pattern.

"Come at me, girl. Come and get me," Jules bellowed at her, teasing her with the tip of his fine rapier.

Jeanne moved, a sequence of aggressive footwork.

"*Bon, bon,* good, good," her uncle encouraged. "Now… advance!"

Lifting the toes of her front foot, she curled it up to slip both feet forward.

"Advance!"

Same move again.

"Advance, advance!"

Again. Twice. First step, a quick one.

"*Bon.* Now… get ready."

Sweat dripped down her forehead, burned as it rolled into her eyes. She dare not spare a second to wipe it away. More trickled down her spine, annoying her blood-engorged skin. She dare not take a moment to blot it.

Her forearm burned red hot, muscles controlling her grip on the pommel refusing to give way.

Another parry, another thrust. She moved two steps closer.

The clangs of sword meeting sword echoed as the thin rapiers came together time and time again, reverberating in the hollow, stone chamber. Jeanne panted now.

The old empty chamber in the basement of the grand chateau of Versailles became a void in time and place, their bodies and grunts of exertion all that existed.

Jeanne listened, as vital to swordsmanship as their grip on the pommel. She listened and waited, parrying to keep her uncle moving. There it came. Just the right *sshing* that spoke a good slash…a grunt from her uncle. She had him on the defense. If he grunted more than she it was a good day; today could be such a day.

A feint, a parry…she pressed him almost to the wall.

Today, she thought. *Maybe today shall be the day of my victory…for I am a Musketeer.*

The smallest grin tickled the corner of her mouth. Parry, thrust, lun—

The chapel bells gonged; their vibration rose through the soles of their thin, flexible shoes.

The combatants froze.

"Is that—," Jeanne began.

"The chapel calls!" her uncle cried, pulling off his headgear, his white mantle of hair falling upon his shoulders.

"I am lost!" Jeanne threw off her helmet, chocolate brown hair spilling out as gear hit stone with a thud.

Jeanne tossed her sword to Jules who caught it deftly by its grip.

"Our secret, *mon uncle*?"

Her uncle tossed his niece a tart glance. "You need ask?"

With a small grin and a slight shake of the head, Jeanne bolted for the door.

"Tomorrow, dear man, *oui*?"

"Of course, *ma petite*." Jules shooed her with a wave and a fond smile at her quickly retreating back.

Down the hall and around two corners, up one flight of stairs and down three hallways, to the closest latrine Jeanne ran. From the basement of the main building—the small one that had been Louis XIII's hunting lodge—to the back side of the south wing—just one of the many expansions made by his son—she flew. She loosened the small ribbons and strings holding her costume together as she ran, impelled by long strides of well-trained legs.

Jeanne Yvette Mas du Bois thanked the good Lord she'd spent much of her childhood in the labyrinth of a castle; she knew every winding inch of it. Yet she cursed it as she ran. It was 1682, for goodness sake. Two decades of improvements and still very few privies and most on one side of the massive palace.

In the abandoned corridor, she reached the water closet, her water closet. She slammed the door behind her and instantly felt trapped; no more than a box in the wall containing a wooden bench with a crudely covered hole from which emanated the foulest of odors, her chest heaved as she gasped for breath depleted by the long and convoluted trek. She breathed only through her mouth.

Dropping to her knees, she pulled up two boards from the crude wood flooring, retrieving the bundle of clothing sequestered beneath. Sloughing off the old knickers, shirt, and bucket-top boots that once belonged to her brother, she bundled and tied them, stashing them where the other clothes had been, the appropriate if rumpled morning gown.

"Millions of *louis* he spends on Aubusson and Gobelin tapestries," Jeanne mumbled as she began to dress herself, "but hardly enough privies for half the people living here. A glorious sink hole, indeed."

Uncounted were the drunken nobles or lost visiting diplomats urinating, defecating, or vomiting in any private corner of the mazelike corridors, staircases, or window embrasures, their struggle to reach a privy or *chaise percée* in time proving fruitless.

The drunks were the worst, their inebriated state dissipating any inhibitions for public elimination. They behaved quite raucously about the whole endeavor. Their obnoxious laughter disgusted Jeanne as did their hygiene habits.

Yet, somehow, the chateau remained clean; accidents disappeared quickly at the hands of the thousands of servants indentured for just such service. Louis XIV insisted Versailles, now *La Maison du Roi* as well as the seat of France's government, be kept immaculate. An adult response to the squalor he had lived in as a child in the Louvre.

Almost dressed, the feminine and frilly stockings and undergarments of a wealthy young noblewoman soaked up the sweat still flowing from her pores, stuck to her skin. There was naught to be done; to not appear, as she must every morning, at the King's Chapel Royale, would be to provoke certain misfortune, and there remained but a minute since the first gong of the bell.

Still lacing up the front of her bodice, Jeanne kicked open the door, banging it with a crash against the hallway wall. In the empty corridor, she ran; the hard heels of her bow-festooned shoes clanked against the hardwood floor, the lacy fontange on her head bounced with each step.

Up two flights of turning stairs, she emerged next to the Hall of Battles on the ground floor and burst through the door leading out into the crowded courtyard. She blundered about, instantly blinded by the blazing light of the hot August sun reflecting off the white marble outer walls of the chateau.

It would be unseemly to run; her feet fluttered in the fastest walk possible. Upon her face a practiced smile firmly in place as she returned greetings to the multitude whose faces were but a blur. Colors and shimmers, but not a one did she see.

Back into the building, the north wing now, through the small corridor filled with courtiers and commoners–there for a glimpse of their sovereign–quickly to the door of the chapel.

Mon Dieu! The words a scream in her head.

The King led the precisely contrived procession up the aisle; the ducs, marquises, and comtes already across the threshold, the barons poised to enter.

She had missed her place! She—the daughter of the Comte de Moreuil, Gaston du Bois—must enter before the barons. To break this code of conduct, one imposed by the King himself, could bring the harshest of punishments.

She must do what she must. Wringing her hands, Jeanne bit her bottom lip, lowered large chocolate brown eyes, dipped her head, and pushed past the barons and their wives, tight-lipped women scowling at her.

If she had not already been, Jeanne would now be the juiciest tidbit on the tip of every wagging tongue today; gossip the second most preferred pastime of the courtiers, a short step behind currying favor.

She slipped into the pew where her mother and father sat; grateful the Comtesse de Cordierer and her daughter separated them.

The King, now firmly ensconced in his tribune, took no notice of her late arrival; the same could not be said for her father. She dared not turn or glance in his direction for the ire in his eye would surely burn her to the bone. The heated waves of his wrath found her.

Mademoiselle le Thibault, the comtesse's daughter stared rudely at them, wide eyes bouncing between Jeanne and her father, a spectator at a highly entertaining game.

Jeanne berated herself for giving one such as this fodder for her lurid mill. She did her best to still her twitching hands and shuddering foot. Taking deep breaths of incense-laden air, Jeanne calmed.

Father Herbert, the parish priest of Versailles, took his place at the balustrade font, vestments of mulberry tenting over his vast paunch, tall miter giving the false impression of height. Raising his arms wide as if to embrace the entire congregation, he launched into his sermon with a booming voice.

"The people of the noble land of France must thank God and the King for the greatness in which we reside. It is by their power and by their hand that we grow and prosper with such exuberance."

He made no reference to the pope or to Rome; no priest serving the crown had any desire to spend the rest of his days in the Bastille. This sermon would serve no more purpose than to praise the King. Louis championed Gallicanism, the purely French movement whose intent meant to diminish papal authority and increase the power of the state, specifically the power of the Sun King.

"Look around you, I pray, for in these very walls is built the power of our great sovereign."

The chapel was a paradigm of Louis' affluent dominance: the gilded scrollwork, the beautiful caryatids and atlantes sculptures, and, most especially, the altar painting. Almost as long as the wall upon which it hung, *Meal at the House of Simon the Pharisee* had come as a gift from the Republic of Venice in 1664, a testament to how far reaching Louis' fingers of power stretched.

Louis XIV sat tall in his velvet seat, large dark eyes raised innocently to the heavens, lids fluttering prettily now and then as the priest spoke so eloquently of him, the shy smile upon his face that of a child being praised. He craved such praise like a starving child, like the many starving who lived in his realm, craving food, any food. No matter the truth of them, words of homage thrilled him.

The expounding priest banged his fisted hand on the pulpit before him, voice rising to the heights of a screech.

"We must do whatever our King and our Lord ask, for to serve them is our only purpose in this mortal life!" The flush on Father Herbert's face spread and darkened like the culmination of his oration.

Louis slumped in his high-backed armchair, shoulders slumping, clearly disappointed the sycophantic sermon ended. He lowered his face, the self-deprecating grin slipping off the corners of his mouth.

Jeanne's hands, poised peacefully upon her lap during the sermon, began to wring once more like a washerwoman wrings a drenched cloth. Silently she cursed the brevity of the thirty-minute service. With a sidelong glance down the pew, she dared a glimpse of her father's countenance.

Like the priest's, his face burned crimson as if all the blood in his body congealed beneath is thin, white carapace. From brow to the hairline of his white wig, a dark vein pulsed with each rapid beat of his heart.

A growl rose from Jeanne's stomach, the painful knot of foreboding twisting within her. She knew what lay in store, knew with assurance it would be terrible, for she had suffered her father's wrath many times, too many. She couldn't avoid the coming storm, but she could try to outrun it.

Jeanne gathered her wide, long skirts in her fists, rushing from the pew, and jostling the Duchess standing in the aisle, standing in her way. The prim, powdered woman squeaked in protest. A quick glance over her shoulder revealed Jeanne's father pushing passed her mother, the Comtesse, and her daughter, meaningless obstacles between him and his prey.

Jeanne hurried ever faster, attempting a decorous if frantic escape, but her father would not be so deprived. He came upon her with wheeling strides of his short legs and grabbed her roughly by the arm. He spoke not a word as he flew down the aisle, teeth bared in an angry snarl disguised as a smile, his daughter in tow. Jeanne curled her spine, slumping, eliminating the inch she rose above her father, an inch forever infuriating him. He yanked her along like a recalcitrant two-year-old, her humiliation mounting as they careened through hundreds of shocked courtiers.

Since May, and the court's official move to Versailles, the population had grown exponentially; close to ten thousand people now lived within the resplendent walls. The vast but crowded hallways forever crammed with courtiers, commoners, and peasants, some hoping for a chance to petition the King, others merely hoping for a glimpse of him. Past all these speculative, scrutinizing eyes, Gaston pulled Jeanne like a dog on a leach.

Through one gilded and jeweled salon after another, Gaston marched swiftly along, feet pounding on the marble and dark wood floors below his feet as if, with each step, he crushed them or his daughter. The long curls of his high wig flew out like a banner proclaiming his importance. Jeanne ran to keep up, her heavy skirts and the many layers of taffeta and silk beneath making it difficult to take long strides.

Gaston's grip on his daughter's arm tightened as they strode through the palace. The clutch of his hand squeezed her muscles, flattening them to a thin layer of flesh. The pressure of each finger like a dagger threatening to puncture.

Her father panted, unused to such physical strain. Her own lungs burned. Encased in the tightly tied bodice, she could take only short, shallow gulps of air; she longed for the unrestraint of her dueling clothes.

With but a few more steps they rushed through the Buffet Room and onto the staircase leading to the uppermost floor. At the top, the trapped August heat smacked them. Père yanked her down the long corridor to the entrance of their suite. Wrenching the door open to the dark, low-ceilinged hallway, Gaston launched his wretched daughter from him. Jeanne landed on the small foyer's floor on her knees.

Jeanne turned a fearful glance up to her father, loosened, disheveled hair falling across her face. She rubbed her arm where the pressing of his gouging fingers still panged.

"To your room," Gaston growled the rumble of a wild animal.

"*Oui, mon Père*," Jeanne whispered, scrambling to her feet.

Her legs tangled in the folds of her skirts. She tumbled once more to her knees, the pain of breaking blood vessels stabbed her. Afraid to look at her father, she tried again, this time making it to her feet. With three quick steps, she made it to her bedroom, entered the room, and closed the door. With backward steps, she reached the bed she shared with her sister and fell upon it, gaze glued to the door, expecting her father to crash through it at any moment.

Her hands would not—could not—be stilled; she watched them shake as if they belonged to someone else. Jeanne pulled her legs up, wrapped her arms around them, and curled her body into a ball as if to stave off the assault she knew would come. Slowly rocking on her curved buttocks, she waited and prayed.

* * *

He paced back and forth in the small room that served the Du Bois family as salon, study, and dining room, crossing the carpet of maroon and gold, arms flaiying the air about his head. Adelaide Lomenie Mas du Bois sat as still as possible on the small upholstered chair, silently suffering her husband's outburst. Adelaide kept her mouth shut, lips paling with the tight clasp. To open them would be to beg to suffer much worse than a verbal lashing.

"Is it not enough that she should return here in shame, but that she should flaunt her misbehavior in front of the entire court? It is an outrage!" Gaston's face flowed purple, almost black under the white, powdered wig; spittle flew from his mouth with each venomous word. "I should have begged Mère-révérend Robiquet to keep her at the convent, or begged the King for the money to keep her there."

Jeanne heard every word, every growl, her father uttered; the almost paper-thin walls did nothing to contain the verbal onslaught. She grimaced, the chagrin and terror of returning to Versailles still fresh, still caused sleepless nights and the urge to run somewhere, anywhere. It was but a few days ago since she had been turned out of the convent where she had spent seven years—seven years of living in hell. The salivating tongues of the courtiers dripped with delight at the scandal of the dreadful behavior that had prompted her removal, humiliating her father even more.

"She is a disgrace to my family, to me, to the King. The whole world knows my daughter has the tongue of the devil speaking to the nuns as if she were their equal, or worse, their better. Now they know she has the soul of the devil as well. They see for themselves that her behavior is no better than the filthy peasants who beg at the gates."

"She is but young, Gaston," Adelaide murmured, a timid whisper, golden-eyed gaze holding fast upon the tight knot that was her hands in her lap.

Gaston whirled on his wife, piercing her with his steely, black-eyed gaze.

"Young? No! She is impudent and unruly, completely out of control. Bernadette is two years her junior and yet she is the perfect young woman, gracious and polite, affable and charming. She will be married and gone within the year." Gaston threw one hand upward toward the door as if pushing his youngest daughter through it.

The mention of her sister sent Jeanne's eyes to rolling. Her own words for the blond, plump beauty differed greatly. She loved Bernadette dearly but her sister's obsequiousness, her blindingly obedient behavior infuriated Jeanne. A fury only fueled by the knowledge of the truth, Bernadette was the beauty, while Jeanne was...passable; or so she had heard far too often from her father.

Gaston stood before his wife, his reddened face inches from hers, hands straddling, one on each arm of the chair. The deep wrinkles of his skin cast grotesque shadows on his face in the dim candlelight of the small room. Adelaide trembled, squirming back against the cushion.

"Your worthless womb. One son was all you managed to spit out of it."

Jeanne slid off the bed and crawled along the floor; her father's voice had become that of the madman that lived within him. He stood close to the edge now, close to the point where ranting anger no longer sufficed. Jeanne felt the coward, with her back to the door, bracing it to keep her father out while her mother defended her, sacrificing herself for her errant daughter as she had so many times before.

Adelaide looked up to her husband, her shroud of timidity falling from her shoulders; anger sparked instead.

"God chooses whom he shall bless with sons. Do you hold the same contempt for the Almighty?

Flesh smack against flesh, echoing against the walls of the small chamber. Adelaide's head bounced off the wing of the chair and a small stream of blood began to dribble from her nose.

Jeanne jumped to her feet, a hand trembling toward the doorknob, fingers quivering with every quick beat of her heart. A sob escaped her lips; bile of anguish and despair rose up her throat. Salty tears ran down her face and into her mouth; she tasted them on her tongue, the taste of fear and self-loathing.

"No, Gaston. Please, no."

A mewling whisper—her mother's—found Jeanne. She venerated courage; she loathed tears, especially her own.

She flung open the door. Her father stood before her mother, arm drawn back, poised to strike her mother once more.

"*Non, Père. Non!* It is me you hate, strike me!" Jeanne hated the crack in her voice, in her determination it revealed.

Gaston spun with a snarl, arm still raised, white-knuckled fist high in the air.

Adelaide flew from her perch, launching herself between father and daughter.

Jeanne stumbled as her mother's body forced her backward. Reaching out, she grabbed her mother's shoulders, trying in vain to remove Adelaide as the target.

"Stop!"

The shouted command came from the door. As one, the combatants spun.

"Raol," Jeanne whispered her brother's name, lowering her head onto her mother's back in relief.

"Père, come." The dark-haired, amber-eyed young man, features so like Jeanne's, strode across the room in a few long strides. He reached up, gently pulling his father's arm down as he turned the man away from mother and sister. "You must come. The *Conseil d'Etat* is beginning. People are wondering where you are."

His son's words worked their magic, Gaston forgot his wife and daughter as if they no longer existed. As he moved toward his son, the ravages of rage slowly slithered off his face, strained jaw muscles relaxed into prominent jowls; the snarl on his lips slid into a smile.

"Ah, Raol, I would be lost with you. You have brought your father the only pleasure he has ever known." Gaston headed toward the door on the arm of his son.

With shocking abruptness, he turned on his heels, the monstrous mask of fury once more defiling his face. His gaze upon Adelaide and Jeanne darkened with undisguised loathing. Both women jumped back.

"She is your fault, your doing." To Adelaide, he spoke of Jeanne as if she were not there, could not hear. "If you cannot control her, you will suffer the consequences."

Gaston turned from wife to daughter, nostrils flaring as if assaulted by a foul stench.

"Come, Père, come," Raol urged, placing his large hands firmly on his father's shoulders, turning and steering the older man back toward the door. With a quick glance over his shoulder, he offered his mother and sister a shy smile peeking out from under his fluffy, sable-colored mustache, a tender panacea offered to ease their anguish.

* * *

Jeanne knocked softly on the closed door.

In the desolate abyss that was the churning wake left behind by his father and brother, she and her mother had embraced, released with their shared survival, two soldiers rising from a desecrated battlefield.

Jeanne had tried to apologize but her mother's ravaged and bruised face had stolen all words from her tongue. Adelaide had kissed her lips, left the room, and closed her bedchamber door.

Contrite daughter had waited anxiously for her mother but could wait no longer; the words of regret clogged her throat like a half-chewed piece of food and she longed to spew, ridding herself of the choking guilt.

"Maman?" she softly called, knocking once more, this time cracking open the door without waiting for words of encouragement.

Adelaide lay on her back on her bed, motionless save for the slight rise and fall of her chest, eyes tightly shut. Jeanne tiptoed to the bedside, peering down at her mother. Fresh tears sprang to blur the vision of the large bruise spreading like a puce stain on the side of her mother's face. Jeanne took the few small steps to the small room's corner where the pedestal holding a water pitcher and basin stood. Gathering a cloth from the shelf beneath, she poured cool water into the basin, soaking the cloth.

Turning back to the bed, Jeanne gasped, dropping the cloth to the hardwood floor. Her mother stared at her with lifeless intensity.

"Ah, dear Maman, you are awake." Jeanne rinsed the cloth once more, ridding it of the clinging dirt from the floor. Sitting on the edge of the bed, she gently placed it on her mother's marred skin.

"Why must you antagonize him so?" Adelaide sound meager, diminished. She spoke without gesture or expression.

"I do not mean to, Maman, truly I do n—not." Jeanne's dark eyes avoided her mother's golden ones. She held the cloth to her mother's face until the heat of their bodies stool the coolness from it. Jeanne dunked it again in the chilly water, bringing it back to her mother.

"Can you ever forgive me?" Jeanne's swelling tears of contrition spilled over and ran a course of repentance down her cheeks.

The corners of her mother's mouth rose in the slightest of smiles. Adelaide brought a hand up, cupping her daughter's face.

"Do I not always?" Lowering her hand, Adelaide braced herself, pushing against the silk coverlet, struggling to sit up straight. She leaned against the carved wood of the headboard, gripping her head as if it were about to fly off her shoulders.

Do you want me to call the physician?" Jeanne rose from the bed, alarmed by the whiteness of her mother's golden skin blanching against the pale against the darkening bruise.

"No. No, I am fine. We must not let anyone see me." Adelaide almost shook her head; pain stopped her at the first twitch. She reached up and captured her head with her hands once more.

"I will always forgive you, *ma petite*. But I do not know how much longer I can protect you." Adelaide raised a shaking head; Jeanne took it, sitting once more by her mother's side. "Things are not as they were when you left for the convent. Your father's situation is more precarious than ever."

Adelaide spoke freely, free of any fear of interruption. As a member of the state council and a fairly well-placed courtier, her husband would be wherever the King was. Gaston rarely returned to their rooms except to sleep, too afraid not 'to be seen'.

"The King has wrenched all power from the noblemen." For a moment, Adelaide pressed her lips together to the point of bloodlessness. "It is but a masquerade he acts, letting them believe they advise him. The Fronde has left our King paranoid and controlling."

Mother leaned toward daughter, grasping the young hands. Jeanne flinched at the feel of such cold hands. She gathered he resolve, cupping the hand in both of hers, warming it, wishing she could give back all she had received.

"They are powerless men, these nobles, reduced to petty games and intrigues to give their life meaning. They are humiliated and frustrated by the machinations the King forces them into. It is no wonder they lash out at any around them less powerful than they."

"But we are his family!" The words flew from Jeanne's mouth like wayward birds and she unable to catch or contain them.

"Who is more powerless than their wives and daughters?" Adelaide scrunched shoulders up toward her ears. "Your father is one of the few noblemen still to serve in Louis' government and it is only because he possesses a financial education. His position is tenuous at best. Why do you antagonize him so by speaking thusly?"

"It is not my intent, Maman." Jeanne turned from her mother, walking to the open doorway, poised in the egress as if to take flight. "And it is not my fault."

It was not her fault her father suffered at the hands of the King. Louis XIV ruled by absolute monarchy, rumored to have proclaimed forthrightly, "*L'État, c'est Moi,*"—I am the State. It was his complex set of unwritten laws and codes of behavior: who may enter the room when, who may sit, who must stand, who may eat and when. Noblemen now held only honorary positions and pensions. Life was nothing more than a struggle for trivial distinction and privileges.

Louis would do anything to keep the nobility from uniting against the Crown, as they had during the Fronde over thirty years ago. The memories of the ten-year-old King, of the deprivation and despair during those years, colored all his decisions; he ruled by them, dedicating his life to punishing them for it.

He filled his high council, the *Conseil d'en haut*, with promoted commoners, usurping the nobles, finding it easier to dismiss an elevated commoner than to strip a comte, and all his descendants, of the title. It was the reign of the lowborn bourgeoisie, as the Duc de Saint-Simon had so aptly named it. The rest were the King's puppets, dancing to the threat of court banishment or a life in the Bastille. These impotent men could but displace their frustration on those weaker than they, their women.

Jeanne turned back to her mother, hands pressed against her stomach as if, under the yellow embroidered bodice, her intestines fought to gain their freedom. Her long shadow, cast by the guttering candles, shook upon the wall behind her. With small, rapid movements she shook her head back and forth, long brown curls flowing like waves about her head.

"I am not like the other girls. There is...something...wrong with me." Her deep brown eyes pleaded for understanding.

Adelaide's mouth formed a ghost of a smile, a benevolent acceptance of a mother to her wayward child.

"I know, *ma chère*, I know. But you can try. Why did you not try harder at the convent?"

"Ah, *morbleu*!" Jeanne's hands flew dramatically in the air. "I could not stand it, Maman. The girls, they are beyond stupid. They are ludicrous, puerile. They fainted in horror at the least little thing, or worse, giggled incessantly for hours and hours."

Jeanne ran the few steps back to the bed, falling upon it with such force that her mother bounced upon the feathers.

"I cannot bear a life where the most momentous decisions I have to make are what to wear and what to serve. It is too meaningless and trivial. I want to learn things, study, be a part of the world. I can n—"

Adelaide raised a hand, silencing her daughter.

"Do you think you are the first woman to long to break the shackles imposed upon us by the virtue of possessing a womb?" Her mother's words hissed out from between closed teeth. "If so, you are greatly deceived."

Jeanne saw her mother's frustrated tears, the vein popping on her forehead, her red splotchy skin and, for the first time, saw true anguish, anguish at her own wasted life.

The young, suddenly frightened girl did not know what to do to relieve the pain of this woman, this angel who had given her life and so much more. She did the only thing that came to mind.

Jeanne stuck out her tongue and rolled her eyes as she'd seen the King's jesters do.

Her mother's face went blank—then split wide; she barked a laugh of pure delight. Her eyes popped and one long, slim hand flew to her chest as if to contain the swift skip of her heart.

The pall of despair lifted. Still laughing softly, she gazed upon her daughter with soulful eyes, bright with the turmoil of her emotions. Adelaide reached out for her daughter and pulled her into a tight embrace.

"Oh, *ma petite*, you are and always will be the breath and death of me."

Jeanne smiled from the safety of her mother's bosom, memories of such sanctuary taken there over the years flitting through her mind like passing scenery. She inhaled the musky, flowery scent of her mother and squeezed back with all the force of her overwhelming love.

"I will try harder, Maman. I really will."

Adelaide clucked her tongue.

"*Non, ma chère* Jeanne, you most probably will not."

~Two~

She stood before the cloudy mirror wondering if the distorted reflection she saw in it was her own or if it had magically captured the image of another, one of the perfectly mannered, perfectly obsequious courtiers clogging every inch of Versailles. The sage-green silk bodice hugged her tightly, fitting to the exact form of the binding corset beneath it. Satin ribbon trimmed the low-cut bodice, elbow-length sleeves and hem and created bows embellishing the full skirt and slight train. The large felt hat in the same sage green boasted one fluffy white ostrich feather.

Jeanne peered closely at her face; her eyes looked darker, deeper, and her skin glowed with tawny effervescence.

"Humph," she grunted to the woman staring at her. "This is far too feminine garb for the likes of you. But it will have to do." Jeanne, neither familiar nor comfortable in such elegance, had promised her mother only a few hours ago that she would try harder, and she would. With a determined flick of her chin and a giggle as the aigrette wiggled high above her head, she left the unfamiliar reflection behind.

Exiting through one of the lower gallery doors, into the back courtyard of Versailles, Jeanne hid her face in the large shadow cast by the brim of her millinery. The sun blazed; her eyes squinted in defense. Through narrowed lids, a colorful mosaic appeared before her—red, blue, green, yellow: every color of the spectrum blurred in her vision. Slowly her pupils adjusted to the light and her full, wide mouth turned up in a bow.

Courtiers. Like petals fluttering around the pistil, these creatures, prodigiously garbed in every color of the rainbow, shimmered brightly in silk, satin, and brocade. Women with piled-high coifs adorned with all manner of hat and lace, and men with their long, flowing curls blowing in the breeze and topped with plumed hats, vied for prominence.

Jeanne's nostrils quivered in delight at the freshness of both air and water. She took her first step toward the entourage as they assembled between the two grand pools of the Water Parterre, the first section of the immense gardens spanning over two hundred and fifty acres. Her heart beat wildly; moisture beaded under her many layers of clothing. This was her first social outing since her return, her first time among the gossiping courtiers, and she anticipated a cold reception.

"*Ma chère, ma chère* Jeanne!" A high-pitched call reached her ears. Jeanne turned, her heart bursting with joy.

Pushing and shoving, two young women struggled out of the cluster of courtiers, rushing toward her, arms and smiles wide and welcoming. Silk and satin enveloped her, two strong bodies pressed her between them.

"We heard you were back."

"Why have you not come to us sooner?"

Jeanne laughed, putting one arm around each of the women, relishing the acceptance she felt in their embrace, heard in their words.

"*Pardieu.* I am sorry," Jeanne giggled. "But I am here now. Come, let me look at you."

Jeanne released her friends and stepped back. Powdered and beauty-marked, Olympe de Cinq-Mars, daughter of the Marquis de Solignac, stood afire in brilliant red silk. Her jet-black hair and eyes burned with her intensity. Paling in visual impact, Lynette La Marechal, daughter of the Duc du Vermorel, shimmered sweetly in yellow brocade, long blond curls pulled back softly to reveal her delicate skin and pale blue eyes.

"How I have missed you both," Jeanne almost sobbed, the emotional reunion with her two dearest friends overwhelmed her.

Heedless of prying eyes, she kissed each one tenderly on the lips. Here in their arms, she found consolation in returning to Versailles.

"How do I find you, *mes amies*? What is about?" Jeanne asked, taking each woman by the hand.

"I am to marry soon," Olympe answered first, not surprising Jeanne. "My father is in negotiations with quite a few hopefuls. Papa says many vie for my hand, but he will not concede to just anyone. Maman says every courtier in the country will attend my wedding. Well, the ones who matter, at least."

"How wonderful for you, *ma chère*." Jeanne smiled at Olympe, seeing how little her friend had changed. Even as a young girl, Olympe's wistful wishes had dwelled on court intrigue, fashion, and to one day making the perfect match.

"And you, ma petite." Jeanne turned to Lynette, swinging the hands of her friends as they headed slowly toward the bevy of courtiers. "Is there a handsome young cavalier waiting for you?"

Lynette hid behind lowered lids and the pink flush spreading across her pale skin.

"*Non, chère* Jeanne, it is not a conventional marriage which I seek. My papa has petitioned the King to allow me to enter the Convent de La Bas Poitou."

Jeanne stopped, arms pulling ahead of her body as her friends took another step or two.

"Truly?" Jeanne's wide eyes gaped at Lynette.

Unlike Jeanne, Lynette had completed her education at the abbey near Toulouse. Her letters had always been a window into the depth of her piety.

"It is what I desire above all else," Lynette assured her, chin jutting up and out.

Jeanne smiled at her friend's conviction.

"When will you know?"

"Soon, I hope."

Jeanne hugged her, face close to her friend's comely countenance.

"Do you feel well? Have you been ill?" Jeanne's thoughts became words with little heed, one of her least appealing habits, but Lynette's pale skin and the purple smudges under the familiar orbs troubled her.

"No. I am fine and have been." Lynette patted Jeanne's hand still clasped in her own. "Have no fear, dearest."

Jeanne smiled, nodding, yet lingering concern niggled her.

"And you, you rascal." Olympe pulled Jeanne along to continue their stroll, looking sideways through narrowed dark eyes. "Is all we have heard true?"

"Too true, I fear." Jeanne cast her eyes down with contrition, but the feigned repentance was an unconvincing mask before these two friends.

"You are the chatter of the chateau," Olympe chided. "Could you not contain yourself for one more year?"

Jeanne shook her head vehemently, one long curl coming loose to fall blithely down her neck.

"It is a miracle I did not get ousted sooner." Jeanne's mouth turned up in a devilish grin, a decidedly malicious spark lighting in her sable eyes. "In truth, my dears, I did everything I could to get evicted."

"*Non,* shh, do not say such things." Lynette surreptitiously cast her gaze about. "Why? Why would you wish it to be so?"

"Why would I not? The place was abhorrent, the instruction trivial nonsense, the girls brainless twits, and the nuns naught but veiled monsters."

Jeanne closed her eyes tightly, repulsed by the memories. To revisit her seven years at the convent was to recall a nightmare that lasted all night. Just speaking of it brought the horrors quickly back; even the smells, the harsh lye soap, the burnt porridge, and the sickeningly sweet incense, came back to clog her sinuses. But it was the blind, slave-like obedience demanded from the Sisters that she could not abide.

"How can my love of God be measured by how deeply I curtsey to the nuns?" Jeanne demanded self-righteously.

Olympe giggled loudly; Lynette shushed her again.

"You really must watch your tongue," Lynette warned softly, teeth clamped tightly together. "You are a part of Louis' court now. There are ears everywhere. You must control your words."

"Ha!" Olympe barked, holding her chin a smidgen higher and flashing a sensual smile at two young soldiers as they passed. "Advising Jeanne to hold her tongue is like advising the world to stop turning. It cannot be done."

Jeanne giggled, joyful at being among those who knew her well, yet accepted and loved her regardless.

"What will you do?" Lynette stopped and turned to face Jeanne, searching her friend's face under tightly knit brows.

"She will marry, of course." Olympe rolled her dark eyes at Lynette.

Jeanne remained silent but shared a telling look with Lynette. She longed to pour her heart out, to tell of all the unrequited dreams fermenting in her heart. Lynette put an arm around her friend, stifling the barrage about to burst, and turned Jeanne toward the large group. They were but a mere few paces away; to speak would be for all to hear.

The three young women arrived at the edge of the clustered courtiers. Jeanne held firmly to her friends, trepidation tightening her grip. A few of the gaudily plumed beau monde turned to glance at her; a few whispered to their friends, snide giggles erupting here and there. A few reared quickly away, nostrils flaring as if they smelled something distasteful. Surprisingly, a few afforded her shallow curtseys and barely perceptible bows.

"There, you see," Lynette whispered gently, "they welcome you back with open hearts."

Jeanne almost guffawed aloud. "If these are open hearts, then I am King Louis."

As if the mention of his name summoned him, the crowd parted and the great sovereign strutted into the center of the circle.

There are men others will instinctively follow, for whom they will act with blind obedience. Louis XIV was such a man. Some called him the most handsome man in France. Jeanne thought it was his persona, his courtesy, reticence, and an almost inhuman tranquility, which made him appear larger than life. In reality, Dieudonné de Bourbon the man was only five-five, just an inch taller than Jeanne herself. His vast selection of wigs, worn in lieu of his own hair for the last ten years, added inches to his stature. His deep-set, heavy-lidded, dark eyes carried the secrets of the universe within their depths. The full-lipped mouth topped with the tightly manicured, curving mustache showed the devilishly playful side of the Sun King.

Louis had changed little in the seven years since Jeanne had last seen him; while slightly rounder at the middle, he still projected the bearing of greatness, perhaps more than ever in the midst of his magnificent palace. The long, dark curls of Louis' periwig flowed over his coat of dove-gray silk, one boasting thick, silver-embroidered buttonholes running all the way down the full skirt of his jacket. Inches and inches of Venetian lace flowed from cuffs and collar. Scarlet, tightly fitting trunk hose matched the deep red heels of his diamond-buckled leather shoes and the deep red of the many plumes of his dove-gray felt hat.

Jeanne stood on the outskirts of the entourage, grateful Louis had not noticed her. The moment when she must face him would come, but she did not wish it to be today. The King knew her well; as a small child, she had spent many hours playing in the royal nursery with the Dauphin, the King's son and heir. But it was the child Louis would remember; Jeanne knew not what he would think of her, the woman, and despite herself, she cared deeply of his opinion.

The bevy of people began to rustle, anxious to be off on one of the King's walks; they jostled and pushed in their eagerness. Off to one side of the King stood a ravishing blond woman, resplendent in violet satin and lace.

"Pray, Lynette, who is that woman?" Jeanne used her gaze to point.

Lynette rose up on tiptoes to see around the piled-high hair and towering hats obstructing her view. A distinctive light sparked in her soft blue eyes.

"Why, my dear, that is Athénaïs herself."

Jeanne's mouth formed a small but perfect circle, surprised and delighted to finally see the woman. Athénaïs, the Marquise de Montespan, was the King's powerful, titular mistress, famous for her beauty and sophistication. In the full sun of mid-morning, Athénaïs glowed. Her radiant and abundant blond hair, the shimmering cerulean eyes, and the perfect pink mouth, like the opening of a rose, sat supremely above the slim but curvaceous figure.

"She looks so young," Jeanne whispered for her friends' ears only. At forty-one, the marquise was only three years younger than the King.

"Evil never ages." Olympe smiled, staring at Athénaïs.

"Evil?" Jeanne's brows rose high on her forehead, creasing the soft, pliable skin.

"Not now," Lynette hissed to her friends, moving to stand between them like a mother separating her wayward children.

Françoise-Athénaïs Rochechouart de Mortemart was not the first mistress to warm the King's bed. The French people had long come to accept the King's behavior; he had married for the political health of their country. He deserved to find satisfaction wherever he could. His subjects could not begrudge him whatever joy he might find, even if it was in the arms of a mistress or two.

The path to be the most favored had been difficult for Athénaïs, she herself a married woman. For the King to cuckold another man was a scandalous affair—though conversely, the more women the King conquered, the greater his power grew. After years of Athénaïs's beauty and glamour infecting the court, the people had come to grips with her married status. Even the church acknowledged the King's right to a titular mistress and recognized Athénaïs, giving her the same power as the Queen, just as the courtiers and commoners did.

"Where is Louise?" Jeanne asked, referring to the previous favorite, Louise de La Vallière.

"Usurped and dismissed," Olympe eagerly responded. "Years ago."

"Where?" Jeanne asked, even as Lynette fiercely pinched the soft skin of her wrist.

"The Carmelite convent." Olympe slapped Lynette's hands away from Jeanne's, getting a tight-lipped scowl in response. "Sister Louise de La Miséricorde."

"*Non?*" Jeanne's eyes popped wide.

"*Oui.*" Olympe beamed.

Jeanne smiled back at her friend, as much at Olympe's obvious delight in gossiping as in the gossip itself.

"And who, pray, is that?" Jeanne tilted her head at the austere, darkly garbed, full-figured woman standing near to Athénaïs.

"Ah," moaned Olympe with the delight of the obese man as he sits down to a feast. "That is Madame Françoise Scarron, the governess to Louis and Athénaïs's children. Now, she is making things quite interesting. They say—"

"Mesdames, Mademoiselles, Messieurs." The King's deep vibrato captured everyone's attention. "Let us walk."

With many a "Yes, Your Highness," and "*Certainement*, Your Majesty," the procession began. They followed obediently behind the King as he strutted off on his red leather-covered cork-heeled shoes. Olympe leaned toward Jeanne, whispering a conspiratorial "later" as she winked one dark eye. Jeanne winked back delightedly, turning her attention to the head of the procession and the King.

"Ah, *chère Duchesse*, it is such a pleasure to have you with us this fine day. It is such a joy to show my home to someone who has never seen it before."

Jeanne studied the King's guest. Her brows knit at the gaudiness of the duchess's *accoutrements*.

"She must be a supremely strong woman," Jeanne said to Olympe over Lynette's head.

"How so?" Olympe asked.

"To be able to hold oneself upright under the weight of all those jewels must take mammoth strength." The Duchess had served as the mistress to many. As each affair ended and she was dismissed by an apologetic but completely satiated married man, she had been given another magnificent piece of gemmed adornment.

"She wears them like medals she has earned in a war," Olympe whispered.

"Has she not?" Jeanne's lips curled in a cynical smile, gaze upon the woman turning hard and cold.

With such a reverent audience, Louis lauded the splendor of Versailles in great detail.

"The bricks were formed by hand, one by one. Do they not match perfectly those of the original building?" His question was rhetorical; his enjoyment was in the sound of his own voice and the greatness of his home.

Versailles, located on the main road between Normandy and Paris, sat upon the vast private property of the Bourbon family.

"So close, we are, so close," Louis continued, pointing to the north and south wings, those allocated to the Secretaries of State, where the work still progressed.

Scaffolds stood like the building's external skeleton while thousands of workers flitted to and fro like ants on a farm, scurrying to the notions of the King. Twenty years ago, when the renovation work had begun in earnest, there had been close to thirty thousand laborers on the grounds.

"My chateau is almost finished."

"Chateau? He still calls it a chateau?" Jeanne hissed harshly. "*Mon Dieu*, it is the size of a small village."

"Shush!" Lynette remonstrated, eyes narrowed in warning.

Jeanne looked back over her shoulder. From this vantage point, far into the garden, she could see almost all of Versailles in one glance. The group of buildings forming the entire palace stood on a slight rise overlooking the village. The huge additions and front gate pilasters echoed the original exterior of warm russet brick and creamy stone with a roof of blue-gray slate. The front faced east and emphasized a hospitable aspect by enclosing three sides of a black-and-white marble quadrangle courtyard, the breathtaking Cour de Marbre.

"How can France and Louis afford such lavishness?" Jeanne continued, heedless of her friend's warning.

"He is obsessed. The cost is trivial," Olympe murmured, gaze narrowing at Lynette as she gave her warning friend a warning of her own.

"Now on, on to my water gardens." The King continued his narration, turning now and then to include the rest of the party, his voice loud and resonate. The courtiers hung on every word though they had all heard them many times before; they followed in a precise procession like a herd of cattle trailing after their leader.

"I've spent hours and hours, days and days designing the magnificence you see here." Louis spread his arms wide as if to embrace the entire estate.

"I am sure Le Nôtre, Caysevax, and Le Vau will be delighted to hear that," Jeanne snipped off the names of the real designers in her friends' ears.

Without a turn of her head, Lynette poked her elbow hard into Jeanne's stomach.

"Oof." The air rushed from Jeanne's lungs. She gave Lynette a small, sheepish smile but said nothing more.

"I will take you through my favorite route." Louis turned the group to their left and immediately the delightful fragrances of exotic flowers and orange blossoms assaulted the senses.

"Do you know the King is writing a book about these gardens?" Olympe asked.

"*Oui*," Lynette chimed in, a look of relief at the appropriate conversation quite evident on her pale features. "It is said the treatise will give, in detail, the correct path to take through the grounds."

From the *Parterre d'Eau,* they walked to the Orangery and then onto the Ballroom Grove. Within the massive, asymmetrically designed landscape, sunken garden rooms existed between box hedges, blossoming archways, and delicate trellis work, each area spectacularly furnished with stone and marble chairs, benches, and tables, and hung with silken drapes and tapestries.

A pond symbolizing each season, centered by bronzed tritons and nymphs, stood as a reminder that the Sun King controlled not only the days but also the year. As the King strode forward, the water park came to life. Louis approached one of the fountains, and its sleeping mechanisms sprang into action, spurting water in a torrent of tender teardrops spraying in a circular pattern, sending gentle, cooling sprinkles upon the whole entourage, each drop glistening like a tiny jewel in the bright sunlight.

The courtiers dutifully oohed and ahhed. Jeanne, unfamiliar with the spectacle, stopped, mouth agape and eyes wide like a child sighting their first shooting star. Lynette and Olympe smiled fondly at Jeanne, the adoring, watchful parents. Jeanne sent them a giddy grin, turning back to the exhibits. Once the King passed the first fountain, its geyser ceased to flow, and the cessation of sound and movement left a silent, empty void. Jeanne jumped as the adjacent fountain spurted into action, jets of water gushing out with a roar just as the King moved by it. A colorful, almost mythical, rainbow formed in the mist, capturing the King in the zenith of its arch.

"Is it magic?" Jeanne turned her face to the sun, and the soothing droplets of water flowing over her features stuck to her skin like gems, sending her face into a sparkling reality.

Olympe came to her and with a charitable grin, took Jeanne's arm, pulling her away from the water.

"Silly woman," Olympe chided. "See those men?"

Jeanne turned to where Olympe pointed and spied the inconspicuous guards stationed at each fountain. Dressed in dark green velvet tunics, pants, and hose, the slim cavaliers blended into their environment.

"Their sole purpose is to make certain these waters flow for the King," Olympe continued, prompted by the confusion on Jeanne's face. "They whistle, dear, when the King approaches, each with a different note. It alerts those manned at the switches when and which water to turn on."

Jeanne glanced round, seeing the other men sitting below the line of trees, dressed in the same camouflaging outfit, hands posed on metal levers. Bemused appreciation quirked upon her lips.

"Brilliant."

"Ah, *oui*," Olympe agreed, pulling Jeanne's hand, stepping quickly with her to catch up with Lynette and the rest of the group.

Jeanne listened with rapt attention as the King prattled on for another half hour as they passed sculptures and fountains and ponds and basins until the tour ended its almost circular path at the back entrance to the palace only a few feet away.

A few of the older courtiers took their leave of the group with graceful bows and curtseys, no doubt in need of rest after the long walk. Others hung about, pretending to be deep in conversation. In truth, they watched.

With a bow to Athénaïs and Madame Scarron, Louis allowed himself to be led away by the Duchess.

"No doubt she is petitioning the King on behalf of a paying customer," Olympe jeered toward the elaborately plumed woman. "Everyone knows it's the only way she can continue to dress and gamble as she does."

Jeanne watched the retreating back of the woman, the corners of her wide mouth lowering perceptibly.

"Come, dearest Jeanne," Lynette broke her friend's sad reverie, "my maman would be so delighted to see you."

"*Oui*, Lynette, it would do me much good to see her as well," Jeanne replied, shaking off her despondency.

"Olympe? Olympe?" The call came from behind them, and the three friends turned to see two young women and a cavalier walking briskly toward them. The small, auburn-haired girl in the lead waved her hand frantically at them.

"Bonjour, Mademoiselle de Chouard," Olympe said, looking down her long, straight nose at the women before her.

"Is it true, what we have heard? Are you to wed Monsieur de Loisseau?"

"Oh, dearest Daphne, is he one of those who wishes my hand?" Olympe looked round. "There are so many, I cannot keep track."

Jeanne blanched at her friend's egotistical rejoinder, astonished when the group laughed in response.

"With such a wit it is no wonder they are lining up at your door," the young man said, taking Olympe's hand and brushing his lips across her translucent skin.

Olympe bowed. "Monsieur La Porte, Mademoiselle La Vienne, Mademoiselle de Chouard, pray say hello to Lynette, whom you all know, and to Jeanne, whom I should hope you remember."

Jeanne recognized Daphne de Chouard from chapel, having seen her pray with great vehemence on more than one occasion.

"Ah, Mademoiselle La Marechal, a pleasure as always to see you," Daphne greeted Lynette; her companions nodded their enthusiastic agreement. "We were just speaking to your father. What a wonderful, kind man."

"Many thanks, mademoiselle." Lynette offered them a small curtsey, giving Jeanne a gentle push forward.

The courtiers's eyes stabbed at Jeanne for a brief moment, then the trio turned away.

"Keep us informed, Olympe," Daphne called over her shoulder.

"We wish to be the first to know of your betrothal."

Olympe waved a limp hand at them, turning back to Jeanne. She watched with Lynette as anger and embarrassment splotched their friend's face.

"Do not bother with them." Olympe twisted Jeanne away. "They are no one to be concerned with. You must learn to know the court. The plotting is constant on a grand scale, and whom to plot against is of most importance. From the Queen to the King's many paramours, the ministers and the courtiers, they are all in it."

Jeanne said naught, her mouth moved as if searching for words, but none revealed themselves. Lynette twined her arm through Jeanne's, pulling her forward toward the chateau.

"You must learn not to let the machinations of the courtiers affect you so, *ma chère*." Lynette stroked her friend's arm softly.

Jeanne crooked one shoulder, a smile that wasn't almost upon her lips, gaze, no longer sparkling with the water gem's prisms, trained upon the backs of the retreating courtiers.

"I know, I know, yet I have little tolerance for their hypocrisy. There is truth to the fashion of courtiers wearing masks, for some are indeed two-faced. They profess profound piety, yet their behavior speaks of anything but. They judge and belittle others they perceive as beneath them and hate any they deem as competition."

Jeanne stopped, turning to her friends.

"I ask you, is this how God intends for his most righteous followers to behave?"

* * *

She held her heavy-heeled shoes in her hand as she tiptoed on stockinged feet down the long, empty corridor. On the floor above her family's rooms, Jeanne stealthily made her way to the farthest chamber. The oppressive heat of midafternoon pressed thick around her; the sweat slid down her brow and between her breasts. She'd excused herself from Lynette and Olympe, bemoaning the need for a nap, but instead, she'd headed for this classroom, her refuge, as it had been almost every afternoon since her return.

Jeanne smiled gratefully as she reached the portal, thrilled to see it open, no doubt those within hoping for a stray breeze or two. She slipped into the room, gracefully dropping to her knees, sliding the rest of the way into a small cubbyhole as she did. From here she could hear everything taking place in the room and, when she dared peek out, could see those within as well. For the most part, she kept herself utterly still, not wishing to expose her position, for to reveal herself would be to incur expulsion and more disgrace.

In her mind's eye she pictured the room and all its details: a dozen or so young boys, aged from six to sixteen, wearing flamboyant clothing and bored expressions, lanky limbs draped across the scarred wooden chairs as they pretended to pay attention to the tutor. Bright light from the one wide-open window cast strange shadows across their faces, throwing their high cheekbones and long, straight noses into stark relief.

"The Romans believed in many gods, some of whom our own King pledges allegiance to, such as Apollo." The tall young man perched on a chair at the front of the room spoke with elegance.

His clothes showed signs of wear and overuse. The son of a lowborn baron, as were most tutors, the instructor was rich in knowledge but little else. Jeanne quivered at his voice as well as the subject matter.

The study of history was one of Jeanne's favorites and one intentionally omitted from her own formal education. The convent deemed it recreational study; nothing recreational was ever allowed at the convent. She'd received on basic instructions: reading, writing, arithmetic, and diction. She had gleaned her love of history at the convent, but not from the nuns.

Had she been twelve or perhaps thirteen? Jeanne couldn't remember. She'd been assigned to clean the convent library; a library the priests from the adjacent monastery accessed as well. Dusting the shelves with a dirty, ragged cloth, she'd picked up *Julius Caesar* by William Shakespeare. When she dropped the old tome on the floor, the pages had fallen open, revealing, like a freshly burst flower reveals its stamen, all of the magnificent secrets hidden within. By the second page, Jeanne was enraptured. The gladiators, the Senate, the law. Her mind whirled as the words spun her back through the ages.

For many weeks, Sister Marguerite had allowed Jeanne to clean the library, until they discovered the young girl sprawled beneath a heavy oak table, sound asleep, Chaucer's *Canterbury Tales* as her pillow. Forbidden to ever clean the library again, the damage had been done; her love of history, books, and learning had become as much a part of her as her own soul.

"The intrigue among the senators was a many-layered briar patch." The sarcasm lay heavy in Monsieur de Postel's voice; the similarity of the times he spoke of to the present day apparent to him and Jeanne, if not to his pupils.

Jeanne smiled, silently congratulating this man for his insight. She admired teachers, thought teaching a noble profession, one she'd considered for herself, but only for a moment. A woman could only teach as an instructress at a convent, and the thought of ever again entering one of those dismal, depressing places was abhorrent.

He has accepted his position well, she thought, hearing no dissatisfaction, only enthusiasm, in his voice. His father had been a member of the lower cabinet, a much more esteemed position than his son the tutor held. But M. de Postel was a Huguenot.

Louis' grandfather had passed the Edict of Nantes eighty-four years ago, giving Protestants protection to practice their faith in freedom. During the last few years, the relations between the Catholics and the Huguenots once more scratched and strained. Slowly, with inconspicuous stealth, the King now weeded the Protestants out of positions of authority at court as his gardeners weeded the vast grounds of Versailles. Once a lawmaker, Baron de Postel was now one of the many tutors situated at court charged with the early education of the nobility's children.

Jeanne leaned in and risked a quick glance at the man pontificating with such exuberance. His long, bony arm stretched outward, an imagined sword held firmly in his hand.

Why can I not be as accepting of my fate as he? Jeanne wondered. Pulling herself back into her hiding place, she closed her eyes to brimming tears and her mind to all such errant thoughts, allowing only the words of the past to enter.

~Three~

"You will be all right, you know." Olympe stood at her elbow, her jet-black hair festooned with small yet brilliant diamonds, a tower of ripples upon her head, her bright red lips slashing across her pale, powdered face.

Jeanne answered her friend with a helpless, fearful expression.

"I think not, *ma chérie*," Jeanne whispered, furiously flapping her fan in her face to stave off the heat of anxiety warming her skin.

Her eyes scanned the stupefying scene before them. Everywhere she looked there were prodigious piles...of hair, of jewels, of food. Jeanne stood at the entrance to the Venus Drawing Room, stunned by the abundance of it all. On every table, massive mounds of food rose to extreme heights. Dishes cradled in silver baskets sparkled on every square inch, filled to overflowing with meats, preserves, and fresh fruit. On every woman, and some men as well, the huge piles of hair matched the pretentious piles of jewels adorning their bodies. Jeanne looked on in growing disgust, the urge to flee growing stronger and stronger.

It was her first appearance at a *Soirée d'Apartements.* Here, most every evening, the obeisant, hedonistic behavior of the courtiers climaxed in an orgy of mastication, music, and mayhem.

Olympe stepped before her friend, eyeing Jeanne critically from tip to toe.

"You look magnificent."

Jeanne pierced Olympe with a pointed stare, nostrils flaring, wishing to pummel her as she had done so many times during their childhoods.

"I look like a whore."

Jeanne held her fan, covering her exposed chest with the silk and pearl confection. She had never worn a gown with such a design: the triangular-shaped bodice whose lowest narrow tip began at her groin, rose wide and flat to the bust. Lavishly embroidered and adorned with bows and jewels, the stiff, flat cardboard below the fabric supported the breasts, pressing them up under the lace until the translucent globes almost burst out the top. Jeanne felt as if she stood naked before the world.

"Ah, *ma chère,* then we are all such women." Olympe laughed raucously, stepping aside, pointing into the vast and crowded room with her own fan. Jeanne followed the path, seeing the multitude of similarly dressed women. Some were not so modest;

their dark nipples peaked out above the ridiculously low décolletage. They laughed, ate, and drank, indifferent to the decadent picture they created.

Olympe shook her head with a chuckle; Jeanne's distaste so clearly wrought on her features.

"Come, Jeanne, eat a little. It will make you feel better, truly." Olympe took Jeanne by the arm, leading her to the food-laden tables.

Jeanne followed in silence, taking her first tentative steps into the room, as watchful and on guard as if she entered a haunted forest. The women meandered along the breadth of the long, damask-covered table set with gold- and silver-gilt platters, stepping in and out of the many eating, drinking, and chatting courtiers. Stewards passed between the guests carrying silver trays overflowing with fruits and other delectable tidbits.

Olympe quickly filled her porcelain plate with quail and veal, bringing the carved pieces of meat to her mouth with gloved hands. Jeanne, foregoing the meat as she often did, made for the fruit, the display a work of art all its own. Perfect piles of peaches, caramel colored pears, and red, green, and auburn apples rose in a triumphant tower before her, their fresh and sparkling aromas a panacea to her perfumed clogged nostrils. Choosing a pear, she placed it on her plate, the gilt-edged stoneware heavy in her hand, carved it into small pieces and began to eat as she stood quietly by Olympe's side.

"Would you care for some *Piquette*?" a dashing chevalier asked Olympe, one of many such men flocking around her. Before she could answer, the handsome young man reached across the table, grabbing a glass of the watered liquor made from a second pressing of the grapes and handed it to Olympe, the long flounces of his cuff lace almost dipping in the pale pink liquid.

"*Merci*, Alain." Olympe accepted his offering, lowering her head to take a sip. She reached out with her red tongue, sensuously dipping it in the liquid, drawing back a few droplets into her open, waiting mouth, her dark eyes never leaving Alain's blazing blue ones.

Jeanne turned away from her friend and the debauched behavior, dismayed but not surprised to see it come so easily to Olympe. She took meager bites of her food, washing it down with raspberry wine, the sweet and sour fruit flavors mingling on the back and sides of her tongue. Olympe's behavior was not unlike most of the other women in the room, but Jeanne had no wish to watch it; she moved her gaze to study her surroundings.

The Venus Drawing Room, like all the State Apartments, had been part of the King's private suite of rooms when Jeanne had left for the convent. Similar to the other seven rooms of the *apartements*, the interior decoration was Italian in style. The white, beige, and green marble walls coupled with the trompe l'oeil statues of Meleager and Atalanta, were topped with gilded scrollwork above doors and panels. Her vision was drawn upward to the painting above, the pale pink flesh of the naked women and cherubs soft against the blue sky and dark clouds.

"It is by René-Antoine Houasse. He is a genius, no?"

Olympe stood beside Jeanne once more, face raised to the masterpiece above their heads.

"She is the Goddess of Love." Olympe pointed to the lounging woman in the center of the painting. "Louis named the room for her."

"Do you still paint?"

Olympe grinned. "Ah, so you remember."

"I still have the one you gave me."

The friends laughed with pure delight as they remembered the splash of colors and splotches of paint Olympe had called The Garden and given to Jeanne when they were small.

"Come to my room soon. I will give you a better one."

"It will never be as dear to me as the first," Jeanne said.

"What is the jest? What do I miss?"

Jeanne and Olympe spun to the familiar voice behind them as it rose above the clatter and music rumbling around them and embraced Lynette.

"Where have you been, *ma petite*?" Jeanne asked.

"In prayer." Lynette lowered her face shyly.

"Oof, where else?" Olympe chided.

Lynette gave Olympe a moue, circling her arms through that of her friends. "I am hungry, is there anything good to eat?"

Jeanne laughed and strode with her companions toward the still conspicuously laden tables. While Lynette ate, Jeanne studied her small friend. Lynette's attire did not match the lascivious vestments of most of the other women, a fact which pleased Jeanne greatly. But she did not feel the same of what else she saw; Lynette's skin still appeared sallow, though the bright blue silk of the seed pearl–and-sapphire-encrusted gown should have given it a glow. After a few meager bites of meat and a couple of mouthfuls of fruit, Lynette put her plate on an empty tray carried by a passing steward.

"I need something sweet, my dears. This way, Jeanne." Lynette led them off, away from the table and through to the next room.

Bawdy laughter filled it, drawing them in. A billiards table stood in the center of the marble floor. Attendants moved in and out with trays bristling with goodies: cookies, cakes, and candies, anything and everything to satisfy the sweet tooth. To wash them down they offered small, delicate crystal glasses of anisette, frangipani, or celery tonic.

With a chocolate-covered cherry in one hand and an anisette in the other, Jeanne sighed contentedly. Her shoulders no longer pinched her neck, and her foot tapped merrily to the sounds of the music.

"*Oui*, there is nothing like chocolate to soothe the soul," Lynette agreed.

Jeanne smiled a wide, closed, full-mouthed smile and nodded, unwilling to miss a moment of the delicious flavors assaulting her taste buds. The three young women stood with the handsome marble Bernini bust of their King behind them, smiling at each other, too intent upon their cocoa cuisine to speak.

Three older women rose from the cushioned bench in front of them. Bowing to Lynette and Olympe, eyeing Jeanne with dubious curiosity, they indicated, with a tilt of the head and an open palm, for the young girls to take their places.

"Merci, Mesdames," called Olympe to their slowly retreating backs, taking the offered place on one side of Jeanne while Lynette accepted the place on the other.

"Are you sure we can sit?" Jeanne asked, finally done gorging herself, wiping the sweet brown smear from the corners of her mouth with the small linen napkin in her hand.

"*Oui*, not to worry, here we get a reprieve from the King, but at the soirées only," Olympe assured her.

"Ah, *oui*, it's not often—"

A resounding crack of billiard balls striking each other furiously interrupted Lynette and the accompanying cheers cut off any conversations.

Jeanne turned her attention to the game table and the players around it. One of the players, the younger of the two, was strikingly beautiful. His natural blond hair, curly and full, fell almost to his waist, his pale skin glowed like cream of pearls, and his blue eyes shone deep and brilliant. He wore tight breeches that sculpted his powerful thighs and a beautifully tailored forest green velvet coat boasting a full skirt and thick, gold-embroidered buttonholes. His tightly fitting trunk hose, embroidered at the ankles with golden threads, displayed muscular calves, and his long, square-toed shoes were simply adorned with a single gold buckle.

"Chevalier de Lorraine," Olympe whispered in Jeanne's ear, eyes twinkling.

Jeanne's gaze latched upon the other player, quite obviously older but just as richly garbed. Jeanne had never seen such a peculiarly presented individual. His high bouffant-styled hair rose at least a foot off his head, and the heavy makeup he wore—powder, rouge, lipstick, and kohl—disguised pockmarked skin and bloodshot brown eyes. Plumed in a suit of pink satin trimmed with silver braid, he sashayed on high jeweled heels down the billiards table toward his opponent.

"Oh, you nasty boy." The effeminate man waggled a limp hand at his adversary. "You've taken my balls!"

The double entendre was not lost on anyone, and riotous, lewd laughter bounced off the huge, golden walls.

"Monsieur," Lynette whispered the title from behind her own napkin. "The King's brother."

"The King of Fops," Olympe announced.

"Oh, *mon Dieu*," Lynette squeaked. Jumping to her feet, she reached down, grabbed her friends by the hand, and pulled them off the bench and away from the Prince and his game.

"You must not speak so," she chastised Olympe once they were securely away, hidden almost, in a far corner between the softly playing string quartet and the warmth of the marble and gold fireplace.

"Nonsense. The truth of the King's brother is a secret to no one, except perhaps our friend here," Olympe countered, patting Jeanne on her arm.

Jeanne's perusal bounced back and forth from Lynette to Olympe, then back across the room to the astounding man in pink.

"She needs to be informed." Olympe insisted.

"Quite possibly, but it should be done privately, where no prying ears could misconstrue information for slander." Lynette crossed her arms tightly against her chest, small chin tilted up; a fortress before her taller, forceful friend.

"Very well." Olympe gave a nod of acquiescence, turning to look around them dramatically. "Is it safe here, do you think?"

"*Oui*." Lynette hissed the word, perturbed at being patronized. "But be quick about it."

Olympe turned to Jeanne, a look of pure mischief upon her beautiful face.

"Philippe, the Duc d'Orléans, is the King's younger and only brother," Olympe stated with a self-important tone.

"Yes, of course, Olympe, I do know that," Jeanne cut in impatiently. "I do remember him from my younger days. But I do not remember him like... this."

"He has changed much from when you last saw him," Olympe continued unperturbed. "He prefers, well, his sexual preferences are obvious, I think."

"But he is married, *non*?"

"*Oui*, and for the second time, but only because his brother insists upon it. His inclinations are not the worst of it, I fear. It is how he practices them that is such a scandal."

Jeanne's brows furrowed. "Surely the King would not allow his brother to practice perverted behavior publicly?"

"Well, he does seem somewhat subdued when out and about," Lynette offered.

"If you call prancing about in women's clothing and behaving more feminine and frivolous than you or I," Olympe countered, "then yes, in public he is discreet. But what takes place behind closed doors is startling, shocking."

"What people do behind their own—" Lynette tried.

"What ordinary people do in private may be their own business, but the King and his family are allowed no secrets." Olympe scanned the room. "It is those nasty 'secret' behaviors that wag the tongues of spite. You know what men can do to other men when they are cruel and depraved."

"He walks a fine line," Lynette agreed with a frown, unable to turn away from the flaming fop. "The King has ruined many a courtier for debauchery, drunkenness, even the uttering of obscene language in public. He would have no qualms treating his brother in the same manner."

"The King does not care for his brother?" Jeanne asked before she could restrain her own tongue, disgusted to find herself caught up in the sort of gossiping she so deplored.

"He barely tolerates him," Olympe stated matter-of-factly, reaching for another liqueur from a passing tray. "He shunts him aside as did his mother and Mazarin."

Jeanne remained silent, holding her inquisitive tongue though she yearned to learn more of the King's mother and the cardinal who helped raise him and his brother. A tray heavy with small squares of cake topped with sugar rosebuds floated before her on the arm of a passing attendant. Jeanne reached out, capturing one of the treats, and popped it in her mouth before such salacious questions could escape.

"You must let us show you around, dear Jeanne," Lynette said with a broad smile, eagerly changing the topic of discussion. "There are so many of our friends who would love to see you again. They may not recognize you, you know, and that is why they have not greeted you already."

One side of Jeanne's mouth curled precariously upward. "Oh, I think they are all quite aware of who I am, Lynette. I simply do not believe they are as eager to speak to me as you seem to be."

"Worry not, dearest," Olympe tutted. "Your scandal will be old news within a few short days, and you will become an established part of court life."

Jeanne chewed on her treat and Olympe's words. To pass among the courtiers unnoticed and anonymously was indeed a goal; to be one of them most assuredly was not.

"Ah, here's just what you need." Olympe nodded while offering the perfectly practiced public smirk Jeanne now easily recognized to a passing marquise. "She tries so hard to hide her growing belly, but she is fooling no one."

Jeanne's eyes betrayed her this time as they roved over the young woman's torso, looking for the telltale bulge.

"She should go to the country until it's over, to save herself and her child from discomfort," Lynette suggested softly.

"She is afraid to lose her place at court," Olympe snipped. "Though if the King finds out Madame de Printemps carries Monsieur La Viger's child, she will never be allowed at court ever again. Married men may fraternize all they want, but a married woman must remain chaste, except to her husband."

"She will make an admirable mother. She is very kind." A tender smile softened Lynette's lips as she watched the woman pass from the room.

Jeanne's brows rose high in astonishment.

"No, you are very kind, *ma chère*." Jeanne circled the waist of her friend with a loving arm. "I have never known anyone else who always finds something good to say about another, no matter who they may be. You are truly the best of us."

The sweet and shy Lynette said nothing; she lowered her head as a small smile spread across her blushing cheeks, blossoming beautifully under Jeanne's praise.

"Look at these three beautiful women standing all alone, such a disgrace." A deep male voice broke the tender moment and the girls turned to find the Duc de Brissac, a dark and dashingly handsome young man, accompanied by a group of friends.

"Ah, dear Etienne, you've come to welcome our Jeanne home, *oui*?" Olympe greeted the dashing duc, kissing first one cheek and then the other.

"But of course, of course. Dearest Jeanne, how wonderful to see you again." Etienne exchanged the same kisses with Jeanne. "Is it not so, my friends?"

"Oh, yes, yes," came cries of delight from two other men and three young women, and, for a few moments, Jeanne flourished in the embrace of strong arms and a cloud of heady perfumes. She remembered these lavish people from her childhood and appreciated their welcome more than she would have thought.

"Is it true that Monsieur de Perronette has gotten himself another mistress?" one of the women asked the group. Jeanne blew a sigh of discontent, falling silent as the discussion typically turned to gossip.

"Have you heard from Monsieur d'Artagnan yet, Jacques?"

D'Artagnan. The word dispelled all other words, all other sounds.

Keeping her eyes upon her own cartel of consorts, feigning interest in their puerile palaver, Jeanne inched her way toward a small bevy of three cavaliers leaning up against the marble wall, drinking bright red and purple spirits as they watched the crowd and talked quietly. The mention of the name d'Artagnan meant only one thing: these men were Musketeers.

Charles de Batz-Castelmore, the Comte d'Artagnan, was France's most renowned Musketeer as well as their leader, a post he'd held ever since the death of Monsieur de Treville and d'Artagnan's service to the King in the arrest of Nicolas Fouquet. The King's former finance commissioner. Fouquet had taken more than his fair share of the country's wealth and suffered in the Bastille still. Her brother's stories of the great d'Artagnan had lit the fire of Jeanne's imagination, a fanatical obsession with the Musketeers.

It was under Henri IV at the turn of the century that the special force of bodyguards had first been formed; they carried the then popular carbines and were aptly named Carabiniers. When the newer muskets became the weapon of choice under Louis XIII, these soldiers—the greatest in the land—became the Musketeers.

"He is considering my petition. Hopefully, he will contact me soon," the young man said enthusiastically. "It might be only a matter of days until I wear the uniform of a Musketeer."

"You will not look as good in it as do I," the third gentleman chided, and the friends laughed softly.

"Did d'Artagnan tell you about any of his adventures? He loves to regale the new applicants whenever he has the chance. They seem to grow grander as he grows older."

Jacques nodded his head, taking a sip of his sherry. Jeanne took two tiny steps closer, longing to hear the man's tale. "He told of the time when he, Aramis, and Porthos saved the—"

"Jeanne!" The bark of her name erupted beside her, scaring her to wit's end. She jumped, long, lithe hands coming to her heart. She dared a glance at the three men she had intruded upon without their knowledge.

They too were interrupted by the bellow, noticing Jeanne and her proximity to them for the first time. All three smiled seductively at her.

"*Oui, Père*?" Jeanne asked her father, eyeing the tall, skinny young man who hovered at his elbow.

"What are you about? Why do you stand here alone?" Gaston snapped, not waiting for her to answer. "Please make your respects to Monsieur de Polignac."

The long-legged, pallid man next to her father took Jeanne's hand, bending over to brush his cold lips across her skin as his pale, lank hair fell about his elongated face. Jeanne felt his fine bones through his thin membrane, and her own hand felt large in its small grasp. She curtseyed politely as he gave her a leg.

"*Enchanté*, Monsieur de Polignac," Jeanne said.

"Please, mademoiselle, pray call me Percy."

"As you wish, Percy." The instant Jeanne spoke his name, his thin, bony face became recognizable. Percy de Polignac was the son of the Baron l'Haire and a member of the King's lower council, part of the *no-*

blesse de robe... newer judicial nobility. He served on the finance committee with her father. She had seen him earlier in the evening, smiling at her from across the mammoth food tables, but had not recognized him.

"It is such a pleasure to have you back at court." Percy kept her hand in his, and his watery, gray eyes lingered on her décolletage, the tiny pink tip of his small, pointed tongue slipping swiftly out of his lips like that of a snake about to devour her whole.

Jeanne pulled her hand from his, flipped her fan open, and brought it up to her chest, waving it as if to cool a flush from her face.

"It is a pleasure to be back, monsieur," she said, no longer wishing to address him informally.

Gaston, uncharacteristically quiet beside them, nodded his head in silent satisfaction, turned on his heels, and strode away.

"*Bon.* It is done."

"What, Father?" Jeanne asked to his retreating back. If he heard her, he chose not to answer.

"What do you speak of? What is done?" she asked again, again ignored. It struck her—a wretched thought, a horrifying thought. She flashed back to the invidious individual before her; the salacious, pleased expression across his bland features confirmed her worst suspicions. Her stomach spasmed. Her hands covered her abdomen as if to push away the sudden gnawing ache.

Percy ogled her. His already thin lips disappeared altogether as his scurrilous smile spread across his ashen skin, but Jeanne could not quell the small denying shake of her head.

"There must be—" she began.

"Jeanne." Olympe came to her side. "We are all adjourning to the Mars Drawing Room for some dancing. Won't you join—*mon Dieu*, what is the matter?"

Olympe grabbed Jeanne's hand, gaze scouring her friend's stricken face.

"What—?"

"We would love to dance, would we not, Jeanne? Please lead the way, Mademoiselle de Cinq-Mars."

Percy took Jeanne by her upper arm, his pointy fingers clasping her where her father's bruises flourished. Before Jeanne could respond, he led her toward the doorway and the next *apartement*.

"Of course, monsieur." Olympe gave him a graceful nod of her head, Jeanne a sidelong look of concern.

Numb and silent on Percy's arm, Jeanne followed Olympe into the next chamber. She longed to talk to Olympe; she longed to scream and run. He had warned her, her father had, but she had not taken his threats to heart.

Along the blood red silk walls of the Mars Drawing Room, courtiers watched as couples swirled upon the shining parquet floors, the bright colors of their couture blurring together, the swish and rustle of the lavish fabrics adding to the grand music that swallowed them in its loud embrace. Percy led her to the dance floor.

"Shall we?"

His obsequious expression sickened Jeanne; she longed to slap him until some semblance of strength infused him.

"Of course, monsieur." Jeanne accepted his outstretched hand, watching with disgust as her quivering fingers took their place within his flaccid ones. As the hard heels of their shoes clacked on the wooden floor, adding their clicking to the symphony of other shoes, the musicians playing from the galleries on either side of the chimney breast switched to a rondeau, and Jeanne and Percy took position.

With gentle and soft nudges, Percy led her through the slow and intricate steps. Almost processional in style, the difficult and complex steps of the rondeau demanded purposeful and specific arm and hand gestures. Precision was as crucial as with the soldiers drilling on the battlefield. Jeanne felt Percy's graceful yet placid prompting, watched the elegant movements of his arms and hands and felt like an ox beside a sheep. Revulsion rose in her like the bile in her chest and she looked down to hide her naked face. She noticed Percy's pointy ankle joints protruding from the thin, tightly fitting silk hose, surprised by their slim and delicate appearance.

He is more a woman than I, she thought, balking away from this equally disturbing sight. When her eyes latched on to the painting above her head, Veronese's *Mystic Marriage of Saint Catherine,* the urge to laugh, to guffaw and cackle with complete mad abandon, overwhelmed her. Jeanne bit into her full bottom lip until the bitter flavor of her own blood burst in her mouth.

"We make a wonderful couple, do we not?" Percy whispered in her ear; Jeanne felt a small spray of spittle on her skin as he spoke.

Beyond hope she looked up at him, her upper lip curling in repulsion, words of disgust and denial caught in her throat as Percy guided her into the arms of another, switching partners in the next stage of the dance.

"Mademoiselle," said the Duc de Brissac, the young man she'd so recently become reacquainted with. Relief found her in his warm, full-lipped smile and felt the powerful arm on the small of her back. The difference between him to Percy was like wet to dry; one dripped with virility while the other lay dusty and barren.

"Oh, monsieur, how wonderful to see you again," Jeanne effused, her voice catching with emotion.

"Indeed?" He smiled down at her, moist lips parting in a sensuous smile as one dark brow rose upon his smooth forehead. "But it has only been minutes since I last saw you."

Etienne pushed her into an extra twirl; her delighted laughter danced with his.

"Some minutes crawl by like an eternity in Hell," Jeanne responded but only laughed more at the duc's confounded expression.

Jeanne moved like a gazelle under Brissac's sure and compelling direction. The music swelled, and the compulsory steps brought all the dancers closer together. Percy blessed her with lingering, longing looks until the final stanza brought them into each other's arms once more, where they finished with a flourishing flail.

"That was delightful, dear Jeanne," Percy said between bated breaths.

"Thank you, monsieur," Jeanne responded, already missing the exhilaration she'd felt in the duc's arms.

"I look forward to many more delightful dances." Percy's crusty, chapped lips rubbed against the back of her hand. She pulled away as if they scalded.

"Your prowess as a dancer is quite overwhelming," Jeanne deftly recovered. "I must compose myself. You will excuse me, *oui*?"

Jeanne rushed from the room, just beyond the archway outside the Mars Drawing Room without waiting for his response. She leaned against the opposite wall, arms quivering as they held her balanced against the hard wood.

"No, it cannot be," she groaned softly.

"*Ma chère, ma chère*?"

Jeanne turned on her heels at the feminine calls. Her friends swam in her tear-filled eyes.

"What is happening? What is wrong?" Olympe asked as Lynette gathered her into short and plump arms.

Jeanne looked at the dear faces, agony twisting her fine features.

"My life is over."

~Four~

"Why? Why is your life over?" Lynette insisted, arms firmly around Jeanne's back as the three women stood alone in the deserted egress.

Jeanne shook her head, kept shaking it, silent lips quivered on a blanched face.

"You must speak to us." Olympe took Jeanne by the shoulders, giving her a small yet fierce shake. "We cannot help you unless you tell us what is wrong."

Jeanne's head stilled; a narrowed squint focused on the familiar face.

"My fathe–"

The blaring horn obliterated her words; she jumped in fright, head twitching on a vein-strained neck, gapping russet eyes flitted back and forth.

"Calm, *ma chère*, calm yourself." Olympe took her hands, patting them softly. "It is time for the King's *Couvert*. They will all be coming."

Olympe could barely be heard as a throng of people poured out into the passageway like a rushing flood from an overflowing dam. Her ersatz façade firmly back in place as she nodded to the passing courtiers.

Jeanne pushed her shoulders back and tilted her chin up, anger and determination stilling her quivering.

"The *Couvert. Oui*, of course, of course." Jeanne nodded. The Kings of France had taken their evening meal in this most public manner for decades. Attendance was as natural a part of a courtier's life as his or her own meal taking. "The *Couvert*, of course."

Jeanne twined her arms through those of Lynette and Olympe and the three friends crossed the outer walkway of the State Apartments. They merged into the flux of courtiers like hapless salmon pulled upstream. Jeanne smiled and nodded, fingers digging into her friends' arms, passing through the astounding beauty of the Hall of Mirrors as if blind, barely acknowledged their arrival at the doorstep of the *Antichambre du Grand Couvert.*

Jeanne moved quietly along with her friends as they shuffled among the other courtiers for their proper place; positions were assigned by rank. Jeanne followed Olympe and Lynette when a Blue Boy signaled, with a nod of his head and a flick of a long, thin finger, for them to enter. They took their place in the second row of the standing nobility, flanking the windowed wall and one long side of the massive table dominating the chamber.

The rectangular room boasted four entryways, a marble fireplace, and the King's table, perfectly set to the rigid specifications required by the King. Atop the pristine white linen, glistened silver and gold platters, crystal and lead goblets, and brass and glass candelabras.

In front of Jeanne stood another row of standing courtiers; before them sat a row of a few chosen women perched on velvet tabourets. To the left, another crowd stood in the doorway.

The line of commoners began in the guardroom and ran through the loggia, down the Queen's Staircase, and out into the *Cour de Marbre*. Jeanne looked through the window behind her and followed the long furrow of poorly dressed people crossing the black-and-white squares of the courtyard. The line seemed to stretch on without end, the warm summer night bringing out more of the inquisitive people. They waited calmly and patiently; their excited whispers swirling among them like vines through a fence as they waited for the King to appear.

The swish of fabrics and tap of heels stopped, and the room burst with warm, redolent bodies. Jeanne turned away from the window, her sight falling naturally straight ahead, and gasped. Heads snapped to her; Olympe nudged her with a sharp elbow. Lynette grasped Jeanne's hand as she followed her friend's line of sight: directly across from them stood Percy de Polignac.

Percy stood in the third row against the small, far wall, yet his head rose above the others around him like one of the King's menagerie giraffes. His simpering smile shone clear against his pallid skin. In the row in front of him, glaring at Jeanne, stood her father. Gaston's face was a hard slate; his eyes held her prisoner—a prisoner he delighted in torturing.

"I must go," Jeanne said, looking down at her feet.

"*Non*, be still," Olympe hissed, taking the hand Jeanne had just freed from Lynette's grasp. With the other, Olympe pulled delicate linen from its place over her waist ribbon. Without looking at Jeanne, she dabbed at her friend's face, patting away the beads of moisture blossoming above Jeanne's upper lip.

"The King," a faceless voice announced.

Louis stood in the doorway, entering the room from the *Salon de l'Oeil-de-Boeuf*. A magnificent quiet greeted him, and Louis gave a nod of his head at the threshold. Resplendent in blue velvet and coifed with a towering wig of dark brown curls, he took his place in the large armchair covered in rich, red brocade next to the Queen's.

Marie-Thérèse sat low and small in her chair, her back stiff, her complexion colorless, eyes vacant as she acknowledged her husband with a small bow of her mousy brown-haired head. With their backs to the fireplace, their Royal Highnesses had an unrestricted view of every Prince and Princess of the Blood seated on the folding stools around the huge rectangular table.

The King sat in his chair. Monsieur rose from his seat at the other end of the table and strode with great purpose to his brother's side, his plum-colored high heels clacking noisily against the hard floor. With a deep and dramatic bow, Philippe handed Louis a napkin, which the King accepted perfunctorily. As Philippe rose, Louis met his brother's eyes, the small smile on the King's lips never reaching his dark eyes. If Philippe saw the slight, he gave no sign of cognition and backed away, still bowing. The napkin-passing complete, the King's meal began.

Led through the waiting throng by a large, halberd-brandishing Swiss Guard, servant followed servant, each weighed down by a heavy tray covered with silver-embroidered gold cloth, creating a celebratory parade of cuisine. Unlike any other cavalcade, this one brought with it arousing aromas stimulating salivation and gastrointestinal growls. As the food traversed into the room, the commoners bowed or curtseyed to the feast as if it were the King himself. Men doffed their hats, sweeping the ground with the plumes. Women curtseyed so low, their gowns blossomed in puffs around them. The whispered words flowed down the line of plebeians like a trickle of water from a slow, thin stream as each muttered in a low, reverent voice, "*La viande du Roi*,"—The food of the King. Bringing up the rear of the procession came the High Steward, the Gentleman Butler, the Gentleman Usher, additional kitchen officers, and their individual staff.

They placed the first service, or the meat course, before the King. The silent staff snapped off the shimmering cloths with great flourish, revealing piles of glistening, tempting food, and Louis chose a selection from each tray. Soon the King's large plate overflowed with stewed, spiced duck, partridges in cabbage, galantine of chicken, and fillet of beef with cucumber and pigeons.

The King took his first bite and the guard holding back the public allowed them to enter and to file quietly past the main table.

Slowly, astonished at the dazzling sight of the King, plainly but cleanly attired bourgeois husbands and wives, dirty-cheeked laborers, pale-skinned clerks, and nondescript artisans tiptoed by. None were disappointed, regardless of their high expectations or the extreme efforts they'd endured to attend the King's meal. Many of these families had saved their meager extra funds for a full year in order to make this trip. Piling themselves into wagon after wagon, they'd traveled for hours to catch this momentary glimpse of the King at table.

"There are so many of them," Jeanne whispered to Lynette, who merely nodded her head in agreement, raising a single finger to her pursed lips. The long line of inquisitive people passed in complete silence. The Royal Family devoured massive quantities of food, making it impossible to speak with each other, even if they were so inclined. The nobility surrounding them, so ingrained to this ceremony, so complacent in the face of its grandeur, watched in bored, tedious silence. Jeanne saw it on their faces: the indifference, the ennui of truth exposed and unmasked in this humdrum, everyday moment. Behind the glitter and glitz lay this banality of life, the true face of a courtier.

This face will be mine.

The thought seared Jeanne's mind, and she reached up a shaky hand to press against her forehead as if to force this painful thought from here. Like a drowning person grasping for a lifeline, Jeanne concentrated on the soft music floating out of the gallery, produced by a quartet of violin players. They played the same three songs over and over, music designed to keep the mass of spectators calm and to induce good digestion for the King.

Bulging salvers of the second service replaced the half-empty trays of the first. Veal, hens, rabbits, and a variety of salads soon vanished in the Royal's gluttony of consumption.

Jeanne's mouth fell open, out of disgust, not hunger. The King's appetite was famous, though she had never seen it for herself. Most people now used the fork utensil, which had come into fashion a few years ago, but Louis still ate with his hands and fingers, the digits dripping with gristle as he licked them or wiped them on the large linen napkin on his lap with fastidious frequency. She wondered how he could eat so much; it was well known that he shunned the practice of purging that the Queen and so many courtiers participated in.

"Drink!"

Jeanne jumped at Louis' bark.

"A drink for the King!"

Now she flinched right. The Principal Cup Bearer approached a side table and bowed dramatically. Straightening up, the small, thin man accepted the gold tray heavy with the King's covered glass and two crystal pitchers, one filled with wine, the other with water, from the Chief Drink Tester. These two men, followed by the Chief Goblet Tester, walked in slow procession to the King's table and bowed in reverence.

Jeanne watched as first the Principal Cup Bearer and then the Chief Drink Tester pulled tiny silver-gilt cups from small vest pouches, poured in a few drops of wine, and took a sip. Would they fall over dead and enliven the evening's events? Every eye in the chamber watched hopefully. When they remained standing, the Chief Goblet Tester made the same assessment of the water, and he, too, survived. At the lack of dramatic death, the Principal Cup Bearer bowed to the King, uncovered his glass, and offered Louis the two pitchers. Louis barely acknowledged the three men as he helped himself to the liquids.

"Thank heavens he was not choking," Jeanne whispered to Olympe, who, despite her best efforts, grinned at her friend's chiding of the elaborate ceremony.

Louis sipped from his goblet while scanning the room over the rim. He gave neither acknowledgment nor recognition, but there would be consequences for those who were not in attendance.

At that moment, three women came to stand in the doorway and for a split second, the king's passive countenance brighten. His eyes widened just a fraction and the corners of his mouth gave a slight upward twitch. Louis rose slightly, hardly leaving his chair, and offered these ladies a barely perceptible nod of his head. Such gestures did not happen often, and the room buzzed quietly at the turn of events. Jeanne couldn't resist the pull of curiosity and craned to see which women deserved such attention. Two were unknown to her, but the third she recognized from this morning's promenade.

François Scarron stood regally in the doorway, the lead in the triumvirate of tardy attendants. Her thick black hair, shot with strands of gray, rose regally yet modestly from her somber countenance. Dressed, as always in dark gray silk, she projected the physical essence of her pious personality. The Queen and her rival shot optical daggers at the commanding presence. Jeanne glanced in Olympe's direction, and her talebearer friend quickly, and with great relish, rushed to her aide.

"She is the widow of the poet Scarron. Athénaïs herself brought her to the King, and now she wishes to kick herself for it. François spends more and more time with Louis of late. More than—"

Lynette pulled Olympe away from Jeanne by the elbow, inserting herself between her two friends, putting an end to their disruptive discourse.

Jeanne turned back to the Royals and their table, shocked to see yet another service now laid out before them. There was partridge pie, fruits, and vegetables from Versailles' own gardens, fried sheep testicles, and slices of roast beef spread with kidneys, onions, and cheese.

Jeanne shifted her weight from foot to foot, feeling the fatigue and weakness spreading through her legs. By the time the King took the last few bites of his meal, Jeanne felt tremors of debilitation shaking her legs; over an hour had passed since the ceremony began. She understood why every courtier dreamed of a loftier rank, not only for the prestige but for the privilege of a seat, a custom and goal hundreds of years old. She bent slightly to rub her thigh muscles, ashamed to be the only one.

They are so accustomed to it, they feel no fatigue.

Jeanne looked at her friends, at the other women around her. She looked across the room at her father and mother and behind them to Percy. They all looked the same, like statues formed from the same mold. She reached up to her own face, feeling her features with cold, weak hands as if to see herself through their touch.

Do I already wear this vacuous mask? Will this audience, this observer role, be the highlight of my every night for the rest of my life?

Her thoughts—her fear—struck her like a hammer. All the saliva in her mouth dried to sand. The floor seemed to rise up and tilt, and she swayed forward, bumping into the woman in front of her. The rotund, elderly female turned her garishly painted face to Jeanne, her upper lip curling in distaste. Behind Jeanne's back, Olympe and Lynette's eyes met.

"We must get her out of here before she faints," whispered Lynette, taking one of Jeanne's arms. With a nod of agreement, Olympe clasped Jeanne's other arm and the three young women slipped quietly from the crowded chamber.

~Five~

"How dare you? How dare you leave before the King?" The hiss came at them from behind like a snake's approach.

The three young women whirled round on their leather heels finding Gaston du Bois, his face gnarled and red, burning with anger.

"Monsieur du Bois, she—"

"Be still and away, Olympe," Gaston ordered with a flip of his hand, not looking at the young woman. "And you as well, Lynette, away."

Gaston had known these young women since they were crawling upon the rug. He knew as well their parents, whose rank stood far above his own, but tonight his actions flowed unguarded by any concerns of propriety.

Jeanne took a step, hoping her enraged father would want her gone as well.

"Do not dare," he barked, capturing her shoulders in his firm, clutching grasp. "Why? Why did you leave the room before the King?"

"I...I...felt ill, Père," Jeanne struggled to control her fear. "I did not want to embarrass you or Maman."

"How considerate of you. What a good daughter you are." His right hand jerked up, stiff, hard, stubby fingers pushing against Jeanne's shoulder, driving her back against the wall.

Jeanne bit her lip to keep from crying out, rubbing at the soft flesh under her collarbone.

"Do not try and deceive me. Nothing you do is ever with merit. You've realized my plans for you, have you not?"

"Yes, Père, I have, but—"

"And you thought to escape, to run away, as you always do."

Gaston's black eyes narrowed to slits, intent upon Jeanne's nose. To look her in the eye would be to look up, something he would not do to his middle child.

"Père, I—" Jeanne pushed off the wall.

"*Non*, stop. Do not say a word more. You will not escape your future, nor will you escape this night. To the *Coucher*. You will say good-night to the King with the decent women." The elderly man's bloodless, thin lips curled in a snarl. "You will pretend, no?"

Jeanne groaned inwardly as her father pulled her toward the back of the palace to the private chambers of the King. She dragged her feet as if her small struggle could make her father give up the quest. Tired and overwhelmed, fraught with fear at the path being paved for her life, she could not abide the thought of any more of her father, Percy, or the court.

The King's public ritual of retiring was shorter than his morning routine, the Lever, but it was as replete with pitfalls as any other courtly custom. Held in Louis' new suite of chambers, those located at the heart of the chateau, the ceremony allowed courtiers of good standing to say good-night to their king.

A few steps through the Salon de l'Oeil-de-Boeuf and they stood at the threshold to the King's Bedchamber. Jeanne forgot her fears; her jaw dropped in awe as she peered into the private bedroom of the King.

She had not seen this room since her return, and she could barely believe these were the old rooms of Louis XIII. The chamber appeared as if forged of gold, seeming almost to glow with the power emanating from its inhabitant. The walls were covered with gold fabric interwoven with crimson in the lustrous patterns of Lyonnais silk repeated on the upholstery. The humongous bed, the centerpiece of the room, boasted a huge canopy adorned at each corner with matching gold and crimson vases holding pure white ostrich plumes so tall they grazed the ceiling with their feathery tips. Above the bed, a relief carved in gold depicted the citizens of France watching over the sleeping King.

Jeanne stood silently in the small antechamber filled to bursting with the eager attendants as they waited for the *en cas de nuit* to be brought in. In a moment, with the large tray held respectfully before him, the King's Premier Valet de Chambre carried in the light snack kept by the bed every evening in case Louis should feel hungry during the night. Three loaves of bread, two bottles of wine, a decanter of water, and three cold dishes weighed down the salver.

Louis stood against the gold-encrusted balustrade surrounding the bed and, with a tic of his bewigged head, signaled the guards to allow the courtiers to enter. The women were first. Entering by the west door, passing before the King, and exiting through the east egress, they dropped a quick curtsey in front of his Royal Highness as they passed.

Jeanne hovered at the back of the line, held firmly in place by the clutching hand of her father. Gaston watched the procession intently, knowing Jeanne's placement was of the utmost importance.

"Go, now." Gaston pushed her away from him without any further warning, and she tripped at the rude thrust.

Recovering her balance, Jeanne took her place between two other women of a like age. One she recognized as another comte's daughter, the other she did not remember at all. She leaned to the left to look past the young lady in front of her and caught a glimpse of the parade as it made its way past the King. To most women he gave a shallow nod, to some a slight bend from the waist. To Athénaïs and Mme. Scarron, who walked together, he gave his most famous bow. With one foot thrust out before him, balanced on the floor with a pointed toe, he swept his right arm grandly above his head, swinging it quickly down while bending in half, until his hand almost met his forward foot. Slowly and gracefully he rose from his genuflection, a self-pleased smile spreading across his face. As the women passed on, Louis returned to a standing position and nodded to the next woman in line.

Jeanne took her turn before him, dipping into her most solicitous curtsey. Rising up, she stole a glance at the King's countenance. Louis' gaze captured her in its powerful grip, intently perusing the young face before him. A hint of recognition and interest flickered in the dark depths. With a small nod, he released her, and Jeanne moved along and out of the room, taking a deep breath, feeling the surge of air she had deprived herself of for the last few moments.

* * *

Gaston and the other male courtiers waited in silence as the women made their good-nights. His right foot, encased in the worn, buckled high-heeled leather shoe, tapped the parquet floor impatiently. The hand thrust deep into the pocket of his breeches worried over a small coin. Finally, the last woman in line made her way past the King, who then moved himself to the small private room off his bedchamber. Here, with other members of his family, Louis would spend a few casual moments, conversing about the day's events with his children, cousins, and sibling and enjoying his dogs.

Gaston jumped into action as soon as the King disappeared behind the partition, and with two large steps stood next to Percy and his father, Pierre, the Baron l'Haire.

"So, you've seen her, *oui*, de Polignac?" Gaston wasted no time on small talk and pleasantries.

Pierre turned and looked down at the abrupt man beside him. Like his son, the baron stood taller than most of his contemporaries, bland with the same pale and wan coloring of his offspring.

"Comte de Moreuil." Pierre nodded, returning a greeting that had not been offered. "If you speak of your daughter, then *oui*, Percy was quite excited to point her out to me."

Percy nodded his head enthusiastically as he bounced on the balls of his feet.

Gaston turned his dispassionate glance to the young man. "He is convinced. And you?"

Pierre's nostrils flared perceptibly.

"I also took note of the King's notice," l'Haire said, frowning.

"I'm told she is beautiful," Gaston spoke through clenched teeth. "No doubt it is this comeliness that caught the King's eye."

"Beauty can be a burden," Baron l'Haire said softly.

"And it can be a great boon to those desiring greater privileges."

The baron stood silent in the face of such flagrant frankness.

"So, what will it be?" Gaston asked.

The baron's answer was stymied as the King reentered the chamber.

Kneeling by the side of his mammoth bed, Louis prayed silently for a few minutes. Crossing himself dramatically, he rose and stood against the gold railing. With theatrical exuberance, he searched the room and all its inhabitants slowly, carefully. He studied each face, determining who would hold the candle for the entire *Coucher.* Who had played his games best this day; who had pandered the most? The privilege was the culmination of each day's manipulations; he gave it out stingily and with great care.

"Marquis de Lamballe, if you please, sir," Louis announced.

A short, round, middle-aged man strode to the front of the room with his chest puffed out. An obsequious smile lit his face as he picked up the golden candelabra and took his place before the King.

Things moved swiftly now, and the Comte de Fresnay, as the highest-ranking noble in attendance, presented his sovereign with his nightshirt. Louis stood impassively as the exquisitely embroidered midnight blue nightshirt of Lyonnais silk flowed over his torso. Of his own volition, Louis donned the matching nightcap and the gold and lace slippers. Attired for the evening's rest, Louis cut as fine a figure in his sleep garb as when decked in full court attire. Given his nocturnal proclivities, this finery was as thoughtfully considered as any of his other outfits. No one knew if he would stay abed or for how long; the rumors of the secret tunnels throughout the palace and the King's aberrant nightlife were neither invented nor exaggerated.

Louis added the final touch, the matching embroidered dressing gown, nodding in the direction of the Premier Valet de Chambre.

"Gentlemen, pass on!" the man called out.

With another regal bow, Louis dismissed the male members of his court and entered the sanctuary of his canopied bed.

Without looking back, the men processed out of the chamber. Here, unlike most rooms of the palace, the lowest members departed first; remaining longer in the bedroom of the King was a prize to be treasured.

Gaston watched the Baron l'Haire and Percy quit the room. He hated the thought of them leaving without another word, but not enough to relinquish the more prestigious place he had earned. He walked slowly, disappointment and anger weighing down his legs.

"Comte de Moreuil?"

A few feet out of the chamber, Gaston stopped at the call. The baron and his son waited just beyond the threshold. He stepped sprightly to stand by their side.

Pierre put out his hand.

"We accept the troth of your daughter, Jeanne Yvette Mas du Bois."

Gaston grabbed the extremity thrust before him, a ghost of a smile almost cracking the usually pursed lips, and shook it fervently.

"It is done."

~Six~

She trampled a circular path into the worn yet still beautiful Aubusson carpet; the small, single shape she created wound round and round. Her downcast stare focused on the intricate pattern of mauve roses and green ivy as they intertwined, a maze of loveliness almost covering the entire floor of the small sitting room.

Adelaide sat in one of the two padded wing chairs. She watched her daughter in silence, holding her hands in her lap, hand that still shook her. Jeanne's nostrils quivered with the smell of fear emanating from them both, growing stronger as they waited in the hot, dense air of the windowless room.

The outer door burst open; the two women jumped like frightened deer. Gaston strut into the room. Jeanne's heart froze in her chest at the sight of his mouth, the corners looked almost turned up. She had never seen him so happy.

Jeanne looked to her mother but found no refuge in the elder woman's face. Adelaide's twisted expression a contrast and consequence of her husband's delight. Jeanne felt a shiver, need not look to know her father now stood in the room.

For a vacuous moment, Gaston percolated in complete silence. His meager chest rose higher with every breath he took; he crossed his arms purposely upon it.

"It is done." The well-pleased man gave a jaunty twitch of his unruly, bushy brows, then turned upon his heel and headed for his bedchamber.

"No, Father, it cannot be true," Jeanne begged.

Gaston froze in mid-step. "It is quite true, and you will never say no to me again," he growled at Jeanne without turning.

"Not Percy de Polignac. There must be someone else." Jeanne took a step toward her father. "I have no wish to marry, but if I must, surely there is someone else. Percy is... is nothing, a weak, meaningless man."

Gaston whirled round, marching back across the room.

"I do not care a whit for his manner nor his bearing." He stood inches from her, his words spewing from him like lava from the cavernous depths of his rage. Jeanne jerked away as the spittle flew from his lips to slap her face. "His father has money and is foolishly willing to part with some of it...for you. Their family home is far from here, where you will live, and wither, far from my eye."

Jeanne could deny her father's abject hatred writ indelibly upon his face, but she could ignore it. "I... will... not."

Gaston roared. His right arm swung up by his side. Jeanne flinched, bringing her arms up and squinting in defense. But the blow never came.

"You will." He commanded with rigid menace, trembling with barely contained rage. "You will, or I will sell you to the highest bidder."

Father and daughter moved not an inch, locked in a battle of wills. Jeanne looked at her mother's red, tear-stained face, and her shoulders slumped; to be sold into servitude, as any nobleman could do to a daughter, would be to break her mother's heart. Surrender was unavoidable. She clamped her mouth shut tight and nodded.

"Go to bed," Gaston demanded, lips curled in a grimace of triumphant victory.

Jeanne looked from his abhorrent face to her mother's dear one and back; a warning or perhaps a request.

"Go to bed," Gaston growled once more, cutting short any consolation between mother and daughter.

Without another word, Jeanne crossed the room, entered her small bedchamber, and closed the door behind her with a soft, final click.

She stood with her back against the door, her breathing quick and shallow. In the bed they shared, her sister's body rose and fell as she slept peacefully. In the thick quiet Jeanne strained her ears to catch any sounds from the room beyond the door. She would not allow her father to abuse her mother again. She knew not what she would do if she were to hear sounds of punishment, but she knew she would do something. No longer did she have anything to lose.

I have nothing.

The searing thought repeated over and over in her mind, a litany of despair. As the minutes ticked by, the already-small room closed in upon her, the walls drawing nearer and nearer. She could stand it no longer.

Jeanne turned and grasped the door handle. Stealthily she turned it till a crack of light shone through. One dark brown eye cast about the room and found it empty. She opened the door, rushed through it, and out of the apartment.

Jeanne flew down two flights of stairs and out the door in the corner of the *Salle des Hocquetons.* The hot, sticky night air hit her face like a slap; the sounds of tree frogs and crickets resounded like a funeral dirge. Down the path, through the North Parterre, past the Pyramid and Bath Nymphs, she ran. The hot air cool on the streaks of moisture, tears she didn't know she shed. She made her way down the long Water Avenue until she circled the Dragon Fountain next to the Fountain of Neptune.

Throwing herself to the ground, Jeanne sat at the edge of the water on the rounded concrete while her chest heaved with exertion. The black of night the blanket she wrapped herself in; keeping her hidden from the thousands of eyes living at Versailles. It felt safe, the darkness, safe to be free and unafraid; she allowed her feelings to flow unfettered from her spirit. As her ragged breath burned her lungs and the sweat dripped down her body, soaking through the frilly garments lying against her skin, Jeanne stared at the massive arrow-shot dragon sculpture dominating the center of the fountain. The great beast showed no fight as two dolphins circled him and four silver swans attacked him from both front and rear.

Why must I always fight? Why can I not surrender?

Her mind struggled with her soul as her lungs struggled for air; the argument prodding at the very purpose of her existence. This burden that was her fate weighed heavy upon her shoulders.

What is wrong with me? Why do I have these feelings? What kind of a woman am I; where do I belong? Why can I not be satisfied with what has been offered me? I want to be more, learn more.

Jeanne cringed at the memory of lessons forced upon her over the years, from needlepoint, dancing, and the basics of writing to the rules of precedence and how to enter and exit a room properly.

How utterly ridiculous, she thought, *when there are so many books to be read, histories to discover, languages to learn. They push us to become wives and mothers, yet there is nothing taught on motherhood or the economics of running a household.*

The troubled musings whirled around her as fireflies glowed amidst the shrubbery and time ticked by.

The palms flattened against her face were sodden with tears. Jeanne took them away but continued to hold them up. She studied the appendages held inches from her face. The fingers were long, tapered, and graceful. She noticed the calluses on the pads of her hands, formed over the years of drudgery at the convent. Jeanne rubbed her thumbs across them, feeling each rise and fall, reading them as a blind man explores his world. The hardened lumps of flesh lent more strength to her hands' already-powerful appearance.

These hands were meant to do something more than pull at thread or flutter a fan.

Jeanne dropped her limbs to her lap and looked around. She could have been sitting upon a wayward planet in the sky. Jeanne alone existed in the vast and endless gardens. She strained her vision to see to their border, straining to see the world lying beyond this castle and its rigid boundaries.

Could she run away and become a nanny or a governess? Such positions were not gotten without references. To use her real name would be to ensure that word of her whereabouts would get back to her father and he would come for her. He would see to his threat of servitude or, worse, to a life for her in the Bastille. She could use another name and become a shop girl, live in a one-room closet all alone as the moments of her life flowed by with no meaning.

Jeanne started, curling herself into a frightened ball as she heard voices in the distance. She held her breath as the mutterings grew closer, and she searched the darkness in alarm.

"To the switches with you, Leo," a voice commanded, and Jeanne relaxed, breathing once more as she saw three of the thousands of men who cared for the grounds walking in the avenue behind the fountain. She half listened to the snippets of their words, their talk of the mechanics of the fountain at her back. She paid them no real mind, lost in the darkness of her thoughts.

"*Commencer, commencer*," she heard one of the men yell.

With a boom like thunder, the fountain behind her burst into life. The rush of the water shrieked through the night as the many hydraulic-powered spouts exploded with the eruption of liquid. Huge and engulfing, the noise drowned out all other sounds.

In this void of anonymity, Jeanne screamed.

~Seven~

"To retreat is not to be defeated, but to step back, once or twice, is to throw your opponent off his guard, *oui*?" Jules instructed from behind his headgear, his voice echoing against its hard shell as it echoed in the empty basement chamber.

Jeanne nodded, understanding. She thanked the good Lord for her uncle this morning and these lessons that drove the many disquieting thoughts born the night before from her mind.

"Ah, *oui*. Then, *en garde. Bon, bon*." Her uncle acknowledged her proper form of the starting position.

"Now, retreat," he ordered.

Jeanne's back foot lifted off the ground as her front rolled to the heel. Then, quick and together, they moved with a flash and she moved a step backward.

"*Bien*. Retreat, retreat." Jules gave the order for her to make the same move again, twice.

Back, back she moved. On the second step, first one foot moved and then the other, completely out of sync, and Jeanne stumbled, sword arm lowering as she tumbled, leaving her body open to attack.

With an advance, lunge, and thrust, three moves executed as a single dance maneuver, Jules brought the blunt tip of his foil hard against Jeanne's chest. Her head dropped, chin to chest, staring at the finishing point in defeat.

"You are dead, *ma chère*."

"*Oui, mon oncle*, you speak the truth."

Jules removed his helmet, allowing his long, curly white hair to flow freely down his back. Cupping it under one arm, he lowered his sword and closed the space between them with a few small steps.

"What vexes you, dear Jeanne? You are here, but your spirit lies elsewhere."

Jeanne looked at Jules through the round holes of her helmet, eyes aching with sadness and despair.

"My father has sealed my fate. He has arranged my marriage to Percy de Polignac, son of the Baron l'Haire."

"Percy de Polignac?" Jules mused, chin wrinkling in consideration. "Tall string bean of a fellow?"

Jeanne smiled faintly. "*Oui,* you have him to rights, *oncle*."

"What can be so bad? One day and one night together, then you each go your separate ways, live your separate lives." Jules shrugged his shoulders dispassionately; such a marriage was typical in their world.

"Lives? What life will I have?" Jeanne took a step toward her uncle with the same aggression as if they still dueled. "Floundering around, following in my husband's footsteps wherever they may lead. Watching while the insipid man does nothing to better himself or the world in which he lives."

Jules shook his head. "You should not have been born a woman."

"Perhaps." Jeanne nodded though not knowing she did so. "But I am glad to be a woman. I do long to feel life growing within me and to nourish that life into a grand human being. But why can I not have a more productive and satisfying life as well?" Jeanne rolled her eyes dramatically. "A female courtier has no real life. She has naught to do but be social. We play cards, listen to music, dance, attend the King's ballets and operas...and talk. Endless hours of conversation, mostly about each other or the King."

Jules looked behind him as if someone had entered the small, reclusive chamber. "You should not say such things."

"Of course not," Jeanne responded bitterly, arms flaying the air about her as her harangue continued. "The King even controls the words from our tongues. Heaven forbid anyone should talk of the condition of our country or its people. We would be on the King's naughty list for months if we did. No, men must talk only of hunting and horses, while women are limited to scandal and frocks and nothing more."

Jules stepped to within inches of his niece. He tapered his eyes, peering into the holes of Jeanne's headgear, searching her face for something he found elusive.

Jeanne felt her skin warm under his intense stare. Moisture beaded under the heavy, padded protective gear she wore. She squirmed. She knew she should be embarrassed by her emotional outburst, but her anger refused all shame.

"Where does such deep dissatisfaction come from, ma petite?"

Jeanne touched her fisted, gloved hand to her chest.

"From here, *mon oncle*. From deep inside my very soul."

Jules brought a hand up to her shoulder, squeezing it with gentle reassurance. There it was, the depth of her fathomless sadness drowning in the endless pool of her dark eyes.

"Then you leave me no choice." Jules lowered his hand and turned from Jeanne, striding toward the long, bulging bag of gear he brought with him to every practice.

Jeanne almost cried out, thinking he meant to leave, thinking he would never again partake in these lessons, her only respite in a life filled with disappointment and delusion.

"*Non, bon oncle, non.*" She ran behind him.

But instead of putting his sword away, Jules reached into the well-worn canvas bag and pulled out a long rosewood box. The reflection of his smiling face shimmered on the deep, rich, highly polished surface.

"I planned to wait to give you this, but I think now is the time." Jules reached over and took Jeanne's sword out of her right hand and thrust the dark red shining box at her.

With slow deliberateness, Jeanne removed her headgear and accepted the gift in stunned silence. She looked down and saw her own confused countenance reflected on its mirror-like surface.

"Go on, *ma petite*, open it." Jules' smile shone wide beneath his bushy white mustache.

The box opened in half on smooth, silent hinges.

"*Sacrebleu*!"

Jeanne's mind doubted what her eyes beheld. Upon the lush, mahogany-colored velvet lining the box's interior lay a brand-new sword. With her left hand, she held the box still while the right retrieved the sword from its depths, handling it as tenderly as she would a newborn babe.

"It is a *colichemarde*," Jules announced proudly.

"Oh, good *oncle*," Jeanne whispered reverently, gaping at the face of the dearest man she ever knew. "A *colichemarde*! This must have cost you a thousand livres!"

Not only was the sword new, the first new sword she had ever possessed, it was of the newest, highly coveted style, the most popular type among Frenchmen at the moment. A strong parrying weapon with an agile point, perfect for the double-time fencing style so in vogue of late. Heavy at the hilt, it tapered to one-third size by the point, perfect for the now-accepted parry-riposte method.

"It is perfect for your height," Jules said, shaking his head at the size of his niece. "So tall, five-four, amazing. As tall as most of the young men. Certainly taller than us old ones. And you fight just as well, my dear. Come. Come let us try it out, shall we?"

Jules retrieved his own sword, pulling on the hard headgear and taking his place in the middle of the room.

Jeanne turned the sword back and forth in her hand, delighting in the weight of it and the gold and silver pommel that fit so perfectly in her hand. She swung it left, then right, hearing the wonderful whish as it cut the air, the sound like a single, perfectly tuned instrument playing her favorite song. The control she commanded on the smaller sword in stark contrast to the lack of it in her life.

Donning her crude helmet, she lowered the weapon to her side, unable to stop herself from glancing down to see it there so close to her body. With complete abandon, she ran across the room and threw her arms around her startled uncle, her headgear banging roughly against his.

"Dear, dear Uncle, you are too good to me," Jeanne said, the front of her helmet pressed against his shoulder, her voice deep with emotion.

"You are pleased, dear one, yes?" Jules' own voice cracked a bit.

Pulling just a smidgen away, their smiling eyes met through the holes of their gear.

"Magnificently so." Jeanne leaned forward another inch, helmet touching helmet, eyebrows rising in a mischievous tic. "Ready?"

"Ha!" Jules yelled, pushing her from him, flashing into position as did Jeanne.

Steel hit steel in a resounding ching. Jeanne felt more powerful than ever with such a splendid tool in her hand. She advanced step after step, moving her uncle around the room as if she controlled a puppet by its strings.

To the corner she brought him; now if she could just force him to—

"This way, Henri, quick!"

From just outside their door the cry boomed and, on its heel, more shouts, grunts, and the clanging of steel upon steel.

Jeanne and Jules froze, listening in wonder and confusion. Jules understood first, threw off his helmet, and ran to the door. Jeanne followed quickly just as he threw open the portal.

In the wide, dim corridor, four darkly garbed, dirty and scruffy men attacked two Musketeers with brutal intent. No manners or polite dueling this—they slashed, thrust, punched, and pushed with great ferocity. Grunting with effort and exertion, the two Musketeers fought with a sword in one hand and a dagger in the other, two weapons against two foes each. Their arms swung and stabbed so fast they were a blur.

With a hard grunt, one Musketeer's back pounded against the opposite wall as a kick found struck his stomach. He faced Jules and Jeanne, rooted in the doorway. With a jerk of his head, he lashed sweat-sodden gold hair out of his eyes.

"Help us, for the love of God, help!"

Jeanne lunged out the door. Jules grabbed for her, grasping naught but empty air.

"*Corboeuf*!" Jules swore and, with a bounce on his feet, launched himself into the fray.

Jeanne threw her sword up, intercepting a villain's thrash aimed toward the golden-haired Musketeer, pulling him off, allowing that the soldier to battle only one foe. She fought with every iota of strength she possessed. No pretty form and thoughtful, choreographed movements, just naked aggression and defense.

A hand wrapped itself around her heart, squeezing and clenching; its beat erratic and flurried. Another found her guts, gruelingly twisting and constricting her intestines into knots. The pain of her own fear almost doubled her over. Sweat broke out on her smooth brow. She ignored both.

Her opponent's sword plied against her again and again, driven on in a relentless quest to sever whatever part of her it could find.

Concentrate, concentrate, her brain ordered, speaking to her in her uncle's voice.

Parry, parry, advance … thrust! The words formed her subliminal prayer. Her arm screamed as the muscles twitched; she refused to listen to that particular wail.

Retreat, jump, thrust, retreat.

Jeanne leaped and lurched as the steel foil led her about the corridor, bulging eyes flickering between the sword and the eyes of the one who held it.

She searched for the tell; the sign revealing where next he planned to flail it. There it was. She saw him lean just slightly to his right.

Advance, advance, thrust!

She struck bone; she felt it. The jolt of collision juddered through her hands and up her arms as if the man's life force escaped through her weapon and out her limb. Her arm froze as it pulled back from the thrust.

At her feet lay her foe. A maroon stain appeared upon his chest, flooding the room with the fetid odor of blood. Jeanne looked to her own torso, expecting to find the same such growth, to the tip of her sword, stained with scarlet liquid.

Her rapid breath echoed in the hollowness of her helmet, and her heart beat loud in her ears. She remained, to her vast surprise, unharmed.

I have killed and lived, she thought, and such a thought sent her blood boiling through her veins. With a warrior's cry, she turned to the villain beside her. For a second, she watched as the scoundrel attacked the other Musketeer and her uncle as well.

The foe fought with more skill and strength than the man whose life she'd just taken, but she had tasted the puissance of spilled blood and thirsted for more.

With a stunning overhead blow and grunt of exertion, the miscreant staggered the Musketeer to the floor. A small, sneering smile stained the man's face as he stepped forward, raising his sword above his head, its point aimed directly downward over his opponent's body.

Jeanne leaped into the space between sword tip and body, raising her own sword to deflect the downward thrust aimed to end the Musketeer's life.

Sword locked with sword, muscles bursting with adrenaline-driven strength, Jeanne pushed at her large adversary, holding him at bay for a few precious seconds—seconds in which the fallen Musketeer regained both his senses and his feet.

"Off!" The King's guard screamed, and somehow Jeanne knew.

With shocking abruptness, she released all force toward her opponent and took one quick step to her left. The bandit's mouth fell open in shock. Yellow, ragged teeth gaped from the hole that was his mouth. His body froze, poised forward as if falling from a precipice, finding instead the tip of the Musketeer's weapon. He continued to fall as the soldier drove home the sharp steel, and together they dropped.

The villain lay dead on top of the dazed but unharmed soldier, the Musketeer's sword run completely through his heart.

"Off!" the young man yelled again, but this time he spoke to the dead, heavy body as he shoved it off his chest.

Jeanne reached a hand down to help the Musketeer to his feet. The young man clasped Jeanne's shoulder in gratitude, the only thanks they had time for. Together they turned to help Jules and the other Musketeer, still engaged in combat.

But the numbers had turned, and the strongest of the criminals lay dead; with but a few thrusts of swords and a few short moments until the remaining two evildoers threw up their arms in surrender.

"Forsake your weapons," cried one of the Musketeers, and the two nefarious men dropped their foils to the floor and stepped back, raising their hands in capitulation.

Jules rushed to Jeanne's side, ignoring all others in his haste to ascertain her condition. Jeanne's hand reached for her own helmet, but her uncle roughly pushed the protective device back down as he narrowed his eyes with a small warning shake of his head.

"Are you all right? Are you harmed?"

Jeanne answered with her own shake, realizing that to expose her sex would be to reveal their activities and condemn them both.

"I'm fine," she said with voice two octaves lower than normal.

"You were brilliant." A hand slapped Jeanne's shoulder so hard she stumbled two steps forward. Righting herself, she turned to the man behind her.

The golden-haired Musketeer stood with his hand thrust out in greeting. Without a word, Jeanne took it, only to find her arm pumped roughly and repeatedly.

"It would appear I owe you my life. I cannot thank you enough." Keeping Jeanne's gloved hand in his, the young man made a deep bow. "I am at your orders, monsieur."

Jeanne fought against years of training and instead of curtseying dropped a small bow of her own. "It was my greatest pleasure," she said in her deep voice, almost laughing at the truth of the statement. The thrill of the fight still thrummed loudly in her veins; her head buzzed from the unique surge of power she had wielded with her sword and her will. Jeanne felt her uncle's intent stare as he stood stiffly by her side but refused to look his way, even as he shook hands with the Musketeer, accepting the younger man's gratitude.

"Do you train to be a Musketeer?" the soldier asked.

"It has always been my greatest desire," Jeanne replied huskily, with complete and utter sincerity.

"Come, Henri, we must get these reprobates to the Bastille." The other Musketeer kept the two criminals in check by sword point and began to lead them back along the cement corridor.

"*Oui*, Antoine, I am right behind you." Henri raised a hand, addressing Jeanne still. "To be a Musketeer is your wish, is it? Then I will make you my protégé. Meet us at the Café de l'Oiseau tonight. I will buy you dinner, and we will see what my friends and I can do for you. The Musketeers are always in need of a sword as talented as yours. Especially now, it would seem."

With a rough, masculine cuff to Jeanne's shoulder, Henri made a quick bow and sprinted, sword still in hand, down the hallway, his majestic gray-trimmed, royal blue tunic swaying as he went.

Jeanne and Jules watched the cavaliers lead the criminals away. The drip of seeping moisture through a crack in the cement rang in the ensuing silence like the gong of a bell.

"You cannot do this," Jules whispered, knowing his niece's thoughts all too well.

"I can and I will." Jeanne pulled off her headgear and threw it to the ground. Reaching up, she pulled all the pins out of her coiffure, allowing her hair to fall in waves to just past her shoulders, the loose chocolate brown curls twirling around her face.

"All the young chevaliers wear their own hair, not the periwigs."

She turned to face Jules with hands firmly planted on her hips. "How many times have I heard that when I wear my hair down, all I would need is a mustache to look just like Raol?" Jeanne insisted, referring to her older sibling.

"*Oui, oui,*" Jules stammered, "but—"

"No buts, *mon oncle*, not this time, please." Jeanne grabbed the befuddled man by both shoulders. "If you love me, you will find me a mustache."

Gaston moved up a step in the long line as it crawled forward. He had been all the way at the end of it when he first arrived at the Hall of Mirrors early this morning, and though it felt like many hours since, it had been just one. This Thursday, like most, Louis granted private audiences during council hours, allowing each petitioner to plead their case to him in private, where even the most embarrassing of requests could be discussed. Like most Thursdays, the line grew long and moved slowly. Gaston struggled to contain his eagerness. If his request were to be granted, the largest thorn in his life would be plucked as assuredly as a dark, wilted bloom is trimmed from the vine. The hopeful man saw the reflection of his own twisted smile in the mammoth mirrors lining the stunning room as he passed them one by one.

"Next!" the tall Swiss Guard barked over and over, finally to Gaston.

He jumped forward. With a bow to the guard, he entered the Council Chamber, the room next to and to the north of the King's Bedchamber. The narrow space appeared larger with so few inhabitants under its high cathedral ceiling. A large black marble table commanded the room; other than the surrounding, armless chairs and the two six-branched candelabra sitting upon the table's dark surface, the room stood empty. Louis' dominating presence filled it to capacity.

Gaston traversed slowly and with great trepidation. He had been in this room many times, but on those occasions, ten to twenty other men had accompanied him and the penetrating and intimidating focus of the Grand Monarch was never solely his.

At the far end of the table, Louis XIV sat quietly on his armchair of blue velvet embroidered with fleur-de-lis and a single gold crown. In silence, the King perused papers strewn across the hard, cold surface before him. His greyhounds lay curled up in their usual spot, asleep before the glowing fireplace. Insulated from any noise from without by the heavy blue drapes at both windows and doors, this room held the secrets, both large and small, of an entire nation.

Gaston tiptoed forward. He stopped and stood silently a few paces away from Louis, afraid to speak or to make any indication of his presence.

"What can I do for you, my good comte?"

The King spoke without movement, without lifting his brown-wigged head or looking at Gaston.

"M-y lord," Gaston stammered, then remembered himself and bowed low to his sovereign.

"Yes, yes." Louis waved a hand toward the supplicant before him, impelling Gaston with an impatient gesture to get on with it.

"I...I've come before you today, Your Highness, to ask, in the name of my daughter, Jeanne Yvette Mas du Bois, for your permission and your blessing to wed the son of the Baron l'Haire, Monsieur de Polignac."

Louis looked up from his papers, eyeing the small man closely, bushy dark brows raised in interest...or was it amusement.

"You are marrying your daughter to Monsieur de Polignac? Percy de Polignac?"

"*Oui*, Your Highness, with your permission."

The King chuckled softly, his powerful baritone rumbling in his chest. He sat back in his large chair and pulled the ends of his crimson velvet lounging jacket across the flounce of his shirt.

"She will devour him," Louis stated matter-of-factly, as if reporting the weather fine, and without further comment turned his attention back to his work.

"Your Grace?" Gaston prompted with a raised, furrowed brow.

"From what I remember and what I've heard, monsieur," the King spoke to his papers; if Gaston heard as well, so be it. "Your daughter is a firebrand and Monsieur de Polignac is a simpering poltroon."

This said, the King looked back up, his inquisitive gaze intent upon the face before him.

"Do you dislike your daughter so much?"

Gaston felt the pressure of the King's dark, piercing gaze.

"Does any man truly love his female children?" Gaston raised his slim shoulders to his ears. "They are a drain on one's resources and can bring the family neither honor on the battlefield nor rightful heirs."

The King smiled at the deftness with which the comte evaded the true question.

"I wonder, comte, do you even know your daughter?" asked Louis, a man who loved all his children dearly.

Gaston shifted uncomfortably as if somehow his trousers had suddenly grown tighter.

"I am not sure I understand, Your Highness."

"No," Louis laughed, his broad chest rising and falling with mirth. "I am quite sure you do not. But give it no more thought," Louis reassured the jittery Gaston, who looked fairly stricken at his King's words, with a stilling, raised hand. "You have always served me well. I give my permission and my blessing."

The door to the chamber flew open, and a Swiss Guard entered on fast-moving feet.

"Your Highness." The military man bowed low. "Please forgive the intrusion."

Louis nodded in his direction.

"There has been an…incident in the castle." The guard, though young, knew well to couch his words in front of the Comte de Moreuil. "Your presence is requested by Monsieur Colbert."

Gaston's eyes widened, for the King's senior advisor to call for him, it must be quite the event indeed. Jean Baptiste Colbert had served as Louis' chief minister for close to twenty years, but his swiftly declining health, though not unexpected in a man of sixty-three years, found his involvement in government affairs declining as well.

Louis nodded his head. "I will be there presently."

The King rose and made to leave the room by the side door leading to his private bedchamber. Gaston, having thought himself entirely forgotten, made for the door to the Hall of Mirrors.

"Comte?" Louis held him from leaving.

"Your Highness?" Gaston turned back with a jerk and a bow.

"May I suggest you keep the two young people away from each other as much as possible until the deed is done? Better the mystery than the reality."

Louis turned and left the room.

"Your Highness." Gaston bowed to the retreating figure and gladly quit the Council Chamber.

Gaston walked past the many hopeful petitioners still waiting in line, musing over the King's parting words. Their meaning eluded him no matter how desperately he scrutinized them.

But no matter, no matter at all, Gaston thought, feeling his spirit lift at the gift of the King's acquiescence. *I am done with my devil of a daughter.*

~Eight~

Fully dressed in a day gown of yellow with lace and pearls, she lay on her bed, staring at the ceiling and listening to the activity outside her chamber door.

"Make haste, Adelaide, Bernadette. It is already two o'clock," her father barked.

"*Oui*, Gaston, we are coming," came her mother's singsong answer.

Clacking hard heels undulated from close to far. A loud click and the door to the suite closed behind the retreating figures of her parents and sister.

Jeanne jumped off the bed as if a musket shot burst in the air. Alone, at last, she was alone. With a shoulder push against the tall dresser she and Bernadette shared, she turned it outward until it opened off the wall like a door. Squatting down, the many layers of her skirt billowing with air, Jeanne pulled at the slat of wooden flooring laying against the wall. Looking down at her beautiful *colichemarde*, Jeanne stared at it for a moment. But soon her reverence passed, and she reached for the delicate, deadly sword, a starved child reaching for a crust of stale bread.

Swish, swish. Jeanne flayed the thin sword through the air, cutting the atmosphere around her. Keeping her eyelids tightly closed, Jeanne used her mind's sight to envision herself once more in the cold, dank basement corridor. She felt the shock as her sword met her enemy's, felt the tension run through her limbs. Her breath came in quick, hard gasps as her struggle continued and she relived the thrilling moments over and over again.

* * *

"Adelaide? Gaston?" Jules scratched at the door to the Du Bois suite of rooms as he opened it a crack, peeking through the slit.

"They are not here, good *oncle*," Jeanne called, moving swiftly from her bedroom to the common room to find her uncle already entering. "They have just left with Bernadette for a turn in the gardens."

Jules closed the door behind him. With forefinger to pursed lips, he remained mute until he joined his niece in the sitting room, kissing her fondly on both cheeks.

"I know, *ma chère*, I know. I saw them leave. I've been waiting for them to go since earlier this morning." Jules' dashing features broke into a delighted grin. "But there were others in the corridor, others whose ears are much larger than their discretion, and I made the show for their satisfaction."

Jeanne laughed at her uncle's mischievous actions and the delight he took in them. "But why? Why such a show?"

Jules took a sack from off his shoulder where it had been resting and untied it. "Because I needed to find you alone but had no wish for anyone to know of this particular meeting."

"You speak in riddles, *mon oncle*. But I must say, I am intrigued." Jeanne took a seat in one of the armchairs, gazing in fondness at the bright and spirited countenance of her uncle. One glance at what he removed from his bag and she bounded back up to her feet.

"Are those what I think?" Jeanne squeaked.

Jules held up clothing—pieces of men's clothing. A brown cloth coat trimmed with leather, buckskin knee breeches, and a shirt of lawn with ivory lace at collar and cuff.

"*Incroyable*, they are beautiful!" Jeanne exclaimed, grabbing for the pieces and holding them up to her body.

They were, in fact, a bit careworn, but still the garments' quality was evident. To Jeanne, they looked more like a key, a key to a chain she carried both night and day.

"Well, I am not so sure of that, but I did think they would fit, both your body and your adventure." Jules pulled more items from his magic bag: linen hose, leather gloves, bucket-top boots, and a brown felt hat adorned with a single white plume. "They recently belonged to a young gentleman of high position but low resources. Though I dare say, he shall not miss them."

From his own waist, he removed his leather baldric.

"For your *colichemarde*," he explained, handing her the sword holster.

The last item he retrieved was small, so small he held it cupped in his palm, holding it out to Jeanne but concealing it beneath his bent digits.

"Do not ever doubt my love for you," he said and slowly unfurled his fingers.

Jeanne laughed with pure delight. Grabbing it, she threw her arms around her uncle's neck.

"I never have nor shall I ever," she whispered into his shoulder.

Pulling away, she held the tuft of hair with her fingers, petting it as she would a small creature.

"But where—?" Jeanne began as she gazed down at the inch-long pieces of hair melded together with a sticky hardened substance.

"I happened upon your brother earlier in the day, did I not tell you?" Jules put the fingers of both hands in the small pockets of his waistcoat, strutting about the room as proudly as a conquering warrior. "Yes, indeed I did, and at the barber, no less."

Jeanne's long fingers flew to her mouth, trying unsuccessfully to quell the giggling. Raol's hair…of course. The exactness of the color startled as if it grew from a single head, not both of theirs. She held the piece against her face, sticking out and curling up her upper lip, trying to balance the mustache in place with her facial contortions.

"But how—?"

"Where are your marks, my dear?"

"Of course, Uncle, of course," Jeanne chirped and ran to her room. She found the small, round ornate box where she and Bernadette kept a variety of face patches. Next to it, as always, stood the small apothecary jar of pine tar. Using a small brush normally employed for face powder, Jeanne painted a thin layer of the gummy substance onto her mustache. Putting the brush down, she took up the mustache and, with the aid of the small, cloudy mirror above the vanity, affixed it to her upper lip.

"Ha!" Jules laughed from his position at the room's door. Jeanne tossed him a wink, unable to shift her gaze from her mutated reflection and her laughter joined his. A hilarious picture indeed; the masculine facial hair appeared preposterous when sandwiched between her perfectly curled and piled coiffure and her low-cut, overwhelmingly feminine bodice.

"Wait, dear man, wait." Jeanne flew from the room, pulling the pins from her hair as she went, shaking it free when they were all removed. In the sitting room, she grabbed the fine shirt and held it to her chest, covering her own clothes beneath it.

"What say you now, good man?" Jeanne asked in her deep, gravelly male voice born in the basement the day her true courage had been born as well.

The smile faded from Jules' face, replaced with sincere astonishment.

"*Mon Dieu*!" He exclaimed, stymied at the sight he beheld...a younger, smaller Raol now stood in the chamber.

Shock receding, his delight rose once more. He gave a leg and a flourishing bow to the person before him.

"Bonjour, Monsieur...Jean?" He pronounced her name with the masculine inflection.

"Jean-Luc," the disguised character responded. "At your service, good sir."

Her uncle laughed at her clever choice.

"There is more to being a man than wearing men's clothing and a mustache," Jules lectured Jeanne as she removed, a trifle painfully, her mustache and put it, with the clothes, back in the bag, while pondering where she would hide them.

"Now, *oncle*, I am quite sure I can act stubborn and self-possessed," she responded without looking up.

"Impertinent wench," he chided, cuffing her smartly on the back of her head. "I am speaking of mannerisms and affectations."

"I know, good *oncle*, I know." Jeanne completed her packing and stood before Jules. "Teach me. Teach me to be a man."

Jules crossed his arms, one hand coming up to cup his chin thoughtfully. "It helps that you are not a very feminine woman."

"I beg your pardon, sir?" Jeanne huffed, feigning great insult.

"Oh, you know what I mean," Jules explained. "You are not silly, prissy...overly giggly."

Jeanne nodded hesitantly. "Ah, *oui*, but I'm still not sure if I should be insulted."

"You shouldn't. Now, on to business. Be sure to make your gestures larger and not so delicate—you want to be thought a man but not a fop. Be sure to bow, not curtsey. Be sure to grab things. Do not delicately lift them, with your pinkies up."

Jules continued his lecture, pacing around the room as he thought of mannerism after mannerism, the intricate yet subtle things that distinguished a gentleman from a lady. Jeanne stood quietly, enraptured and intent, trying with all her might to commit to memory all of his instructions.

"But most of all"—Jules stopped before her—"you must walk like a man."

"*Walk* like a man?"

"*Oui*. You must walk as if you possessed..." Jules stammered, his discomfort obvious. "Well, my dear, men have...well, you see..."

"Ah, yes, of course." Jeanne finally understood and tried not to giggle. "Their...manhood, *oui*?"

"*Oui*," Jules huffed gratefully. "You see, it does make one walk differently."

"Really?"

"Really. For one thing, the stride is longer." Jules demonstrated as he walked through the room to the front door and back. "But mostly it is the position of the legs. They are not positioned the same as with women."

Jeanne stared at Jules with one raised brow.

"They are not as close together."

Jeanne stared for a moment more, then shook her head.

"Well, of course not. They couldn't be, could they?"

"Well, for some, unfortunately, I suppose they could. But not I." Jules puffed up his chest, and Jeanne bit the inside of her lip to stifle the laughter. Turning quickly, she marched the same path Jules had just taken, imitating his manner as best she could.

"*Bon, bon*," Jules praised as if they were again at the duel. "The stride is good, the forcefulness of the shoulders, correct. But the legs are still not set wide enough apart." Jules considered her intently.

Jeanne watched his determined contemplations, as he looked past her, as his eyes brightened with discovery.

"Of course," he barked. Stepping toward her swiftly, he reached behind her, grabbing something from her mother's embroidery box, holding it triumphantly before her face.

"Good lord, *oncle*, you cannot mean?" Jeanne stared at the item in his hand—her mother's pincushion. Made of a soft fabric and stuffed with cotton, it was funnel-shaped at one end, expanding to a small ball at the other.

"It is perfect." Jules pushed it into her hand. "Go. Go put it…there."

Jeanne shook her head at her uncle but did as he bid. Behind the closed bedroom door, Jeanne lifted layer after layer of silk and taffeta, finally finding the top of her long stockings and shoving the cushion firmly in place, a plain satin garter keeping it there. Lowering her skirts, she fluffed them down and strode from the room, legs forced much further apart as she did.

"Well, it works," she reported, entering the room with a decided swagger. "But I care not for this. How can you men stand this? It is quite uncomfortable!"

"You should talk, my dear," Jules said, gesturing, with a tic of his head, at her firm, high breasts. "Those cannot be a joy to carry around all the time, either."

"Ha!" Jeanne barked with laughter, then froze in panic. Grabbing her breasts, her eyes bulged and her mouth gaped open. "My breasts!"

"*Oui*, you will have to bind them. And tightly."

"Ah, *oui*, bind them, of course." Jeanne calmed; her uncle had obviously given great thought to the details of her disguise.

Jules gave her shoulder a fond pat. "I must take my leave. I am sure your parents and sister are not much longer for the park."

"True, *oncle*, true," Jeanne agreed, though she trembled at his leaving, as though his absence would make the reality of her evening's adventure all the more real.

"But I must ask two things of you, *ma chère*." Jules stood before her, raising her chin with his hand so their gazes met unimpeded.

"Anything for you."

"If you love me, you will die before telling who gave you these items." Jules nodded at the bag at Jeanne's feet.

"Never question my love, *cher oncle*."

"If your aunt found out, she would laugh till she cried, in private only. In public she would punish me, quite severely I am sure."

Jeanne smiled, picturing her aunt chasing her uncle down with the strap she used to threaten her children.

"And secondly, you must come to me first thing in the morning. Immediately after chapel, when your aunt will be with the other Bas Bleu. I will not rest until I know you are safe."

Jeanne nodded, smiling, warming with his concern.

"Nor could I go long without knowing every juicy tidbit," Jules said over his shoulder as he made his way to the door. At the egress, however, he stopped abruptly and turned back to Jeanne.

"Are you sure, Jeanne, truly sure?"

Jeanne tilted her chin up and squared her shoulders. With the deep, gravelly voice of Jean-Luc, she assured him. "I have never been this sure of anything."

~Nine~

"Jean-Luc" hailed a coach and jumped onto the lower step before it came to a complete stop.

"To the Café de l'Oiseau in Clagny, my good man!" "he" shouted to the postilion.

Jeanne threw herself onto the padded seat cushion of the carriage and almost giggled out loud. She put her gloved hand to her chest to keep her heart from leaping out. Through the layers of men's clothes, through the glove, she felt it beating with all the naked fear coursing through her; it banged against her ribs like a mallet on a drum. The sweat dripped down her arms and her gauze-wrapped breasts; she inhaled the fetid odor of her own secretions.

What kind of man would I be if I did not smell a little?

Jeanne almost giggled again, amused at the question she posed to herself. As the carriage turned out the chateau's gate and onto the Place d'Armes, Jeanne felt her breathing finally returning to normal.

Gone was the pounding sound of her heartbeat echoing through her ears. She felt almost herself for the first time since leaving her suite of rooms. She felt most like herself for the first time in her life.

As soon as her family had left for the evening's *Soirée d'Apartements*, she had morphed into "Jean-Luc", stuffing her gown and undergarments in a bag.

That first step out of the family suite as "Jean-Luc" had been the greatest of traumas. As the adrenaline surged through her, she kept her face cast down to the ground, certain she would be caught and imprisoned immediately. But as she strode through the manse and out into the garden, where she stashed her bag under a hollow pedestal, she moved virtually unnoticed. Such anonymity gave her strength, though it did little to calm her nerves. The only people to show any notice were, strangely enough, a few young women, friends of Jeanne's who smiled and giggled at the dashing sight of "Jean-Luc." Within moments, Jeanne began to feel the freedom bestowed upon a man. To walk alone, without friend or chaperone, was a liberating experience, and the imitated man's swagger Jeanne affected had become one of delight like a child set free to run in the green fields after hours in the classroom.

To be here, in this carriage, alone and on her way to a town, was an amazing reality. Jeanne looked out the window, seeing the sights as the road led from Versailles to Clagny, one of the three towns surrounding the palace, as if with new eyes. To the north lay Trianon, to the east, St. Cyr. But it was to the south of

Versailles, only two kilometers, to the town of Clagny that "Jean-Luc" traveled. Jeanne had never been to Clagny; it boasted many a café and bistro as well as the Hôtel Treville, home to the Musketeers and their famous captain. Boisterous, raucous, and just a bit wicked, Jeanne had never been allowed to enter the village's confines, until tonight.

* * *

"Jean-Luc" stood just inside the heavy oak door, peeking into the Café de l'Oiseau as a child peeks around the corner to the bottom of the tree on Christmas morn. A single wide-open room, the café boasted a bar of dark wood running along one back corner and in the middle, there rose a square, stone fire pit. Hanging above the licking flames, quails and pigeons, fish and roasts churned on a spit, dropping their juices onto the fire with a sizzling splash and a burst of tantalizing aromas to tickle the nostrils and excite the palate. Jeanne swallowed back the saliva that formed naturally in her mouth. Rough-hewn wooden tables and chairs covered every square inch of remaining floor space. Each table claimed at least two inhabitants; most were crowded.

Jeanne scanned the café's loyal clientele, rambunctious and rowdy men accompanied by a smattering of women. The patrons' dark clothing of leather with touches of lace, homespun gowns with a few ribbons here and there, clean yet worn, proclaimed them to be the merchants and the bourgeois filling the city by the hundreds. The shabbily dressed yet merry serving wenches danced their way through the maze of tables and groping hands, trays heavy with mugs of ale and dishes of carved meat held high above their heads.

"This is him. It must be. This is our savior!"

Jeanne flinched. Henri, the golden-haired Musketeer, strode toward her from deep in the front corner of the room, pushing chairs and those in them brusquely out of his way.

Henri slapped her on the back with his left hand as his right grabbed hers, pumping it heartily. Jeanne responded in kind, remembering from her uncle's tutelage how a fierce grip spoke of masculinity.

"You are my rescuer, are you not?"

"*Oui*, Monsieur. *Bonjour*. I have found my way to the right place, I see." Jeanne's throat constricted as she forced the air through tightened vocal cords. The thought of speaking unnerved her, but she found herself pleased. She lowered her chin to her chest to produce the deeper tones and made a mental note to avoid the movement overmuch.

"That you have, indeed. I've been telling my friends about nothing but your prowess with the sword all evening. If you did not come, they would think you were a figment of my vivid imagination."

Henri smiled, and Jeanne found herself enchanted by the lopsided, full-lipped grin. Such errant thoughts fled as her new friend brought her toward his table.

"But pray, tell me your name so I may introduce you to this miserable group of rapscallions," Henri chided, producing the desired jeering and cursing from his compatriots.

"I am Jean-Luc de Cassel." Jeanne matched Henri's wide strides as they made their way through the room.

"And I am Henri Boucher d'Aubigne, at your service. Gentlemen," Henri announced, banging a pewter tankard on the table, capturing the attention of the three men around it, "I am most pleased to introduce Jean-Luc de Cassel. If not for him and his mastery with the sword, I would not be here with you tonight."

"Well, no matter, we are pleased to meet you nonetheless," teased one of the men, who stood and reached out to take the hand Jeanne offered. Jeanne grasped his hand firmly but faltered as she took a good look at him; she had never seen a man so beautiful. Perfect blond hair flowed in waves to his shoulders. Ocean blue eyes and a thick mustache over exquisite lips made him look like a doll rather than a real flesh-and-blood person.

Henri gave the man a good punch in the arm. "Do not be fooled by Laurent's beauty or his sarcasm, Jean-Luc. He is a decorated Musketeer and an expert swordsman himself. Jean-Luc, Laurent de Ventadour."

Jeanne gave a slight bow. "It is an honor to make your acquaintance, sir."

"It is an honor to shake the hand of my rescuer as well." The man stood and bowed to Jeanne, the one Henri hand called Antoine, the other Musketeer in the morning's tussle. She recognized his mousy brown hair and rather nondescript countenance. Though not unattractive, he appeared plainly handsome next to the shining Laurent. "Antoine de La Ferte, monsieur. I am at your orders."

"Merci, monsieur," Jeanne responded with an answering bow. "But please make no more fuss of my actions. I did no more than anyone would have done in such a situation."

"Perhaps, perhaps," Antoine conceded, "but none too many could have done it so skillfully."

"I hear you fought like a Musketeer?" declared a deep baritone voice, so deep it seemed to echo out of a cave, and Jeanne turned to a black-haired, black-eyed man.

"I hope so, mon—" Jeanne stammered, unable to finish as the man took her hand in his and it disappeared. She followed his face as he rose to a height Jeanne had never imagined possible. Standing tall, he was a good six or seven inches above her, vast and broad-shouldered with a head like a small boulder and no real neck to speak of separating the two.

"Do not be frightened, Jean-Luc. Please make the acquaintance of Gerard de Gramont." Henri sat back in his chair, grabbing an empty one at the next table for Jeanne. "To make war is by far Gerard's most passionate desire. He wishes for nothing more than to die with honor on the battlefield. But though he may look like a bear, he is naught but a pussy ca—"

Gerard lifted Henri out of his seat and off the floor with hardly a movement and barely an effort, staring down into the surprised face of his friend.

"Or perhaps he is truly a bear," Henri said, feigning fear. Gerard dumped Henri back in his chair and sat himself. As broad as he was tall, Gerard's muscles bulged and stretched the sleeves of the thin white shirt he wore under his waistcoat of black leather.

Jeanne could not help herself. "What did your mother feed you to make you so?" she asked.

"Everything," Gerard responded with a surprisingly sweet smile; Jeanne joined the others' laughter.

Finally at ease among these men, Jeanne relaxed into the chair as she accepted the cup of wine rather than the ale first offered. She grabbed the receptacle as taught, not by the handle, but by the base of the mug with a firm grip. Her first sip of the fruity beverage slipped out her mouth and down her chin, unaccustomed as she was to drinking with a mustache.

"You are all Musketeers?" she asked, inconspicuously wiping her mouth.

"No," barked Laurent, surprising Jeanne as well as his compatriots. "We are, in fact, of the First Company of the King's Musketeers, the greatest of all Musketeers. The same company of the great Athos, Porthos, Aramis, and d'Artagnan."

Jeanne would have thought the man bragged if not for the pride shining in his eyes.

"We heard you fought like a man possessed, yet with great skill and cunning," Gerard said, wiping the froth of ale from his mustache with the back of his large paw of a hand. "Where did you come by your skill?"

"From one of the King's own fencing partners, Monsieur du Mas," Jeanne boasted, proud of her uncle. "He is my current sponsor at Versailles."

"Have you seen much action?"

Jeanne felt the scrutiny of M. de Gramont's dark eyes. She twitched nervously in her seat, almost reaching up to scratch the irritating mustache sitting so uncomfortably upon her lip.

"No, monsieur, not real action. I have been studying for many months now, but today was, in fact, my first kill."

"Wonderful," Antoine barked raising his mug toward Jeanne's direction. "Felicitations, good sir."

"Hear, hear!" the others joined in.

"We felled two of the miscreants," Henri explained to Laurent and Gerard.

Jeanne swallowed a deep draught of wine, finally accustomed to drinking with hair on her lip. "Where are the other two? What has happened to them?"

"Well, my dear fellow, they are in the Bastille, where else?" Antoine explained. "They will be paid a visit by the Marquis de Louvois soon if they have not already."

"May God have mercy on their souls, the poor bastards," Laurent said with a smile.

"The Marquis is sure to get the truth from the criminals, one way or another," Henri piped in. "If it were not for you, Jean-Luc, Antoine and I would not be here, and their fate would not be in the hands of Louvois."

"Please, dear sir, I beg you. Mention it no more," Jeanne said modestly, yet her heart beat faster at his praise.

"Is it true? You wish to be a Musketeer?" Gerard asked. "Is that not what Henri told us?"

"It has been my dream since I was but a small child, flaying at my siblings with my small wooden whinger." In her truth burst sincerity.

"You seem quite young?" Antoine asked. "How old are you?"

"I am seventeen," Jeanne replied, unconsciously sitting taller and straighter in her chair.

"Bit of a scarecrow, aren't you, boy?" Gerard playfully slapped Jeanne on the back, causing her to lurch forward and spew the wine in her mouth.

"Sometimes size doesn't matter, good sir," Jeanne responded, wiping her face as Gerard had with the back of her hand, but failing to join in as the others roared with laughter. She smiled to hide her confusion, obviously missing some private jest she did not understand.

"True, true." Laurent nodded his head, still smiling with amusement. "But you must have at least two years of military experience to qualify for the Musketeers."

"Of this I know," Jeanne persisted. "I am hoping my two years as page to my cousin Raol du Bois will be enough." Jeanne offered the carefully composed story she'd crafted during the carriage ride.

"You squired with Du Bois? Where?" Henri grabbed the large tray burdened with various meats the serving maid placed in the middle of the table.

The four men attacked the food with complete abandon as if they had not eaten in a fortnight.

"It was during the last two years against the Dutch. We were there when William III was defeated at the Mont Cassel." Jeanne wracked her brain to remember all the details of her brother's letters, letters she had read over and over. "I was with Du Bois when we marched into Freiburg."

"Ah, *oui*." Laurent nodded and smiled, reaching out with his hand for a chicken leg. "I was there as well. We were brilliant in our victory, yes?"

"I thought so." Jeanne grabbed some fish from the plate as the others did, without the use of a serving utensil, feeling delightedly wicked in doing so.

"Perhaps you are right, Jean-Luc," Henri spoke through a mouthful of pigeon. "Perhaps that would be enough to satisfy the requirements. We will be happy to speak of you to Captain d'Artagnan, will we not, gentlemen?"

Jeanne watched in silence as the three other men nodded, raising their glasses to their lips in salute.

If I were indeed Jean-Luc, I would be thrilled beyond description, but I am not.

She raised her mug to her lips, almost draining it of the pungent liquid. Her long hand gripped her cup, her knuckles straining white with the force of her grasp. Jeanne pulled away for a moment, if only in her mind, back to reality. She could never live among these men as a fledgling Musketeer did. She could never join in triumph as their enemies were put down, never send them running like frightened children from the scarred ground. She could never serve beside these men on a battlefield where the glory of honor was scented with men's waste as they voided themselves in the last moment of life. She could never do any of it. Her hand clasping the mug slammed against the hardwood table, the few drops remaining at its bottom splashing out.

"Our friend needs more wine!" Gerard called to a passing serving maid.

"*Oui*, it would seem I do." Jeanne stared at her empty glass and the glistening globules on the marred wood with as much surprise as the man beside her.

"Where is Raol these days?" Laurent raised his voice to be heard over the quartet of musicians who had taken up their instruments, regaling the room with a spirited song. "I believe I remember him."

"He is teaching at one of the regional academies." Jeanne pushed her plate away from her, having had her fill of the trout.

"Regional academies?" Antoine asked, still stuffing his face with all manner of victuals.

"*Oui*," Jeanne replied, her voice warming with pride for her brother. "The ones contrived by Monsieur Colbert. Companies of cadets in outlying regions, such as Picardy where Raol is, are formed into one academy. The governors of the province run them, but it is retired soldiers that do the teaching. They instruct in musketry, drilling, fencing."

"Sounds like a good job for you, Gerard," Antoine said to the large military man. Gerard bobbed his head as he stuffed yet more food down his throat.

Jeanne continued, a smirk tickling her mouth.

"They also teach math, geography and... dancing."

"Hah! Not for you after all, Gramont," guffawed Laurent.

"What do you mean with such hateful words?" the burly Gerard barked, rising from his seat. "I am a great dancer, better than Louis himself."

The huge Musketeer reached out and grabbed the nearest serving wench, abducting her so abruptly, her already loose and falling dirty blond hair became even more disheveled. With spasmodic movements, the lumbering giant of a man led the maid through clomping, jerky maneuvers.

Laughing along with the others as they all rose from their seats to clap along with the music, Jeanne smiled at Henri.

"He would do much better sober, I think."

"No," Henri laughed, watching the hilarious exploits of his dear companion, "actually he does much worse then."

The music changed quickly, from the slow baroque to a spirited, lively tune.

"Now we do the gavotte," Gerard cried to his partner as she tried not only to keep her feet but to keep her feet from being trampled by the mammoth Musketeer as well.

Lifting the woman's rag doll-like arms above her head, Gerard began to twirl her to his left. But instead of completing the complicated maneuver, his monstrous right foot landed forcefully on her left. Stunned, he released the woman's hands without pulling his lead, sending her flying across the room, where she landed with a loud and resounding thud.

There was a moment of stunned, shocked silence—a moment quickly filled with uproarious laughter. Gerard, seeing the wench slowly rising to her feet and noting that she was, for the most part, unharmed, he turned to his audience and gave them a deep bow, sending them all into more gales of laughter.

"You are a buffoon!" Laurent cried to his friend. Rushing over to the still-tipsy serving maid, he graciously brushed the dirt from her skirt, taking special care where the fabric curved around her taut derriere. Finding the shape much to his liking, the devilishly handsome man cooed softly in the girl's ear, leading her back to their table and plopping her on his lap as he took back his seat.

"Are you all right?" Jeanne asked, leaning toward the young woman. "What is your name?"

"Melisande, monsieur, and I am fine, *merci*."

The comely woman nodded, accepting the large mug of ale Laurent offered her. She took a deep swig of the brown liquid, raising her chin to get every last drop. Laurent stared at her lips, licking his own as he watched beads of moisture drip from Melisande's full, pouty mouth.

"I am undone."

Jeanne heard him moan and watched amazed as, without further preamble, Laurent's lips captured Melisande's mouth. She tried to pull her eyes from the private moment but could not, hypnotized by the sensual act displayed before her, an action she'd never glimpsed so closely before.

Laurent released his hold upon the wench, hefting her up higher upon his lap as they shared a small, private smile. From the corner of his eye, he saw the inquisitive attentions of the young cavalier. Laurent turned and faced Jeanne with raised brows and a devilish smile.

"Would you care for some?" he asked, with a tic of his head in Melisande's direction, offering her as he would some victuals. "She is really quite superb."

"Me?" Jeanne heard the squeak in her voice. She grabbed her mug, taking a deep draught of the fruity liquid. "Not for me, *merci*, monsieur. I can see she belongs to you completely."

Laurent bowed at the waist to Jeanne, accepting the compliment as he acknowledged her refusal. Turning back to the dazed young woman, his full lips attacked hers once more.

"These are the best times of our lives—the best such rascals as we can hope for."

Jeanne turned to Henri, touched by his philosophical words as he too watched the carnal conduct.

"Rascals?" Jeanne laughed. "Surely you gentlemen are noblemen, as are most Musketeers, no?"

She studied these legendary men; men she considered to be the best her country had to offer. They were certainly the most celebrated swordsmen in the whole world. They were also a legion of devil-may-care fellows, perfectly undisciplined toward all save their captain and their King. Here, in this café, as in cabarets and hôtels surrounding Versailles, they imposed their power upon all. As the sun slept they became half-drunk, spreading themselves about, shouting, twisting their mustaches, and clanking their swords.

"You are partly correct, though some of us are of the lowest nobility, such as yourself, a cousin of a cousin of a comte or duc. While others…" Antoine's eyes slipped sidelong to glance at Henri.

"Others hold a more lofty position."

Henri eyeballed his friend, and though he spoke to Jeanne, his gaze remained affixed upon Antoine. "But we do not associate ourselves with those so privileged, do we, Antoine?"

"Oh, no, of course not." Antoine's sarcasm was not lost on Jeanne.

"Why do you not live at the palace?" Jeanne queried.

"All here are too lowly ranked to deserve such sumptuous accommodations, thank heavens." Henri raised his glass toward the ceiling, taking a large swallow of the dark red liquid.

"Thank heavens? You would not wish to live at Versailles?"

"No, thank you indeed." Henri banged his mug on the table. "To belong to a class which has privileges but no usefulness, to drown in the pool with the other courtiers, to lie and backstab, to flatter while loathing, to claw and dig and work one's way up to possibly holding the King's undergarments someday? And perhaps, merely perhaps, after years of this, to be cursed with a minister's position, which is no more than a puppet for the King?" Henri took a deep breath to finish his harangue. "No, not for me is such a life."

Henri's words were like a priest's sermon. To hear such statements, sentiments reflecting the deepest secrets of her own thoughts, startled and exhilarated her. Was it possible this man felt the same as she did?

"I understand you completely," she said, unable to say more, gaze intent upon his full lips.

Henri turned to her, filling both his cup and hers with more wine. "I believe you do, Jean-Luc. I believe you and I will be great friends."

The two likened souls raised their glasses, toasting their newfound kinship.

* * *

It stood at the end of the Rue Saint-Antoine. The gray stone castle rose up as a black silhouette against the murky sky: a huddled giant, ominous and imposing. Its tall towers reached for the firmament like hands reaching out from a grave.

The three-hundred-year-old Bastille fortress had been built as part of the defensive structure of Paris. The Mad Monarch, Charles VI, had turned it into a prison, a penitentiary of such abominable affliction, the mere mention of its name pierced the heart with abject fear. Once it had housed only political and religious prisoners and society's everyday criminals. Under the Sun King and his father, it had come to devour seditious writers and young rakes taken at the request of their own families, families who no longer cared to deal with the wildness of their offspring.

Since the Fronde, just the mention of the Bastille instilled fear and trepidation in even the highly ranked, for at the behest of a *letter de cachet*, a sealed royal order signed by Louis XIV, anyone could be taken away, swallowed by the stone monster. Many entered through its tall wooden doors, but not all came out. Some claimed that when they passed by late at night, when all life lay still and quiet around it, the screams of the inhabitants could be heard from the street.

The gong of the famous Bastille clock announced the hour. Adorned as most large timepieces were with figures, these representing a saint in bonds, its carillon could be heard through the castle, by every inhabitant, as it slowly, methodically, mercilessly noted every moment of their captivity.

The Marquis de Louvois swept his long, dark cloak around his shoulders as he swiftly turned the corner and entered the dark closet serving as office for the warden and the turnkey. A tall and imposing man, he was, nonetheless, dwarfed by the masked man accompanying him.

"Where is your master? Where is Gourville?" Louvois' dark eyes searched the small, dimly lit chamber as he searched for the Bastille's governor.

"M-marquis de Louvois." The small man, weighed down by his belt full of keys, jumped to his feet as he stammered. "I...I do not know, Excellency."

François Michel Le Tellier, the Marquis de Louvois, had been Louis' Secretary of State for War since 1666. Lately, his long fingers seemed to reach into so many more affairs of state, slipping into the prominent position of senior advisor as Colbert's life slipped away from him.

"Find him. And be quick about it," Louvois snapped.

The turnkey darted past the Marquis and his henchman, rushing up the long flight of stone stairs leading to the upper floors of the prison.

Louvois paced for a moment in the small office, barely able to move in the confined enclosure, and strode out to the hall; still narrow, it allowed him at least a few steps in each direction. His long face burned red with annoyance as he followed the servant's path. The circular staircase edged the interior of the tall tower as it wound its way both up and down. Lanterns whose low, flickering flames cast strange shadows upon the rock wall, umbrae that appeared to move with the slightest breeze, dimly lit the way.

Not even a minute passed and the jangling sound of the turnkey's return echoed through the hollow hall.

"Marquis, Marquis, I am here." The small, stout Gourville scurried behind the key holder. "I was not expecting you today. What brings you to our fine establishment?"

"Fine establishment?" Louvois looked squarely down his wide nose at the warden, one incredulous brow raised high. "The two brought in by the Musketeers earlier, have you spoken with them?"

"Just long enough to give them a welcome they are not soon to forget." The governor smiled like a wolf that had just swallowed a vole.

Louvois smiled in kind, quite familiar with Gourville's welcomes, one given to every inmate with the tip of a whip. "Which one screamed first?"

Gourville rubbed his hands together as he remembered. "Govin."

"Take me to him," Louvois barked and began his descent down the castle.

The warden and turnkey rushed to pass him, to lead the way downward. The behemoth in the shroud brought up the rear.

Two floors down and the stench of filthy, rotting human flesh became oppressive. Louvois' nostrils quivered in distaste. Reaching the appropriate door, the warden beckoned for the turnkey to do his job, unlocking the heavy steel-enforced door. Gourville pushed it open and stepped aside, allowing Louvois and his companion to enter. As the warden made to step over the threshold, Louvois halted his progress.

"Leave us," the marquis commanded with a rude twitch of his double chin.

The warden's face scrunched with words he dare not say, placed the lantern he carried on the floor, gave a small leg, and hesitantly left the room, closing the massive aperture behind him. With a last peek into the room through the two thin slats, Gourville motioned for the guard of the hall to stand before the door.

Inside the room, Louvois turned to the captive, finding him in a pile of limp flesh in the darkest corner of the small chamber. The fecund odors of sweat, urine, and feces pulsed from him like heat from a flame.

"Govin, do you know who I am?"

The beaten man raised his grime-ridden countenance and looked at the person before him, straining to see in the dark of the chamber. With a shrug of his shoulder and a shake of his head, he denied such knowledge.

"I am the Marquis de Louvois."

Govin gasped, pushing with his feet, his stained boots scraping the ground as he tried to gain a foothold, pushing himself farther back against the wall and into the corner. He needed no further introduction. Unlike Colbert, Louvois preferred violence, bent on the brutal destruction of all he deemed unworthy.

"Ah, I see you do know me." Louvois stepped closer to the miscreant now trembling in fear. He bent his knees, lowering his large body to the same level as Govin's. "Why were you at Versailles?"

Govin stared into the frightening face so close to his own, stared silently.

The back of Louvois' hand met Govin's face; the savage strength of it split the prisoner's lip. He wiped at it with the tattered sleeve of his coat but still said nothing.

"Very well. Campan?" Louvois called and rose, straightening his cramping legs. Without looking over his shoulder, the Marquis gave a flick of his hand and the masked man he called Campan took two large steps to hover over Govin.

The captive's eyes widened as they rose. A small, deep moan of fear escaped his closed lips.

The henchman reached down one mammoth hand, grabbing Govin by his hair, pulling him to his feet as he pulled strands of it out by their roots. Campan stood the prisoner in the middle of the room, fastening the manacles hanging off the end of the chains embedded in each side wall onto his wrists. With one grasp of his collar and one tug, Campan stripped Govin of his coat and shirt, leaving Govin's pale chest and whip-scarred back exposed and vulnerable.

Louvois slowly stepped around the captive to stand before him.

"I offer you one more chance, out of sheer generosity of spirit. Why were you at Versailles?"

Govin spoke not a word, head hanging limp upon a dirty neck.

"Very well," Louvois said again and stepped back.

The first blow pounded his midsection, pushing every vapor of breath from his lungs. Govin doubled over as much as he could with his shackles holding him in place, not enough breath left in his lungs to groan in pain. The second, third, and fourth blows struck his face, one after the other, splitting his lip, eyes, and cheek. The shadows on the wall danced as huge, powerful arms flayed through the air, as Govin's head rolled on his shoulders as his stringy, dirty hair flew in the air from each impact. The gray stone walls soon glistened with droplets of blood, the bright red blazing against the cold ashen rock. Between each blow the same question.

"Why?"

As his eyes swelled shut, as his consciousness tattered with each blow, Govin heard Louvois' powerful, angry voice reverberate through the chamber and his bruised brain.

"How dare you attempt to assassinate the King of France?"

Campan's fist struck Govin's nose. The crack of breaking bone echoed in the dank air.

"The most powerful sovereign in the world!"

Campan's curled hand struck him like a hammer in the back, the pain resounding through his kidneys.

Through split, blood-dripping lips, Govin finally spoke.

"Not... King... Queen."

All movement stilled; all sound ceased.

"Who?" Louvois simply asked in the vacuum and the beaten, defeated man gladly gave up the name.

Louvois gestured to Campan with his chin, and the giant of a man left the room at once. The marquis took one last look at the inert man before him and left the room as well.

"Take him away," Louvois called casually over his shoulder to the warden standing with the guard waiting outside the door.

"Put him in the lowest cell," he ordered, referring to the putrid, ordure-filled, vermin-infested subterranean rooms on the bottom level of the Bastille. "Even if France wins every war for the next millennium, the King will never pardon the likes of this wretch."

~Ten~

Uncle Jules opened the door the instant Jeanne made the first scratch upon its surface as if he had been waiting there just for her.

"You are all right?" Jules swept Jeanne into his arms before she said a word. She nodded her head enthusiastically as he held it tightly against his shoulder.

"I am more than fine, *oncle.* I am magnificent." Jeanne thrummed with lingering wonder. "It was amazingly easy. It was … amazing."

Jules shook his head at her but smiled nonetheless. The dark circles stained circles about his eyes as his worry for his favorite niece had ruined his night's attempts at sleep.

"Come, *ma chère*, come in and tell me everything." Jules beckoned Jeanne into the two small rooms comprising his family's entire living space and closed the door behind them.

Jeanne took two steps in and stood in the heart of her uncle's sitting room. Through an open door to her left, she glimpsed her two young cousins in the only other room, the one used as a sleeping chamber for the entire family. Immediately her body began to bake in the oppressive heat, moisture seeping from every pore of her body.

Stationed directly below the roof of the palace on the third attic floor froze in the winter and sweltered in the summer, yet Jules and his family, not as highly placed at court as the Du Bois clan, felt naught but gratitude to have them at all. Since May, the waiting list for such rooms had soared into the hundreds; some nothing more than windowless closets split in half horizontally, where the courtier slept on the bottom while their lackey or servant slept on the top. Those desperate enough fought and gambled over such rooms with great regularity.

Less lucky courtiers, numbering in the hundreds, paid for expensive lodgings in town—rooms they barely ever saw or frequented. In the lofty climb up the scales of the Versailles privilege ladder, to even hope to get a room there, they must be constantly seen within its walls. They arrived at the chateau at the crack of dawn, attending all the King's daily events. During the King's private moments, these poor sycophants with no room to rest in could but stand about in antechambers until the King emerged once more. Day after day they watched the King like a dog watches his master. If not watching him, they talked of him. Most often the day didn't end until the

King completed his *Coucher*, when these exhausted individuals would fly home to grab a few hours' sleep only to start all over again at dawn's first light.

Jules' position as fencing partner to the King gave him the luxury of these two boxlike rooms. He often ruminated on what would happen to him and his family when he became too old and feeble to continue his regular dueling with Louis.

Jules sat Jeanne in one of the two small armchairs as he sat in the other.

"How did you get there? Did you have any trouble finding it? Did anyone seem to wonder at your appearance?" The questions came as his strikes when they dueled. Jeanne let him spew. Once he paused, floundering for breath, Jeanne told him every moment of her magical evening; moments she had relived over and over as she lay wide awake all night after successfully sneaking back into the palace, her family's suite, and her bed.

"They are going to speak with Captain d'Artagnan. They have invited me to the Hôtel Treville. Can you believe it?" Jeanne's story finished, she threw herself back against the chair, breathless.

Jules stared at his niece, her twinkling eyes, her flushed cheeks blazing through the thin coat of powder she felt obliged to wear while moving about the castle.

"I am happy for you, of course, ma petite. But...but I never expected you to continue this folly. Surely last night was a onetime event, *non*?"

"Oh, *bon oncle*, it cannot be, it can't." The zealous desire in which she burned she spread upon her uncle as she grabbed his hands. "But what are you doing? Where do you see this charade taking you?"

Jeanne slumped back, the look of impassioned obsession ebbing from her face.

"Nowhere really, *oncle*. I am not a fool. But to experience such freedom as belongs to a man is a stolen joy." Moisture beaded on her forehead but not just from the heat. "And perhaps to train with the Musketeers, to feel once more the surge of power through my arm. That is all I wish for."

"But the risk, *ma chère*. You could be imprisoned...or worse," Jules argued.

"And when I am imprisoned by a loveless marriage," Jeanne continued as if her uncle had not spoken, "I may take the memories of these moments out, like treasures from a box, and relive them over and over. And in those memories find the joy once more, perhaps a bit faded, if only for a stolen time now and again."

Jules stared at his niece in wonder; how she came by such aged wisdom befuddled him. He mourned the loss of her carefree, girlish innocence.

"Very well, continue with your masquerade. But make me a promise." Jules leaned closer to Jeanne, grabbing her by the shoulders, their faces just inches apart. "Promise me you will take care and guard yourself."

Jeanne's head tilted an inch to the side, gaze upon the dear man softening. "I promise, *bon oncle.* I do most heartily promise."

"*Chère* Jeanne, *chère* Jeanne!" The squeal of two young female voices broke their tête-à-tête as Jules' daughters came rushing out of the bedchamber.

The six- and seven-year-old girls flocked to Jeanne's side, throwing their arms about her and pushing her back into the chair, laughing with delight at their greeting.

"Mademoiselles, you overwhelm me." Jeanne fiercely hugged them back, relishing the love they so easily offered her. "What are you about? What is afoot?"

"We are awaiting our governess, cousin. She is due any moment," Michelle informed her; the elder sister, she was a pretty, younger version of her mother, with keen intelligence sparkling from her big eyes.

"Will you stay, Jeanne, will you stay?" Susanne begged. She was a petite little doll, with brown hair and dark eyes like her father; she seemed still a babe to Jeanne. Susanne jumped up and down as she awaited Jeanne's answer. Her bright green dress, puffed out by three layers of the lacy petticoats peeking out from under the skirt, bounced with every hop. Jeanne could not have said no to the little pixie face and its upturned nose for all the *louis* in France.

"Of course I will stay, of course. Do I not always?" Jeanne laughed again as the girls threw themselves upon her once more. A scratch came at the door, saving Jeanne from any more of the children's accosting, and the two excited girls rushed to open it.

"*Bonjour*, Madame Dremont, *bonjour*," they shouted to the woman who stood outside the portal.

"*Bonjour, mes petites.*" Mme. Dremont strode purposefully into the room, removing her hat and handing it to Michelle to hang on a hook. Tall and thin, with pointed chin and cheeks, she reminded Jeanne of the nuns who had taught her at the convent. Mme. Dremont reached down and gave her charges a tight hug, and there Jeanne saw the resemblance end.

She may be a stern-looking teacher, but her heart is warm and loving.

Jeanne sighed with gladness; her beautiful young cousins would not suffer a childhood similar to her own. Jules had long ago promised Jeanne they would not be sent to any convent, but taught, as were many a courtier's children, by one of the bourgeois governesses who made their way through life by teaching the nobility's children.

"Get your books, my dears. We will read some more today."

Jeanne smiled and went to stand against the back wall of the sitting room as the tiny sprites ran to the bedchamber to retrieve the small tomes they seemed to treasure so much. Fairy tales of knights and dragons soon appeared in her mind's eye as Mme. Dremont's voice filled the room.

"And when he took his sword—"

"You will not give that to her, I forbid it!" The female screech ravaged the air like the dying plea of a mortally wounded animal.

"How dare you give her such when I have so little?"

"When he took his sword—" Mme. Dremont raised her voice, hoping to drown out the ruckus from the next room. As she did, so did they.

"You will only lose it at the gaming tables if I give it to you." A male voice growled like a raving bear.

"Madame de Fabiole hates that her husband gives more jewels to his mistress than he gives to her," Michelle informed Jeanne with haughty superiority, reminding her so much of the grown gossips infesting Versailles.

"But Monsieur de Fabiole hates how his wife loses everything at the tables," Susanne informed her with a giggle; Jeanne wondered if her youngest cousin understood the hearsay she passed on. Jeanne prayed she did not.

Jeanne and Mme. Dremont shared that very adult look, concern over what these impressionable minds saw and heard. Both knew there was naught to be done. In a community where everyone knew each other's most intimate secrets, it was nowhere so obvious as in these upper-story rooms where the paper-thin walls left nothing to privacy. The four females sat in silence as the tirade continued, Mme. Dremont giving up any attempts to read over it. She sat in tight primness, hands clasped firmly in her lap, lips pursed upon her face, until it petered out, the argument ending in the slam of a door and the sobs of a woman.

"Very well," Mme. Dremont announced. "Let us continue. When he took his sword—"

Again, Mme. Dremont was interrupted, this time by a scratch at the door.

"Could you answer that, *s'il vous plait*, Jeanne?" Uncle Jules called to her from the other room.

"*Bien sur, oncle*, of course," Jeanne called back, signaling to Mme. Dremont to continue with a wave of her hand.

Jeanne opened the portal...and the world dropped from below her feet.

In the space of the open portal stood a smiling Henri d'Aubigne.

Jeanne's hand flew to her upper lip...should she not have her mustache on?

Her hand flew again, to the side of her face, would Henri recognize "Jean-Luc" in the woman standing before him.

"Are you all right, mademoiselle?" Henri stepped in swiftly, grabbing Jeanne by her upper arm as she swayed and paled before him.

"She is fine, monsieur, *ca va*." Jules rushed to greet his guest and aid his niece. Putting a supporting hand at the small of her back, he stepped halfway between them. "How may we be of service, kind sir?"

"But how wonderful...it is you!" Henri cried at Jules, grabbing the elder man's free hand and pumping it fiercely. "My other savior, how remarkable indeed."

"Please, young man, your compliments confound me. How surprised I am that you would remember me."

The panic gripped her tighter or was that her uncle's hold upon her arm. Her breast heaved as she gasped for air. If he remembered her uncle, surely he would recognize her.

Jules felt her rapid breath on the back of his neck. With a half turn in her direction, he gave her a small shake of his head. Henri would not recognize the young woman before him for the young man he considered a fellow; there was no mistaking the look of a man wholly assessing the countenance of a woman...his gaze lingered on Jeanne's rich chocolate hair piled high in curls upon her head, on her full, wide lips. Henri's eyes fluttered politely, yet not without interest, over her small, high breasts and tiny, tightly cinched waist. This young man would never believe her to be a one herself, no matter how well-crafted the disguise.

"Of course I would remember you. I am doubly pleased that my quest should bring me to your door to offer my sincerest thanks in person. Henri Boucher d'Aubigne, at your service." Henri bowed deeply to Jules, and Jeanne relaxed, pleased at his charm and manners.

"I had no idea it was the famous Monsieur du Mas to whom I owed my gratitude."

"Did you not?" Jules ushered Henri into the room.

"Is it true, sir," Henri marveled, "that you have studied with Philibert de La Touché and Wernersson Andre de Liancour?"

Henri spoke the names of two of the most illustrious sword masters France had ever known as if they were the words to a prayer; very few men had had the pleasure of working with the King's fencing masters.

"Ah, *oui*, it is true," Jules said humbly as he shooed his wide-eyed, fascinated daughters from the room.

"Come, my dears." Mme. Dremont corralled her charges into the bedchamber and closed the door as their unrestrained giggles erupted.

"Please have a seat." Jules beckoned to Henri and Jeanne, taking a place behind Jeanne's chair. "May I introduce you to my niece, Jeanne Mas du Bois."

"Surely not?" Henri sat so as not to insult his host, but his excitement kept him on the edge of his seat. "Are you related to Raol du Bois?" Henri asked directly to Jeanne.

"I am proud to call him brother, monsieur," Jeanne said, no squeaked, as she heard so many of the inane, desperate femme fatale's of Versailles do. As much as she might have wanted to deny it, there were far too many ways for Henri to learn the truth. Truth is always easier than lies when hiding.

Jules camouflaged a laugh behind a hand-covered cough.

"Then this truly is the most amazing of coincidences," Henri exclaimed.

"A coincidence, you say?" Jules asked.

"Oh, *oui*, monsieur. You see, I came to find the sponsor of a new acquaintance, Monsieur Jean-Luc de Cassel, in hopes of finding Jean-Luc. But never would I have imagined his sponsor is the other man to whom I owe my life and that this man is also the uncle of Raol du Bois. It is truly quite amazing." Henri sat back with a slap across his knee.

"Quite," said Jules with an obvious sarcastic twang only Jeanne understood.

"You look for Jean-Luc?" Jeanne asked quickly, drawing Henri's attention away from her mocking uncle.

"Do you know him, mademoiselle?" Henri asked.

"*Oui*, monsieur, I am quite familiar with him."

Jules turned away, his cough turning to a whoop.

"Are you all right, monsieur?" Henri asked, half-rising from his seat to attend to Jules.

"Fine, fine, young man, be not worried." Jules kept the cavalier in his seat with a wave of his hand. "I'm afraid Jean-Luc is not here right now."

"'Tis true," Jeanne spoke before her uncle could say any more, doing her best not to let the irony of the conversation get the better of her. "He is with Monsieur d'Esconde, a cousin of mine."

Jules looked down upon his niece, eyebrows quirked unevenly. Frederick d'Esconde was indeed a cousin, but one who lived far to the south and studied to be a priest at an abbey.

"May I give Jean-Luc a message for you?" Jeanne pushed, anxious to discover what brought Henri in search of her alter ego.

Henri hesitated, searching both her face and her uncle's.

"I believe I may trust you," he finally announced. "You who have saved my life and you who are sister to a highly decorated soldier."

"Of course we are trustworthy," Jeanne insisted. "Any message for Jean-Luc will stay between us and go no further."

"Oh, of that I can most certainly assure you," Jules answered, more for his niece than their visitor until she pinched the hand he rested on her shoulder.

"It is well." Henri sat forward and lowered his voice, conscious of the ears behind every wall of the palace. "The miscreants we apprehended yesterday have confessed. They did indeed attempt an assassination as we suspected. But on the Queen, not the King."

Jeanne knew she should breathe, should blink; she could do neither.

"Why would anyone wish to kill the Queen?" she barely managed to whisper.

Her own mother served as an attendant to the Queen; Jeanne knew the woman quite well, having been welcomed to her side during her childhood days. The French people may have felt the Spanish princess Marie-Thérèse had her flaws, but surely none wished her dead.

"That is what we must find out," Henri declared. "In my gratitude, I wished to include Jean-Luc in our endeavor. He seems anxious to prove himself and has earned a place by our side."

Jeanne tried to restrain it, but a wide smile flourished upon her face. She wiped it clean when she caught Henri staring at it.

"We have learned from one who overheard the Marquis de Louvois'...conversation, shall we say, with one of the captives, the residence of the man who hired the criminals. We are going there this very night."

"And you wish for Jean-Luc to accompany you?" Jeanne asked.

Jeanne ignored her uncle's pinch upon her shoulder.

"But of course."

"Then I assure you I will get him the message, good sir."

"Then I am indebted to you as well, mademoiselle." Henri reached out and took one of Jeanne's hands, brushing his lips as light as a feather across the back. Jeanne could not stop the shiver that undulated through her from the delicious sensation.

"But—" began Jules.

"Why do I not recognize you, Mademoiselle du Bois? I thought I knew all the young women at court." Henri gave Jules no quarter as if he were no longer in the room.

"Really, monsieur, you know them all?" Jeanne taunted Henri, flirting without knowing she did so.

Perhaps it was the way he looked at her, the way he licked his lips as he spoke to her, that turned her into someone she barely recognized.

"Only in passing, I assure you." Henri gave a dashing half smile. "But if I had met you, mademoiselle, there is no possibility I would have forgotten."

"Jeanne has been at a convent for many years." Jules refused to be ignored this time. "She has just returned to Versailles."

"To stay, I hope?" Henri explored, a question and a request.

"It would seem, monsieur," Jeanne replied, lashes fluttered as she dropped her gaze.

"It was most kind of you to stop by." Jules reached out to take Henri's hand and lead him to the door, clearly exhausted by the course of the discourse. "We will be sure to pass on the message to Jean-Luc."

"You are most kind, Monsieur du Mas." Henri rose and followed Jules to the door. With a swift and sure move, he returned to Jeanne. "I look forward to seeing you again, mademoiselle."

Bowing over her hand, he brought his lips again to her silky skin.

"And I you," Jeanne said, surprising herself. "Please make free to call me Jeanne."

"Jeanne," Henri whispered the word, a caressing sough.

"Bonjour, monsieur." Jules came to Henri, physically leading him to the door and out by the young man's upper arm. "*Bonne chance.*"

"*Bonjour,*" Henri called over his shoulder before the door closed.

Jules turned to his niece, hands firmly and indignantly upon his hips.

"Really, *oncle*, is that any way to treat such a nice young man? A Musketeer?" Jeanne smoothed invisible creases in her skirt, her fixed upon her lap.

"What are you about?" Jules roared at her, something he had never done before. "Have you gone mad? What has possessed you?"

"I do not know, *oncle*." Jeanne looked up, revealing the naked truth writ upon her face "He... affects me."

"Affects you?" Jules bellowed. "He could have you hung."

"But he won't." Jeanne rose, stood defiantly before her uncle.

"He makes no connection between myself and Jean-Luc, nor will he ever."

"Perhaps, perhaps," Jules conceded, "but you surely cannot mean to keep your rendezvous with him this evening?"

"I can and I will."

"Impossible! Inconceivable!"

Jeanne took two steps toward Jules; they stood merely inches from each other.

"Someone is trying to kill the Queen, my Queen," Jeanne hissed, a screaming whisper. "I must stop them. I can and I must."

* * *

Henri stood on the other side of the closed door immobilized by what had transpired within, at the people he had met. Monsieur du Mas was something of a legend among the Musketeers, one of the few men given permission to raise a sword to the King. Yet it was not this iconic man who imprisoned him. Those chains belonged to Jeanne. He shook them off only when a man emerged from the door to the left, a man whose cockled face became more so at the presence of the Musketeer.

Henri tipped his head, quickly making his way through the winding, contorted hallways of the chateau. Though he passed many a breathtaking masterpiece along the way, Jeanne's eyes, their deep sable color, were all he could see. He would not call her a classic beauty; no one would. Jaw a bit too square, chin a bit too strong. And her breasts... well, there was only so much the purposeful undergarments could do with so little to work with.

But those eyes and all he saw in them. Something deep inside her captivated him, her... spirit, he could think of no other suitable word. It burst in the sparkling depths of those eyes, or perhaps how she quirked, barely perceptibly, one brow or one side of her mouth as if she knew something you didn't, as if she found something amusing you knew nothing of. He knew only the desire to be assumed with her, by her. He would find a...

He returned greetings from passing acquaintances, hardly knowing what he said or to whom.

He had seen so much in those beautiful eyes and the intriguing countenance brimming with intelligence and curiosity, compassion and concern. He felt the skin on his forehead crinkle. He had seen other things there as well, hidden secrets, pain, and longing, but from what, for what, he could not conceive or guess. Such mature dolefulness on one so young perplexed as greatly it saddened.

Making his way out to the *Cour de Marbre* and the still cool morning air, Henri passed three young women, gaudily gussied up, waving their fans and batting their eyes at him.

"Mademoiselles." Henri offered a small bow to the three young girls; their giggles echoed off the marble floor and stone walls.

Jeanne does not behave like these silly girls. The thought jumped into his head unbidden. It reminded him so much of something his mother had once said.

"You will find plenty of girls falling weak to your charms, my young buck." The still-beautiful woman had smiled at him over a dainty cup of tea. "But finding a real woman? That is not so easily done."

Henri laughed even now at this memory and felt a touch of longing for his dear maman. It had been a while since his last visit; he was sure he would get quite the verbal thrashing from her sharp tongue—one that dictated his childhood, one that had made him the man he was—if he did not make an appearance soon.

The loss of husband and father had drawn the two together; Henri had been the man in his mother's life for many years. There would always be an empty place in each of their hearts where the man's absence dwelled, yet theirs was a caring, content, and companionable relationship, one that graced Henri not only with a wonderful childhood but an adult refuge, one he felt lucky to possess.

I would like to tell Maman of Jeanne.

Once more his thoughts surprised him.

Turning the corner of the south wing, he jumped back, muscles flinching with the sudden effort. Sidling up to the wall's edge, Henri peered around the corner, seeing the faces clearly now that the glare of the strong sun no longer clouded his vision. Four formidable women approached, regally yet elegantly attired, talking merrily yet without the same flighty twitters and giggles of the young women he'd passed. Henri pulled back, recognizing well one of the mature faces as that of Madame François Scarron. Turning quickly, Henri headed back into the chateau and the anonymous exit of the Lower Gallery.

~Eleven~

With the inclusion of a table, the two armchairs pulled up to its ends, and a tabouret placed at its side, the sitting room transformed into a dining room. At Adelaide's orders, two of the thousands of serving girls brought their midday meal from the humongous kitchen two floors below. Jeanne sat through the private dinner with her mother and sister, barely touching her food, unable to still a shaky foot or a tapping finger.

"What is it that disturbs you so, Jeanne?" Adelaide delicately dabbed her large linen napkin to each corner of her mouth then laid it gently in her lap.

Jeanne used her long, three-pronged fork to move some salad from one side of her plate to the other and back again, staring straight down while the fingers of her left hand tapped out an impatient rhythm.

Bernadette, seated on the tabouret to Jeanne's left, kicked her sister's shin under the table with the pointy tip of her bow-festooned shoes.

"Ow," Jeanne snapped, answering her younger sibling with narrow-eyed annoyance.

Bernadette's plump, round face blushed, but she merely inclined her head toward their mother, her small, round mouth pursed tightly.

"*Excusez-moi*?" Jeanne turned to her mother.

"I asked what bothers you," Adelaide repeated.

"Oh, nothing, Maman. There is no bother. Why do you ask?"

"No bother?" A single thin brow rose up on Adelaide's forehead. "You are like a pot of broth about to boil over, my dear. In truth, I have never seen you so vexed."

Jeanne dropped the fork she held in her hand. It rang strong and true against the heavy porcelain plate. She clasped her hands tightly together in her lap, stilling them against her legs. She took a deep breath through her nose and exhaled slowly, centering herself as her uncle had taught her during sword lessons.

"I am fine, Maman, truly. I... I am just not used to so much leisure time. In the convent, we had scarcely a moment to ourselves all day." Jeanne grabbed the thought out of the thick air surrounding her, hoping it would satisfy her mother and her nosy sister, who hung on her every word.

Adelaide reached out, and Jeanne offered a hand in turn across the table.

"I am sorry for all you suffered there, *ma chère*," Adelaide frowned. "Though much of your trouble was your own doing."

"I know, Maman, I know." Jeanne rolled her eyes impatiently.

"But it is over now. Life at court can be quite pleasant."

"And quite dull."

"If you'd just learn to make the most of your situation," Adelaide said, ignoring her daughter's rude comment. Taking back her hand, she served herself some fruit from the small pyramid before her. "Today the King is at full council, and we female courtiers are free to engage in our own pursuits, at least for a few hours. I am quite sure your friends are up to something fun and interesting. Why do you not go find them?"

Jeanne stood up so fast she almost knocked her chair down. With the swift reactions of a seasoned sword fighter, she grabbed the back of the chair as it tilted precariously on its back legs, lifting it straight off the ground with a bulging bicep, and righted it before it crashed to the floor.

"You are right, Maman." Jeanne ignored the baffled expressions of her mother and sister and the questions, almost kicking herself for her manly actions before these two utterly feminine women. "I will go find Olympe and Lynette. I am quite sure they will keep me amused for some time."

With a most womanly curtsey, the best Jeanne could manage, she excused herself and rushed from the room.

* * *

Jeanne pushed against the back doors of the Lower Gallery, releasing herself into the fresh air as a trapped animal is released from its cage. She tilted her chin up to the sun, letting it shine full on her face, and breathed deeply of the blossom-perfumed air in the massive gardens. Flinging her arms out by her side, she spun around on her heels, delighting in the freedom of the outdoors. She trembled with joy as a warm, strong afternoon breeze brushed against her like a lover's tantalizing hand.

Her blissful smile froze and faded under the weight of the many judgmental eyes upon her. Jeanne stifled her feisty spirit, donned her wide-brimmed straw hat, and tied the ribbons under her chin. With as much mustered grace she possessed, she made her way down the avenue between the two ponds of the Water Parterre. Looking around, she nodded politely at those she recognized, smiling and bowing her head, altering her behavior to that of the well-mannered courtier as she continued to feast on the delights of the outdoors.

Through the haze of the sun, insects glowed in its rays, looking like fairies dancing on the breeze. Butterflies looped and played around the humans as if taunting them with their freedom. Turning to her left, where the tangy smell of the orange groves beckoned, she spied a group of painters, women painters, at the edge of the Maze Grove. Jeanne's full lips spread in a smile; where there were female artists, there was Olympe. With a bouncing step, Jeanne turned and headed toward them.

She soon found the tall, dark, beautiful woman among the other more commonplace females facing the center avenue of the Maze Grove. Olympe towered over the women around her, concentration locked on the vista before her. Silently Jeanne crept up behind her friend, gaze flitting from Olympe's canvas to the scene she depicted. In both, the edges of the scene were exactly delineated by the tall, full, tightly pruned, dark green yew trees bordering the lane. The long, light brown dirt of the avenue stretched out to the edge of infinity, to the vanishing point, growing smaller as it went, to end at a mysterious green door of foliage, one that beckoned the adventurer to enter, to see what truly lay at the threshold of art and reality.

"You have become a master," Jeanne burst with an incredulous whisper, unable not to.

"Oh!" Olympe jumped, startled, and turned, relaxing in recognition. "It is you, *ma chère*."

"*Mais oui*." Jeanne threw her arms carefully around her friend, heedful of the splotches of paint on Olympe's smock. Made of light gray homespun, the smock, the same as all the other women painters wore, mirrored the shape of their gowns: tight and fitting above the waist, their skirts flaring out full and wide, reaching the tops of their bowed or beribboned shoes.

"How wonderful to see you!" Olympe returned her embrace, still holding her palate in one hand and her brush in the other. "What brings you here?"

"Oh, *mon ami*, I am so full of news and excitement I cannot contain myself," Jeanne explained. "I was acting such a silly-nilly I had to get away from Maman before she thought I was mad."

"But why? What makes you so unsettled?" Olympe trilled, captured by her friend's exuberant and glowing face.

"Quiet, if you please, Mademoiselles."

The two women jumped at the command from an older yet still powerful male voice. Jeanne turned to see none other than Monsieur Charles Le Brun walking toward them. She pushed herself down into a deep curtsey.

"Forgive me, sir." Jeanne's respect for the renowned artist banished her giggles. "I had no intention to disturb. It was a coincidence to find my dear friend here."

Charles Le Brun, First Painter to King Louis, looked down at Jeanne, his plump cheeks puffed full of indignant air, his goatee warbling as he spoke.

"Very well, you may watch. But do so in complete silence, *oui*?"

"Of course, sir," both Olympe and Jeanne assured him.

"Humph," M. Le Brun declared as he stalked off to another of his students, readjusting the small barrette upon his long wig of dark curls, his long painter's cloak swaying as he went.

"Your teacher is Monsieur Le Brun?" Jeanne hissed to Olympe, unable to contain her astonishment.

Charles Le Brun, considered by many to be the greatest artist in all of France, was not only a painter, but a decorator, artist, and designer of royal furnishings as well. Together with Mansart, he had created Versailles' greatest accomplishment, Le Galarie des Glaces, the Hall of Mirrors. Detail-obsessed, he had designed every facet of the chamber, down to the smallest component, even to the composition of the door locks.

Olympe nodded her head in silent affirmation; her pride at her triumph clear in her black sparkling eyes and glowing cheeks. With a tic of her head, Olympe brought Jeanne over to a second canvas, another painting she'd just completed.

Jeanne gasped at the brilliance before her. An intricate piece depicting the center front of Versailles, its brilliant colors leaped off the canvas—the red of the brick, the blue of the tiles, and the cream of the stone. The minutest details of the glimmering ironwork balcony running above the central entrance off the *Cour de Marbre*, the overflowing flower boxes and grasping vines, and under the windows of the first floor all the glorious gilded ornamentation lionizing the Sun King breathed in full life upon the canvas. At the center of it, like the center of Versailles, the central windows captured the eye, drawing the observer in closer. The shapes within teased and tickled the brain, shimmering images of figures only half-discernible. These were the windows into the private chambers of the King. Olympe's obscure interpretation spoke of the mystery of their renowned sovereign as well as the people's obsession with him.

In silence, Le Brun stepped up behind the two women, sharing this moment of study with them. With long, stained fingers he rubbed his goatee as he pondered the work in front of him.

"She is the only woman with any talent in the entire kingdom."

His pronouncement made, Le Brun spun on his heels and walked away.

Olympe's gaze met Jeanne's, wide with shock as they shared a quiet, youthful giggle at the man's pomposity.

"Did you hear what he said?" Jeanne entreated, smile so wide her jaw ached with it. "What a great compliment, from such a man. Extraordinary. You could become a master yourself. It is possible with such acclaim from this man. You are thrilled, *oui*?"

Olympe's smile faded; she abruptly turned back to the painting in progress.

"Of course, it is the approval I dreamt of when I first picked up a brush."

Jeanne tilted her head to the side and her brows knit as she stared at Olympe, studying the abrupt change upon her friend's countenance.

Unable to fathom her secret, Jeanne remembered what she had started to tell Olympe, the adventure she longed to share with her compeer, to make it real by making it known.

"You will not believe what I am about—"

"I am to marry the Vicomte du Ludres," Olympe disseminated darkly.

Jeanne's hand flew to her mouth, all and every thought of her own exploits drying on her tongue. She was to marry the Vicomte du Ludres? The lecherous despot and hedonistic heathen? A filthy-rich and powerful man who had nothing else to offer a young wife, not good looks nor charm?

"I am so sorry." The words slipped out of Jeanne's mouth before she could catch them.

Olympe spun on her heel, away from the painting, glaring at Jeanne with eyes narrowed to slits. The heavy silence hung between them, broken only by the cold scream of two sparrow hawks as they passed low overhead and the coo of the doves in the distant orange trees.

"Do not pity me, not me. I will have everything." Olympe stepped closer to Jeanne. "I know my place. It is more than I have ever wished for myself."

"Has he said he loves you?" Jeanne asked, eye to eye with her friend.

"He...he has complimented me on my dancing," Olympe said with great fraudulent conceit; for most young women of the court, this was a lofty accomplishment.

"But your painting, your art..."

"I will continue my work. You know what marriages such as mine will be—they are made entirely for wealth, rank, and property. Once we are wed, I will be free to continue my interests. The vicomte will never notice my petty actions with the distraction of his busy schedule." Olympe's voice quivered as it faded to a whisper. They both knew a man like Du Ludres would never allow such a thing. No matter how powerful or rich, for French men it was about control, the control they commanded over all around them, especially their women. Jeanne said nothing, could think of nothing to say, but the pity in her eyes spoke volumes.

"If you love me, you will say nothing more than best wishes," Olympe begged, brushing away the unbidden tears with a brusque, angry hand. In the stark truth reflected off her friend's face, she faltered, helpless. Throwing her palette to the ground, she stomped away without another look back, off toward the north wing of the palace.

"Best wishes," Jeanne whispered to the empty air, rushing off as well, wanting—needing—to be gone from this place, toward the refuge and truth she lived hidden in the sanctity of Jean-Luc's skin.

~Twelve~

'Jean-Luc' entered the open double-doors of the Hôtel Treville silenced by awe, much as a religious fanatic enters a great chapel; the urge to fall to her knees in abject respect almost overpowered her. Instead she feasted on the myriad sights, sounds, and smells within. The large, circular, and spacious two-story foyer teemed with men. Young and old, of every size and shape, some swam in the sea of royal blue and silver tabards; others swagger in leather and lace, high bucket-top boots, swords clanging from their hips where they hung from their scabbards. Plume after plume bobbed through the air, rising high from the hats sitting jauntily on their heads. Musketeers all.

The Hôtel Treville named for the famous commander of the Musketeers who had ruled over Athos, Porthos, Aramis, and d'Artagnan who had long since passed from this world replaced by the new commander of the Musketeers, Charles de Batz-Castelmore,

Comte d'Artagnan. Out of respect for the man he had loved so well, who had taught him so much, Captain d'Artagnan insisted the original name of the chateau remain.

Stone benches ran along the first half of the two walls running away from the front door; upon them sat the elite, the ranked soldiers, the best of the best. From the end of the benches, two circular staircases completed the round shape of the room, leading up to the second floor and a single door leading to the buildings more private chambers.

In the middle of the room, two men dueled under a multileveled chandelier whose candle flames flickered in the erratic zephyrs of the thrashing swords, and in every crack of space around them other men watched, heckled, laughed, and gambled upon the outcome of the duel. The room buzzed with activity: voices both loud and low, laughter and guffaws, and the clanking of swords. Men came and went in a never-ending parade, armed to the teeth and unmindful of anything or anyone that got in their way.

Completely unnoticed still, Jeanne gathered her courage and stepped into the fray, feeling both out of place and inconsequential. Searching for Henri or any of the other men she'd met last night, she pushed her way through the unrelenting throng. As a gowned and beribboned Jeanne, she knew a path would be cut for her through the mass of chivalrous men; as 'Jean-Luc', they totally ignored him, a thought both pleasing and confusing.

"Ah, here he is now."

Jeanne turned to her left, spying Gerard de Gramont and Antoine de La Ferte standing in the small space between the left bench and the left staircase.

"Come along, come along." Antoine caught sight of Jeanne and beckoned to their friends on the stairs above him. Jeanne saw Henri and Laurent wave back and push against other men to make their way to the bottom of the steps.

"Good fellow, how wonderful to see you here." Henri greeted with a hearty slap on her shoulder. "I am most pleased the lovely young lady gave you the message."

"That she did," 'Jean-Luc' assured him. "She is to be trusted."

"You know her well, this Jeanne du Bois?" Henri asked, jostled against Jeanne as the small group passed close to another duo of Musketeers. Jeanne felt his hard chest and abdomen brush against her arm, and she stiffened, struck by the awkward leap in her stomach.

"Very well, monsieur," Jeanne replied, glancing about, evading his gaze.

"I would very much like to hear more about her." Henri's honey-colored eyes twinkled in the candlelight.

"None of that now," Gerard interrupted, giving Henri a push in his back, heading him toward the door. "We must be off. Now that Jean-Luc is here, we must be about our business."

"Of course," Henri agreed, albeit reluctantly, leading the small troupe through the crowd and out into the street.

Jeanne drank deeply on the fresh air of the still-warm night. The crystal-clear sky above their heads glittered with a multitude of stars in the black, moonless atmosphere.

"This way, Jean-Luc," Laurent called as the fivesome turned down the narrow, cobbled street heading south, away from Versailles.

"We travel on foot?" Jeanne asked, still unsure of their destination.

Yes, our goal is but a few streets down," Antoine assured her.

At the end of the Villeneuve St. George, the group turned left, entering the seedier side of the village surrounding Versailles. Here the dilapidation rose in complete incongruence to the magnificence of the palace, grim decay sat at the feet of Louis' glory. Unlike the homes and structures around the Hôtel Treville, the buildings bordering this slim avenue were neither large nor comely. Most were two-story buildings with fading, broken clapboard finishes, shutters hanging askew, and broken glass in their dark windows. Piles of rank garbage lined the gutters of the stone street, and the stench of sewage assaulted the senses.

Henri came to walk beside Jeanne.

"Our mutual friend told you the target of the criminals' swords, *oui*?"

"She did." Jeanne nodded, matching Henri's large strides. The clank of their swords joined with the click of their hard heels on the cobbles, creating a powerful percussion rising up behind the raucous yells and laughter floating out of the windows they passed. "But it makes little sense to me. Our Queen may not be overly loved, but she wields little power. What would be the advantage?"

"Ah, you see things clearly, my young friend," Henri praised. "That is exactly what we hope to find out."

"What are we sure of?"

"Not much, I'm afraid." Antoine joined in the conversation, taking up the position on the other side of Jeanne. With Laurent and Gerard side by side before them, the young cavaliers traipsed down the street as if it belonged to them and no others. People strolling about quickly jumped from their path, and the beggars lining almost every lane shrank from their presence.

"One of the guards at the Bastille used to be a part of our own company," Antoine explained. "I exchanged greetings with him when Henri and I brought our captives in. He came to me with the news that Louvois had indeed interrogated one of them. Though my friend could not hear everything said behind the closed door, he did hear two extremely telling pronouncements: 'Queen' and 'Vanneau of Rue Aynard.' "

"This afternoon, while I came to find you, Laurent and Gerard took their meal at a local café. It took only the purchase of a few flagons of wine to find out a Vanneau did live on Aynard, at number ten, to be exact." Henri finished the story.

"So it is to the Rue Aynard we go?" Jeanne asked.

"*Oui*," the two men chorused.

A turn to the right and another to the left and they arrived at Aynard. Dimly lit by only a few high lanterns, shadows lurked coal black and mysterious in the alleys and spaces between the buildings. The houses were abysmally small and decrepit, simple one-story structures boasting nothing more than a front door and a small window. Number ten stood in the middle of the avenue. Its gray clapboard looked almost ghostly white in the starlight, the large wooden numeral one stood proud but the zero hung askew, a missing top nail sending it lopsided like an egg pushed onto its side. Shuttered tightly, both door and window shone naught but pale yellow light out of the large cracks around the entranceway and niche; soft sounds, distinctly human, slithered out.

"Someone's home," Gerard whispered, and the four men around Jeanne jumped into action. With an economy of hand gestures, these Musketeers who had fought beside each other for years passed silent communications to each other, taking up their positions as if assigned by some higher power. Antoine and Laurent flattened their bodies to the right side of the door while Henri did the same to the left, pulling Jeanne by the scruff of her neck to stand beside him. Gerard stood before the door. A nod to each side checked their readiness, and he rapped a knuckle hard against the cracked wood.

"Open up in the name of the King's guards."

All sound from within ceased. The Musketeers and "Jean-Luc" held their position, silent, ready.

Two drunk, shabbily dressed men passed on the street, swerving in a zigzag path and slowing down at the curious sight of the Musketeers flanking the ramshackle structure.

"Move along," Laurent whispered, raising his sword toward them, using the glittering point to indicate the direction. "There's nothing of your business here."

The bedraggled carousers quickly fled the scene, and Laurent turned back to Gerard with a satisfied nod.

"Open up in the name of the King's guards!" Gerard growled more loudly, banging repeatedly on the door with the large outside flat of his curled fist.

A shuffling noise came as their answer, a scrape, chair legs against a stone floor perhaps. Jeanne's jaw muscles clenched; her breath came ever faster. The man standing next to her stood at the ready, his sword out of its scabbard and in his hand, knees and elbows bent, poised to strike. Yet somehow Henri appeared completely composed. His smooth, burnished skin showed no sign of tension; his full lips appeared to be almost smiling.

Jeanne shook her head, a small, incredulous shake.

The beam of light from the crack of the door slowly grew larger; it opened.

With a steel shing, Gerard pulled his sword out of its sheath. Just a slit of a face showed through between the small space of door and threshold; a feminine blue eye, a hint of pale skin surrounded by strands of dirty, stringy dark blond hair appeared.

"What do you want?" a small, timid, distinctly female voice inquired.

"We wish to talk to Vanneau." Gerard took a step closer, to better hear the soft voice.

"He is not here. Go away."

The door began to close—stopped by the monstrous booted foot of Gramont as he planted it firmly between wood and jamb.

"Where is he?"

A soft sob broke the silence.

"I do not know nor do I care." Another sob, the voice distant, removed from the door.

Gerard turned to Henri; heavy, thick black brows knit in confusion as he raised his broad shoulders in a shrug. Henri answered in kind, then twitched his head toward the door. Gerard pushed at it; it easily gave way—no one stood or held it closed against him. Gerard entered with Henri and Jeanne following close behind. The one-chambered structure couldn't hold them all; Antoine and Laurent remained outside in the doorway; they listened with eyes trained on the dark, deserted street.

The woman sat at the rustic, coarse-grained table in the center of the single-roomed abode. Upon the table one candle guttered and flickered, its flames licking the interior of the room with long, wavering shadows. Along the back wall stood a dresser and a bench on a floor of broken and chipped flagstones. One bed lay in the far corner; thatches of hay stuck out at all angles from large holes in the threadbare sheet, one rough blanket sat in a pile upon the mattress; no curtain hung around it. The tangy, green smell of cooking vegetables invaded the small space, erupting from the bubbling liquid in the black pot hanging over the meager fire in the hearth on the right wall.

Henri took a few steps and stood beside the woman. Her once white gown was a grimy brown rag, the stretched and over-worn fabric falling off one shoulder, and a tear ran down one side seam of the stained skirt. With elbows on the table, her head hung in the cradle of her hands.

"What is your name, madame?" Henri asked, voice soft and tender.

The woman looked up at such a voice, and Jeanne cringed. The bruises on the woman's face were dark and plentiful. The swelling on the right eye almost closed the lid, the one on her forehead rose in a large lump, and the one by her mouth still trickled blood where it split her lower lip in two places.

"I am Lenore."

"Who did this to you?" Henri gently took the woman's face by the chin, turning it this way and that to get a good look at the devastation.

"Who else?" The woman gave a sad half smile. "My husband."

"Vanneau?" Gerard asked.

"*Oui.*"

"Why?" Jeanne asked without thought. "Why did he hurt you so?"

"Because he can." The woman turned to Jeanne as she answered. "He was... displeased and sought to release his displeasure on me."

Jeanne saw her mother in the woman before her; no beautiful clothes, no glittering jewelry, but they were one and the same. She stepped to the back of the room and, pulling out a linen handkerchief, dunked it in the ewer of cold dirty water resting upon the dresser before returning to the woman. With delicate hands, Jeanne placed the cool cloth against the woman's eye and the bruise still spreading across her fair skin.

Lenore flinched as Jeanne's gloved hand grew close to her face, then relaxing at the sight of the handkerchief, shoulders slumping in relief at the feel of the coolness on her hot, damaged skin.

"Why was he displeased?" Gerard paced to the back corner of the room, mission uppermost in his mind.

Lenore looked up at him through her one good eye but said nothing.

"Do not protect such a man." Jeanne squatted down on her knees, bringing herself even with the woman in the chair. "He deserves no such fond consideration."

Lenore studied the face of the cavalier before her. A silent nod of her head seemed to mark her decision, but still she spoke not.

"Why does he want the Queen dead?" Henri asked the question, and if shock was his goal, he achieved it.

Lenore's eyes sprang wide, even the bruised one. Her defeated, bowed body snapped to rigid attention.

"He...he does not want her dead," Lenore corrected, unmitigated panic contorting her decimated face. "He was merely hired to see it done."

The Musketeers exchanged silent, guarded looks.

"Who, madame? Who would hire him to do such a thing?"

Lenore shook her head, releasing more stringy strands of dirty hair around her face. "I do not know. I have no name."

"Did you see anyone? Can you describe him?" Gerard prodded.

"It was not a man but a woman. She wore fine and fancy clothes with many jewels and ribbons. I dared not listen too closely, for surely my husband would punish me for such curiosity, but I did hear her say he should come for his payment to the palace itself."

Lenore spoke her last words with grave conviction as if shocked as well to hear such an order came from Versailles.

"A noblewoman," whispered Henri.

"Who lives at Versailles," Gerard spoke through clenched teeth.

"Someone comes," Laurent hissed, turning from his post into the still-open door. "Make haste."

Jeanne jumped to her feet. Gerard and Henri crossed the small floor to stand at the back of Antoine and Laurent.

"Who goes there?" a gruff voice called. "Who dares stand in my house without an invitation?"

"Six," hissed Antoine beneath tightly shut teeth.

Jeanne drew her sword, her stomach twisting in a familiar knot. There twisted exhilaration in that knot, she would not deceive herself...fervency she craved. From the bottom of her vision, she saw her mustache quiver and bit her top lip to still it. She flexed her hand on the hilt of her *colichemarde*, felt the power of her arm muscles contract. A small smile came to rest upon her lips.

The six men now stood in the street directly in front of the Vanneau house, six large men, raggedly dressed yet armed to the teeth. Swords and daggers glistened from each and every hand. Broken and brown teeth stood within gnarled, open mouths. No wigs adorned their heads, just long, greasy plaits of their own hair hanging past their shoulders.

"We are the King's Musketeers," Gerard answered, pushing past Laurent and Antoine to stand like a mountain at the head of the range. "We have come for Vanneau."

"For me, monsieur?" A black-haired man stepped out of the group. Shrouded in a long, dark cloth coat, dark hat, and boots, he held a sword in one hand; in the other, a bottle. "Well, I must say, I am quite flattered. Imagine, Musketeers, coming to visit me."

Vanneau turned to the degenerate group behind him who laughed dutifully.

"You will come with us, Vanneau," Gerard ordered.

"Unfortunately, gentlemen," Vanneau turned back, "I would rather see you rot in hell than accompany you anywhere."

The declaration made, Vanneau cocked his arm back and hurled the bottle at Gerard. The large man stepped quickly to his right, and the glass sailed by him, landing in a shattering of pieces on the stone beneath his feet.

Gerard roared with rage, throwing himself into the center of the villains, taking on two of the miscreants, including Vanneau himself. The rest of the ruffians scattered, swords leading to the other Musketeers.

All thoughts of fear and trepidation left Jeanne's mind as she engaged her opponent. As a bird flies with no apparent effort, Jeanne fought with the natural instincts of a warrior and the heart of one as well. Sword in one hand, dagger drawn from her boot in the other, she thrust and parried, stabbed and feinted.

Metal clang against metal, low grunts of effort and pain the accompaniment.

The sweat of exertion drenched her. Jeanne saw only the eyes of her opponent, waiting, watching for clues as to where his sword would next strike.

Back and farther back she moved him, pounding her sword against his, so many thrusts and cuts; she forced him to defend himself, allowing him no room for aggressive, offensive moves of his own. Jeanne pushed him across the uneven cobbles, backing him against the dilapidated structure across the avenue. She had him; she saw it—the fear and the panic.

She had never know such ecstasy.

Jeanne brought her arm back, hanging on the precipice of the kill, lusting for it. She shifted, body poised to reach out—

Her feet flew out from beneath her; something hard swept them off the ground.

The back of her head cracked against stone. Her mind lost hold of reality. Images wavered in and out of her consciousness. Musketeers and criminals floated above her, locked in battle. The sounds of the fray echoed hollowly as if they came from out of a long, narrow tunnel. The street's dampness seeped into the back of her clothes, cold and clammy on her hot skin.

One man stepped out of the dimness. One snarling, filth-ridden face hung above hers. He said something. She didn't hear him. She hear only the sound of her erratic heartbeat pounding in her ears.

The dagger rose above his head; a grimy, white-knuckled fist held it fast. It pointed directly at her chest. She tried to raise her hands, her sword, but they wouldn't move, weighed down by a stone under feet of heavy water.

The man smiled and lunged. Jeanne closed her eyes and prayed.

A roar came out of the distance. A man, a sword, passed between Jeanne and her assassin. The sword met the dagger with a loud peal. The dagger launched through the air and out of her field of vision. She saw the back of a Musketeer as he pressed against the criminal. The cavalier's hat flew off his head as he pushed forward. His golden hair glowed under the starlight.

The criminal gasped. His mouth fell open; his eyes bulged in panic.

Jeanne's vision blurred; she saw no more.

* * *

When she tried to sit up, a crushing pain overwhelmed her and she started to fall. An arm, a strong, powerful arm, caught her shoulders and gently lowered her back down. Her head came to rest on a pair of large, firm thighs. Reluctantly, she opened her eyes and looked up. Above her shimmered the smiling face of Henri.

The golden eyes, the firm lips. Jeanne reacted as a woman, smiling shyly back. Reaching down, she felt the cool smoothness of her buckskin pants and flinched in a panic. Reaching up, she felt the mustache still in place and heaved a deep sigh of relief.

"You are fine, as handsome as ever," the man above her said with a half grin.

"Very amusing," Jeanne replied in her best "Jean-Luc" voice. "Help me up, please."

"All right." Henri pushed tenderly at her shoulders. "But slowly this time, *oui*?"

"Yes, yes," Jeanne agreed. Like a snail rolling up into its shell, Jeanne sat up in a deliberate, drawn-out motion. Instinctively, her hand went to the back of her head as the crushing pain struck at her once more, slightly relieved this time. She found Henri's hand where he held a cloth upon her.

"Hold it there for a few more minutes," Henri said, releasing the cloth to her custody.

Jeanne felt the cloth and a damp, sticky, thick wetness upon it. Blood, her blood.

Henri got up and came around, squatting down before Jeanne, looking closely at the face of his friend.

"Better?"

"*Oui*, better." Jeanne couldn't help but grin at the dashing, hopeful countenance before her. She looked away quickly; 'Jean-Luc' would not look at a fellow warrior in such a manner. Thoughts of Henri flew from her mind as she took in the devastation around her. Bodies lay everywhere, decorating the dark, still street in mud-coated, blood-crusted piles. Beyond the circumference of the fray, timid shadows of onlookers stood quietly in rapt curiosity.

"They are all dead," Henri assured her, looking strangely sad. "We will learn no more from them."

Jeanne nodded with understanding; to have taken at least one alive would have assured them of more clues to the mastermind of the reprehensible plan.

"Gerard, Antoine, Laurent?" The names came quick to Jeanne's lips. She didn't think any of these bodies belonged to them, though she looked for them with still blurry vision.

"All fine, a few wounds," Henri assured her. "None as bad as yours. They are there."

Jeanne followed Henri's outstretched finger and looked into the gloomy interior of the Vanneau house. Flanked by the three cavaliers, Lenore sat at the table still, turned in her chair, looking out the open door. The narrow, pale ray of light seeping out the fissure glowed on the lifeless body of her husband, prostrate on the cold stone ground, the congealed puddles of blood glowing bright red against the dark gray of his clothes and skin. Vacancy dominated her bruised face. Jeanne squinted, making out the shapes as Gerard lifted her almost lifeless hand and place a small, drawstring purse in it. The coins within tinkled as Lenore wrapped trembling fingers around it. The empty face left the remains of her husband and for a brief moment locked upon Gerard's. Without a word Lenore rose, walked out into the street, and left the scene of carnage, a silent wraith disappearing into the fog and darkness.

Jeanne made her slow, tender way to her feet joining the other soldiers.

"Will you live, Jean-Luc?" Antoine asked good-naturedly.

"I believe I will, thank you, good sir."

"Do not thank me," Antoine said. "Thank Henri. He saved your scrawny hide, not I."

"You fought valiantly," Henri assured her, cutting off her words of gratitude before they began. "He used a desperate trick to save his life."

"I owe you my life, sir," she said and bowed as deeply as the pulsing pain in her head allowed.

Henri smiled and bowed as well. "Then we are even, for I already owed you mine."

Jeanne tried to recall the maneuver that had sent her to the ground, but couldn't. She had had him, his life had been hers to take. She smarted from the denial of her bloodlust as surely as her head ached from its collision with the stone. "Though I should like to learn that trick, if you would not mind."

"Hah! It will be me—"

"Enough, enough I say," Gerard bellowed, stepping away from the group and, with his bloodied face turned up the street, looking back the way they had come. "Let us congratulate each other over some ale while we fetch a doctor to put Jean-Luc's head back together."

"Hear, hear!" cried Antoine and Laurent as Henri took Jeanne's arm, throwing it and clasping it around his shoulder with one hand while supporting her back with the other. As Jeanne and Henri followed the others on the roads back to the Hôtel Treville, Jeanne did everything she could not to think about how exquisite Henri's body felt so close to her own.

~Thirteen~

By eleven the next morning the sun blasted the earth with an unmerciful dose of heat from its perch in the cloudless deep blue sky, smiting the small creatures roaming the earth.

As she crossed the *Cour de Marbre*, Jeanne removed her wide-brimmed hat, squinting in the brightness bouncing off the stone walls and marble floor. Though the millinery afforded her protection from the scalding sphere, she longed to feel the air through her hair and upon her head, still beating with dull pain. Instantly her moist scalp tingled as a faint breeze brushed against the thin layer of sweat hiding beneath her silky, cocoa-colored hair. Like a warm and loving hand, the heat from the sun touched the blood-crusted wound and a measure of pain lifted from the laceration and blew away on a zephyr.

Many of her acquaintances milled about the courtyard. Adorned in bright colors, the thin fabrics and lace they wore glowed in the brilliant light as they called out to her. Surprised, secretly pleased by these gestures of friendship and acceptance that seemed to increase with each day she spent at the palace, she waved and smiled shyly back but would not be deterred.

Jeanne had known where she would head this day from the instant she awoke. Her sleep had been short, and the memories—both frightening and invigorating—had haunted her through the brief, peaceful hours, but their message came clearly and she would not be daunted.

A Friday morning found the King with his private confessor for a time; Jeanne would speak to the Queen.

She crossed the marble terrace and reentered the main building of the chateau through the vestibule to the Queen's Staircase. Entering the shade, she sighed, closing her eyes, adjusting them to the dimness, feeling comfort the change of temperature afforded in the sun-blocked stone enclosure. As the coolness washed upon her like a cleansing bath, so did the sights and sounds of the riotous activity within the small confines of this plaza.

The black-and-white checked marble floor at the base of the Queen's Staircase was barely visible, so many people and objects covered its shiny surface. Vendor stalls of every shape and size, garnished with cloth hangings of every color and texture, lined the walls of this long antechamber.

In this famous vestibule, artisans and craftsmen sold their wares as they had done for decades. Generations of families survived the harsh life of a commoner with the profits from the commodities they sold here, living the life of a gypsy as they followed the court from palace to palace, chateau to chateau. Wherever the King and his cortege established themselves, these peddlers accompanied them, unable to make a living without the conspicuous consumption of the courtiers. The permanent move of the King, his court, and the government to Versailles gave these merchants the most stable existence they had known in years, allowing them an immutable setup of their displays in allotted locations.

Jeanne ambled down the narrow passageway, swerving between the stalls, eyeing the wares for sale. Of the finest quality in all of France, perhaps in all of Europe, only approved vendors sold their goods at Versailles, all heavily scrutinized and dissected before permission to sell was granted.

The vendors—both men and women—were well-groomed and well-dressed, their clothes simple but clean and free from tatters. Most catered to the nobility though some offered less costly items to the general public, appealing to the commoners who shopped after visiting the park. From silks, filmy laces, good wines, grand paintings, to fashionable canes, and jewelry from the best goldsmiths, if it was to be found in France, it was found at the court marketplace.

Jeanne hovered at the beauty aids, unbidden thoughts of Henri flitting through her mind as she perused the creams, lotions, patches, and perfume bottles that held but one fragrance. At his court, Louis allowed no scent save that of orange blossoms; all others were strictly forbidden: they bothered his sensitive nose and olfactory senses. Never before had Jeanne cared for such things, but she found her eye pulled to them as her thoughts targeted Henri once more. She shook her head, clearing her mind, and continued down the aisle, passing the vendors offering snuff and pipes and the men gathered around them. Women were prohibited from the use of tobacco in any form, for the King detested the smell of it on females, claiming it ruined them and their natural delightful essence.

In between the more permanent and substantial kiosks stood other sellers, those who used only baskets to display their wares. Here were herbs, sweetmeats, handkerchiefs, hand mirrors, purses, maps of Versailles, guides to the park, and the most popular item of all, embellished fans.

Without making a purchase, Jeanne walked the entire length of the plaza and began the climb up the magnificent staircase, running her hand along the balustrade of dark green marble. At the top of the stairs, she turned right and circled around to enter the Queen's Guard Room.

The large chamber looked much as she remembered. Tall screens hid camp beds, tables, and racks for the guard's weapons while almost hiding the beauty of the red marble walls gilded and glowing under the five crystal chandeliers.

"Mademoiselle du Bois, *bonjour*," a tall, dark-haired young man called to her, his long-legged strides bringing him swiftly across the room.

Jeanne peered at the young man, looking intently under his triple plumed hat.

"Jacques?" Jeanne's eyes popped in recognition. "Jacques de Fremont, is that you?"

Jeanne remembered the young, silly boy who would never sit still in the children's classroom. Never would she have imagined he would grow to such a size and dashing countenance. In his red and gold tabard, he looked utterly dapper and debonair.

"*Oui*, it is I." Jacques kept his hazel eyes locked upon hers as he bent over her hand. "I am happy indeed to see you here."

"*Merci*, Jacques. It is good to see you as well." Jeanne felt herself bat her lashes at him.

What is happening to me?

"I saw you the other evening at the soirée, but you were quite occupied with Monsieur de Polignac." Jacques pursed his lips, scrunched his long, straight nose as if he tasted something sour. "Are the rumors true? Are you to become his wife?"

Jeanne fall the moisture in her mouth dried up and turned to dust, horrified to hear the court already twittered with rumors of the match.

"Nothing is sure until it is done." Jeanne smiled mysteriously.

"Then I may still hope?" A small smile played at the corners of Jacques' mustache-topped lips.

Jeanne dropped her chin, feeling her cheeks burn, turning the same pink as her pearl-trimmed gown.

"I like to believe there is hope for us all," Jeanne said, neither dissuading nor promising anything to this man she wished to call a friend. Though tempted by his comely appearance, it was another's face that came to mind.

"Make way, Fremont, I wish to pay my respects as well." Another young soldier, not as tall as Jacques and blond haired, vaguely familiar to Jeanne as well, pushed Jacques aside to take her hand. Within but a few seconds, male attention inundated her.

"Enough, enough now," a deep voice barked, one aged with wisdom, and the flocking young men jumped to attention. They parted and made way as a handsome, white-wigged gentleman strode purposefully into the room. This man Jeanne recognized immediately.

"Ah, the young Mademoiselle du Bois. I heard you were back with us." The Queen's High Chamberlain, Monsieur de Villemont, took Jeanne's hand, giving it a chaste yet fond kiss.

"Thank you for remembering me, monsieur." Jeanne curtseyed deeply to the gentleman she had known as a child. "It does me well to see you."

M. de Villemont put his arm out for Jeanne and led her forward to the large door at the other end of the antechamber.

"I am quite sure Her Majesty will be pleased to see such a friendly face as well," said Villemont as he opened the large double doors leading into the Salon des Nobles, the splendid room where the Queen held her official audiences. Under the Italian-styled ceilings, the marble-lined walls of green were edged with gilding and adorned with paintings depicting the virtues of this Queen and all who had come before her.

Jeanne stepped into the room, surprised at how many women already occupied the square-cushioned tabourets lining the walls, their green upholstery matching exactly the green marble of the walls.

Even had she not been sitting in the large armchair positioned just to the left of the cold fireplace, Jeanne would have recognized her Queen anywhere. Now in her early forties, Marie-Thérèse d'Autriche had changed little, though the loss of four of the five children she had given birth to had grayed her already-colorless complexion and hair. She still dressed simply, with a childlike coif. As short and stout as Jeanne remembered, the Queen held herself with the same icy-stiff and proud bearing as when brought from Spain twenty-two years ago.

A middle-aged, comely woman rose from her chair near the door and approached Jeanne, a quizzical expression upon her face.

Jeanne curtseyed deeply to her.

"Jeanne Yvette Mas du Bois," Jeanne said, maintaining her reverent pose.

The woman nodded, waggling the high wig of white curls sitting upon her head, and walked to the Queen. Leaning toward Marie-Thérèse, she whispered the name into Her Majesty's ear.

Like the flash of a struck flint, the Queen's small eyes lit up, giving a sparkle to her plainly pretty face. "Thank you, Madame du Roure. Come, my dear, come!" she called to Jeanne, one small, plump hand beckoning her forward.

Jeanne approached her Queen, dropping into her deepest curtsey before the imposing woman.

"Just look at you, how beautiful," Marie-Thérèse fussed at Jeanne like a fond, not-often-seen aunt. Jeanne's mother had been a lady-in-waiting to the Queen since before Jeanne's birth, and Marie-Thérèse had seen much of Jeanne as a child. "God smiles upon you, my dear, I see it."

Jeanne rose slowly and smiled, not surprised at the quick reference to the Almighty. Marie-Thérèse's Spanish and deeply religious beliefs were always uppermost in her mind.

"Please sit with me." the Queen gestured to the small stool to her left, astonishing Jeanne with the great privilege. "Tell me everything. Where have you been? What have you been up to?"

Jeanne obliged the Queen, detailing her years at the convent, leaving out the misbehavior spurring her return, quite sure Marie- Thérèse knew all the details. Marie-Thérèse smiled and nodded, amused at her young friend's story as she petted one of the three fluffy white miniature poodles sitting obediently at her feet.

"And have you come to court to stay?" Marie-Thérèse asked at the end of Jeanne's dissertation.

"I have, Excellency."

"Wonderful, wonderful." The Queen clapped her hands in delight like a child at a circus, juvenile behavior that matched her appearance. "Though you should have come to me sooner, you naughty girl."

Jeanne nodded humbly. "I would have done so, Your Highness but I thought sure I would have seen you at a soirée."

The whispering voices of the other women in the room, the soft hissing swirling around the Queen and Jeanne while they spoke, dried up like a thin stream under days of bright sunlight.

"My apologies, Your Majesty." Jeanne bowed, immediately contrite, though what she was apologizing for, she didn't clearly fathom.

"No mind, my dear." Marie-Thérèse picked up one of her dogs and sat it on her lap, where she lavished it with attention, stroking the animal's back, scratching it behind its ear and under the diamond-encrusted collar. "I do not attend many court functions these days. I prefer it here with my dogs and my pets."

Jeanne nodded silently, acknowledging as fact the rumors of the Queen's unsociable confinement. She turned to the far corner of the room and saw the Queen's "pets," the group of brightly dressed dwarves who were always in Her Majesty's company.

"The King still asks me to attend. I try to when I can." Marie-Thérèse spoke softly, eyes intent upon the animal in her lap. "I do so wish to please him."

A wave of sadness for this woman roiled over Jeanne even as Marie-Thérèse's innocence baffled her. No matter how the King humiliated her with other women, she would never betray her husband. Not only would she not, she *could* not; to cuckold a King was to commit high treason, punishable by death. To Jeanne, what the Queen must have endured through the many years of Louis' involvement with La Vallière, and now to be completely eclipsed by the brilliance of Athénaïs, seemed unimaginable. Perhaps the rumors rang true; perhaps the Queen did cry herself to sleep most nights. It would certainly explain the red-rimmed eyes and heavily powdered face. Never more did Jeanne feel grateful not to be born a royal.

"Chocolate, please," the Queen called, breaking the awkward moment. Attendants jumped to her bidding, and the lavish wheeled tray of porcelain cups and pitcher rolled in and set before her. The gloom about her lifted as she imbibed the rich, dark, warm liquid she loved. Jeanne accepted the fine cup offered, tentatively tasting the drink she had never experienced before. As the thick, sweet fluid flowed upon her tongue, she closed her eyes in pure delight.

"It is utterly delicious, is it not?" Marie-Thérèse smiled at Jeanne's obvious pleasure. "Tell me, *chère* Jeanne, tell me. What will you do now you are a permanent fixture at court?"

"I-I'm not sure just yet, Your Highness," Jeanne stammered, wishing she could share the truth of what she dared to do, dared to believe she could be.

"I have given thought to working at the Hôtel des Invalides."

Since her return from the convent, Jeanne had often thought of offering her services at the infirmary for the soldiers and the poor. But that was before she'd met Henri, before the birth of 'Jean-Luc.'

"Really?" The Queen's eyebrows rose, as did the squeak in her voice.

"Why would you want to work there?" Madame d'Abrignys, another of the Queen's most devout attendants, chimed in.

"Why, to help the poor, of course," Jeanne retorted to the woman she now thought of as daft.

"The poor? Ridiculous!" a full-figured woman scoffed, rising from her tabouret to come join the conversation. Her large breasts bounced above the dark green low neckline. "I am sick to death of hearing about the poor. One can't walk about anywhere without being bothered by the greedy beggars. Not Paris, not St. Cyr, not even here at Versailles."

"You are correct, my dear Duchess," said another woman. "I've seen them myself many, many times."

"There are many poor among us, madame. It is society's burden." Jeanne looked up from her dainty cup.

"Nonsense," the duchess huffed. "Why, I heard Monsieur Colbert saying just the other day that the royal revenue has tripled in the last few years."

"*Oui*, the King's coffers fill higher each day, but the people of this nation, its commoners, are starving." Jeanne's emotions loosened her tongue. "They cannot even afford bread."

Every other woman in the room stared at Jeanne with pure consternation darkening their features. Jeanne realized the treacherous sound of her words and held her breath, ready for a resounding verbal thrashing.

Before any rebuke came, the double doors of the salon burst open and two servants lugging large silver trays filled to the brim with fruit, cakes, and pastries entered the room.

"Well, then, if they have no bread," twittered Marie-Thérèse, eyeing the delicacies with greedy abandon, "let them eat cake."

Jeanne fell silent. Though the Queen spoke in jest, no matter how distastefully, her jest was were to stifle the discussion, the likes of which she cared little for.

"How have you been, Your Majesty," Jeanne asked between small bites of pastry hoping to turn their conversation. "Has your health been well? Has anyone been bothering you?"

"*Mais oui*, but of course, I have been fine, just fine." Marie-Thérèse stared at her young visitor, perplexity clear in her narrowed gaze, waving the confusing questions away like an annoying, buzzing insect whirling about her head. "Tell me, dear, how do you find it back at court?"

The Queen stared pointedly at her, and Jeanne knew she should stop her inquisition.

"I have been made to feel most welcome, though I must confess, I still feel as if I am on the outside looking in much of the time." Jeanne looked at the women in the room, gathered together in small circles, their highly piled hair, powdered faces, and sparkling jewels competing for brilliance. Their gowns of satin and silk, beads and lace all looked so similar, it was as if they wore uniforms of a club, a secret society Jeanne felt she would never, could never, join.

"I remember feeling much the same when I first came to France." Marie-Thérèse nodded her head, a far away, longing look on her small features.

Jeanne knew not how to reply; she remembered the stories her mother told her of how the court would laugh at the Queen and her foreign, Spanish ways; how the Queen would sob night after night. Though she loved and idolized Louis at first sight, Marie-Thérèse found the frivolous, hedonistic court life shocking. She kept herself apart from the start, making no effort to lose her Spanish accent. Some said she hated all things French, from their manners to their cooking.

Jeanne set her cup in its saucer and the chime of expensive porcelain rang in their ears.

"But France would not be France without you now, Your Majesty." Jeanne smiled at the Queen she loved so much, just as her mother did, looking toward the majestic Gobelins tapestry depicting Marie-Thérèse in a garden as magical as Eden, surrounded by birds, butterflies, and all manner of magical creatures. "Surely it is only a greatly beloved Queen who would be immortalized in such a way?"

Marie-Thérèse reached over and took Jeanne's chin lovingly in her hand.

"You are so innocent, *ma petite*. What you do not know is how many feel France would be greater without me."

Jeanne's dark eyes grew wide. She searched the small face, wondering if this woman knew of the attempt on her life.

"What do you mean, Your Highness?"

The Queen retreated into her high-backed, gilded chair only to lean forward once more.

"The King has not been here in many a night," the Queen said, tears pooling in wide, girlish eyes. "He has not come through that door since…I cannot even remember when." Marie-Thérèse glanced at a paneled portion of her gilded wall, and Jeanne could just barely make out the edges of a concealed portal, one like the many others leading through the vast network of secret passages winding through the chateau.

"Have you seen her?" the cherubic Queen whispered to Jeanne.

Jeanne almost asked who the Queen meant, Athénaïs or Madame Scarron, but realized it would only add insult to the woman's already-raw emotions. "*Oui*," she answered simply.

"That woman will be the death of me," Marie-Thérèse exclaimed softly.

Before Jeanne could reply, before the shock of the Queen's statement receded from her thoughts, one of the Queen's dwarves flipped across the room as if beckoned by her melancholy. He stood no taller than a prepubescent boy, with the face of an angel above the deformed body and twisted legs. A close-fitting skullcap of blood red adorned with bells and baubles sat upon his head. His snug-fitting doublet of red and black boasted no trinkets; instead lace cuffs and a proportionately sized sword garnished his ensemble.

The Queen clapped her hands in delight at the sight of him.

"Have you come to entertain us, Theo?" But her delight fled like a frightened animal at the sound of an interloper. The doors burst open and the commanding figure of the King stood at the threshold.

Everyone in the room jumped to their feet, curtseying or bowing.

With knees still bent, Jeanne sidled away from the Queen.

Louis strode into the chamber, stopping abruptly when he caught sight of the dwarves. Did the King hate the minions because they antagonized him or did they antagonize him because he hated them? The discordant relationship between the two parties was widely known and conjectured upon.

With a look of disdain for the dwarves, Louis marched across the room to his wife. Did Theo first flip toward the King or did the King first swing his walking stick at Theo? Louis roared with anger and impatience, swinging again as two other dwarves joined in the frolicking around the King's legs. To the King's consternation, the little people dodged his assault, flipping end over end, bells and bangles creating a riot of sound until they were safely out of his reach and quiet reigned once more.

Reaching his wife, Louis quickly brushed his lips against the back of her small hand.

"*Bonjour, ma chère*," he said with little emotion, "I see—"

From their corner of the room, the dwarves began to shake their rattles, creating such a cacophony, the King could not speak another word.

Louis' eyes narrowed, and he turned to the Queen, a low growl rumbling from deep in his throat.

"Theo," Marie-Thérèse called without looking away from the King, "one of your bells has come loose. Please go and see to it."

"*Oui*, Madame," the small man called, answering her as he had so many times before. To the King's relief, the dwarves quit the room by the side door, but not before Louis and everyone else in the room saw the smug smiles on their painted faces.

"How does your day fare, Louis?" Marie-Thérèse asked, hoping to allay his anger.

Louis turned to his wife and regaled her with an account of his activities thus far. Jeanne heard just snippets of the conversation, mostly talk of the festival to take place in a few days. In a matter of minutes, Louis bowed to his wife and to the other women still standing about the room and quickly left as commandingly as he'd arrived. Jeanne, seeing Marie-Thérèse once more on the verge of tears, moved quietly beside her.

"He has done his duty." Marie-Thérèse stared straight ahead, tears welling again, mouth frowning. Taking Jeanne's hand with her left hand, she squeezed it tightly while pulling out an embroidered, lace-trimmed linen from her waistband with her right. "I will not see him again for many a day."

"I'm sure it is just his busy schedule keeping him from your side." Even as Jeanne said the words, she heard their ring of falsehood.

Marie-Thérèse looked up at her young friend with a small, pathetic smile. "You are kind to me, *ma chère*, just as you were as a small child. It is truly wonderful to have you back with us."

Jeanne bent her knees to squat beside the Queen's chair. "I am happy to be back with you as well, Your Highness. But I would ask a favor."

Marie-Thérèse turned toward Jeanne. "If it is in my power, dear girl, of course you shall have it."

"Please take care of yourself." Jeanne cast her gaze cautiously about the room. "Watch yourself and those around you carefully."

"Whatever do you mean, Jeanne?" The Queen flinched back.

"You—" Jeanne continued.

"Daughter."

Jeanne felt the hand clasp her upper arm, and though it did not hurt, she felt the slight pull and stood up accordingly. Next to her stood her mother; Adelaide's face twitched with barely suppressed anger. Jeanne hadn't seen her enter the room and didn't know how much Adelaide had overheard.

"Lynette was just looking for you, Daughter. I told her you would be along soon." Adelaide smiled, words slipping through tightly clenched teeth. "Make your respects to the Queen and run along now."

"Of course, Maman." Jeanne curtseyed to her mother, then turned back to the Queen. "Thank you for seeing me, Your Highness."

Bending down, she brushed Marie-Thérèse's cheeks with a kiss, one on each side, and took a chance, whispering as her lips came close to the Queen's ear. "Beware, not everything is as it appears."

~Fourteen~

Jeanne sat quietly in the tenth row of chairs lined up from wall to wall in the masculine Mars Drawing Room. Up until the permanent move of the court to Versailles, this room had served as a guardroom, and it retained its military decor. Helmets and trophies decorated the cornice in alternation and historical battles were commemorated in the small ceiling cove paintings framed in gold. Tonight the room overflowed with row upon row of chairs and tabourets quickly filling up with animated courtiers. A new production of the play Les Fâcheux was about to open.

To Jeanne's left, Lynette sat quietly, a rosary in her small, delicate hands, her rosebud lips moving soundlessly in prayer. Strangely, Jeanne felt like praying as well. The dark circles around Lynette's eyes were so much darker than just a few days ago. Thin and gaunt, the cough Lynette tried to suppress came more and more frequently.

On her right Olympe fidgeted, looking here and there; the vibrant young woman seemed unable to sit still for a moment.

"There is the Duc de Vivonne. He is Athénaïs's brother," Olympe haughtily informed Jeanne, identifying each and every attendant as they entered the room, adding her own little bit of scuttlebutt to the description. "It's said the King is to make him the Captain-General of the Galleys."

Jeanne nodded vacuously at each announcement. As more and more courtiers filled the chamber, their chatter buzzed and hummed through the room, the sound growing louder. Raucous laughter resounded against the marble walls, and the clatter of heavy heels on the shimmering marble floor forced Olympe to raise her voice.

"Ooh la la, there is the Abbé de Choisy, and in men's clothing no less."

These provocative words caught Jeanne's attention; she turned with raised brows to her garrulous friend, following the path of her gaze to the corpulent middle-aged man with the long, curly white wig. In a jacket of deep purple-embroidered silk and a waistcoat embellished with beads the colors of the rainbow, the flamboyantly attired man sauntered down the aisle, a young woman on each arm. He passed Jeanne and Olympe, taking his seat in one of the rows closer to the front.

Olympe leaned closer and lowered her voice. "He is a well-placed courtier and a church historian, but he loves to dress in women's clothing. It is rumored he lives openly in Paris as the Comtesse de Sancey."

Jeanne laughed, quite sure Olympe exaggerated, but her friend stern look stifled them. "'Tis true?"

"*Oui*!" Olympe insisted.

"Does he...ah...is he like Monsieur?" Jeanne asked, referring to the openly homosexual brother to the King.

"*Non*, but his tastes are bizarre, to say the least." Olympe grinned. "He has sex with women, so they say, but he forces them to dress like men."

"Strange indeed," Jeanne said, staring at the man in front of them.

"Ah, there is Madame d'Aumont, Madame Lamoignan, and the Duchesse de Richelieu." Olympe twisted in her seat to see the entrance of these highly placed nobles.

Jeanne watched the older women nod and greet friends and acquaintances as they made their way into the room, unable to walk side by side in their wide silk and brocade skirts. She turned away and slumped in her chair; she'd had enough of such talk and such people. The isolation she shared with the Queen fell upon her slumping shoulders once more. To be wrapped in solitude in such a mass of humanity. Such loneliness grew as deep as a bottomless pit...a ghost condemned to walk among throngs of restless spirits haunting the world, surrounded yet wholly forsaken.

"Excuse me, mademoiselle, would you mind if I sat next to Mademoiselle du Bois?" The question, posed to Olympe, froze Jeanne's breath in her lungs. That voice, the deep modulation of Henri d'Aubigne, sounded like the ring of a bell in her ears. Jeanne thrust her derriere back in her chair, pushing her spine straight, smoothing the yards of her gold-embroidered skirt.

"Well," Olympe purred like a cat as she rose and moved one seat over, allowing Henri to sit between them, "it would be my great pleasure."

Henri reached down and took Jeanne's hand, tenderly kissing her warm skin. "How wonderful to find you here, mademoiselle. How are you this fine evening?"

Jeanne opened her mouth, but not a sound came out. All her words forsook her at the sight of Henri in fancy dress attire. His knee-length silk coat of cerulean blue hugged his firm, muscular torso, accentuating the 'V' shape from slim waist to broad shoulders. The matching knee breeches did little to disguise his powerful thighs, and the gold stockings hugged his large calves tautly. The gold edging on coat, breeches, and waistcoat matched the golden flecks glimmering in his eyes as he looked down at Jeanne, his darkly burnished gold hair hanging in waves around his face.

"She is fine, monsieur." Olympe provided the answer where Jeanne could not.

"*Oui*, Monsieur d'Aubigne, I am indeed well," Jeanne finally managed. "How nice of you to join us."

"*Merci*." Henri smiled, his gaze intent on Jeanne.

"Ahem." Olympe feigned a small cough.

"Oh, *pardonnez-moi.* Monsieur Henri d'Aubigne, may I please introduce you to my dearest friends, Mademoiselle Olympe de Cinq-Mars and Mademoiselle Lynette La Marechal."

"*Enchanté,* Mademoiselles." Henri took each woman's hand, brushing his lips across them as he bowed from the waist.

"A pleasure, monsieur," Lynette said softly, coming out of her reverie to be social, smiling shyly at the handsome man.

"*Enchanté* indeed," exclaimed Olympe, raising her shoulders and eyebrows at Jeanne over Henri's bowed head. "And how do you know our dear Jeanne, monsieur?"

"We have a mutual acquaintance, Mo—" Henri began.

"*Oui,* many mutual acquaintances." Jeanne cut him off, the hands of desperation strangling her throat at what he almost revealed among the prying ears of the courtiers; she could feel them breathing down her neck, or craning theirs to see what took place behind them Swallowing back the lump, she continued, "My Uncle Jules, for one."

"Yes, of course," Henri agreed, "Monsieur du Mas and also—"

"Do you attend many concerts, monsieur?" Jeanne asked, frantic to keep the conversation away from 'Jean-Luc.'

"No, not many," Henri said, laughing heartily. "In truth, this is my first in many a year."

"Really," Olympe crooned. "Whatever brought you here tonight?"

"I heard there were to be some special attendants," Henri answered Olympe, then turned back to Jeanne. "Some of the court's greatest beauties. I wished to see for myself."

"I hope you are not disappointed, monsieur," Jeanne murmured, chin dipping demurely.

"Not at all, mademoiselle." Henri leaned closer to Jeanne.

"Please, call me Henri."

"Henri," Jeanne said breathlessly; the sound of his name felt like cream upon her tongue.

The lights dimmed, and the smell of melting wax and doused wicks filled the room as servants ran about putting out the sconces adorning the walls every few feet. The murmuring crowd quieted to a hush and the seven-piece orchestra began a slow, deep ballad. Henri leaned even closer, whispering into Jeanne's ear, talking of silliness, making her laugh into her hand through the entire performance. Olympe and Lynette tilted their heads forward, listening to the couple, sharing their own silly grins and amazed looks over the close-tilted heads of their friend and this mysterious man whose effect upon her was so obvious.

The music ended, the candles were relit, and Henri and Jeanne still leaned toward each other, seeing nothing but each other, impervious to the movement around them as the courtiers rose, making their way to the doors like fish in a fast-moving stream.

"Did you enjoy the concert, Monsieur d'Aubigne?" Olympe finally asked, growing weary of waiting for Jeanne and her gentleman friend to return to reality. Still, neither Jeanne nor Henri noticed Olympe or Lynette as they stood on each side of the smitten couple like guards watching over a treasure.

Olympe gestured to Lynette, waving a hand in Jeanne's direction. Lynette pressed her lips tightly together, shaking her head. Olympe stamped her foot, eyes narrowing in dire warning. Lynette rolled her eyes, her shoulders slumping. Taking a deep breath, she reached down and put a hand gently on Jeanne's shoulder.

"Jeanne?" she called softly, blushing from the tips of her fingers to the roots of her hair. "Jeanne, dear, do you still want to attend the poetry reading with us?"

"Who?" Jeanne asked blankly. She noticed the hand upon her shoulder and followed the arm up to the crimson face of her friend. The spell shattered. "What? Yes, yes, of course."

Jeanne and Henri jumped to their feet, as the real world came into focus.

"Did you enjoy the concert, monsieur?" Olympe asked again.

"Ah, *oui*." Henri nodded and smiled, pulling on the bottom of his waistcoat. "I can honestly say I have never heard anything like it."

"That's because you never heard any of it," Olympe said quietly under her breath.

"Please, Mademoiselles, do not let me detain you further."

"That's quite all right, monsieur," Lynette quickly assured him, stepping around him and Jeanne to take Olympe sternly by the arm. "It has been our great pleasure to meet you."

"And mine." Henri bowed.

"Would you care to join us for the poetry reading?" Jeanne asked, not sure whether she wanted him to or not, not sure if she could bear being near him much longer, yet not sure if she could bear to be away from him.

"*Non, chère* Jeanne." Henri took her hand in his, lingering over the soft crème-colored skin, caressing it with his thumb as his golden gaze caressed her face. "I am afraid I have monopolized you long enough. I would never wish to come between you and your friends."

Jeanne smiled, his words and his sentiment so unlike those of most young men, who wished for nothing more than to constantly be the center of a woman's attention regardless of anything or anyone else.

"I have greatly enjoyed our time together." Jeanne amazed herself with her candor.

"As have I, *ma chère*," Henri whispered the endearment, his lips meeting the hand in his.

Jeanne felt her abdomen tighten, felt the small hairs rise on the back of her neck. Speechless, she curtseyed on knees that shook and trembled.

Henri bowed and turned to slip down the row of chairs and out into the aisle. He saw Olympe and

Lynette just a few steps ahead of him, making their slow way out of the room.

"Will you and your lovely friends be attending the festival a day from now?" he called.

"Oh yes, we are all excited about it." Jeanne smiled broadly, a little girl anticipating the arrival of a new trinket.

"May I look for you then?" Henri asked hopefully.

"It would only make the day more delightful," Jeanne assured him.

Henri's crooked smile widened. With a small yet familiar nod of his head, he took his leave. "*Bonne nuit, ma chère.*"

"*Bonne nuit, cher* Henri."

* * *

"It is all your fault, as usual."

Jeanne stepped into the small foyer of the Du Bois suite, thoughts of Henri still whirling in her mind, tickling the edges of her mouth into a grin, when her father's voice assaulted her. She faltered, mystified at the cause of his anger.

"What have I done, Père?" Jeanne doubted his annoyance came from any discovery of 'Jean-Juc.' He appeared peeved, agitated, but if he were to learn of her other life, his anger would be apocalyptic.

"Your future family is causing quite a stir about the chairs." Gaston stood in the middle of the small sitting room, his pointed face flush with anger.

"My future family?" Jeanne's puzzlement swelled until she felt almost light-headed from it.

"The Polignacs, of course." Gaston squinted at his daughter, jaw muscles clenching at her feigned ignorance.

Jeanne felt the blow to her gut as if her father had used his fist; her hand reached instinctively up to rub and soothe it. To consider the Polignacs her future family was to consider the end of her life. She couldn't fathom what those abhorrent people had to do with furniture.

"Chairs?" Jeanne stared at her father askance, thin brows furrowed on her forehead. "What chairs?"

"These chairs," Gaston bellowed, flaying his arms about dramatically, indicating the two armchairs, the two armless chairs, and the two tabourets he had arranged in a circle in the small room.

"What do the Polignacs care what kind of chairs we have?" Jeanne stepped into the room, standing in the empty circle between the chairs, turning this way and that as if the answer to the puzzle lay hidden among them.

"Because, you stupid girl, we will be using them in but a week's time, when they come to dine with us, and they are being quite ridiculous about it."

Jeanne's head snapped in her father's direction. "They are coming to dine with us?"

"*Mais oui*, but of course, to make the arrangements." Gaston threw his hands up in a huff. "He is merely a baron but expects the armchairs, claiming they deserve them since his wife is the daughter of a marquis."

The Battle of the Chairs was a common one at court these days. The prestige associated with the three types of seats, originally instigated as one of Louis' twisted manipulative machinations, now served as a point of serious contention whenever courtiers socialized.

"I am a comte and a member of the State Councils, I shou—"

The front door opened and Adelaide entered, returning from her duties with the Queen. Gaston launched back into his tirade, offering no greeting or compliment to his spouse.

"You must do something, Adelaide. The Polignacs are being uncommonly difficult." Gaston stood before his wife, hands perched on hips, bewigged head bobbing and weaving as he spewed his frustration.

They are being difficult? Jeanne mused. *Surely, Maman has much experience dealing with difficult people.*

But as she looked at her mother, Jeanne felt a stab of fear.

Adelaide looked deathly pale. Her normally golden, glowing complexion looked yellow, like old, faded parchment, all the more wane against her deep maroon velvet dress. Her mother's held her hands clasped tightly together, yet Jeanne noted their trembling. Her coiffure was askew; never had Jeanne seen her mother out and about when not perfectly groomed. But it was the look in Adelaide's eyes, the golden eyes much like Henri's, which truly frightened her. Adelaide had been crying, there was no doubt, but worse, they looked like they had seen horror itself; they were changed—aged and terrorized.

"I will not capitulate, I will not," Gaston ranted without stopping for breath, showing no acknowledgment of Adelaide's unease.

"I will take care of it, Gaston, worry no more about it," Adelaide said, her voice a pale ghost of itself.

"Oh, you will. You will take care of it." Gaston ceased his fidgeting, pulling the ends of his lounging jacket tightly about him as he crossed his arms in front of his chest. "I can bear no more of this. I must rest." He turned away, entered his bedchamber, and slammed the door shut.

Jeanne rushed to her mother as the wham of the closing door still resounded through the suite.

"Come, Maman," Jeanne took her mother by the arm with one hand, supporting her back with the other. "Come sit down."

Adelaide obeyed silently, allowing her daughter to lead her with no resistance.

Placing her mother in an armchair, Jeanne rushed to the small buffet along the opposite wall and poured a large glass of wine. Handing it to her mother, she pulled a tabouret directly in front of Adelaide and sat, leaning forward with her elbows on her knees.

"What has happened, Maman?"

Her daughter's words broke Adelaide's stupor. She looked up.

"The Queen has been poisoned," Adelaide spoke with the monotone of dispassion, with the emptiness of one in shock.

Jeanne flinched as if struck, barely moved, until she did. She rose, crossed to the buffet, and poured another glass of wine; this one she gulped before returning to her stool.

"How? When?"

"Barely an hour ago." Adelaide took a large swig of the dark red liquid. "We had just finished a game of L'Hombre when she began to look pale. Within a matter of minutes her hands, feet, and face began to swell, grotesquely distorting her appearance. Soon she could not talk, could barely breathe. We could see her throat…swelling." Adelaide closed her eyes and rubbed at them with her free hand as if to push the visions from her memory.

"Does she…" Jeanne faltered, afraid to even speak the words, "…does she live?"

Adelaide nodded; Jeanne sighed so hard her lips fluttered before she chugged back another mouthful of nectar.

"We called for Fagon immediately." Adelaide referred to the King's first physician. "He bled her, of course, but first he gave her something that caused her to regurgitate. It went on for so long, till she had nothing left in her. But it worked. The swelling receded and her breath came back. She suffers still, though. Her throat is raw; she can barely talk or swallow. But she lives."

Jeanne stared at the inside of her chalice and the few inches left of the wine. "Did Fagon say he was certain it was poison?"

"He did," her mother whispered as if she spoke of the devil himself.

Jeanne threw her head back and chugged down the remainder of her drink.

Adelaide leaned forward and took her daughter brusquely by the shoulders. "What were you talking so quietly about with the Queen this afternoon? What do you know, Jeanne?"

Jeanne met her mother's inquisitive look, afraid to tell her, afraid not to.

"I heard—please, Maman, do not ask me from where," Jeanne begged, "I heard there had been an unsuccessful attempt on Her Majesty's life a few days ago. The…the person who told me seemed to feel it would not be the last. I meant to warn her."

Adelaide stared at her daughter, searching the countenance so dear yet in some ways so unfamiliar.

"Are you in danger?"

"No, Maman," Jeanne assured. "I am not." Jeanne's eyes dropped in contrition; the slight distinction between herself and 'Jean-Luc' did little to ease the guilt of the lie.

Adelaide pulled her child against her, their bodies crashing as powerful as the love that passed between them. She held Jeanne for a few silent minutes, her arms saying all she felt to this precocious offspring she loved so dearly.

"I must return." Adelaide rose, strength returned from the unburdening and the wine. Leaning down, she kissed Jeanne tenderly on the forehead in farewell.

Jeanne watched her mother close the suite door quietly behind her.

"I must tell Henri."

~Fifteen~

"You've got him, Gerard, you've got him!" Antoine yelled, jumping to his feet as he cupped his hands around his mouth.

"Go in for the kill!" Henri cheered from his place beside Antoine, hands pumping the air.

Arranged on blankets of the softest linen, the small but merry group could see both tilting yard and fencing court, combatants in the tournament fighting valiantly on both. Gerard the Giant fought valiantly in the fourth round of the fencing duels, demolishing all who opposed him in record time.

On the tightly cropped lawn beside the Obelisk Fountain, toward the back north corner of the vast Versailles gardens, Jeanne and Henri, Olympe and Lynette, Antoine and Laurent could see almost the entire large field, typically quiet, bursting with life with today's festival events. It spread out before them, tents and booths of every size, shape, and hue, colors glowing bright under the blazing light of a summer sun like a living tapestry, a painting come to life as courtiers milled about everywhere, glorious themselves in their best, most vivid garments.

Jeanne jumped up and down beside Henri, her iridescent pink gown shimmering in the bright midday sun, thrilled at Gerard's prowess and triumphs. Her hand flinched by her side as she dueled along beside him, in her mind if not on the field. Never had her petticoats scratched her skin so much as they did in that moment. And yet Jeanne enjoyed this year's Feast of St. Louis more than any other she could ever remember. Her wide mouth spread from ear to ear; her laughter rang free through the warm afternoon air, unencumbered by any thoughts of impropriety.

Begun in the thirteenth century, the Feast of St. Louis commemorated the life and death of Louis IX, who died on this day, August 25, in the year 1270. Renowned for his strong, fair rule and his personal piety, he had led the Seventh and Eighth Crusades, earning him sainthood in 1297. To share this year's Feast with Olympe and Lynette, Henri and 'Jean-Luc's" other friends made it a day of both thrills and joy, made it all the more poignant. It was a fête of great proportion, more lavish and extravagant than any remembered, the first held on the grounds of Versailles.

"To his right, Gerard, his right," Jeanne screamed before she could stop herself; her hand flew to her mouth, but too late to seize the words. She looked furtively at Henri, fearful of his reaction to her unladylike behavior, raising her other hand to fix the errant strands of her rich brown hair coming loose as she bounced up and down.

"*Oui, oui,* to his right," Henri yelled, laughing in delight, throwing an arm around Jeanne's back as they bounced up and down. Jeanne heaved a sigh of relief, relaxing, enjoying their mutual frenzy, yet so conscious of his muscular limb against her, like a line of fire scorched across her back.

Did Gerard hear them or did he see the opening for himself? No doubt the subject would be argued vehemently among his friends for weeks to come. Gerard took quick advantage. A feint, a lunge...his sword struck hard against his opponent's chest protection—a coup de grace.

The white flag flew high in the air, like a dove released with joy from its cage, tossed by the referee. Gerard thrust his beefy arms upward in triumph, pounding the air above him with meaty fists, a broad smile splitting his huge face dripping with sweat, the beads sparkling in the high sun as the man blazed with his victory.

"Bravo, bravo," Antoine, Henri, and Jeanne yelled, waving to their exultant friend across the vast and crowded field.

Jeanne threw herself down upon their quilt, laughing and reaching for her goblet of wine before it overturned, gulping a large draught to ease her scream-roughened throat. Henri landed beside her with a similar plop.

"You know so much of the duel. You are astounding," Henri complimented.

"Our Jeanne has always been something of a ruffian, I'm afraid." Olympe sat primly on a corner of the blanket, her yellow day gown of silk garnished with the satin petals of a daisy lay perfectly arranged around her to exhibit her figure to its best. Beside her lounged Laurent, resplendent himself in his most dashing ruffle and lace shirt worn with a sleeveless leather doublet and black satin breeches. The two beautiful people had given little time or attention to anything else save each other since Henri had introduced them earlier this morning. Olympe stared at Laurent's low-buttoned shirt and the few inches of his bronzed, muscular chest it revealed, while Laurent's lascivious look barely left her magnificently displayed bosom.

Henri laughed. "My own sister was a bit of a nymph as well, a delightful playmate."

Jeanne rewarded Henri with a tender smile that softened her features, thanking him for his defense. Their gaze caught, held, locking them together in this moment, this private void. She watched his eyes as they drank upon her face. She stilled beneath his evocative scrutiny. Like a painter's brush tenderly rendered, Jeanne felt their touch as his golden gaze caressed her cheek. Self-conscious under his deep perusal, Jeanne licked her lips and swallowed the puddle of saliva pooling in her mouth, unconscious of the sensuality of the act. She watched in amazement as Henri's eyes snapped open, fluttering up then back to her mouth. His large Adam's apple pulsed up and down, he bit his lower lip tightly.

On the other side of the blanket, Lynette sat quietly; next to her lounged Antoine. Of a similar disposition, they kept each other comfortable in silent companionship. She held a dainty fringed parasol over her head as she watched the goings-on with heavy-lidded, pale eyes. Antoine plucked small blades of grass from the ground, split them longways, and threw them up in the air, sending them twirling back to the ground like faeries come to land upon Earth. Lynette's shy, amused smile brought a sparkle to his eye, a slight upward curve of his lips.

"Perfect," Antoine said as he spotted two young servants walking toward them with large, overflowing baskets. Within minutes, a bountiful picnic lay before the young celebrants. Fish from Versailles' own stream came on silver platters. Newly-laid eggs cuddled together in a bowl of crème porcelain. In linen-lined baskets came fresh-baked baguettes accompanied by tiny cups of just-churned butter, a simple salad, and fresh fruit. A box of little cakes with colorful frosting and toppings completed the banquet.

As the companions ate, conversation dwindled and the sounds of the day waxed and waned about them. Orchestral music floated on the breeze; voices and laughter rang out from the field, a murmur like a babbling brook away in the distance. The languid wind rustled the shrubs and trees, and nature's hum sang in chorus with the loud buzz of the cicada and the twittering of bright red and blue robins.

Henri fed Jeanne small pieces of baguette, dripping with butter, the enticing aroma of the fresh-baked rolls still strong as he took them out of the basket.

"We will have to finish soon if we are to see Gerard win in the final round," Henri said, taking a bite of a hard-boiled egg. "You enjoy watching the duels, yes?"

"*Oui*, very much." Jeanne sighed, looking away to the dueling court. "You gentlemen don't realize how lucky you are to participate in such sport."

Henri stared at her youthful, healthy face, the glowing skin, the full lips and bright eyes. "It must be quite frustrating to always watch and never participate."

Jeanne turned quickly to see if he mocked her. She found only sincere empathy in his golden gaze. "You are quite right, sir."

"Yet we men should be envious of you women." Henri looked down at his meal.

"Envious?" One brow arched incredulously upon Jeanne's forehead.

"Ah, *oui*." Henri brushed the long, waving strands of hair off his burnished face. "To possess beauty and intelligence...well... are women not the most blessed?"

"We are, sir. You are quite right," Olympe piped in, taking a bite of a full, luscious strawberry, letting the pink juice run down her red lips. Laurent quickly dabbed at the liquid with his linen napkin.

Jeanne just smiled and shook her head at Henri's folly and Olympe's overt sensuality.

"It is the lunacy of men not to take advantage of such a valuable commodity." Henri rose to his knees, strong thighs stretching and flexing. "To ignore such a vast resource of ideas and inventiveness seems to me to be a waste."

Jeanne could no longer chew or swallow the pieces of carrot in her mouth, so shocked, so delighted, was she by his words. She stared up at him, her smile reverent.

"Oh my," Lynette whispered softly, gaze locked upon her friend and Henri. Antoine, Olympe, and Laurent nodded their heads almost in unison.

A rousing cheer rang out behind them, and they all turned this way and that to see what had caused the ruckus.

"The King," Olympe called, rising to her feet with the help of Laurent's strong hand. "The King comes."

Everyone rose to their feet and strained to see their ruler as he came toward them.

Louis rode on the back of an open single-person chaise, a single-seated wheeled chair drawn by one man. In his arms, the King cradled a baby, an infant wrapped in a royal blue blanket embroidered with silver and gold. As Louis drew near the crowds, he raised the child high for all to see, his usual mask of placid stoicism vanquished, replaced by beaming pride. In his arms, his newborn grandson, the son of the Le Grand Dauphin, another Louis, this one the Duc de Bourgogne, born just nine days ago.

"Huzzah," the six young people called in rousing congratulations.

Their cries joined those of the crowd, raised and joyful voices forging a grand cheer of good wishes for the King and the continuation of his blood.

"His first grandson, imagine," Henri said almost wistfully as they watched the King continue his parade through the gardens then turn and head back toward the castle, a glowing orb that seemed to move as if on wings, floating just feet off the ground.

"He must be so thrilled."

"It is a real love, I think," Jeanne said softly, happy for her King, who seemed to never bask in the light of true happiness.

Stepping around their linen perch, she came to stand next to Lynette, putting an arm around her friend, whom she knew loved babies dearly. "Could you see him? Did you get a glimpse of the baby?"

"I did." Lynette gave a slight nod accompanied by a thin smile.

Jeanne saw the hollows in her friend's cheeks; the trough of shadows ran deep below Lynette's high cheekbones, brought into prominent relief by the glow of the midday sun.

"Have you eaten an—"

Lynette started coughing, a racking, hacking sound rising from her lungs like the barking of an angry dog. She covered her mouth with one hand, the other grasping at her chest as if to jail the spasm within her ribs.

Antoine and Henri rushed to her side, each holding one arm as the woman continued to convulse. Laurent thrust a goblet into her hands, not caring whose it was or what it held, as long as it was liquid.

Jeanne watched, paralyzed with worry, feeling more helpless than she ever had before, feeling more fear than when 'Jean-Luc' had faced the fiercest of enemies. Finally, between bouts, Lynette managed a sip or two of fluid, bringing the cup to her mouth with a shaking hand, only able to keep it still enough with the firm assistance of Antoine's hand over hers. Slowly the coughing eased and her breathing returned to something resembling normality.

"Pray forgive me," Lynette said, her voice straining through her aggravated throat, and bowed her head low.

Olympe took two steps and stood before her friend, wrapping her arms around her. "There is nothing to forgive, my pet, nothing whatsoever." Releasing one arm, Olympe beckoned toward the blanket and the few morsels of food still remaining in their containers. "Why do you not sit down and have some of the oranges? They are the King's best."

Lynette managed a small, shy smile, but shook her head. "No, *merci*, dear Olympe. I think... I think I will return to my room for a quick rest."

"Please, mademoiselle." Antoine raised his arm, holding it perfectly horizontal, his elbow thrust toward Lynette. "It would be my greatest pleasure to escort you."

Lynette, giving the shallowest of curtseys, took his arm with one hand while accepting her forgotten, fallen parasol from Henri with the other. As the strong man led the weak woman away, stepping around other groups of revelers perched on similar blankets, Lynette turned back and threw a small kiss toward Olympe and Jeanne.

"We will see you later, *ma chère*," Olympe called cheerfully with a wave.

Jeanne put two fingers to her pursed lips and raised them to her retreating friend, unable to speak through a throat closed tight.

"How long has she been like this?"

Jeanne turned to find Henri once more by her side.

"Since I've been back, I think," Jeanne answered, watching Lynette's departure, so grateful to Antoine for lending her his strength. "A week, maybe more."

"More," Olympe's voice delivered the news, bereft of all its buoyancy. Jeanne saw her jaw muscles clench under her smooth, powdered skin as she too watched their friend, the third cornerstone in their pyramid of friendship, make her wearied way through the flower and bush-strewn paths.

"Has she been seen by a doctor?" Laurent asked.

"I'm not sure," Jeanne said. "Olympe?"

The stolid woman shrugged her shoulders silently.

"We will get d'Anseau," Henri assured them with an agreeing nod from Laurent, referring to the Musketeers' own physician.

In silence, Henri reached over the few inches separating them and took Jeanne's hand in his, squeezing it with gentle reassurance. Jeanne allowed him to carry her burden, if only for a moment or two.

"Olympe!"

The thunderous voice screeched out from behind them. The remaining group swiveled on their heels, shocked out of their musings, squinting as they turned in the direction of the blazing sun. Olympe's shoulders slumped; her chin fell to her chest.

"*Oui*, Papa. I am here."

The Marquis de Solignac marched toward them, round and red-faced, elaborately attired in dove gray brocade with silver trim, the tendrils of his white wig streaming out behind him.

"I have been searching for you for hours." The marquis gave no salutation to Jeanne or the two men as they curtseyed and bowed to the elder nobleman. "The Vicomte du Ludres has been asking for you all day. How dare you embarrass me in this way?"

Grabbing his daughter's arm roughly, the Marquis de Solignac pulled her away without another word. Following with irresolute effort, Olympe gave Jeanne and Henri a half wave while she bestowed a look of blatant longing upon Laurent.

"Come," the marquis barked with a tug on his wayward child.

They lost Olympe to the crowd as it enveloped her.

"The Vicomte du Ludres?" Laurent spoke the words as if he tasted something detestable. "Surely not?"

"*Oui*, I am afraid so." Jeanne's head spun, first toward where she had last seen Lynette, then twisting, turning to Olympe's path. Despair brewed, bubbling in her eyes, a deep furrow formed between thin brows.

"Come, my dear," Henri coaxed gently, still holding her hand, pulling her with tender playfulness. "Come, our giant is just about to plunder another hapless victim."

Jeanne allowed herself to be led with a small, grateful smile.

She reached out her other hand to Laurent, and the dashing cavalier eagerly took it. The three strode off to the dueling cloister, leaving behind the strewn morsels of their morning and their meal, giving no thought as to who would clean it up.

* * *

Jeanne found herself completely crushed, squished in the tiny circle between three large men, including a severely sweaty and pungent Gerard, as they bounded up and down, screaming incoherent triumphant hoots and hurrahs. At the exultant moment of his complete victory, Gerard had jumped the fence separating the dueling area from the spectators, embracing his dearest friends with humongous, muscle-bulging arms, trapping Jeanne in the middle of their embrace. She let out a helpless, unbidden squeak, and the three men separated, but just a few inches, enough to let her breathe.

"You've done it, good man." Laurent slapped Gerard heartily on the back. "Well done, truly well done."

Gerard accepted the praise with a slight bow of his large head, glorying in the kind esteem of his comrade.

Henri reached past Jeanne and grabbed one of Gerard's beefy fists, raising it high over their heads.

"Behold," he yelled, capturing the amused attention of all around them. "Behold Gerard the Giant, the greatest swordsman in all of France."

Thunderous applause and great shouts of acclaim rose around them. The immense man smiled humbly, and his ruddy face blossomed with a rosy blush. He raised his other hand in acknowledgment, and the ovation subsided. Looking down at Jeanne, he took her hand in his mammoth mitt.

"It is a pleasure to meet you, Mademoiselle du Bois." Gerard brushed his thick lips across the back of her hand. "I have heard so much of you from Henri. I see he does not exaggerate the depth of your beauty."

It was Jeanne's turn to blush as she dropped into a deep curtsey. She was no great beauty and she knew it, yet his words flowed over her like fine silk.

"*Enchanté*, monsieur." Jeanne looked up at the Hercules before her with unfeigned admiration. "It was a true pleasure to watch you today. You have earned your victory quite brilliantly."

"She knows so much about the duel, Gerard," Laurent informed him, twirling one end of his long mustache as he watched a trio of young damsels swish and sway past them. "It is quite uncanny."

"It's true," Henri confirmed to Gerard, seeing his cynical expression. "You should have heard her, yelling out directions. The perfect ones."

"Ah, then perhaps it was your voice I heard and not an angel's after all." Gerard once more brushed his lips to her hand as Jeanne laughed. She hoped her amusement would disguise her fear, wishing to kick herself for her unrestrained behavior. "I hope I can get to know you better, *chère*, perhaps after I have made myself more presentable?"

Gerard stepped back and, with a grand gesture, indicated his still duel-garbed, dirty body.

"It will be the highlight of my day, monsieur," Jeanne said in all truth; having liked the man as 'Jean-Luc,' she felt certain Jeanne would find him equally engaging.

"*Très bien.* Then, please, give me but a few minutes and I will return much more comely. Even this one will pale beside my beauty." Gerard began to walk away with a sauntering gait and a tic of his head toward Laurent.

Henri and Laurent burst into laughter, and though she tried not to, Jeanne giggled behind a cupped hand.

"I'll be waiting, good sir." Turning to Henri and Laurent, she gave them a push in their friend's direction. "Why don't you two accompany him, make sure he finds his way back. I think I will take a moment and check on Lynette."

Laughter subsiding to a chuckle, Henri took Jeanne's two hands, capturing them in the cave of his, gently kissing the tips of her digits as they slipped out of their hiding place held tight against his chest.

"Of course, *ma chère*, what a delightful idea."

Jeanne saw the empathy and understanding in his kind, happy face.

"Thirty minutes, no more. We will meet again by Apollo, next to the Canal."

Jeanne nodded happily. "Till then."

"I will count the seconds." Henri released her hand and turned with great strides to join Gerard and Laurent.

Jeanne held her hands to her chest, hoping to still the trembling heart below. As soon as the trio was out of sight, Jeanne walked as swiftly as possible away from the castle, toward the towering, camouflaging towers of the Colonnade and the clothes of 'Jean-Luc.'

* * *

She scanned the area like a soldier sneaking into enemy territory. Her heart thudded swift and loud in her ears. The sweat under her shirt and leather waistcoat ran in rivulets down the indented pathway of her spine. She longed to scratch under the itchy paste holding her mustache on, but she dared not.

I must be insane. I must.

Jeanne berated herself as she clomped her way through the gardens of Versailles, using her best mannish swagger as she strode purposefully in the buckskin-leather, bucket-top boots. Her molasses eyes flicked here, there, and everywhere, looking for her family or anyone she knew well. Seeing Madame d'Abrignys walking toward her among a small group of women, Jeanne quickly turned her glance, put her hand up in front of her face as if to block the late-afternoon sun, and swerved dramatically to her right.

She hurriedly jumped off the Royal Avenue to slip through the bushes of the Bosquet des Dômes. Like a mongoose on the hunt, Jeanne slid her way through the thick shrubbery to emerge at the crest of the Apollo Fountain.

Taking a moment to pick the broken pieces of green leaves and stems from her attire, she scanned the area for familiar faces. Just beyond the rushing water, Henri and his trio of friends stood on the grassy knoll between pool and the beginning of the Grand Canal. Their handsome faces bore grand smiles; they leaned toward and away from each other, a playful swat here, a hearty slap on the back there.

Jeanne straightened her back, jutted out her chin, lowered the wide brim of her felt hat, and took her first broad step toward the gallant group. As she rounded the northern curve of the intricately designed pool surrounding the mammoth fountain, Antoine caught sight of 'him.'

"Look, *mes amis*, here comes our young friend," he said, pointing at the approaching 'Jean-Luc.'

The other three rugged faces all turned her way, and Jeanne held her breath, fearful that this time, like each time, her disguise would fail.

"*Bonjour, bonjour*," the men called warmly.

"We were wondering where you were just a few minutes ago," Henri informed 'him,' bestowing upon 'Jean-Luc' one of those backslaps, a gesture which Jeanne felt sure passed as appropriate and accepted affection between men. "We'd hope to see you today. We've been having a most wonderful time with our mutual friend, the Mademoiselle du Bois. She is a most delightful woman."

Jeanne smiled, pleased to hear Henri's praise of her other self, thrilled to see the spark burst in his golden eyes at the mention of her name.

"Where have you been hiding?" Laurent queried.

"I have been in the service of Monsieur du Mas most of the day," Jeanne said in her deep, gravelly voice, easily sounding extra low and rough today after all the cheering for Gerard this morning. "Unfortunately, I must return in a few minutes."

"That is too bad indeed. It has been a most enjoyable festival thus far. I'm sure the rest of the events will be equally as grand." Antoine regaled 'Jean-Luc' with the details of Gerard's dazzling display at dueling. Jeanne hoped she responded with appropriate enthusiasm, oohing and ahhing at moments in the story where it seemed most natural for someone who had not seen the entire performance.

"I am deeply sorry to have missed it. Congratulations, good man," Jeanne said, head tilted up to Gerard, reaching up to deliver one of those slaps on his broad, leather-clad back.

Jeanne leaned closer to the men, surveying the groups of people who strode around the grounds near them, some who headed for the boarding platform of the Canal's grand gondolas, so many others who just strolled about leisurely. But she saw none paying any undue attention to her and her fellows.

"Have you learned any more about our...project?" Jeanne lowered her voice to a whisper, remembering to keep the tones deep and coarse.

All four men shook their heads. "Nothing," Laurent responded first. "Why? Have you heard something?"

Jeanne nodded solemnly. "I have. Quite disturbing news, in fact."

Jeanne launched into the tale of the Queen's illness, using the exact words her mother had used to tell the story. She could have shared the information as 'Jeanne,' but she had no wish to involve her mother in any way with this peculiar affair. To continue this masquerade and to do so while retaining her sanity, Jeanne knew she must keep her two worlds apart, as separate as logistics would allow.

"How is she now? How is our Queen?" Gerard said, almost frantic with concern. "Did I not see her on the festival grounds earlier today?"

"You did, big fellow. Calm yourself." Antoine pacified his friend with a soothing voice and a stilling hand wrapped around Gerard's large bicep. "We know she is a favorite of yours. We will do everything to keep her safe, you know that."

"*Oui*, ah, yes, I do." Gerard hung his huge head, black hair falling around his face as he nodded in understanding. "But this is terrible news, most terrible."

"I agree, sir," Jeanne said. "That is why I felt so compelled to share the story with you."

"You've done well, good man. We will be sure to pass on your loyal behavior to Captain d'Artagnan," Antoine assured her.

Jeanne's smile spread under her mustache; it was the highest of compliments.

"I must return. I am sure my master will be missing me by now." Jeanne bowed low and turned away with a wave.

"Come to the *Hôtel* tomorrow," Henri called to Jean-Luc's retreating form. "There is sure to be many a challenge to our triumphant friend here."

"I will," Jeanne called back. "*Merci.*"

~Sixteen~

By the time "Jeanne" returned to the foot of the Grand Canal, Olympe and Antoine had rejoined the group—now larger with the addition of her sister Bernadette and her sister's friend, Angelique de Sance. Not only had Jeanne changed back into the many layers of her feminine attire, she had run through the garden and up the two flights of stairs to Lynette's quarters. Her friend still slept, causing her more concern, and she'd not been able to talk with her.

"Where have you been?" Olympe spotted her first, thrusting her hands on her hips as if she were Jeanne's parent, concerned yet angered by her child's tardiness.

"At…Lynette's." Jeanne words eked out between gasps of fresh air. "She slept still, and I sat by her side for a while."

Jeanne felt great guilt at using her friend's illness as a veil for her secret conduct but believed that when

Lynette heard of her fabulous adventure, her friend would be happy to learn of her part in the subterfuge. Jeanne longed to tell both Lynette and Olympe of her furtive pursuits, believing to tell would be to make the adventures real and not just a figment of her longing and imagination.

"Pray forgive my tardiness. I greatly apologize for making you wait." Jeanne curtseyed to the group and a wink for her sister, whose eyes bulged at the men around her, as did her young friend's.

Henri bent his golden-covered head to bring his mouth close to her ear. "I thought you meant not to return. I was ready to tear the chateau apart in search of you." Pulling back, he bestowed a deep, sensual smile upon her.

"I will always be where you can find me, good sir." The words flowed freely from Jeanne's lips, no thoughts or inhibitions tainting their sincerity. She felt a pull on the short, puff sleeve of her day gown and turned to find her sister at her side.

"*Bonjour, chère.* I am so pleased to see you." Jeanne gave her sister a quick hug. "Where ever did you come from?"

"Olympe found us, and then these...men found her as we were walking past."

Bernadette's plump, young face glowed with her rapture and excitement to be among such dashing, masculine company. "How do you know them?"

Jeanne glanced at the men, at their beauty, their raw masculinity, and felt it too: the pull, the immediate and undeniable desire they elicited from every woman around them. From the corner of her eye, Jeanne caught Angelique straightening her back, pushing forward a chest already large and noticeable, yet looking like a stag caught in the middle of a circle of hunters.

Jeanne wanted to laugh at the palpable feminine responses of her sister and Angelique to the Musketeers but held her mirth.

"That is a long story. One I will be most willing to share with you in, say, twenty or thirty years."

Bernadette tilted her head a smidgen, brows knitting upon her forehead, clearly puzzled by her sister's mysterious words. Jeanne did laugh then and pulled her sibling into another fond embrace. Over Bernadette's head, Jeanne caught a glimpse of someone and her heart froze in her chest. Percy de Polignac and two other men, birds of a feather who appeared equally as puny and placid as Percy, walked straight for them, heading down the diagonal path between the Colonnade and the *Salle des Marronniers.* Jeanne spun on her heels, turning so quickly with Bernadette still in her arms, she almost pulled her sister off her feet.

"Does he see us?" Jeanne hissed at Bernadette.

"Does who—" Bernadette began, quickly spying the tall, skinny whelp of a man heading in their direction.

"*Non,*" Bernadette hissed back with a small shake of her head.

Jeanne clenched her fists, squeezing them in fear, her stomach muscles gripped by a panicked spasm, racking her brain for an escape. Behind her coterie, she saw one of the magnificently plumed gondolas berthing at the dock and its many passengers disembarking.

"Come, come, *mes amis*, a gondola has come just for us." With one hand Jeanne pulled her sister, with the other she reached for Henri's hand, yanking him along as she trotted toward the boat.

The happy group followed her willingly if confused at her haste.

Jeanne jumped on board the vessel, forsaking the hands of the two gondola boatmen poised, one on each side of the boarding plank, with a beckoning, helpful arm. She felt the boat tilt first one way then another as it responded to her jarringly added weight.

Taking a seat in front of the stern boatman, she screened herself behind the single, large center flag mast and the bow-positioned boatman, and heaved a sigh of relief. She could not see Percy or any of his companions; if she could not see them, they could not see her. Her shoulders relaxed as did every other muscle in her body. Bernadette sat opposite her on the bench, pulling Angelique down beside her, shielding Jeanne even more from anyone still on shore. Jeanne thanked her with a silent smile and bow of her head.

"Are you all right, *chère* Jeanne?" Henri asked as he took his seat on Jeanne's right along the far railing of the vessel, his ornamental sword clanking against the side of the boat.

"Oh, yes," Jeanne assured him. "I just did not want to miss this gondola. I thought it a perfect pastime for such a merry group as we."

"How right you are," Laurent intoned as he squeezed himself in between Jeanne and Olympe, taking a hand of each woman and kissing them smartly. "It is a perfect afternoon for such frivolity."

Antoine sat on the other side of Olympe, the last on the bench of seats at the stern of the boat, leaving only Gerard still standing.

With a mischievous smile on his large face, he squeezed his large posterior between Bernadette and Angelique on the opposite facing bench, daintily lifting the yards of their skirt fabric out of the way. The two girls giggled, and the delightful sound blended with the staccato call of two warblers as they passed overhead.

Jeanne studied the flirtations of the men and these young girls, how Bernadette and Angelique hovered around the older males like bees around a honeypot, and a spark of concern lit in her chest. She leaned forward, a crooked finger beckoning Gerard, Antoine, and Laurent to draw closer.

"These girls are still children," Jeanne cautioned with narrowed eyes, with the glare of Jean-Luc during battle.

Gerard turned back to the two females beside him, seeing Bernadette's beauty and the full bosom and pouty mouth of Angelique.

"No, mamselle, they are most certainly women."

"They may be women on the outside, but in their hearts and minds they are but young girls," Jeanne spoke with a cutting tongue. "Dally with them disrespectfully and you will answer to me."

The friendly warning came from a woman, but the power and conviction belonged to a warrior, the truth of her being whether it be known or not. The men listened as they would not normally do to other women except, perhaps, their own mothers.

"We understand perfectly, *chère* Jeanne," Laurent assured her. "Worry no more."

Jeanne sat back against the cushions with a small, satisfied, closed-mouth grin, and worried no more, trusting these noble men without question. In that instant, the gondola forsook the shore, and she turned to Henri and laughed as their heads jerked upon their necks.

The gentle, gliding, quiet motion of the boat was soporific under the beating sun and the high heat of midafternoon. For a while the group rode in silent camaraderie, watching the green shore slip smoothly by, seeing the small gray and white gulls launch themselves from the tall, swampy grassland, their raucous calls piercing the somnolent silence. The group languished on the cushioned seats draped with crimson and gold brocade and watched as the fabric's fringe trailed over the side and into the water rushing away from the slowly moving craft in small, rolling waves.

From behind them, another gondola sailed into view, one of three given to Louis by the Venetian

Republic, passing barely two feet from their own. The passengers on each vessel waved to the others, friendly smiles and calls of *bonjour* exchanged between them.

"There is Karlotta de Pons." Jeanne waved enthusiastically to her friend on the other boat as it slipped away. "It has been good to see her again. I have not seen her mother anywhere though, and I wish to pay my respects."

Jeanne gained no reply but did not miss the shared glance between Olympe and Bernadette and the shake of Bernadette's head.

"She is dead, *ma chêre*," Olympe grudgingly informed Jeanne.

"No, it cannot be so?" Jeanne barked in shock.

"It is, I fear," Olympe assured her.

"When?"

"Ah, *chère* Jeanne," Laurent piped in, "the better question is how?"

"How?" Jeanne's eyes widened, flitting from face to face in search of answers.

"Good question," Olympe teased, bumping her shoulder against Laurent's. But then her playful smile died away, and she leaned close to Jeanne. "Poisoned."

Jeanne's jaw dropped.

"It cannot be," she whispered the words yet again, voice trembling. To hear this word, this despicable word, having just heard her mother utter it only last night, was a disturbing coincidence.

"'Tis true," Olympe assured her again with a solemn nod of her black-haired head. "And she was not the only one to die. There was the Duchess de Fontanges."

"Another dalliance of Louis'." Bernadette nodded spiritedly.

Jeanne thrust herself back upon her cushion, shaking her head as if to stave off the words, even the idea of the words. If she could, she would have thrown her hands upon her ears pretending such words did not exist. "Do they know who would do such a thing?"

"Madame d'Alluye, a dear friend of the grand Athénaïs," Olympe informed her. "But she was not the only one to hang."

"The Marechal de Luxembourg was acquitted," Antoine said the name with dire relief, a friend perhaps.

"Olympe, the Comtesse de Soissons." Bernadette offered.

"Mazarin's niece?" Jeanne stuttered, calling forth the name of the cardinal who had helped Queen Anne raise Louis.

"She was one of the King's first loves," Angelique said, having no wish to be left out of the conversation. "But she was not hung, only banished from court."

"The last to go was Catherine Monvoisin, La Voisin. They say she was a midwife and a fortune-teller who sold love potions as well as poison." Henri took up the story. "And many who claim she was a dear friend of Athénaïs as well."

"Though she was not hung, was she?" Gerard leaned forward to ask.

"*Non.*" Henri shook his head. "She was burned to death."

Jeanne squeezed the hand she held, unable to speak.

"You were lucky to have missed it; it was a terrible time at court, a despicable affair."

"*L'affaire des poisons.*" Laurent twirled the words out slowly on a curled tongue.

"*L'affaire des poisons,*" Jeanne repeated, a frightened whisper.

* * *

Jeanne's cloud of worry scattered with the lively breeze kicked up on the water then through the grounds as afternoon became evening. The shadow dissipated into fragments of troublesome little thoughts deep down inside her as the carefree cortege continued their ride and to enjoy each other's company through the rest of the fête. By the time they made their way to the *Bosquet des Rocailles,* an outdoor ballroom, a coliseum-type creation designed by André Le Nôtre located next to the Parterre and the Fountain of Latona, six more young people, a good mix of men and women, had joined their happy cartel. Having sent their servants ahead two hours ago, the clique strode grandly in, taking their seats as they replaced their seat savers, just four rows from the rounded stage.

Waiting for the first performance to begin, an opera by Lully, Jeanne studied the growing audience glowing in the warmth of hundreds of flambeaux circling the enclosure while listening to their excited twitters and their loud greetings. Here and there among the powdered, primped, and patched, Jeanne spotted a few men dressed in the royal colors of light blue trimmed with silver and gold braid and women in the same colors topped with hats trimmed with white feathers. These were the elite, the King's chosen ones, for the moment at least, a designation which offered them other privileges along with the King's favor. Jeanne did not even care to imagine what they must have done to deserve such an honor.

Following Lully's opera, *Cadmus et Hermione*, came a play, *Le Malade Imaginaire*, the last of Molière's musical comedies infused with elaborate sets and effects, staged not only by actors but by those nobles courageous enough to take part. Olympe leaned over Henri's lap to inform Jeanne of the names of the players, most of whom Jeanne had been gone too long to recognize.

"There is Madame d'Albret—she is a good friend to François Scarron. And that is Madame de Montauban and her two servants. Oh, and, of course, there is the Baron de Seneges—he is quite a good singer."

"Do the courtiers always take part in these pageants?" Jeanne asked.

"Oh yes," Olympe confirmed. "It is a great honor to be included in a performance for the King. What better way to be seen?"

"That is why I have no wish to call myself a courtier," Henri whispered to the two female heads drawn close before him. "Well, one of the many, at any rate."

Jeanne sat back with a smile for Henri, no longer wishing to hear any of the prominent names; she had no wish to lose respect for any more of them. Ignoring the embarrassment these fine people wrought upon themselves, she lost herself to the comedy of the spectacle, finding herself helpless, laughing uproariously with the rest of the audience. At one point, as one manly noble fell to the floor and the one behind him tripped upon the first's body to fly across the stage, almost into the audience, Jeanne actually coughed as the force of her laughter threatened to choke her.

Henri graciously patted her back, his own guffaws shaking his entire body, tears of laughter pooling in his eyes.

Jeanne's attention fell wholly upon the glorious man beside her. Her coughing subsided; Henri took his hand off her back, retaking her hand in his where it had cocooned for most of the day.

I feel I have known him forty years, not four days. How can that be?

But upon those thoughts rode others of such import they erased the fond smile from her face.

What would he think if he ever found out his two new friends were one and the same? Would he turn from me in anger and disgust? Would he hate me completely?

The thought sent fear pumping through her, a desperate fear clenching her tightly in its grasp. Her laughing face darkened; her lips trembled. Henri saw her distress and leaned in closer.

"Are you all right?" His concern distinct in his tender tone, his furrowed brow.

Jeanne feared to speak, afraid her emotions would be set free if she opened her mouth. She squeezed his hand tightly; with a nod and a shrug and a smile of reassurance, she turned back to the play with a deep, stilling breath.

From the stage to the supper table, the courtiers strolled through the grounds ablaze with light; thousands of candles and flambeaux lit the night, fixed on the pathways and on the trees and bushes. The crowds reached the chateau and cooed in delight.

Along each lengthy side of the main building of the castle, the avenues lying to the north and south and continuing into the gardens and down the length of the Water Parterres ran long tables. Each lengthy piece emblazoned with the finest of the King's porcelain and silver, tabourets at each place, enough settings for the entire entourage of courtiers. An outdoor supper awaited each and every guest, attended by servants bedecked in Greek costume.

In the center of these two trestles, between the chateau and the Water Parterre, Louis sat at a small private table. With him his wife, his children, the Prince and Princesses of the Blood as well as a few chosen courtiers, Athénaïs de Montespan and François Scarron among them.

In the cooling but still warm night, the courtiers gorged themselves on every delectable the King's kitchen produced. Capons, partridges, and bisque of pigeon came in the first serving, followed by never-ending veal, fricasseed chickens, grilled turkeys, and petendeaux.

The aromas of meat tantalized the air and mixed with the rich, fresh odors of the gardens, satisfying all the senses as the purely decadent food slid down the throat and into the gullet.

Somehow they ate the dessert as well, drinking crystal glass after crystal glass of the King's best wine. With the dessert came the magnificent finale, a fireworks display like none seen before. The crowd squealed in pleasure and astonishment as the rockets lit the sky as bright as day as if the sun rose again. But it was not the sun scorching the heavens and all that dwelled beneath it, but the Sun King himself. Sitting at the heart of the assemblage, Louis basked in the glory of this triumphant moment, bowing in modesty as the cheers rose up around him.

The explosions ceased, the food stopped coming, and Jeanne threw down her napkin on the empty plate before her, the fifth such decimated trencher if her count was accurate.

"I cannot move. I won't be able to eat for a fortnight at least." She rubbed her swollen stomach unabashedly, a crumb-encrusted smile broad on her face, glowing softly in the candlelight thrown by the gold and silver candelabra.

Henri reached over, smiling in pure enchantment, and wiped the crumbs away from her mouth with a silky linen and a few soft strokes.

Jeanne felt the napkin on her lips, felt Henri's hands so close to her face; his gentle cleaning became an erotic caress. His gaze rose from her lips to her eyes, and Jeanne saw the naked lust, gripped by the same desire.

"I hear there is to be yet another performance," Laurent said, standing behind Henri's chair, puffing away on a cheroot. "In the Salon de Mars. Shall we continue our revelry there?"

"Yes, let's," Bernadette quickly twittered, willing to go anywhere this gorgeous man beckoned.

"Go on without us," Henri said, never taking his eyes from Jeanne's as he stood and, pulling out her chair, reached out a hand, one she readily and willingly filled. "We are too full; we need a walk."

"Too full of each other," Antoine muttered jokingly. "Come, my gallant companions. Another performance, another audience. We must not disappoint."

The festive group made their way to the doors of the lower gallery. Henri and Jeanne, silent, intent upon each other naught else, turned from the tables toward the hundreds of trees in the Orangery. Hand in hand they walked; moisture formed in the cup made by their palms and Jeanne wondered if it came from the heat of the still-warm August night or from the heat they created betwixt them. Passing the small circular pond at the entrance to the grove, the young couple walked in silence devoid of awkwardness. A strong breeze rose up, and Jeanne lifted her face to be caressed by it. Henri turned and smiled, his own long, wavy golden hair flitting out behind him as the silky wind brushed across his face.

A peculiar moan reached their ears. Jeanne labored to hear it better, to fathom the origin of the noise.

"It is the breeze through the trees," she whispered in delight, afraid to silence nature's tender music with her words.

"So you say." Henri leaned toward her. "But I have heard there are ghosts here and it is their cries we hear."

"Ghosts?" Jeanne whispered, shoulders shuddering with a small shiver, though her mischievous smile told him it was a tremble of pleasurable fright.

"*Ah oui*," Henri assured her. "As you know, for many years, thousands of men toiled at the feet of Versailles, expanding it, building it ever grander and larger, as some still do today. At one time a strange fever ran rampant through the workers, killing hundreds a day for many a day. Many believe their deaths were the result of the anomalous odors, smells like the decay of human flesh, which rose out of the ground as they dug at it."

Jeanne stopped walking, enraptured by Henri's tale.

"Some say the spirits of these men live still," he continued, stopping as well, facing her only inches apart, "coming out at night, searching for a way out of the maze they themselves helped to construct.

As they realize they are still trapped within the chateau's clutching grasp, they moan with frustration and loss. That is the sound keening through the night. Or so they say."

Henri finished with a soft smile and a titillating flick of his brows. Jeanne was enthralled by his story, by him. A wail-like screech stabbed the air, high-pitched and shrill. Jeanne yelped, launching herself at Henri. Laughing softly, he eagerly wrapped her in a protective embrace. Jeanne laid her head against his shoulder, clutching his embroidered waistcoat.

"Have I frightened you, *ma petite*?" He looked down at her. "I would have not thought it possible."

Jeanne's gaze fastened upon his lips: their fullness, their moisture. She shivered still, though no longer sure if the palpitations came from the frightening story or from sheer wantonness. For she wanted him badly, she knew for certain, wanted his lips on hers, knew he shared her desire. Without hesitation, she parted her own lips to meet with the onslaught of his. They captured hers, and she willingly surrendered. He wielded them tenderly at first, then with such masterful power he stole the breath from her lungs; she gasped with the thrill of it.

Henri pulled back, searching her face, brows drawn together in concern. She saw it, the solicitude, the respect, and her heart swelled. The corners of her wide mouth twitched with a grin. With a sensuous small smile of his own, he bent his head once more, capturing her full bottom lip with his two, gently pulling and sucking on the sweet flesh as if it were candy.

Jeanne could taste the wine on his tongue, could smell the musky manliness of him. Her head swam with the ecstasy his lips brought her; they were more delicious than any edible delight ever tasted. For a fleeting second she remembered her few juvenile kisses and realized how different, how inadequate, they were.

His lips left hers, and she thought to object until she felt them scorching a path of desire and heat down her throat, to the top of her young breasts, his mustache tickling her tingling skin like feathers, and she moaned with satisfaction and desire. She grew tipsy in his arms, their strength against her back the only thing keeping her from tumbling backward.

From the hollow of her collarbone, his words came as a garbled mumble.

"You have been at the convent for seven years?"

What a strange question. "Uh, *oui*," she acknowledged.

"And you..." Henri hesitated, his lips never leaving her skin. "You are still a maid?"

"Very much so," Jeanne replied with characteristic frankness. Her head snapped up from where it hung back on her neck seemingly devoid of any previous musculature. "Why, am I doing this terribly wrong?"

Henri's stunned laughter echoed through the scintillating silence. He laughed against her neck, his body quivered against hers and he smiled. Henri looked up, looked deeply at her; there lay all his desire still burning hotly behind the twinkle of glee.

"*Non, ma chère*, you do everything right." Henri kissed the tip of her nose with pursed lips and then, to her utter devastation, took a step back, separating two bodies melded so perfectly to one. "It is I who transgress."

Jeanne began to shake her head but saw his face, the face of a Musketeer, and thought better of it. These men may dabble with many a wench, but their honor would prohibit the casual defacing of a maid. This true nobility wrought her absolute admiration, and that of 'Jean-Luc,' and she would not deny or disrespect it. She nodded, understanding, but uttered a deep, unfulfilled sigh as her shoulders slumped in disappointment.

Henri's laughter rang true through the night, and he wrapped his arms tightly around her once more. Jeanne felt no fiery desire but rather overpowering emotion; she languished in it. From far off, strands of music reached their ears, a soft sonata from the strings of tender violins and fathomless cellos. Henri reached down and took one of Jeanne's hands, raising it slowly to shoulder height.

They began to dance.

* * *

The music had stopped many minutes ago, or had it been hours? The moon now commanded the sky, a crescent offering a hook in the heavens.

"I must get you home," Henri said to the side of Jeanne's head where his lips still dwelled as they danced to the music of the night.

"I think I am home," Jeanne replied, emotion naked for all to see.

"As am I," Henri replied.

Did he feel the same profound sense of belonging?

"No, no," Jeanne whimpered as he pulled away from her. Keeping her hand in his, he led her back up the path that would bring them to the chateau. Jeanne followed him, though she dragged her feet like a child on the way to a disagreeable relative's house.

Henri led her through the South Parterre then headed straight, leading them toward the main back-doors in the lower gallery.

"No, this way," Jeanne insisted, taking the lead, turning right at the intersection of the paths and heading up along the south outer wall of the main building. "I know many shortcuts."

Reaching the corner where the main building joined with the south wing, Jeanne opened a small door disguised as a window, leading into a deserted antechamber.

"There would be no one here at this hour," Jeanne assured him.

Jeanne led him up a circular staircase to the *Salon de l'Oeil-de-Boeuf* and through the archways into the Hall of Mirrors. Jeanne heard him gasp behind her. She spun around, expecting to see a threat lying in wait.

"I've not seen this room since it was finished," Henri marveled.

Begun in 1678, the glory of Versailles defined opulence and elegance, with mirrors, glass, and gold. Seventy-three meters long but only ten and a half meters wide, its shape like a vast hallway. The room's ceiling coves depicted the King's military victories and his political accomplishments while ironically anchored on one end by the Salon of War and at the other by the Salon of Peace.

The outside wall boasted seventeen windows while the inside wall, the one abutting the King's own rooms, matched their design with seventeen mirrors. The mirrors' arches were set on marble pilasters with gilded bronze capitals decorated with symbols of France such as the fleur de lys. The solid-gold tables, golden statue lamp holders, and orange tree pots standing alongside ancient figures and busts of Roman emperors led the way down the length of the breathtaking architecture.

"I would never have thought such a place existed." Henri could but gape as Jeanne led him down the long length of the hall and into the Salon of War. Crossing the room diagonally, Jeanne brought them to the far arch and made to turn the corner into the Apollo Drawing Room.

"I have no wish to hear your excuses." A female voice, the hiss of a snake, slid from the other side of the partition. The words froze with a blast of frigid air.

Pulling Jeanne behind him, Henri took the lead, sidling up to the edge of the three-quarter wall. With the stealth born of many years as a soldier, he brought his head to the edge of the screen and turned a sliver at a time until he could see the other side. Turning back to Jeanne, he raised his arms with a shrug.

"I have already paid a king's fortune, and yet the Queen lives still."

Jeanne bit upon her tongue to keep her gasp within as Henri's grasp upon her hand crushed. Jeanne pulled on him this time, exchanging places closest to the opening and, mimicking Henri's motion, sneaked a look into the other room. Barely did she have time to glance into the chamber when she pulled back so fast she almost cracked her head on his.

Wrapping her arms around his neck, Jeanne yanked hard, forcing his lips down upon hers, smothering his yip of surprise with her mouth. Above their locked lips, they communicated silently, Jeanne stifling his questions with a warning look. As the hollow clack of leather heels on the hard marble floor grew closer, understanding dawned on Henri and he released himself to the kiss. Jeanne's held breath returned, and she relinquished herself to the camouflaging embrace.

Their desire would not be denied; it took on a life, a fire, of its own, and the heat so shortly doused lit once more. Jeanne's knees nearly failed her as Henri's smooth tongue drew a line slowly across her lips, outlining them with his moist, hot flesh. The exhilaration surged through her entire body, fear and lust blending in a cataclysmic joining.

What is happening to me? Jeanne thought but made no move to pull away from the shimmering sensations bombarding her. *Have I no resolve, no strength at all?*

The clomping heels entered the room and stilled. Henri moaned with passion, both in welcome relief from the building rapture, an easy and true subterfuge of their ruse. To see lovers locked together in a dim corner, late on the night of a fête, was not a surprising sight. After a moment's hesitation, the sound of walking began once more and passed through the room. Henri released Jeanne's lips and lowered his head to her silky nape. Beyond the rapture of womanhood, Jeanne—ever the warrior in her truth—opened her eyes, searching the chamber in the dim light, peering over Henri's tawny head. At the last minute, the cloaked walker stopped. The head swiveled, the cloak's hood fell back a few inches, and three-quarters of a woman's face revealed itself. Her gaze locked with Jeanne's.

Quickly lowering her lashes, fluttering them in feigned ecstasy, ardor not so imagined, Jeanne broke the contact, succumbing to the demanding man before her. As the sound of the plodding heels drew softer and away, Henri and Jeanne slowly separated. Jeanne's hand upon his chest felt its rapid rise and fall; it came as heavy and ragged as her own; she recognized the dreamy expression on his face, knew it was her own as well.

"Do you know her?" Henri asked with a thin whisper.

"The face is familiar, but that is all. You need to follow her."

"I cannot. I cannot leave you till you are at your door."

Jeanne pushed at his hard chest, and for a moment longed to allow her fingers to linger there. "Do not be silly. I have sneaked back to my rooms many a time. I am not my father's least favorite child for naught. I will be quite all right, I assure you."

With a hesitant nod, Henri inched his way toward the exit the woman had used, bouncing on the heels of his feet, the adrenaline of the pursuit having its way with him. "Are you sure?"

"*Oui*, most sure," Jeanne said persuasively. "Go."

Henri took two steps away from her, darted back, pressed his lips hard against hers, then rushed away.

Dazed and dizzy, Jeanne brought her fingers up to her ravaged lips. "Good night," she whispered reluctantly.

Henri nodded to her from the door. "Be careful, my love."

Jeanne watched him slither stealthily through the Hall of Mirrors, hiding behind the large figurines and statues.

My love? His words echoed in her mind, taking up residence as favorites.

~Seventeen~

Two mornings later, Jeanne returned to chapel, finding the long rows of benches half-empty, so many courtiers still absent, still recovering from the grand pleasures of the Feast. For some, the pleasures had continued all through the night and well into the next morning.

The prelate droned on about the magnificence of King and country, but Jeanne's mind worshipped the memories of that momentous day and even more the epochal night. One image commanded them all: that of Henri.

What am I to do now?

The mass ended, the courtiers filed out in proper order, yet Madame La Marechal, Lynette's mother, remained on her knees in the pew, though the line of ducs and duchesses had already passed from the room.

On silent tiptoes, Jeanne slipped down the pew and kneeled next to her dear friend's maman.

"*Bonjour*, Madame." Jeanne smiled at the hunched-over form beside her.

Madame La Marechal's head snapped up as if struck from behind, her prayer so intent she'd heard nothing of Jeanne's approach.

Jeanne sucked back air in a gasp; the ravaged face of this pretty woman, powderless, splotched, and tearstained, one she had known for a lifetime, unnerved her.

"What, Madame?" Jeanne insisted, none too kindly. "What is it?"

"Lynette," Mme. La Marechal whispered, "is very ill."

Jeanne waited for no more words; she jumped to her feet and ran out of the pew, down the aisle, and out the chapel doors. She ran all the way up the two flights of stairs to the La Marechal suite of rooms on the same floor as her own.

Arriving at the door, Jeanne raised her hand to knock, almost committing a grave faux pas in her urgency to see Lynette. To knock on a door at Versailles was the height of impoliteness. Instead, to gain entrance one was expected to scratch at the door with the nail of the little finger of the left hand. Jeanne did her best, but it was not overly loud—the nail on this finger was still as short as her others; she'd not had time to grow it long, like the other residents of the chateau.

The timid graze sufficed, and a female servant opened the door.

Recognizing the noble young lady, the comely woman led Jeanne to Lynette's small back room. Jeanne rushed across the threshold and buckled to a stop, stricken by the physical appearance of her friend.

Lynette lay motionless in her small bed, her skin a sickly yellow color. Dark circles outlined her sunken eyes and her glorious blond hair lay in oily strands upon the pillow. A weak smile lit upon her face at the sight of her friend.

"*Bonjour*, Jeanne." Her rattled greeting barely made it across the room.

"*Bonjour*, Lynette," cried Jeanne, forcing her best smile upon her face. With quick steps she strode to the tabouret beside Lynette's bed and sat, taking her friend's hand in her own. Jeanne's nostrils flared, assaulted by the onerous smell of dried urine and stale feces, the sourness of sickness and rotting flesh.

"It is so good to see you...You look well...How are you feeling? Has Olympe been to see you lately?" Words rushed from Jeanne's mouth as if their speed could defend against her fear. "Did you hear of Mademoiselle de Broussel and her married lover?"

Jeanne prattled on and on, telling her friend all the trivial happenings at court, for she knew if she would stop but a moment, the truth of her friend's condition would set in and she would let loose the raging sob kept captive at the back of her throat.

Through her friend's entire tirade, Lynette listened quietly, a small, wan smile upon her sickly face, nodding her head at times.

Jeanne knew not how many minutes passed before Lynette's mother appeared at the door. The woman's face told Jeanne everything; there would be no denying what was happening to her most beloved companion.

"Ah, here is your dearest maman." Jeanne jumped to her feet, leaned over, and kissed Lynette's fever-warmed and clammy cheek. "I will leave you in her capable hands."

Jeanne rose from her stool, guilt-ridden but desperate to be gone; she would set free her breaking heart where Lynette could not see. As she headed for the door, Mme. La Marechal came to take her place on the bedside stool. As the two women passed each other, Jeanne reached out and grabbed the elder woman's arm.

"Has d'Anseau been here?" she whispered, referring to the Musketeer's physician.

"*Oui.*" Mme. La Marechal shook her head. "There is naught to be done."

Jeanne began to turn away, but this time Lynette's mother stilled her with a pull on her arm.

"The King insists I move her." Her anger loud in her quiet whisper.

Pain, hot and angry, struck Jeanne, a nearly felling blow. By long-standing tradition, no one, nobility or otherwise, was allowed to die while under the same roof as the King. Even members of his own family were rushed out within seconds of their passing.

Fresh tears fell like cold rain down Mme. La Marechal's grief-scarred face.

"He is allowing us a room at Trianon," she said.

The small pavilion built on the former village of Trianon sat just behind the gardens of Versailles, reached quickly on foot or by a vinaigrette, a single-person, wheeled chair pulled by a solitary man.

Jeanne nodded and flew to the door, a sob choking her. At the threshold she held, unable not to turn back. There she found her friend's shy, tender smile, the one Jeanne had loved to see throughout the best moments of her life, and the pain of the loss to come struck Jeanne with a drowning, crashing wave. Rushing back to the bed, she threw her arms about Lynette.

"I will see you soon, dearest friend, I promise."

Jeanne escaped the room as her tears did her eyes.

* * *

"It will do you good to get away, dearest," her mother assured Jeanne. "It will only be for the day—we return first thing in the morning."

Jeanne nodded silent assent, stepping into the Du Bois family carriage, the bright sun of another hot summer morning tripping itself over the horizon, white-hot streaks flashing across the low sky.

Having fled Lynette's room, Jeanne had returned to her own, sobbing in fear and her own helplessness. Opening the door, she had rushed in, straight into her mother's waiting arms.

"You have been to see Lynette?"

How do mothers know so much? Jeanne had wondered, but only for a moment, and like most children, no matter their age, ran needful into her mother's consoling embrace, the only safe haven in a world gone mad.

"Come to Paris with me in the morn. It will serve as a good diversion."

Jeanne had silently agreed and now found herself firmly ensconced in the small carriage being led away by their two lackeys, bright as the sun in their yellow livery.

As they crossed the *Cour de Marbre*, many a head turned and bowed in their direction; the vehicle's accoutrements a reflection of the Du Bois family's status, one of affluence and position.

Lined with burgundy velvet trimmed with gold braiding, the interior offered comfort. Outside, the gilded body boasted fringe at the top and gilded wheels glowing in the early morning light as the conveyance pulled away from the curb, drawn by two large bays.

Within seconds the carriage passed through the perpetually opened flanking gates of Versailles, which gave onto the cobbled Cour Royale and Place d'Armes, an inviting place where the King gave welcome to all his people, peddlers and beggars the only ones to be turned away.

No matter how poor or lowly stationed, anyone could enter the palace grounds as long as they were properly presented. They must be tidy no matter how humble, the women must remove their aprons, and all men must have a sword by their side. Porters, stationed at the gates sixteen hours a day, offered swords for rent should a gentleman not have one. Even this early in the morning, many families stood in line awaiting inspection, twelve, thirteen children or more walking behind their parents like obedient ducklings. Jeanne stared in amusement and confounded amazement at their sheer numbers.

"He pays them," her mother said, her gaze following the direction of her daughter's.

"*Pardonnez-moi*?" Jeanne turned from the window to her mother perched beside her on the cushioned bench.

"He pays each family one thousand livres for every child past the tenth."

"But why?" Jeanne looked back into the crowd with wide-eyed astonishment.

"He and France need soldiers and servants, *oui*?"

Upon her mother's face, Jeanne saw her own feelings of disgust mirrored on the familiar features. She offered no answer; there was nothing to be said of such things unimaginable, and they fell into silence as the carriage entered the Cours-La-Reine, the main highway into Paris.

The carriage pulled up in front of the Du Bois family's Paris home an hour and a half later, and the two drowsy, bored women disembarked in front of the Renaissance-styled, ten-room chateau. Jeanne had not seen this place, the place of her birth, in many years. Too fearful, a fear bordering on the paranoid, her father refused to be absent from court for any length of time. He was not alone. To do so was to invite the King's displeasure with open arms.

"I am exhausted, *ma petite*." Adelaide patted her daughter's hand. "I believe I'll lie down a bit before supper."

"Of course, Maman," Jeanne said. "I make for the bookseller. I shall meet you back here in time for supper."

"Do not wander," her mother called over her shoulder as an elderly butler helped her up the steep stone steps of the entrance.

"I won't, Maman. I promise," Jeanne called, already on her way across the cobbled street.

It took all the resolve and restraint Jeanne possessed not to run as she turned off the Rue St. Honore onto the dirt-paved Rue de l'Abre Sec, passing quickly between the coaches and sedan chairs clogging the busy city street. The dust rose up off the dirt road in whirlwinds around her. She zigged and zagged, avoiding the piles of horse excrement and garbage lying in the gutters. The dingy smell of hot human and animal rode the passageway, especially dank at the height of the summer season. The clomping of horses mingled with the cracks of whips and the calls of drivers vying for right of way in the crowded boulevard.

Jeanne had no intention of visiting the bookseller, though she loved such establishments dearly, the worlds hidden between the thousands of pages, even the smell of the books all lined up so precisely one after the other enticed her. But she had a much greater quest to complete, one conceived in her mind during the long, tedious ride into the city.

Jeanne could not shut Henri out of her mind; his expressions, his words, his smells, every touch they had ever shared tantalizingly tormented her. Jeanne's thoughts thrilled her and filled her with the utmost dread. She had no notion how to please such a man, and she wanted so badly to please him. She denounced her lack of knowledge unacceptable and worried over it like the nuns worried over their rosaries until she remembered one of her brother's stories. Raol had told her of a woman who knew how, perhaps more than any, to satisfy a man.

Jeanne quickened her pace; her feet moved so quickly her heavy skirts became entangled around her legs as she turned a corner, but she didn't slow down.

"*Mon Dieu!*" Jeanne scudded to a stop.

Coming toward her at a leisurely pace was the Marquis and Marquise de Retz, lifelong friends of her parents.

Jeanne had no choice but to slow her pace and drop into a respectful curtsey to the elderly couple.

"*Chère* Jeanne," the marquise twittered with her age-warbled voice. "It is so nice to see you back from the convent."

"*Merci,* Madame." Jeanne feigned good manners and gentility. "It is good to be back."

"Are your mother and father here in the city with you?" the white-wigged, aged-spotted marquis asked.

"Only Maman," Jeanne replied politely. "She's at home resting."

"Of course, of course," the marquise responded.

Jeanne held her tongue further, though an awkward silence ensued. She should ask after their health or that of their children, but she wallowed in the clumsy quiet.

"Well." The marquis filled the strained pause. "Please give our best to them both."

"Of course, I will, monsieur." Jeanne nodded. "Madame."

With another shallow curtsey, Jeanne continued her rushed walk, grateful for the bizarre rules of manners her society employed, one of which prevented the gossipy marquise from asking where Jeanne was headed. She would be chastised for her abrupt and rude behavior, Jeanne prophesied for herself, but it was better than trying to explain why she was now so far away from the bookseller.

Jeanne turned the corner onto the Bois de Boulogne and immediately saw the Hôtel Sagonne, home of Anne de l'Enclos, or "Ninon," as her many friends called her. Heaving a sigh of relief, Jeanne sprinted toward the stately house just two doors from the corner.

Fairly jumping up the four stairs to the entrance, Jeanne gave the door three rapid knocks, the proper way to gain entry into a lady's home when away from the chateau of Versailles.

"I would like to see Madame l'Enclos, *s'il vous plaît*," Jeanne announced to the elaborately dressed servant who answered the door. Without waiting for him to step back, she pushed her way in the partially opened portal, too afraid of being seen on this stoop to be polite. "Please tell Madame that I am Jeanne Mas du Bois, the sister of Raol."

With a deep, silent bow, the servant turned away, leaving Jeanne in the foyer.

Nervous and impatient, Jeanne fussed with her pile of brown curls, tucking in some errant strands loosened during her sprint, then straightened the layers of her honey-colored silk skirt. Her grooming complete, she looked about in wide-eyed wonder, dazzled by the richness of the décor. Without moving from the foyer, she could see down the long hallway leading straight away from the double front doors and into two of the adjoining rooms. To the left, the walls opened to a dining room of maroon and gold, resplendent with tapestries and elaborate arrangements of fruit, and to the right a salon of deep navy blue and silver boasting large windows looking out onto an elegant garden in the English style.

Jeanne took a few steps forward, her leather heels clacking loudly in the quiet vestibule, and craned her neck to look farther down the mahogany hall. Her heart skipped a beat at the sight of two paintings, side by side, in the inimitable style of Jean Tassel, one of the greatest French artists ever to hold a brush. Her lips crooked up at the riches of this house's owner and how she came by them.

Ninon de l'Enclos was no noblewoman, nor had she married nobility. She was an author, a patron of the arts, and, above all, a famous courtesan. Some of France's greatest men had spent time in her arms:

the Prince de Condé, Gaspard de Coligny, even La Rochefoucauld. These powerful men came for her physical delights, but her wit, her charm, and the high society they found in her home brought them back time and again. Her riches came as favors, gratitude not payment, from the many men who had found comfort in her arms. Jeanne's own brother Raol had learned much within these opulent walls. Even now, a few years past her sixtieth birthday, Mme. de l'Enclos was still amazingly beautiful, even richer than her reputation implied after so many years and so many men.

"This way, mademoiselle."

Jeanne jumped at the butler's call, quickly following him down the long hall and into a small sitting room. She glanced in at the threshold, at the warm affluence of this room, the Aubusson carpets, the silk and brocade curtains. All done in pale pinks and greens, it was much more inviting, much more personal than the other rooms, though just as richly ornamented.

"Come, child, come in," the strong yet sweet female voice beckoned from the one winged armchair upholstered in pale crème and embellished with pale pink rosebuds and green vines and leaves.

Jeanne timidly stepped in and around, finding herself in the company of Ninon de l'Enclos. Dropping quickly into a curtsey, Jeanne barely had time to acknowledge the high-piled blond hair shot through with strands of gray, the pale, twinkling blue eyes, the high cheekbones and still-smooth skin all above a large and grandly displayed bosom.

"Up, child, up," the powerful woman demanded. "Let me see you clearly."

Jeanne did as instructed, standing tall before this imposing woman, glad for the many layers of skirts she wore hiding her trembling knees.

"Ah, yes, I see it now. You look much like your brother, amazing really. Please, *chère* Jeanne, have a seat." Madame de l'Enclos inclined her head to the matching armchair beside her, and Jeanne sat happily.

"I remember Raol quite fondly. I found it a privilege to teach him the language of love." Ninon dispensed two cups of tea from the thin, delicate porcelain by her side, handing Jeanne one without asking if she desired it. "He came to me quite young, which is always better."

Jeanne quietly sipped the tangy, herbal-tasting liquid, needing its fortification; Ninon studying her over her own cup.

"Did Raol tell you himself about his time with me?"

"He did, Madame." Jeanne almost choked on her words. "But…but he didn't…he only said how kind you were to him, how…helpful."

"Ah, a true gentleman." Ninon put down her cup with a rich, solid tink of porcelain on porcelain. "I could tell from just the look of him."

"*Merci*, Madame." Jeanne relaxed a bit, thinking fondly of Raol. "He is a wonderful brother."

The two women continued to sip their tea, silence coming to accompany them as they imbibed the herbal beverage.

"Well?" Ninon asked, lowering her cup, clasping her hands together and placing them pointedly on her lap. "Are you going to tell me what brings you to my door, or do you wish me to guess?"

Jeanne took one more sip, placed her cup down on its saucer, and looked this forbidding woman in the eye. No nonsense must be played here, no silly girlish, coquettish hedging. She saw it upon Ninon's face.

"I have been in the convent for seven years," Jeanne began her story, "and have just recently been...returned home. My experience with men is practically nonexistent, and what experience I have should be better left forgotten, I think."

Ninon chuckled, nodding her head in understanding and encouragement.

"But now...now I have met someone."

Ninon studied her carefully; warm color rose upon Jeanne's cheeks, she could feel it even as her eyes softened and her lids grew heavy, as her breath came faster and the pulse beat quick in her throat. "And I want...I need to..."

Words withered in her throat; she searched to no avail for those that would express all she felt, all she wanted to feel, all she wanted to make Henri feel.

"You want to make him love you?" Ninon replied to her angst.

"I believe he already does," Jeanne said, and in the jut of her chin and the straightening of her shoulders, she showed Ninon her own power and self-possession. "I want to please him, though, and I don't know how."

Jeanne slid from her chair to sit at the feet of this goddess of love. "I have read book after book of history. I could wage war and win with the knowledge I have obtained there, but I know nothing of what pleases a man." Jeanne confessed, eyes wide and up to the experienced woman.

Ninon leaned forward, placing her translucent-skinned hands upon this confused soul's shoulders, looking down at her not with the amusement Jeanne expected, but with respect.

"To know one's deficiencies and admit to them is a sign of great character." Ninon nodded decisively. "Much more genius is needed to make love than to command armies. Come, sit yourself comfortably." She handed Jeanne a pillow, keeping the young woman close but comfy and content. "I will tell you everything, *chère fille*, everything."

~Eighteen~

"Have you seen Lynette today?" Jeanne asked Olympe the next morning, reining her tawny Palomino beside her friend's black stallion in the *Cour d'Honneur* of the Grand Stables.

"*Oui*." Olympe nodded, resplendent in her scarlet red riding attire, her full lips the same brilliant color, pulling tight on her reins as her horse bucked toward Jeanne's. "There is no change."

Jeanne hung her head clad in the huge cavalier's hat of orange felt with stark white cascading ostrich plumes. Dressed like all the other women in the uniform appropriate for the hunt; her deep orange velvet jacket, cut in a masculine style, enhanced what little curves she possessed. Her stock, the same white as her plumes, yards and yards of the cravat wrapped several times around her neck, ending in a large knot. The ends of the scarf fanned out to perfection against her upper chest, splayed like the open wings of an eagle, showcasing the intricately embroidered ends.

"I saw her yesterday afternoon when Maman and I returned from Paris," Jeanne said as more and more courtiers joined the gathering. "It was a short visit. We spoke only a few words, and then she fell asleep."

This morning the King had called for a hunt, and, under the first cloudy sky they'd seen in many a day, it was to the hunt they went. Though an accomplished rider, this was Jeanne's first royal hunt; her own nervousness made her horse twitch. Renowned as a major social gathering, all of France knew hunting as one of the King's favorite pastimes.

To the left was Monsieur, the King's brother, effulgent in a pomegranate hunting costume, and by his side both the Chevalier de Lorraine and his wife, Elizabeth Charlotte the Palatinate, the one the court called Madame. The big-boned, broad-faced, buxom woman seemed to follow the movements of the King much more than her own husband. The Prince de Condé and his son the Duc d'Enghien were present as were Brienne, d'Humieres, the Princess d'Armaganac, and Louvois.

"Where is the Dauphin?" Jeanne asked Olympe, searching the thickening forest of faces.

"He does not partake of the hunt." Olympe continued quietly at Jeanne's raised her brows response. "He is frightfully lazy—we hardly ever see him. He finds happiness sitting around all day long reading."

Jeanne recalled the man she had spent some time with in the children's court of honor when they were no more than toddlers upon the rugs. A well-spoken intellectual, the King's son loved art above all else, even more than he wished to be King. To grow in the shadow of such a tree as Louis XIV would be an ominous undertaking for anyone; better to sprout leaves of a different color than to try and match those of his father.

The pounding of hooves resounded as three women rode up from the trail, their gold, yellow, and brilliant green costumes bright against the browns and dark greens of the forest. Athénaïs and two of her maids rode into the center of the group, sending other horses shying away, creating a circle within which she served as the nucleus. Men doffed their hats as both women and men bowed to her from their saddles. The blond beauty acknowledged their homage with a curt nod of her head. Searching the grounds near the rustic stables with her intense deep blue eyes, Athénaïs noted each and every face of the courtiers around her.

Turning to the far dirt trail where carriages, filled with those who wished only to watch, lined up one after the other, Athénaïs's gaze held, her expression changing from wide to narrow. At a small tic of her head, one of her maids brought her brown and white gelding close to Athénaïs's dark bay and leaned her head close to her mistress. Jeanne saw Athénaïs utter a few words, a mere four or five at most. The attendant nodded and rode off toward the line of carriages. Reaching a shiny black carriage, the woman called into the open window and a face filled the opening.

"It is François Scarron," Jeanne said in surprise.

"Indeed," Olympe agreed. "This should be interesting."

Athénaïs's maid spoke softly to the older, elegant woman, but François said nothing. Her gaze found Athénaïs's. Much was said between them in the silent communication, a frown on the lips of François, a wide smile on those of Athénaïs. François pulled her head back into the carriage' within seconds the driver snapped his whip and drove the vehicle off.

"She sent her away," Jeanne said as if Olympe hadn't seen it herself. "Athénaïs sent François away."

"If she had her druthers..." Olympe inclined her head toward the tow-headed beauty "...she would send her far away."

Before Olympe could say more, the five-piece ensemble, the one permanently ordered to follow the King around the grounds, began a lively Delelande tune.

"Perfect music to kill by," Jeanne whispered to Olympe, who smiled indulgently at her outspoken, opinionated friend.

The King rode into the assemblage and all talking ceased. He brought his huge gray bay next to Athénaïs and waited until all around him showed a bowed head.

"Welcome, my good people. We shall have ourselves some fun today, *oui*?"

Cries of agreement met the King's words, and the participants began to talk amongst themselves once more. The horses stomped and twitched as grooms completed the final preparations. Jeanne and Olympe found themselves beside Louvois and some of his comrades.

"It is brilliant, if I do say so myself." Louvois' double chin waggled as he bragged to the group around him. "There have been enough sweet requests and rewards—it is time we bring the Huguenots to heel."

Jeanne shared a wary expression with Olympe. The difficulty over the Protestants had plagued the nation for centuries, and though King Henri IV had offered them some protection and some civil rights with the Edict of Nantes eighty-four years ago, the French Protestants of the day found themselves once more under threat. Under Louis XIII and Cardinal Richelieu, those Protestants willing to convert had been rewarded both financially and socially; with Louvois in power, such peaceful, civilized practices slowly disappeared.

"I rid myself of my worst soldiers while forcing the damned Huguenots to leave once and for all."

"So you put the soldiers in their homes?" One jowl-faced man asked, a smile broad on a face sprouting burst blood vessels on nose and cheeks.

"I do," Louvois assured him. "I send the most obnoxious and despicable soldiers and billet them in the homes of the most stubborn Protestants. There they are free to do whatever is necessary."

Jeanne shuddered at his atrocious words. The War Minister of France actually sanctioned his most beastly soldiers to wreak havoc upon his country's own people, Protestant though they may be.

"Well, how does it go?" the man prodded.

"Marvelous, splendid indeed." Louvois thrust out his barrel chest. "Thousands have converted, but even better, thousands have left."

Jeanne shook her head, ashamed of her own countrymen. *What a cowardly way for France to rid herself of those they perceived as unworthy*, she thought. *What a loss of some of the country's greatest citizens, nobles, and artists.*

"If it is not Mademoiselle du Bois, as I live and breathe." Louis rode up on quiet hooves and brought his horse beside Jeanne.

Jeanne lifted herself an inch off her saddle and bowed to the King.

"Your Majesty, how kind of you to remember me," Jeanne said, surprised he recognized her from the child she had been seven years ago. Seeing the King in his modest hunting attire, Jeanne found Louis to be at his most attractive. Here Louis refused to gussy up; no laces or bows hung from his garb. The simple cloth of his brown riding habit flaunted only sparse embroidery with gold thread around the buttonholes and pocket flaps, collar and cuffs. Thigh-high black leather hunting boots finished the ensemble.

"Oh, I remember well the spirit, mamselle. It is not often one sees it within such a fair countenance." The King stared intently at Jeanne's face, not turning away even as Athénaïs pulled her own horse up next to the King's. Drawing closer, the King's mistress listened closely as her lover addressed yet another beautiful young courtier. "Though I must say I am astounded at the womanly beauty you now possess."

"*Merci beaucoup*, Your Highness." Jeanne squirmed under the earnest attention of both the King and Athénaïs. The King exaggerated the truth of her comeliness merely because she was a woman; Athénaïs knew it as well as she. Jeanne searched for something to distract them, and for a moment thought she saw a familiar face, one haunting her dreams both night and day.

"I most heartily agree," Athénaïs piped in smartly. "Why, it seems like yesterday that I saw her playing on the floor with the Dauphin."

Jeanne felt the intended sting of the woman's words, met it with silence.

"She would still make a good playmate for Auguste, would she not, Your Highness?" Referring to their eldest, their twelve-year-old son, Athénaïs circled her horse round to come between Louis' and Jeanne's. "You must come and see us in the nursery, Mademoiselle du Bois."

Jeanne nodded in silent acceptance at the offhand invitation.

Louis' eyes roamed over Jeanne's small but firm, high bosom.

"A playmate for Auguste? Perhaps." Louis chuckled smoothly. "But only if he shares with his father."

Athénaïs's snide smile evaporated; her verbal poison backfiring upon her. Before she could say more, another horse rode up to the threesome.

"*Bonjour*, Your Highness. Are we ready to bag ourselves a fine stag?"

The sound of his voice was that of deliverance. Jeanne turned to find Henri astride a spirited white roan. He was her vision come to life, more handsome than she imagined in his tight-fitting buckskin jacket with a thin strip of fur on cuff and collar and spurred leather boots.

"Monsieur d'Aubigne, is it really you?" Louis cried in a genuine, fond greeting, turning to Athénaïs. "We never see him at court do we, Madame?"

"No, not nearly often enough. Monsieur." Athénaïs nodded to Henri, but Jeanne thought her warmth a façade, that the woman, in truth, held no fondness for him.

"What brings you here after all this time?" Louis asked. His keen gaze quickly flickered between Henri and Jeanne and a small, lascivious smile spread across his grand countenance. "Ah, I see."

"I attended the Feast of St. Louis," Henri informed his sovereign. "I had such a splendid time I thought to spend more of it at court."

"Ah, *oui*, that is most obvious." Turning his horse, the King pointed the animal's large, moist black nose away from the small group. "Tell me, Mademoiselle du Bois, where is Monsieur de Polignac?"

Jeanne faltered, sable eyes jumping from her King to Henri's. "I am afraid I have no idea, Your Majesty."

Louis smiled as his horse stomped about. "Do you care?"

Jeanne held herself mute, refusing to be pulled into Louis' intrigue, refusing to be cornered into lying to her King.

Louis laughed heartily at her silence and her sagacity; the powerful sound boomed through the distant trees, and a bevy of black birds launched themselves into the air with loud calls and flapping wings. The King bowed to the young woman and Henri beside her. Clucking his tongue, digging his heels softly into the sides of his horse, he trotted away without another word. Athénaïs following close behind.

Henri turned his horse toward Jeanne's; animals and humans faced each other.

"Who is Monsieur de Polignac?" Henri asked, his voice tight, his face a mask of placidity, yet a vein pulsed upon his forehead. She wished to spare him, and herself, but she could not, would not lie to him any more than she already had.

"He is the man my father is trying to force me to marry."

"No!" Henri yelled, but the cry faded under the screech of two rapid horn blasts renting the air.

The Master of the Hunt, the Duc de La Rochefoucauld, strode onto the stable yard resplendent in his red and gold military-style couture, and the milling group swarmed around him and the King.

The hounds barked and bayed, still held back at the stable door by leashes seized firmly in the usher's hands.

Clad in white leather boots and a dove-gray doeskin tunic, the Master of the Hunt bowed low to his sovereign. Straightening, he reached up with a leather-gloved hand, handing Louis a wooden wand tipped with a boar's hoof. The King accepted the stick with grace, as he did at the start of every hunt. Intended for the King to use as protection against branches during the frantic hunt, it had evolved to iconic proportions of dignity and honor.

A broad smile appeared on Louis' face. He pumped the hand holding the wand into the air.

"Release the hounds!" the Master of the Hunt screamed, and they were off, *La Chasse Royale* led by Louis and no one else.

Jeanne held on to her reins with all her strength, following Henri while Olympe followed her. The fervor of the dogs spread to both horse and human, and the beings plunged into the woods at blazing speeds. Through trees and shrubbery, the hunters followed the yapping hounds. Cresting a hill, Louis, still in the lead, pulled up hard on his reins, causing a domino effect of chaos behind him.

Jeanne stood upon her stirrups and saw what the King did: a peasant far in the distance.

"Get him!" Louis roared, anger thick and dark. Outraged, he spun his horse in circles as he pulled upon the reins, whipping his head to and fro to keep the miscreant in sight as two mounted guardsmen gave chase to the quickly retreating form. "How dare he hunt upon my land? Does he not care that I could hang him for it?"

Perhaps he doesn't care, Jeanne thought. *Perhaps his hunger is too great to care.*

A young stag with only two points peeked out from behind the cluster of firs on the horizon. The peasant forgotten, the riders surged through the trees, snapping the overhanging branches back into the faces of those behind them. Like the surge of a mountain's melting snowcap, they plunged forward, heedless of everything in their path. The thunder of the hooves pounding down the grassy slope joined the blaring horns, barking dogs, and shouting hunters. The horns announced the view halloo…the sighting of a stag, bringing in the few riders who had lost their way. Soon the copse where the blazing red and yellow maple leaves lit the dark forest filled with horses and humans. The circle of executioners surrounded the stag, its large black eyes darting every which way for the slightest opening, the merest glimpse of an escape route. The animal's flank muscles twitched; its ears stood at perfect attention. Two stomping horses brushed up against each other and quickly jumped apart.

There it was. The stag leaped forward through the space and was gone, lost in the tangle of evergreens. With renewed vigor, spurred on by the baying hounds, the chase resumed.

Jeanne pulled back on the reins, preventing her horse from following no matter how he yearned to go. Henri restrained his own horse, watching the hunted and hunters as they fled. Neither spoke as the rest of the party, including Olympe, surged by them; two islands in the midst of a churning ocean. In the end, only they remained in the clearing, alone in the silence.

"Did you see it?" Jeanne stared straight ahead, following the incensed hunters. "Did you see the desperation, the naked fear?"

"I did." Henri's deep growl frightened her. "I know just how it feels."

Jeanne turned to him; their mutual despair met in the glance.

"Why did you not tell me?" Henri reached out and took her reins in his, holding both horses still and together.

Jeanne shook her head, loosening the bevy of curls upon it.

"Henri, there is so much I need to tell you but cannot. Percy de Polignac is a nightmare, my nightmare, and I refuse to accept him. There has to be some way out of this. I believe it so completely, I did not tell you, for it will not happen."

Henri reached out and put a gloved hand upon her neck, drawing her to him as best he could. "You do not love him?"

Jeanne laughed a genuine, spiteful laugh. "Does the stag love the hunter?" she asked.

Henri jumped down from his horse, coming to stand beside Jeanne's. He held his arms up to her, and she gladly released herself into their care. He lowered her slowly, allowing their bodies to press and rub against each other's inch by inch until her feet touched the ground. Already Jeanne gasped for air, the need for him so strong she could barely stand it.

He moaned as he lowered his lips to hers, and she abandoned herself to him. She found the strength as Ninon's words echoed in her mind. She reached up to his doublet, never allowing her lips to leave his. First the top button, then the next, she unfastened his jacket.

His eyes popped wide; he tore his lips from hers. She accepted his glance and held it, her hands never leaving his coat. At the release of the fourth button, she put her hands within the sides of the jacket, rubbing her palms against his hard chest, feeling the firm, tight muscles spasm under her touch as his chest heaved with his hard, quick breath. She felt his nipples tauten and rise as she brushed across them. Jeanne felt him weaken under her touch, this strong, powerful man, and continued to wield the sword she now fully possessed. Her legs quivered beneath her with the command of it, with the heat of it. She reached down to unbutton more, to reveal more of him to her.

Four horn blasts ripped through the air. Henri grabbed her wandering hands. He held them flat upon his chest, just below his right pectoral. Jeanne felt his heart beat fast against his chest, pounding his ribs as if trying to break its skeletal cage. She looked up, searching his face, seeing the same incomprehensible need and yearning, the same stirring as she felt within herself, and smiled.

"Do not laugh at what you do to me," Henri warned her, but his own mouth turned up at the corners beneath his bushy mustache. "That I could not bear."

Jeanne bit her lips, trying to erase the satisfaction from her face, but it was a futile attempt.

"We must go. We must be seen at the kill site," Henri told her. "And if you do not stop looking at me like that, I won't be able to walk for hours." He looked down as did Jeanne, and her innocent eyes bulged.

Henri's laugh sent shivers up and down the length of her.

"You are such a conundrum." He kissed her softly, tenderly, with a closed, pursed mouth. "And I would wish for a lifetime to unravel your mysteries."

Jeanne licked her lips, wishing to relive the taste of him on her tongue, afraid to say anything, afraid to start talking and reveal all.

"Come." Leading her by one hand and their horses by the other, Henri turned them in the direction of the horn blasts.

Jeanne walked beside him, holding his hand so tightly in hers as if she were trying to fuse them together. The sounds of the forest grew around them as the birds and small animals grew accustomed to their presence. A thought jumped into her clearing mind.

"Why does Athénaïs not care for you?" Jeanne stopped, realizing the blatancy of her question, searching his face for any sign of insult.

Henri pulled on her, forcing her to keep walking, chuckling softly, deep in his chest.

"There is nothing you do not see, is there?" Henri smiled with pride at her. "You would have made a fine soldier, or perhaps a spy."

Jeanne laughed at his jest, praying it would not sound as fake to his ears as it did to her own.

"Why does Athénaïs not like me? That is a good question, ma chère. But I'm afraid the answer is a long and twisted one, not for this place and this time. You are not the only one with mysteries, I'm afraid."

Her face searched his for answers; perhaps they were more alike than even she imagined.

They came upon the kill site; courtiers gathered round the King and joined the onlookers for the first step in the end of the hunt. Dusk descended slowly, like a fuzzy gray blanket. Jeanne and Henri joined the circle in time to see the Master of the Hunt step into it, reaching up to receive the boar-tipped wand from the King. For the first time, Jeanne noticed the stag, down on its side, an arrow embedded deep near its heart, but still, its rib cage rose and fell with its rapid breath. The Master took a dagger from his baldric and looked to his King. Louis nodded, a barely perceptible gesture, and without further ado, the Master of the Hunt slit the stag's throat, the dark red blood pouring from the wide gash.

Jeanne looked up at the sound of the King's laughter, and applause resounded through the obedient crowd.

We are like the stag, Jeanne thought. *Merely a source of amusement for the King, and, if he should tire of us, if a courtier should dare to speak their mind, he would have one of his many minions hunt us down, silence us, and remove us from his sight.*

Henri must have seen her disgust, her aversion, for he tenderly shook the hand he held in his.

"Brace yourself, there is yet more to come. You should see it to the end."

Jeanne searched his face in silent denial.

"Come, mount your horse," Henri instructed her. "We must return to the palace."

Like spellbound children, the courtiers returned to the chateau, following dutifully behind their master, their King. Whether on horseback or in a carriage, they all returned.

An even larger crowd gathered at the Court of the Stags, the third courtyard near the central building of the castle, but not all were allowed through to the inner circle. Only those chosen, privileged people at the hunt may enter the charmed infrastructure.

Henri led Jeanne along, pushing past the unprivileged without enthusiasm. They approached a Swiss Guard armed with halberd, neck ruff full and high upon his tall torso. The two men exchanged a disciplined nod, and Henri, with Jeanne in tow, passed without further question. The other halberd-armed guards stopped all who approached, with great respect and deference, asking their names and titles before allowing them to pass. Those of the highest rank were personally escorted to one of the many second-floor balconies overlooking the courtyard.

"Do you wish to watch from there?" Henri leaned toward her and asked with a whisper.

"*Merci*, no," she replied.

"Good." Henri walked them to the edge of the crowd and stopped, their view into the empty courtyard unencumbered.

Innumerable gold-leaf sconces set the courtyard blazing, their glow reflecting off the balconies and cornices of the pink-bricked palace. The horns blared a regal fanfare, and the King took his place on the center balcony. Athénaïs stood to his left, the Queen taking her place to his right. Before the last note died in the still, hot air, the balcony filled with the Prince and Princesses of the Blood and the highest-ranking noblemen present.

Jeanne found her father at the back of the crowd but felt no panic, sure he couldn't see her in the throng. His hunting days had ended long ago, but he would not miss an event such as this.

The quiet shattered as the whippers-in directed the loudly baying hounds in the circle now lit as bright as day. On tethers pulled by the whippers-in, the gory bundle of the slain stag's intestines came into the light and immediately the acidic, dark scent of blood filled the warm, sticky night air. It took snap after snap of the whips for the three trainers, decked out in their red livery, to keep the hounds from attacking the clump of flesh immediately.

"Back, dogs! Back!" they shouted repeatedly to the frenzied animals.

From the grand staircase, the Master of the Hunt descended, splendid in his red livery bedecked with golden buttons. The silver gilt spurs on his red-heeled, yellow leather boots jangled as he stepped.

Reaching the center of the courtyard, he turned to the balcony above. The King raised the boar wand high above his head.

Handing his own stag hoof–tipped wand to the page behind him, the Master took a few large strides and gained possession of the gory pack. Oblivious to the blood staining the lace and embroidery of his silk coat, the dark man pulled on the bundle, bringing it to the center of the courtyard.

"Tayaut! Tayaut!" the Master cried, taking the forhu and throwing it to within a few feet of the yapping hounds, their agitation nearly a hysterical, fever pitch, still ignoring the whips and shouts of the trainers.

Finally, as the cacophony rose to nearly unbearable heights, the King gave the signal with a small nod of his head and the hounds were released.

"Hallalie, valets! Hallalie!" the trainers shouted to each other.

Like starved flies to honey, the beasts pounced on their prize with all the pent-up ferociousness of freed savages. The trainers, whippers-in, and Master of the Hunt circled the dogs, laying a crack or two wherever necessary, keeping the horde from turning upon each other as the carnage continued. Satisfying their bloodlust, the hounds devoured the stag's remains devoured, all save the gnawed bones. They broke apart and crawled away, growling low in gratitude and satisfaction.

Scooping up the bone fragments, the whippers-in took them off, calling the well-satiated dogs with them. A final blare of the horns sounding the call for retreat ended the ceremony, and the courtyard and balconies emptied out.

Jeanne stood, hard and cold like the statues surrounding the courtyard, paralyzed by such savageness taking place under the guise of social entertainment. The raucous laughter from the milling courtiers sounded surreal; she blanched at their sadistic delight. They would go now and feast themselves; in her mind, they were just like the dogs, no more than animals.

~Nineteen~

As the midmorning sun found its way into the chateau, Jeanne found her way to Athénaïs's suite of rooms in the south wing. Her name gained her effortless entrance into the magnificent antechamber and the rooms grander and more lavishly opulent than those inhabited by the Queen. On the second floor as opposed to the third floor, there were twenty rooms to the Queen's twelve. The power this woman possessed both amazing and appalling.

Olympe had been quite willing, perhaps a trifle too eager, to school Jeanne on Athénaïs's glorious rise to power, how she had used the timid and shy Louise de La Vallière, the King's first real mistress, to bring herself before the King's eye.

Befriending La Vallière, acting as an empathetic, more experienced woman, Athénaïs had allowed Louise to use her to appear livelier to the King through her association with Athénaïs. But as Louise suffered through difficult pregnancies, became quieter and more morose, the King grew tired of her growing frail and introverted nature. Athénaïs, with her powerful beauty, her wit and charm, her sophistication and elegance, dazzled in comparison, dazzled Louis.

At first, Louis and the married Athénaïs kept their affair secret. As the King's furtive paramour, Athénaïs used Louise's open affair to insinuate herself into the Queen's favor. Better than any actress, Athénaïs feigned dislike of Louise for her philandering with the King, pretending to be of supreme piety, while secretly fornicating with the King. Her own piety a barometer for all her actions, Marie-Thérèse had named Athénaïs a Maid of Honor to her court.

Forced to endure the knowledge of Athénaïs and Louis, Louise endured both the pain of the King's disfavor while coerced into helping the two lovers. As Louis and Athénaïs made love in her bedroom, Louise sat alone in the connected anteroom, a ring of embroidery trembling in her hands, ready to deter any who came along, crying silently as she listened to the sounds of their passion from the other chamber.

Jeanne's reverie shattered as the double doors of an adjoining chamber burst open and a small girl, no more than five, came running out. She laughed raucously as she ran, a couture-clad porcelain doll clutched in her hands. Four other children followed close on her heels.

From the back of the large room now revealed, Jeanne caught a glimpse of Athénaïs, radiant in a shimmering blue day gown perfectly matching the color of her eyes. In a room bountifully and capaciously done in shades of yellow and crème, the striking woman stood surrounded by four or five female attendants. Looking up from the papers and fabric swatches they held before her, Athénaïs spied her escaping children and Jeanne standing and waiting in the foyer.

"Ah, Mademoiselle du Bois, just in time." Athénaïs waved a hand in her direction. "Would you be so kind as to stop my children from turning the chateau into a play yard?"

Jeanne obediently dropped into a deep curtsey, turning in the direction of the wayward sprites. Through the winding maze of rooms in the monstrous suite, she caught up with all five of them, each with a hand on the doll, either by a leg, arm, or the head, each pulling as hard as possible.

"Ow, ow, you are killing me," Jeanne exclaimed in a high-pitched, squeaky voice, feigning the voice of the doll. "Why do you torture me so?"

That silenced them all quite quickly, young faces contorting in confusion and puzzlement. Who was this grown woman talking like a doll?

"Monsieurs and Mademoiselles." Jeanne curtseyed deeply; though children, they were still the issue of the King. "I am Jeanne Yvette Mas du Bois, quite pleased to make your acquaintance."

"*Enchanté*, mademoiselle," they responded politely, with neither bow nor curtsey.

"Your Maman has asked me to bring calm amongst you." Jeanne stepped into their power-struggling circle, slowly and gently retrieving the strained doll from their hands. "What has this poor doll done to deserve such terrible treatment?"

"She hit me with it."

"He tried to take it from me."

"We want to throw it to each other."

"It used to be mine and I want it back."

The words hit her from every direction, overlapping and building on one another in both volume and anger.

"Hush, hush, this will not do," Jeanne insisted. "Each of you sit down."

The children looked at each other, at the sparse furniture in this study with just its desk, one chair, and rows of rows of bookshelves.

"Right here, on the floor. That's it. That will do fine." Jeanne sat herself, crossing her legs under the yards of fabric of her full skirts.

"I've told you my name. Now you must tell me yours."

Like their father, these children loved to speak of themselves; it was not long until they each took a turn, standing up and addressing the small group as if they addressed the King's council.

First the oldest, twelve-year-old Louis-Auguste, then Louis César, the ten-year-old second son. Louise-Françoise, the king's oldest daughter at nine spoke before Françoise-Marie, sweet at five, and Louis-Alexandre, a sprite of four.

As the smaller ones told their stories in their soft, little voices, Jeanne's ears tingled as tidbits of sound, voices trickling in from the adjacent room, from beyond the second set of doors leading out of this chamber. One rang louder than of any other, that of Athénaïs herself. Jeanne feigned attention to the children's complaints as she strained to discern the woman's whines.

"If it were not for me this chateau would still be the dingy hunting lodge of his father. How dare he ask her opinion as well as mine?"

Unsure to whom she referred, Jeanne knew Athénaïs spoke the truth: the grandeur of Versailles had much to thank her for. At her urging, Louis hired Jules Hardouin-Mansart, Versailles' most famous architect, had worked tirelessly with him and Louis for weeks, months, years bringing the palace to its present glory.

"Does he think she could have made it what it is, filled it as I have?"

In the next room, Athénaïs spewed her anger; Jeanne pretended to dance with the doll on her lap, amusing the children, with one ear peeled to their mother's words.

"These great performers, artists, writers—they are here because of me and no other."

Jeanne absently nodded her head; Athénaïs had helped make Versailles what it was there as well, the glorious cultural center of the world; as Versailles was to palaces, Athénaïs was to women.

"If I were Queen, it would be even grander. The whole country would be as enlightened as we."

If she were Queen? The words seared a brand upon Jeanne's mind.

Could this truly be the goal of this viciously ambitious woman?

"Where is she?"

Jeanne heard Athénaïs bark from the next room. "Is she with the children where I pay her to be?"

The two doors Jeanne strained to listen through burst open and again Jeanne saw the inner sanctum of the King's mistress.

Athénaïs sat in regal anger on a lounge chair of yellow damask, her attendants fluttered and floundered around her, trying anything and everything to appease their mistress.

"Oh, Mademoiselle du Bois, I had forgotten entirely about you." Athénaïs looked at an attendant then up to her coiffure; without another word, the attendant primped and preened at Athénaïs's hair, makeup, and gown until she looked, once more, perfectly groomed.

"Pray, come in. We shall have a short visit, shall we?" Athénaïs gestured two finger at Jeanne as if she called a small dog to her side.

Jumping off the floor, Jeanne dipped into a deep curtsey and made her way into the exquisitely appointed chamber, approaching Athénaïs, who reclined upon her chaise. The piercing gaze held her in captive silence; Athénaïs studied her from top to bottom and back again.

"You are beautiful, if in a very masculine way," the King's mistress said with such contempt it was no compliment.

"You are most kind, Madame." Jeanne thanked her, icicles dripping from her voice.

A hint of a smile tickled Athénaïs's full, rouged lips. "So you give as good as you get."

"Madame?" One of Jeanne's dark eyebrows shot upward, no smile spread her lips, a perfect parody of innocence.

"Sit down, mamselle, you have earned it," Athénaïs allowed with another dismissive wave of her hand, nodding with supercilious satisfaction as her generosity was well met. Turning her head, she called out in a demanding whine. "Heloise, Margaux, some wine and cheese, *tout de suite*."

"*Oui*, Madame," replied two high-pitched voices.

"So, you were deported from the convent, yes?" Athénaïs turned her caustic attention back to Jeanne.

Jeanne felt her teeth grind but contained the retort born on the dust. "You are well informed, Madame."

"You will take a husband soon, I have also heard, a baron's son. What is it, Polignac?"

"It is my father's wish," Jeanne replied, exposing clenched teeth to pass as a smile.

Athénaïs stared at her, the corners of her mouth rising slightly. "I can see by your face it is not your wish."

"I am in no hurry to marry. I have just returned to court. I see no reason to rush."

The clang of a wheeled salver came to their ears and entered from the side portal, pushed by two of Athénaïs's attendants. Jeanne flicked her gaze to them, experienced the briefest moment of recognition. Panic burst upon her like a sudden thunderstorm.

One of Athénaïs's attendants pushing the cart was none other than the woman Jeanne had seen in the dead of night with Henri, the woman who had spoken of the Queen's death.

Jeanne lowered her head and rubbed at her brow, camouflaging her face with the hand while peering out from between the fingers to see. Two glasses of wine were poured and to them along with a plate of soft cheese and slices of baguette.

"Merci, Margaux," Athénaïs thanked and dismissed.

Margaux. Her name is Margaux. The shout slammed about in Jeanne's head.

"Please help yourself, mamselle," Athénaïs offered with a grand sweep of her arms. "You will find I can be quite generous to those who stay within my favor, those who take my advice."

Jeanne grabbed the large crystal goblet and held it before her face, taking one small sip after the other, keeping the lower portion of her face blocked from view.

"And my advice to you is to marry, soon. It makes little difference to whom. Unmarried women at the Chateau soon find themselves in more trouble than they can handle."

Jeanne coughed, choking on her wine; the woman's threat could be no more blatant than if she held a knife to Jeanne's throat.

"Your recommendation is exceedingly wise," she said through her clogged throat, thoughtlessly lowering her hand to put down the goblet, leaving her countenance open in plain sight.

A quiet gasp brought her frightened gaze up. Margaux's critical gaze latched firmly upon her, a glimpse of confusion wrought between narrowed lids and a furrowed brow.

She knows me but does not know from where. I must retreat before the knowledge comes to her.

"I am happy to hear you say so," Athénaïs prattled on, oblivious to Jeanne's discomfort. "I would like for us to be friends. One as spirited as you would compliment my group of friends quite well, I think. I would wish for nothing to come between us, especially so soon after your return to Versailles."

Jeanne took another sip of wine and nodded, bringing her glass even with her face. "I would like nothing better myself."

Jeanne searched the room for something, anything, to find a way out. As if sent by God, Athénaïs and Louis' youngest daughter, five-year-old Françoise-Marie, ran into the room on her slippered tiptoes.

"Mamselle, mamselle," she called as she scampered toward Jeanne, her doll outstretched before her, "could you make Denice talk again?"

Jeanne smiled and instinctively reached down to the sweet-faced child.

"I see you have a way with children." Athénaïs barely spared a glance at the delightful creature that was her offspring. "Very well, be off with you. Please the whelp for a few moments if you can spare them."

Jeanne's eyes flashed between mother and daughter, grateful the youngster showed no understanding of her mother's nasty words. She jumped to her feet and turned to the child, back to Athénaïs and her still-inquisitive attendant.

"It was a pleasure, Madame. Thank you so much for your generosity of spirit and refreshments," Jeanne called over her shoulder, plying the pleasing sophistry she had learned after years with egotistical abbesses.

"*Oui, oui*," Athénaïs waved her along, dismissing the pet who grew tiresome. "But do not even imagine I will make you governess. I have made that mistake once already. Come back after you've gotten yourself a husband."

"*Merci*, Madame," Jeanne curtseyed without turning all the way back then quickly scurried from the room with the tiny girl at her feet.

Jeanne shut the main door to Athénaïs's suite of rooms gently behind her and leaned her back against it, nostrils quivering as she drew in the first real breath she'd dared since seeing the face of the despicable woman who had spoken of the Queen's murder.

Her thoughts swung like a giant pendulum, wondering what Margaux's presence in Athénaïs's rooms signified, knowing it could mean only one thing, but denying that such fiendishness could be true. She desperately needed to talk with Henri, to find out if he had been successful following the woman the other night, to see where she had gone, to see if he missed Jeanne as desperately as Jeanne missed him. She shook her head as the silly thought insinuated its way into her mind.

"Jeanne! Jeanne!"

She spun toward the gut-wrenched sobs, cries of a heartbroken and torn, a wail of despair from the darkest reaches of someone's soul. Olympe ran toward her, her friend's appearance shocking in its own right.

Half of the tall brunette's hair hung haphazardly about her face; the other still bounced upon her head. No powder or rouge adorned her face, only dirt-smudged tear tracks running down her face and her throat. Untended phlegm oozed out of her red-tipped nose. Jeanne threw a hand to her heart, fearful of anything this wraith might have to tell her.

But Olympe only wailed and sobbed more, the howling growing louder the closer she came. Jeanne could take no more; she grabbed her friend and shook her by the shoulders.

"Tell me, Olympe, you must tell me."

Olympe nodded, swallowing her tears. "She's gone. Our dearest Lynette is dead."

Time stopped. The words echo in Jeanne's ears as if they came down a long tunnel. All color drained from the world; it shifted to shades of gray as only black and white merged in her vision. Her hands tingled; a great numbness came to possess her.

Olympe grabbed Jeanne. "If you wish to say goodbye you must hurry. They are coming to get her immediately."

Jeanne began to run before Olympe finished speaking; she knew only minutes remained. She flung a look over her shoulder to see Olympe once more plagued by racking sobs and slithering helplessly to the floor, but Jeanne spared her no pause.

Kicking off her leather-heeled slippers, Jeanne ran through the castle. The shocked faces of the courtiers, their red lips grotesque circles in their pale, powdered faces, assaulted her as she made her way to the lower gallery and out the rear doors. She ran as if the devil himself snapped at her feet. Everywhere she saw scenes of her childhood, and in each and every one, Lynette was there. The tears she did not know she shed streamed back into her ears.

The blue and white tiles of the Trianon rose before her. Jeanne ran through the pink marble pilasters, across the checkered floor, and found her way through the glass doors.

She heard a distant wailing and followed it. Down one small corridor and up the next. She turned one corner, then another, stumbling to a stop.

Lynette's mother sat in a heap on the floor, sobbing in the middle of the passage. A small man dressed all in black backed out of a room, in his hands the front of a stretcher. On the stretcher a sheet-covered body. Before the second man with the other end of the stretcher made it out of the room, Jeanne ran to it. Cries of warning and shock railed against her as she pulled the sheet from the still form below it.

Her precious Lynette lay pale, almost waxlike upon the shroud.

"No, no, it cannot be," Jeanne heard herself murmur. Her eyes begged the attendants to tell her otherwise.

"She sleeps. We must rouse her."

Their looks of revulsion and pity told Jeanne the truth could not be denied.

Bending low, Jeanne brought her lips to her dear one's face, her tears dripping on Lynette's cold skin, covering the lifeless form with mournful kisses.

"You were the dearest friend a person could have." Jeanne brought her lips close to Lynette's ear, believing, because she must, that Lynette could hear her still. "I cherished every moment we spent together. *Adieu. Adieu.*"

Jeanne felt a strong hand on her shoulder, pulling on her.

"We must go, mademoiselle." one attendant tugged at her, while the other tried to push the stretcher along. Jeanne let them go, only releasing her grip on her friend at the last moment, when she could reach her no more, and watched, pain a pounding in her gut, as they took the body quickly down the hall and out of the small chateau.

With hands still reaching for her lost friend, Jeanne felt living, loving arms wrap around her; she collapsed into Olympe's waiting clench.

Their sobs mingled together in a song of sorrow as they stood frozen in the hallway.

"Why, why?" Olympe repeated the words over and over in a stupefied whisper.

Jeanne shook her head, knowing no answer for the timeless question, knowing only one thing.

"God has taken the best of us."

* * *

Surely the sun shone too brightly, the birds chirped too loudly...flowers too colorful...air too fresh...too sweet. It could not be the day she would lay her friend to rest, when they would put her young body in the cold, hard ground and set her spirit soaring into eternity. Yet Jeanne found herself beside the large rectangular hole in the ground, standing beside her family, watching as the six men of the funeral cortege brought the golden wood casket closer and closer from across the vast grounds of the La Marechal family home.

Jeanne stood dry-eyed, her knuckles white as her fists pulsed against her thighs. The muscles in her shoulders and neck twitched and flinched with the anger surging through her body, but she knew of no way to release it. Grief strafed her heart; her mind cried out for them to stop, this could not be, Lynette could not be gone.

Like flotsam floating in the endless ocean, Jeanne careened, lost without her companion, floundering without the calming assurance that Lynette would be there to reel her in should her behavior stretch beyond the confines of acceptable propriety. The voice of her conscience was gone, and her mind wallowed in the quiet emptiness.

The prelate prattled on, but Jeanne heard not a word. She scoured the faces around her, the many nobles and courtiers—no King and Queen, as royalty never stood in the same space as the dead. Her own mother and father, sister and brother. Lynette's family, unrecognizable in their grief. Olympe stood to her right, unable to stifle her sobbing. The service mercifully ended, and the circle of attendants dispersed like a flock of birds scattered in fear, death a reminder of their own mortality. Jeanne turned from Olympe and her family, unable to bear their sad company another moment. While they headed toward the small house, Jeanne turned to the right, intending to walk the paths of the small gardens. She took barely a step before encountering the melancholy aspect of four powerful men.

Her breath hitched to see them there, overwhelmed by the honor of their presence, their great gift of condolence. One at a time they approached her, first Laurent, then Antoine and Gerard, each leaning forward to kiss both her cheeks, not needing to say more than what their attendance did not already say. Henri came last. Jeanne's heart split open to see the sympathy on his dear face. He took two steps toward her, his arms already up, open and waiting for her to enter. Jeanne ran into them, to their refuge, the erupting sob already finding its way to her lips. Where she could not with her family and friends, Jeanne released the gnawing of unbearable grief eating away at her. Against his chest, she spilled her tears, pounded out her anger, and dissolved herself of the guilt for not being at Lynette's side as if unwavering propinquity might somehow have prevented the disease from taking her friend's life.

As the other men discreetly walked away, she railed, screamed, and cried until she collapsed against him, all angst finally spent.

Henri scooped Jeanne up in his arms, never having spoken a single word throughout her entire cleansing tirade, and took her away.

~Twenty~

Jeanne sat on one side of her bed, half dressed, shrouded in somber silence. On the other side, her sister buzzed and twittered, donning layer after layer of beautiful undergarments of silk and lace, the rich fabrics rustling over the sound of her giggles, her servant as excited as her mistress.

"I have never attended the wedding of a nobleman." Bernadette trilled the words, singing them instead of speaking.

"*Non, ma petite*," tutted Tilly, Bernadette's maid since she had been a small girl. "You were at the Dauphin's wedding."

"Tilly," Bernadette chided, her excitement now shrill as her head popped out of the yards of her purple satin gown. "I was only twelve, a little girl."

Jeanne glanced at her discomposed sibling over her shoulder with a fond smile, grateful for her sister's silliness.

"Oh, *mais oui*, how could I be so stupid." Tilly winked at Jeanne from her rosy, round-cheeked face. Seeing Jeanne still clad in only her corset and one petticoat, the middle-aged maid came to stand beside her.

"Let me help you, dear. Bernadette is complete and needs me no longer."

Since Jeanne's return from the convent, her father had still not arranged for a personal maid for her; he was far too busy getting her married and out of his sight. Jeanne smiled with a shake of her head.

"I'll be fine, Tilly, *merci*." Yet she remained motionless as Bernadette flitted her way out of the room with Tilly right behind, still fussing at a few errant strands of the young girl's high coiffure.

Jeanne sighed in the quiet wake of their exit; she didn't blink, festering in a stymied daze.

"We must leave soon, *ma chère*."

Jeanne jumped at the sound of her mother's voice; she hadn't even heard her enter the room.

"Oh, Maman, you frightened me so," Jeanne sighed, a fluttering hand on her chest.

"I am sorry, child, I did not mean to." Adelaide sat beside her daughter on the bed. The older, elegant woman blazed in a red brocade ensemble with rubies around her neck and in her high-piled golden hair. "You really must finish now, though. We have to be going."

Jeanne looked to the silk stocking in her hand, one she'd held for at least an hour, and shook her head.

"It does not seem right, Maman. She is gone bit two weeks. How can we go to a party?"

"This is not a party, *ma petite*, this is the wedding of your dear friend, one as dear as Lynette, is it not so?"

"Of course, of course. I love Olympe as well as I ever loved Lynette. But couldn't they have waited a little longer?"

"Life and death wait for no one, I fear." Adelaide brushed back the tendrils of curls hanging by the side of Jeanne's face. "Nor would Lynette have wanted them to."

"Perhaps," Jeanne conceded. "But it does not seem right that I make merry while she lies in the ground."

"I remember when you were just a child, oh, I have forgotten how young you were, you could not have been more than four or five, and I watched you play in the nursery with Lynette and Olympe. Karlotta was there as well and some of your other friends. Then this frightful boy with one of those wooden swords … what do they call them?"

"Whingers, Maman," Jeanne breathed, spellbound by her mother 's reminiscence.

"Ah, *oui*, he took his whinger and flayed it in front of Lynette's face as if she were a criminal, scaring her terribly. In a flash, you picked up another discarded whinger from the floor and charged the nasty child with it. You attacked him, swinging your little sword like a pendulum, to and fro, while yelling at him to 'get back, get away from her.' " Adelaide mimicked the motions, swinging her arm back and forth, features scrunched, intense. "Your face was ferocious, red with anger, your eyes bulging from your head. The boy froze, stricken with such panic I thought he would faint. But he quickly found his feet and ran from you as if death itself pounded behind his heels. You chased after him, whooping with victory, calling over your shoulder, a beaming smile you gave just to Lynette.

"'I got him, Lynette! For you, I got him!'

"I looked down to where Lynette still sat on the floor. Her eyes were wide, full of astonishment, full of you as they welled with tears of happiness. The love she held for you at that moment, the love she felt from you, transformed her face. She glowed with it."

Adelaide brought her sight back from that day long ago and saw her daughter. Taking Jeanne's chin in one hand, Adelaide wiped away the tears streaming down her daughter's crème-colored skin with the other.

"To have given and received such a love in a lifetime is a cause for great celebration, is it not so?"

"*Oui, Maman,*" Jeanne threw her arms around her, gratitude for the gift of such a precious memory. Releasing her, Jeanne reached out and picked up the rest of her clothing.

* * *

Gaston sat in the winged armchair of his sitting room, wondering what could possibly take so long.

"You put your clothes on, and *fini*, it is done." He harrumphed to himself, blowing pent-up air out of his pursed lips.

A scratch on the door broke his ponderous introspection.

"Come," he barked, rising from his seat, large stomach leading the way.

"Monsieur du Bois, I have arrived." A short man, as round as he was tall, rushed in, a whirl of frantic movements, arms waving and wig curls flapping. "But please, quickly choose, I have many more patrons to see, many more. It is a busy day, monsieur, busy, busy."

Gaston immediately made way for Monsieur Percerin, one of the jewelers from Lombardy, those who made their living loaning extravagant adornments to those families not able to purchase such baubles of their own.

"Very well, show me what you have." Gaston gestured to the small table between the two chairs.

The agitated little man opened his small case, revealing two flat sides lined in black velvet, glittering with diamonds, emeralds, rubies, and more in many different settings and styles.

"That." Gaston indicated with a rude point of his finger. "And those."

"*Trés bon*, monsieur." The jeweler took out the requested pieces and laid them on the table, turning back to Gaston with a raised, open palm.

Gaston clenched his jaw, grinding his teeth as he doled out the two hundred livres, the standard fee for such a rental.

Like so many of the other, poorer nobles at court, he was forced, from time to time, to empty his shallow purse on such extravagances. Louis' own expensive tastes and habits forced them to live above their means. The King expected those around him, those who wished to remain around him, to be as grandly plumaged as himself. The debt they lived under, the same which he forced them into, bound them to him all the more, their leader to whom they must turn for financial sustenance. It was a vicious circle, one of the King's own design and deep satisfaction.

The jeweler nodded his thanks, closing his thin valise with a snap and sprinting for the door. "Do not forget, monsieur, tomorrow at this time or it will be two hundred more livres," he called over his shoulder.

"*Oui, oui.*" Gaston waved him off, returning to his chair to stew in his own bitterness, now with even more fuel for his flames of self-pity. "Have no fear."

* * *

Adelaide and Jeanne came from out of the girls' room, completely dressed and ready to go. Next to her mother's fiery red ensemble, Jeanne glowed in forest green, a hue transforming her brown coloring into a deep, tantalizing richness. The gown plunged low, the taffeta molding her breast and narrow waist, while the skirt hung like a narrow bell. Upon her head sat a lace fontange and in her hand matching gloves and an embellished fan.

Gaston strode across the sitting room to his wife and daughter, thrusting out both hands. Both women flinched backward instinctively.

"Put these on," Gaston barked at Jeanne, opening his palms to reveal an emerald and diamond necklace in one hand, matching earrings in the other.

Adelaide and Jeanne gasped at the magnificence of the stones in the exquisite settings, the deep green of the gems matching Jeanne's attire perfectly.

"What have I done to deserve such adornment, Père?" Jeanne asked while her mother fastened the necklace behind her.

"They are for the King," Gaston replied, looking at his daughter as if she spoke ridiculous nonsense.

"Surely the King will not notice if I'm wearing such finery or not," Jeanne said, unable to keep her hand from feeling the jewelry as it rested at the base of her throat.

"You will be surprised at what the King does and does not notice." Gaston turned on his heel and strode to the door. "Besides, Monsieur de Polignac and his parents will be in attendance. We must somehow assure them that you are worthy of their son."

Opening the door, he marched through it, taking for granted that the rest of his family would obediently follow.

"You look magnificent, *chère* Jeanne." Adelaide squeezed her daughter's arm as they proceeded behind Gaston.

"*Merci*, Maman," Jeanne whispered, but she no longer felt beautiful nor cared if she was or not.

* * *

The short ride to the gates of the Chateau du Ludres took no more than half an hour, the long drive from street to chateau taking half as long. Jeanne craned her neck to see out the window of the coach. This was her first visit to the vicomte's home; she scrutinized the impressive building as she drew closer to it, curious to see what manner of cage her friend Olympe had set for herself.

The Hôtel du Ludres was designed in the classic French style with a façade of sandstone, numerous tall windows, and a balustrade-encircled roof. Between the marble columns, the impressive double doors of the front entrance stood open on this warm, sunny day, welcoming the grandly and gaudily plumed guests into the large foyer.

Behind her family, Jeanne followed the swelling numbers of courtiers filing in. Like sheep herded in the meadow, they made their way toward one of the larger salons where the ceremony would take place. Jeanne stepped across the threshold, eyes adjusting from the brightness of the day to the dimmer room within.

As intended, her gaze followed the curve of the gilded staircase to the high arched ceiling embellished with a vast pastoral painting in the style of Valentin de Boulogne.

Within the mural's soothing colors, the centaurs would never release the scantily clad vixens they held in their grasp. At first glance, the embrace appeared to be a loving one as the powerful, bulging arms of the creatures seemed to gently encircle the pale, tender skin of the maidens. But as Jeanne studied the forms, squinting to see all of the figures and images floating above her head, she saw the teeth-baring grimace of the centaurs' mouths and their narrowed eyes and furrowed brows. The young maidens' lips gaped wide in slack-jawed fright, and their eyes bulged from their sockets. They were prisoners on the verge of torture and molestation.

Jeanne shivered in the heat of the day. For a moment, she thought she saw Olympe's features on one of the maidens and wondered if this art was a portent of her friend's life to come. She offered a silent prayer it was not.

* * *

Jeanne took a glass of champagne from a tray whirling by her head, only half listening as Bernadette twittered in her ear.

"It was so beautiful, was it not, Jeanne?" Her sister rambled on without waiting for an answer. "Olympe looked stunning in her gown, white and gold, such a beautiful combination. Even the vicomte looked regal in his matching attire."

Jeanne restrained her laughter; innocently offered, her sister's proclamation was a telling sign of the groom's older and less-appealing visage than the one of his young, beautiful wife. Suddenly she felt Bernadette's bony hand squeeze her arm, and Jeanne dropped into a curtsey beside her. Lifting her head as two people walked by, Jeanne acknowledged La Grande Mademoiselle pass on the arm of the Duc de

Lauzun. Both now in their fifties, though she a little older than he, these two members of the court's upper echelon had been lovers for many years, and their undisguised love affair was an accepted fact.

Anne-Marie Louise d'Orléans, the daughter of Jean-Baptiste Gaston, Duc d'Orléans, Louis XIII's brother, had loved Lauzun, the sunny, fun-loving Gascon, for all of her adult life. But her cousin the King would not approve of their marriage, leaving her to marinate in the title of La Grande Mademoiselle, for she would not have another. The tall, heavy-set woman, a gentle and friendly sort, glowed on the arm of her heart's desire. Péguilin, as his friends called him, was a minor nobleman but a highly decorated soldier and a favorite of Louis XIV. Most surmised his relatively low status was the cause for the King's refusal.

Jeanne watched the couple greet a circle of guests of a like age or older, shocked at the prestigious people in attendance. Madame de Scudéry, now well into her seventies, still commanded the literary clique revolving around her: there was Gilles Ménage, Paul Pellisson, and Pierre Huet, all scholars and writers alike. The women were some Jeanne longed to acquaint herself with; their reputation as forward thinkers pulled at her spirit. The Marquise de Sévigné was there, as was the Comtesse de La Fayette, and the young Duchesse de Chevreuse who had taken her mother-in-law's place.

Jeanne mused on the company Olympe would be keeping in the future; it was a life of lofty connections, everything her friend ever dreamed of—but how high was the price she would pay?

"Let's find Olympe," Jeanne urged her sister, and the two young women made their way out of the salon toward the grand ballroom. People crowded the hallway as thickly as the heat of the afternoon air. Jeanne and Bernadette pushed through, finally finding space and fresh air in the ballroom; though no less populated, the grand-sized chamber offered more room. The parquet floors shined and reflected the bright sun coming through the south wall of glass doors, each festooned in white silk and garland upon garland of white gardenias, their vibrant fragrance caressing the air. Sumptuously attired guests twirled on the dance floor, their bodies cutting the reflections, sending intermittent bursts of light and shadow through the high-ceilinged chamber. The room buzzed with happy conversation over the tinkling of crystal and the music of the small orchestra in the corner.

"Well, if I have not found the two most beautiful girls here, then I must be in the wrong place," said a soft male voice behind them.

"Raol!" the sisters cried together as they whirled in unison, throwing their arms around their adored big brother at the same time.

"We did not think we would see you here today." Bernadette reached up to kiss Raol's handsome face; he looked even more dashing than usual in his light blue brocade jacket and breeches and exquisite shirt with lace at collar and cuff. "We didn't think the academy would let you go again so soon."

Jeanne felt a wave of grief; the last time they had seen their male sibling had been at Lynette's services.

"Normally true, *ma petite*, but the name of the Vicomte du Ludres has a powerful effect on many people." Raol turned to Bernadette, catching the flash of pain on Jeanne's face. "Would you be a dear, Bernadette, and get me some champagne? I haven't been able to find a waiter anywhere."

"Of course, Raol," Bernadette assured him with a broad smile, all too happy to do anything for the older brother she worshipped. "I'll be right back."

"Your heart still breaks, chère sister?" Raol bent his tall head, chocolate brown curls falling in his face as he looked into his sister's sad expression.

Looking up with threatening tears, Jeanne bobbed her head in silent answer.

Raol's full mouth turned down under his bushy mustache, mirroring the pain he found still so fresh in his sister. Without another word for there were none worthy enough, he lay a strong, loving arm around Jeanne's shoulders.

* * *

He'd searched for her all morning, in every face and every group of courtiers. At long last, he spied her as he stood in front of one of the ballroom's ceiling-tall glass doors. Henri's face softened as he caught sight of Jeanne entering the room. A smile spread with slow pleasure across his face, and he took a step toward her.

His foot faltered, stopped. His smile died on his lips. Who was this handsome cavalier who joined Jeanne and her sister? His heart fluttered as the man put his arm around Jeanne, so familiar, so loving.

Without thought or care, Henri rushed across the room.

* * *

"Mademoiselle."

Jeanne heard the voice, felt her hand being lifted, felt the tender lips cross the back of her hand and closed her eyes in a moment of pleasure and relief, a short-lived reprieve. Her lids burst open, and she saw the look on her brother's face as he watched Henri greet her so affectionately, recognized Raol's familiar, protective look. All fluid dried in her mouth as the two men she loved faced each other for the first time, two men she had hoped would never meet, at least until she'd gathered the courage to tell Henri of "Jean-Luc's" birth. She looked from one dear face to another, watching as their intelligent, wary contemplation took the full measure of the other.

"Ahem." Raol coughed politely into his gloved hand.

"Oh, *p-pardieu*," Jeanne stammered. "Monsieur Henri d'Aubigne, pray allow me to introduce my brother, Raol du Bois. Raol, Monsieur d'Aubigne."

Raol bowed to Henri. "I am at your orders, monsieur."

"*Non.*" Henri bowed, delight bursting upon his handsome features. He grabbed Raol's hand and pumped it with great enthusiasm. Raol was no rival; what's more, he was a friend of Jean-Luc's. "It is I who am at your service. I have wanted to make your acquaintance for some time."

"Really?" One of Raol's brows rose inquisitively upon his smooth forehead, gaze jumping from his sister's face to that of this man who looked at her with naked adoration.

"We have a mutual friend."

"Ah, *oui.*" Raol smiled fiendishly at his sister. "I can see that."

Henri took Jeanne's limp, cold hand in his, caressing her face with his eyes. "Your sister, sir, is a great deal more than a friend—with the greatest respect, of course."

"Of course." Raol bowed, delight pure upon his face.

"In truth, I meant another acquaintance. I refer to Je—"

"Raol!" Jeanne cried out his name as if a knife had stabbed her, so frantic was she to curtail the conversation. She felt just one step away from tumbling off the cliff of hysteria. Jeanne saw the two men jump at her loud exclamation and tried to gather herself. "Oh, *excusez-moi*, but I just remembered something of the utmost importance I must tell my brother."

She took both of Henri's hands in hers. "You will excuse us for just a moment, won't you? It is a matter of grave family business."

"Of course, of course. I will wait right here for you." Henri bowed over her hand and nodded toward Raol. "Pray let me know if there is anything I can do to assist you."

"*Merci*, Henri," Jeanne said with soft politeness. Then, grabbing Raol's arm, she jerked him away and out of the ballroom.

Rushing through the hallway and into the foyer, she moved like a rock rolling upon a steep mountain through the crowds, parting them as the rock parts the trees, leading her brother up the winding stairs. On the second floor, Jeanne burst through the first door she came upon, still with Raol's arm gripped tightly in her own.

From inside the chamber, soft giggling greeted them as well as the sight of two legs, flagrantly feminine ones still clad in lace hose and bowed shoes, bouncing over the back of the couch in the center of the room. As the cushions squeaked in a telling, repetitive song, a deep male voice growled in muttered, ecstatic tones. Jeanne rolled her eyes and pulled Raol away, ignoring his mischievous smile and efforts to crane his neck to see more.

In the next room, sobbing greeted them. Jeanne and Raol stopped for a flash of a moment, taking in the three young women, lavishly dressed, and standing together in a tight circle. A stunning beauty stood in the middle; platinum blond hair piled high, tears streaming down her crème silk skin while the two on either side did their best to comfort her. Jeanne dropped a shallow curtsey to the women and pulled Raol out into the hall.

"I think I should go back in there," Raol feigned concern. "God only knows what drama could cause such a ravishing creature to weep so. What kind of gentleman would I be if I did not offer her my services?"

Jeanne paid him no heed and rushed a few steps farther, along to the third door off the long corridor. She heaved a sigh of relief at finding the chamber empty. Warm and inviting, the large and spacious room, much like the other two salons, boasted high ceilings hung with monochromatic Lyonnais silk, each room dominated by a particular color.

Jeanne released her strangling hold on Raol and paced away from him, her face toward a far window looking out over the circular drive.

"*Mon Dieu*, Jeanne," Raol barked, rubbing the arm where she had squeezed the blood from his skin. "Whatever is the matter with you? What is this great family business?"

Jeanne clasped her hands to her chest, white knuckles protruding as she held her despair so tightly within them.

"There is no family emergency. I . . . I needed to get you away from Henri. There is something I must tell you before you speak with him further."

"Ah, why am I not surprised?" Raol took a step or two toward her. "I think he is quite smitten with you, and, if I'm not mistaken, the feeling is mutual, oui?"

Jeanne nodded her head, jerks of agitation. "It is indeed so. I do care for him, dearly."

"Then why do you look so vexed, my dear? I would think you would be joyful." Raol stared at his sister, confounded.

"Because I am afraid that soon he will come to hate me." The words said, the rest of the story burst from Jeanne like a dam released by an overflowing flood; the whole tale of her disguise and how it came to be, streamed from her lips until the saga ran dry and all her secrets lay revealed. Raol gingerly lowered himself, with visibly trembling knees, into an armchair; though his bottom lip hung from his mouth, no words came from them.

"Say something, please, Raol." Jeanne knelt at his feet, pleading.

"And he has no idea you are one and the same?" Raol sibilated.

"He does not." Jeanne's unblinking eyes never left her brother's face. "Will you keep my secret, brother?"

"Of course, of course," he assured her, head nodding loosely upon his neck. "But why, why would you do such a thing?"

"To do ... something." Jeanne shook her head, floundering. "Something meaningful with my life. Something...that truly thrills me as it serves my country." She stood with fisted hands, defiance twitching her jaw. "Why...why is such a purpose only for men?" Jeanne thrust now open hands toward him. "Why are these to be only for embroidery or…or flapping a damnable fan?"

Raol stared at her, a mystified gaze as her passion set her ablaze. "It is my fault."

"What?" Jeanne barked. "What nonsense do you speak?"

"I treated you as a playmate; I played too rough with you when we were children." He stood and walked to the windows.

Jeanne followed close behind. "Do you think our childhood games make me long for a greater existence?"

Raol turned back to her with a confused shrug of his broad shoulders.

"No, Raol, it is not that," she assured him. "It is my dissatisfaction with my own opportunities and nothing more. Perhaps it is my jealousy that you have known the glories of war, and I will never know any more glory than a well-set table."

Raol chuckled, but with no smile upon his lips. His eyes narrowed as he searched her face. "Is that what you believe, that war is all glory?"

Jeanne gave no reply, seeing a flash of ill-disguised pain in his familiar eyes.

Shaking his head, Raol pulled his dear sister into his arms, held her tight as if to capture her forever in his grasp.

"Be careful what you wish for, *ma chère*. What appears to be glory can in truth be damnation."

~Twenty-One~

She padded from her bedchamber to the sitting room and sat, listening to the unearthly quiet of her family's suite. Her family, like most courtiers, attended the evening's soirée; even the flanking suites rang with empty silence.

She jumped to her feet, wishing she could jump out of her skin, for it fairly crawled upon her bones. She paced back into her bedchamber but, once there, looked around in puzzlement, not knowing why she had come.

She stared at the space below her bed, turning from the dark gap as if to deny its attraction. She paced back into the sitting room, dissatisfaction ever stronger.

Utterly alone. Her in this world, in this life...utterly alone. Lost to her, her two dearest friends, one to God and one to the devil, for that was how she viewed the Vicomte du Ludres. It had been two weeks since Olympe's wedding day, and she had yet to see her friend return to Versailles for any activities. She had seen Du Ludres, looking as bloated and boastful as ever, but not a sign or even a word from Olympe. Jeanne feared for her, for her strong spirit.

Jeanne's own spirit suffered as she searched desperately in the meaningless life at court to fill the hole left by the absence of them. But nothing was the same without them; there was no joy to be found in the endless and repetitious avocations of court life, for if there was no one to find reality within the depths of such affectation, how was it to be endured?

From small room to small room Jeanne paced again. Each time she weaved through her own room, her gaze sidled to the secret place beneath her bed, the place where lay Jean-Luc's attire, drawn to it again and again, like a bee to brightly plumed flowers.

Gritting her teeth she flew out the main suite door and stomped down to the window at the end of the long corridor, finding even this passageway vacuously empty. She stood at the aperture and for a brief moment found solace in the beauty of the Versailles gardens at night, the glow of the flambeaux reflecting light off the shimmering waters, the flowers and trees dancing a small, delicate dance in the evening breeze. But its emptiness mocked her; she stormed away to return to her rooms, weaving the same pattern from sitting room to bedchamber once more; her gaze—frequently, annoyingly—straying to the compartment under her bed.

Back out, through the sitting room, into the hall, straining to look out the glass. Movement from below caught her eye and she stood on tiptoe to see. Two Musketeers, bold and debonair in their blue and silver satin tabards, strutted down the lane and out of sight. Her stomach flip, a sign.

Jeanne ran back to her room and reached for the hidden cache of men's clothing with the same guilt and shame, the same yearning and delight as the abstaining addict reaches for their opium.

* * *

Jean-Luc walked through the gates spilling out onto the Place d'Armes with a swagger worthy of any young chevalier. Young and alive, the night bristled with energy, as did Jeanne did, savoring every moment of her escape and freedom.

Revelers young and old walked the streets, men and women in groups and pairs, laughing, calling, singing, determined to find pleasure wherever it might hide. She passed the Hôtel de Bourgogne, smiling at the sight of the actors' painted faces visible in almost every window. With Jean-Luc's anonymity as a shield, Jeanne relaxed under the cloak of the stars and the dim lights of the single-candle lanterns. Her stride elongated with each step she took, as she was, in truth, forced to do while wearing the cumbersome bucket-topped boots and sporting the pincushion in her breeches, a stride that felt more natural with each step, more true to the being within. The tailored silk jacket swung jauntily behind her; she tilted her chin up arrogantly as if she owned the world. By the time she arrived at the Café de l'Oiseau, the morose Jeanne was merely a ghost of the ebullient Jean-Luc.

* * *

"I've come with a message from Jeanne du Bois," Jean-Luc told his merry comrades once the greetings were over; a full mug of wine and some food sitting on the scarred wooden table in front of him.

"Oh, Henri." Gerard mimicked a woman's voice in a terrible squeaky, high-pitched treble. "Come take me, you wicked man."

Jean Luc bit his lips closed to keep from laughing as riotously as Antoine and Laurent, though Gerard's imitation combined with Henri's blush amused greatly. "Not that kind of a message, but one to do with our mission."

His words quickly quieted the boisterous men down; they pulled their chairs in closer to the table, scraping the chair legs loudly across the planked flooring and leaning in toward Jean-Luc.

His manly voice lowered to a whisper, Jean-Luc told them of Jeanne's encounter with Athénaïs, of the woman's boastful words as well as those revealing her desire to be Queen.

"We shouldn't be surprised," Laurent remarked. "That woman's ambition knows no bounds."

Jean-Luc nodded and continued, speaking faster as adrenaline kicked in, remembering the fear when recognizing Athénaïs's attendant Margaux.

"Jeanne told me you followed her…Margaux…that night." Jean-Luc finished the story, turning to Henri. "Were you able to see where she went?"

Henri shook his head. "She slipped into a secret door. I could not take the chance of following her down it. I did not know the passageways or what I would encounter on the other side."

"You were right to do so," Gerard growled. "The last thing we want is to be found out. If they know we are watching them, they will not try again."

"We want them to try again?" Jean-Luc croaked, aghast, like a pubescent boy.

"Of course," Antoine explained. "We have little left to investigate. Our only hope of capturing the miscreants now is to catch them in the act."

"But what a risk to our Queen!" Jean-Luc pound a gloved fist upon the wood before him.

Henri stilled with a hand to shoulder. "There are more eyes on the Queen than ever, more than she knows. They will not succeed, have no fear."

Jean-Luc said naught, but in silence pictured the innocent, solemn woman the country called Queen, a woman who had shown Jeanne nothing but kindness for all of Jeanne's life. The one who dreamed of wearing a Musketeer's tabard, shuddered at the oblivious nature of their bait.

Henri must have seen Jean-Luc's distress. He refilled his friend's empty wineglass.

"If it will make you feel better, ask our friend Jeanne to spend more time with the Queen. She is an amazingly intelligent and observant woman. She will help guard her, I am quite sure."

Jean-Luc looked upon him, brows knit upon a scrunched face, but found the hint of a smile. "I know she will."

Henri fell into an uneasy silence, staring into his own glass.

Jean-Luc sensed unspoken words on his tongue, longing to fly out. The silence remained unbroken in the loud, boisterous room; the words would come in time.

"Do you know of Polignac?" Henri finally asked.

Jean-Luc blinked against the surprise of hearing that name. "He is the man Jeanne's father has chosen for her."

"She does not…" Henri floundered; he thrust himself back in his chair, running two tense hands across his face and through his hair.

"No, she doesn't. Not … at … all," Jean-Luc said with all the repugnance Jeanne felt for Percy de Polignac.

Henri smiled. "What will she do?"

"Anything she can." Jean-Luc shrugged, not knowing the answer.

"Tell me more of her," Henri asked, his need naked in his tone.

Jean-Luc sighed, wondering how to talk of the truth of such a person.

Behind closed eyes, Lynette's soft, tender face came to mind.

With a shy smile, Jean-Luc began to speak, describing Jeanne as Lynette would, the good and the bad as Lynette had seen in Jeanne more clearly than any other.

Time slipped away, as did the wine down their throats. Their friends came and went around them, with women, with food, with drink after drink. The buzz grew louder in Jean-Luc's ears; there had been enough wine drunk.

"In plain truth"—Jean-Luc slammed the empty glass tankard upon the hard table—"she is not able to come to grips with her place in this world, and her behavior reflects her dissatisfaction."

Henri laughed. "I like a woman with spunk."

Jean-Luc washed him harshly with a skeptical glare, leaning in closer to better gauge his reaction. "You say that now, but will you still like her, and her 'spunk,' in twenty years?"

Henri stared at the face of the young man before him, silent and sullen in his study.

"I am besotted, I must be." He sat back with a laugh, shaking his head dolorously. "For I swear I see her eyes in your face."

Jean-Luc's heart lodged in his throat; grabbing the tankard, finding it empty, and reaching across the table for the bottle. Tossing it back having forgotten to imbibe no more, Jean-Luc took a long diverting draught of the wine.

Wiping drips from mouth with the back of a hand, Jean-Luc turned back to Henri.

"When you see her in your dreams, then you will know it is true love."

Henri leaned in as well, so close, close enough to see the truth of him, the anguish.

"Then it is already too late."

Longing and desire surged just looking at him, heat rose beneath leather and buckskin, gaze marinated on his tawny skin and full mouth. A stirring in thighs signaled the time to go.

Jean-Luc stood abruptly, legs straddled as he pulled the chair out from between them as Raol so often did. Passing behind Henri on the way to the door, he slapped him on the back in farewell, the besotted fugue still haunted his features.

Jean-Luc returned to Versailles, vacillating between joy and confusion.

* * *

"Where the deuce have you been?"

The roar flung upon her before she passed over the threshold into her family's rooms.

The sear of cold fear surged through, muscles shuddering. Her hands trembled on the bundle of clothes she carried in a small pack as if her outraged father could see through the cloth and knew what she held.

"I … I just went for a walk, Père." Jeanne willed her feet to move. "It was such a warm night, I needed some air."

"Until one o'clock in the morning?" Gaston's sharp features blotched with red anger. "Three times I came looking for you. Three times did the Baron de Polignac ask for you."

"I am sorry, Père. I did not know." Jeanne kept her head downcast as she inched her way to one of the chairs in the sitting room. Slipping slowly behind it, she cautiously lowered her pack to the floor, out of her father's sight. "I was just so overly warm."

"From now on you do not go anywhere without telling me." Gaston stabbed a stubby finger in his daughter's direction.

"I am not a child, Père," Jeanne lashed out heedlessly, "and I refuse to remain no more than your chattel. I come and go as I please."

Jeanne's hands fisted at her sides though she knew it not; she stared at her father with narrowed eyes. A monster of anger and frustration grew invisibly between them.

"The King has approved this match, and the Polignacs come for dinner tomorrow to sign the papers. Percy wants you. The baron wants you. There is nothing you can do to stop this." Gaston thrust his pointy chin in the air in triumph, puffing out his chest as he stomped to the door. "I have paid dearly to attend tonight's *Petit Coucher*. Your insolence will not stop me."

The door slammed behind him. Chains of damnation held her fast; her short nails dug into the palms of her hand, leaving crescent marks gorged into her skin. She looked down at the bundle at her feet, and all the stolen moments of the night rushed back to her. A smile of satisfaction spread slowly across her face.

* * *

Bernadette did not snore, though she slept with her mouth gaped open. Turning toward her sister, Jeanne heard Bernadette's soft breath catching in her sister's throat from time to time, a muted tic like a distant clock counting the minutes until her doom.

Once the papers were signed with the Polignacs, there was, in truth, no way out of the marriage. Her life would be forfeit; trapped and bound by God and law. Jeanne kicked the thin sheet off her legs in frustration. Sweat bead upon her in the still, dank air. She stared up at the ceiling as if salvation hid in the white plaster.

I am besotted. Henri's words popped into her mind like the stars in a dusky sky. *Then it is already too late.*

Her skin tingled at her memories. Not just those of Henri, but those of Jean-Luc as he fought beside Henri, those of the blood-lust that was Jean-Luc's, that thrilled and satisfied so completely.

Percy wants you. The baron wants you.

Her father's voice cut the titillating sensations as surely as the ax cut the tree, and she closed her eyes, hoping to shut them out of her mind. They would not be forsook.

Percy wants you. The baron wants you.

Jeanne jumped upward, the glimmer of an answer took form.

But what if they don't want me?

~Twenty-Two~

Jeanne stared at the two dresses laying on her bed. In her corset and petticoats, she stood contemplating them, one arm crossed against her chest, the other with her hand up to her face, index finger tapping her chin.

Plush and stylish, the yellow one boasted an abundance of beadwork, a wide *busquiere*, and yards and yards of Venetian lace. It was also blatantly provocative; the neckline cut wantonly low and the bottom edge of the *busquiere* ended at the top of her genitals in a risqué point. It was a gown for an evening meant for seduction, not a dinner with a potential suitor and his family. It was rumored the Baroness de Polignac was a prodigiously pious woman; to dress the *putain* would be just the thing to disabuse her of the idea of Jeanne as her new daughter.

The other gown, a blue one, was not only out of fashion, the edges were worn, the cuffs and hem frayed, the color faded, and it boasted few adornments. It might be just the thing to show Jeanne would be no trophy on anyone's arm.

To make her devious plan work, Jeanne must attend to every detail. Who knew if what might make her repugnant to one member of the Polignac family would not endear her to another? She had lain awake the entire night, conceiving everything viable to make herself undesirable. Darkness encircled her eyes, marring what beauty she possessed. She could name a list of offenses as long as her arm to the tip of her sword.

The clanging of metal rang loudly from the outer room. Jeanne tapped her foot, impatient with her own indecision. Servants delivered the meal from the kitchens below, placed the banquet on the sideboard in readiness for serving. Her time of decisiveness ticked to an end.

With a cluck of her tongue, she grabbed at the yellow gown and threw it over her head. Any poor person could be gussied up, but shame upon a family would last forever.

Pulling and twisting the gown into place, Jeanne reached down into her bodice and, with a cupped hand, lifted one small, muscular breast at a time so as much of her meager bosom as possible flowed up and over the lace-edged neckline. Looking down at her engorged chest, she set her shoulders firmly into place and made for the door. Catching a glimpse of herself in the filmy mirror in the corner, Jeanne rolled her eyes at the sight but continued on her path of intended self-destruction.

"*Mordioux*!"

Jeanne's swiveled toward the familiar voice.

"Raol!" she exclaimed, shocked to see her brother standing next to Bernadette in the small foyer. "What are you doing here?"

His handsomeness erased by shocked distress, Raol strode over to her, his leather heels clicking on the wooden floor.

"Our father requested I attend tonight's gathering." Raol grabbed Jeanne's upper arm and pulled her back toward the door of her bedchamber, lowering his voice to a hiss. "What are you about? Why are you dressed like this? This is not you."

Jeanne smiled with broad satisfaction, a clever façade to hide her guilt and fear. Under her brother's scrutiny, she felt the fraud she attempted to portray, the many for he knew them all. "I'll take that as a compliment, Brother."

Pulling her arm from Raol's grasp, she turned, unwilling to take him into her confidence, afraid he would try, and succeed, to persuade her to abandon her plan.

Stepping into the suite's common room, Jeanne nodded appreciatively at her mother's ingenious answer to the chair dilemma. Flanking the long table at each head and one on each side were four armchairs, one for each parent. In between were four tabourets, one for herself and Percy and one each for her brother and sister.

Earlier in the evening, Jeanne had overseen the setting of the tablecloth; the crème Dutch yellow linen hung only three inches below the tabletop. Jeanne preferred this drapery much better than the previous custom...tablecloths so long they served as napkins. Thick napkins of a matching material sat tall before each plate, fashioned in a complicated triangular pattern by her father's valet. The obsequiously talented man stood at the side of the buffet ready to serve at the host's pleasure.

As fair fate would have it, her parents entered from their bedchamber at the same time as a scratch came upon their door. Adelaide and Gaston halted, aghast at the sight of their daughter, their eyes flicking from her attire to her face and then to her siblings as if Bernadette and Raol possessed some explanation. Raol avoided their gaze while Bernadette raised her shoulders in a baffled shrug.

"Get the door please, Bernadette," Jeanne asked sweetly, sparing not glance nor word for her parents.

"No—" Gaston cried out...too late.

Bernadette flung the portal wide, there stood the baron and baroness, the thin face of their son popping up from behind.

With a last look of bewilderment for her daughter, Adelaide strode forward with an outstretched hand of welcome, taking the baroness's hand and leading the small woman into the foyer with a curtsey.

"It is such an honor to welcome you here," Adelaide said, the very essence of graciousness. Her own gown, a simple but rich brown with satin trim, matched perfectly in style and grandeur the navy blue one worn by the Baroness.

The small, mousy, gray-haired woman curtseyed in response.

"Thank you, comtesse. It is our pleasure to be here. We have been looking forward to this evening for many a day, especially our Percy." The woman's high-pitched voice warbled as one of her small hands gestured over her shoulder, instructing her husband and son to make their way in from the hallway.

As the two men made their greetings to Adelaide and Gaston, Jeanne stood immobile on the other side of the table. Her heartbeat fluttered in her over-exposed chest, small droplets of perspiration burst upon her top lip. Could she do this? Should she do this?

"We are quite proud of our dear Percy." With her squeaky vibrato, the Baroness spoke once more of her son as if he were a performing pet, her tall husband nodding silently by her side. "Many young girls vie for his attentions, but we were quite choosy in deciding upon his mate."

Jeanne studied Percy's long, pale face, the thin lips, anemic eyes, and high forehead. He blushed as his mother spoke of him, not taking his gaze from the baroness's face, a pet waiting for some more praise and a reward. Seeing him thus, she knew; Jeanne knew she would do whatever it would take to release herself from a lifetime with this weak man.

"Baron and Baroness, *bon soir*." Jeanne thrust herself within the circle of guests, making her greetings out of turn, curtseying low, displaying her bare décolletage to its fullest. She stayed down, drawing out her solicitation as she heard the quick intake of breath, not only from Percy but from his mother and father as well. Rising, seeing their faces, the stunned countenance of the baroness especially, proved all Jeanne had hoped this moment would be.

Reaching out a hand, she placed her limb in the delicate one of her betrothed. Percy leaned over it, his lusterless gaze not moving from Jeanne's brazen appearance, heedless of the shaking plumes stirring atop his hat, almost hitting Jeanne in the face as he moved closer to her. As all the men present were of almost equal standing on the ladder of ascension, they would keep their hats on for the entire visit.

"Good ... good evening, *chère* Jeanne," Percy spluttered, brushing his lips across her skin.

Though she tried to hide it, Jeanne shivered at the coldness of his mouth.

"Please come in, will you all?" She led them into the dining room.

"Yes, of course, come in." Gaston brushed past Jeanne, his face engorged with blood, vibrant against the whiteness of his high, curly wig and lace collar. Pulling out a chair on the far side of the table, he gestured to the Baroness. "Please, Madame, make yourself comfortable."

With a small, tight nod of her head, the short woman took her place in the offered seat, her mouth a stiff, straight line across her face. The baron held the chair for Adelaide, who sat with a nod of thanks. Once Gaston and the baron sat, the four younger people took their seats, and Gaston, with a sharp gesture of his white-wigged head, instructed the servant to begin the meal.

Placing the surtout, the metal-forged centerpiece with compartments for salt, pepper, other spices, and toothpicks, in the center of the table, the buttoned-up valet announced the beginning of the meal.

"What did you think of this year's Feast of St. Louis?" Adelaide asked, sitting primly in her seat with her hands neatly folded in her lap as the first course of soup and fish was served.

Jeanne took an unsteady breath. Her mother appeared composed, acting as the gracious hostess, but Jeanne saw the small beads of perspiration under the curls of Adelaide's high coiffure. She had not considered it, how her actions would punish her mother; for that, she despised herself yet the game had begun and she would play it till the end.

"I thought it magnificent." Jeanne cut off any answer from their guests, plopping her elbows on the table in the most deplorable fashion.

Jeanne forged on despite the stupefaction served her from every face about her.

"It was truly the best one ever, do you not think so, Baroness?"

The older woman barely moved as she took a first spoonful of her soup with a noticeably trembling hand. "I thought it—"

The baroness's voice broke off in a croak, her face turning to a putrid color, a spoiled version of that of the table linen. Unperturbed, Jeanne continued to lean over her bowl and blow on her soup, the act of a peasant.

"I thought the tournaments were some of the best. Did you not think so, Percy?" Raol ladled a small spoonful of soup from his bowl, a swift glare at his errant sister slipping from his eyes.

Percy primly wiped at the corners of his mouth with his napkin. "I could not say. I did not see any myself."

Jeanne gave her brother a contemptuous look as if daring him to see any worth in this effeminate man. Raol ignored her, launching into a wonderfully descriptive tale of the matches he had witnessed. His voice became a calming influence over the tinkling of cutlery on porcelain as the dinner party continued.

The valet brought more food to the table, reaching in with a delicate gold basket, offering bread to the Baroness, the oldest female getting the first selection of any offering.

Jeanne reached out and grabbed a piece before the baroness could, taking a large bite and chewing the roll with an open mouth while slurping noises escaped from between her visible teeth.

"The King looked so very happy with his new grandson." Adelaide raised her voice, a desperate attempt. "Did you see the child, Baroness?"

The small woman stewed like their well-cooked soup, silent mouth open and slack as she stared at Jeanne. She moved not an inch, with no acknowledgment of Adelaide's query. Like a victim of a great trauma or a person who had just witnessed a deplorable crime, one so heinous as to boggle the mind, she was but half there.

Jeanne didn't dare to look across the table at her, sure she would lose her nerve or give way to the nervous laughter bubbling up in her throat; to release either one would be defeat. She searched her memory, recalling all the long, tedious lessons from the nuns on proper table comportment, intending to break each and every one of them. Jeanne stared at Percy, who sat directly across the table. His unanimated, feeble expressions, his dainty and delicate mannerisms, gave her all the inducement she needed to continue her performance.

"Drink!" Jeanne yelled and bit her lower lip as everyone at the table jumped in fright and horror at her call. The valet did not move, so unfamiliar with this manner of request; a person of good breeding merely gave a small hand signal or asked for a beverage with a low-voiced appeal. Gaston cleared his throat with a rumble, gave a curt nod of his head, and his servant moved into action.

Retrieving Jeanne's glass from the row of glasses on the buffet table, where they awaited each guest, the flustered man poured a glass of wine and placed it by Jeanne's plate.

As Jeanne overtly sipped and slurped, the second course arrived, one of three different roasts and salads, the offerings some of the best the Comte de Moreuil's money could afford. Jeanne glimpsed hopeful looks appear on the face of the baron and his wife as the silver platters were placed on the table.

Picking up a slice of roast with her bare hands, Jeanne tore a piece off with her teeth and, with her mouth still overflowing with half-masticated meat, turned to the baron on her right.

"Do you enjoy the hunt, sir? I did not see you when last I took part. It was quite the kill, I assure you."

"I enjoy it not, nor do I have time for such frivolity." The baron shook his head but said no more. Though allowed to participate, it was not a woman's place to discuss such a manly pursuit.

The baron cast a look at Bernadette, who sat silent through the entire meal, her lovely dark eyes cast downward, her movements small and graceful. Jeanne could almost see the thoughtful wish in his eye...why had he not chosen this quiet, well-mannered girl over her churlish, obnoxious sister.

The third course of hot and cold fowl came to the table, and fatigue plucked at Jeanne; the fear and nerves of her charade exhausted her. Flowing with those feelings, she leaned back in her chair with a wide, loud yawn. From under the table, she felt a foot meet sharply with her shin and looked up to see Raol eyeing her with deadly intent. Evading his ire, Jeanne picked up a pigeon leg and cleaned the meat off the bone with her teeth. As the juice of the bird ran down her hand, she licked her fingers, lapping at her digits with a bright pink tongue.

Gaston stood so fast his chair flew out behind him, crashing against the wall at his back. His face contorted in pure fury at this, his daughter's most egregious behavior, but he somehow managed to temper his words. "If you will excuse us." He bowed graciously though shallowly to the guests at his table. "My daughter and I will see to our last course, one we are sure will please you all greatly."

Yanking Jeanne from her chair by her upper arm, he fairly ran with her in tow out into the hall. Jeanne almost tripped on her long hem, gorge rising in her throat. She never expected her father to chastise her with the Polignacs still in attendance.

Out in the hall, Gaston closed the door quietly behind them, his movements restrained and perfunctory. Bringing his face to within inches of his daughter, he hissed at her in hushed castigation.

"I know what you are about, you horrible girl, don't think for moment I do not. If you do not cease immediately, I promise you I will beat you to within an inch of your life."

Jeanne squared her jaw at him, looking deeply into the face so full of hate.

"I would rather wear the scars of your fist for a lifetime than endure a single moment as that man's wife."

Gaston's livid face quivered with his rage. "Very well. Then cease or I will beat your mother till her skin is forever scarred. And when you are in the Bastille, I will beat her still."

The cold, despicable words cut across Jeanne's mind. She drew her head back sharply as if Gaston had slapped her, banging her head on the wall behind her. Words of retaliation caught in her throat, her fists clenched by her side; in her mind, her sword grew from her palm…till she skewered her father in the gullet.

She said nothing, did nothing; there was nothing to do. Gaston had played the one card, the only thing, powerful enough to make her stop, and she had no more resilience to fight him. She should have known it would come to this; she could only hope what she had already done had been enough.

A slow, sordid smile spreading across his face, Gaston stepped back from his daughter, pulled down on his waistcoat, and straightened his cravat. With a triumphant nod, he opened the door, beckoning to the servants just now appearing at the top of the stairs with the cumbersome dessert tray, and strode back into the room with great assurance. A silent, helpless Jeanne followed him.

Gaston and Jeanne took back their seats at the table just as the dessert paraded in behind them, its grandeur eliciting an awed response from even the staid baroness. Carried in by two serving girls, the *Tourte Picarde*, a pyramid of pears covered with custard, the pile so high the women bringing it in could barely see around it. Conversation of the King and Queen continued over the dessert, but Jeanne took no part, barely tasting the lusciousness of the confection as the shroud of defeat hung around her.

The baron and baroness said little themselves, only what minimal politeness dictated. The baroness frequently glanced silently at Adelaide, soundlessly encouraging her hostess to make the necessary move.

Adelaide accepted the intimation. She stood, regally in the face of the disastrous evening, and curtseyed to the table at large.

"It has been our greatest privilege to have you in our home," she said, a most proper end to a meal offered to her guests. "We hope it is just the start of many more such evenings."

The baron huffed noisily, standing with a scrap of his chair and rounding the table to help his wife from hers. "That remains to be seen, comtesse."

"But Polignac, the papers?" Gaston jumped to his feet, rushing to the couple making their hasty way to the door.

"Later, Du Bois." The baron did not even look back over his shoulder as he headed for the door. "Percy, come."

As his father and mother escaped the room, Percy came round the table to Jeanne's side and took one of her hands in his equally feminine one.

"Have no fear, dear." He leaned over, lips to her ear. "I will talk to my parents. I will convince them. My mother and I can surely turn you into the woman your parents could not." With a faint kiss to her hand and a bow to Gaston and Adelaide, he left the room close on his family's heels.

Jeanne stared after him as if she watched a ghost, a creature too unfathomable to be real; surely after her display, he could not still want to align himself with her, he could not still desire her. Dreadful silence descended upon the Du Bois family.

With the lethal quietness of a panther, Gaston reached out a long arm, hand in the shape of a claw, and grabbed Jeanne by the shoulders. With one powerful shove, he threw her against the wall; the impact so intense, all her breath erupted from her lungs. She slid slowly down the wall, gasping in pain.

"Father! Gaston!" The family cried out, whirling round them, but Gaston was not to be distracted. He held up one arthritic, gnarled finger behind him toward Raol and Adelaide, one silent but fatal warning. Leaning down, he put his face to his daughter's. Jeanne stared at the red veins in the whites of his eyes as he bit off his words between his teeth.

"If they deny you now, I will spend every sou I possess to see you rot forever in the Bastille."

Without another word or thought for his child, Gaston turned away and yanked open the door to the hallway and strode purposefully through it.

"Adelaide, come now!" he bellowed from without.

Jeanne's mother began to walk slowly to the door. Each step she took away from her injured daughter brought a look of fresh pain to her face. She followed her husband as her tear-filled eyes drenched her daughter with a silent apology.

~Twenty-Three~

Raol held out his hand to his sister. Frightened gaze intent upon his caring face, Jeanne reached out, accepting his help, using his strength to pull herself up off the floor; her own had failed her.

"What were you thinking?" A harsh whisper.

Jeanne's chin quivered with pending tears so deplored, teeth jammed tightly together. "I cannot marry him, I cannot."

"Run away, *chère* Jeanne, please." The sobbing plea came from the dining room.

Bernadette sat in her chair at the table still, a table strewn with the discarded remnants of the disastrous meal, a mess awaiting the servants.

Jeanne ran to her sister's side, kneeling down before her, wiping away the huge round tears running silently down the young girl's splotched face.

"Where would I go, *ma petite*?"

Bernadette shook her head of golden hair. "I do not know. But I could not bear the thought of you rotting away in the Bastille. I could not."

Raol came and stood behind his two sisters, watching them with brows in a furrow upon his smooth forehead. "She will not go to the Bastille, to you I swear it."

Two pairs of large, moist eyes looked up to him, much as they had for the whole of their lives.

"I do not know yet what I will do, but we will do something."

Jeanne stood and put her arms around Raol's broad shoulders, the moisture on her face staining the dark maroon velvet of his finely tailored jacket.

"Perhaps you would have nowhere to go, but what of Jean-Luc?"

His whisper was so soft, so scathing, Jeanne's mind and mouth numbed. Before she could answer, Raol put a hand out to Bernadette, pulling his other sister into their embrace.

"Come," he said, rubbing their backs softly with his large, wide hands. "Let us go to this evening's soirée, shall we? Let's drink and dance together."

In Raol's big, brown eyes, Jeanne saw her own fear, despair that, for the three of them together, such evenings would soon be coming to an end, and nodded her acceptance with a wan smile. "I think I would like to change first."

Amid their laughter, Raol agreed. "Good idea, Sister. Good idea, indeed."

* * *

They wandered into the Apollo Salon, much-needed aperitifs in each hand, drawn by the choral of music wafting out of the chamber. Often used as a musical venue during *Soirées d'Apartements*, this space usually served as the King's throne room. The eight-foot, crimson-canopied throne, ornately crafted from solid silver, dominated the chamber. It sat upon a dais at the far end, the platform covered with an exquisite Persian carpet. Above the fireplace at the opposite end loomed a life-sized portrait of Louis decked out in his blue and gold coronation outfit. The ceiling, a masterpiece of decorative painting, glowed *The Chariot of the Sun*, by Rigaud. With fresh, lively colors, gods and goddesses cavorted, battled, or rifted across a dazzling azure sky. Finished with gilded moldings, the room was perpetually decorated with bowls of fresh fruit on every table and orange trees in gilded tubs.

"Dance with me, my sweet." Raol put his small, curved glass down on a table and grabbed Bernadette's hand, whirling her away onto the dance floor after she thrust her own glass in Jeanne's hand. Sipping first her drink, then Bernadette's when her own disappeared, Jeanne watched her siblings with heartbreaking fondness; she smiled to see happiness and delight return to her sister's face.

How can I be so selfish? Jeanne berated herself, angry for not giving a moment's consideration as to what her actions might do to the rest of her family, too intent to relieve herself of her father's agreement and, yes, to anger Gaston at the same time. But for all of Bernadette's mature physical appearance, she was still so young, not emotionally equipped to deal with such upheaval as Jeanne had served them all at tonight's meal.

Whatever is to be done next must be done without harm to anyone else.

Jeanne made the promise, turned, and exchanged Raol's full glass for Bernadette's now empty one, taking a sip of the warm, peppermint liquid, movement outside the door catching her eye.

A young couple standing shyly in the aperture, peering into the lavish room with eyes as large as a child's outside a confectioner's shop. Their clean but shabby attire proclaimed them as commoners; the apprehension on their faces told all they were lost. Within moments the two Swiss Guardsmen stationed in the room noticed the couple and approached, bowing politely. The soldiers asked, with great respect and courtesy, for the young people to leave.

Jeanne smiled at the contrary nature of her King, her world. She turned from the door, meaning to take Bernadette's place in her brother's arms, instead floundering in the face of the Baron and Baroness de Polignac now before her. They scrutinized her, frowning in confusion at the modest yet beautiful pink and pearl gown.

"Madame, monsieur." Jeanne plunged into a deep curtsey, unsure how to act or what to say to these people, almost sorry for the discomfort she'd caused them but having no wish to ingratiate herself.

Hearing no reply, she rose, only to find them gone, their backs hurrying away from her with nimble speed.

Jeanne's hand flew to her mouth, covering the wide smile as if to contain the great laughter bubbling in her belly.

"When you smile like that it's as if the sun has come out for a second time in a day."

Jeanne whirled, a tingle unnamed coursing through her. Henri stood but a foot away, devilishly handsome in black jacket and breeches trimmed in gold piping and buttons, white lace at collar and cuff. He wore a crooked smile upon his face and a twinkle in his golden eyes.

"It has been too long, mademoiselle." He whispered the words against the hand he held in his, lingering over her tawny skin.

"It has, monsieur." Jeanne curtseyed, though none too deeply for her quivering knees could not manage it. The music, the laughter, even the voices around them faded to naught more than a low hum; only they existed in this room. "I have not felt much like socializing of late."

"I am most pleased to find you back among the revelers. She would not have wanted you to stop living."

Jeanne stared into his kind face; how well he knew her yet knew her not at all. "You are quite right, sir. Lynette loved my spirit, though many times she struggled to contain it…and me."

Jeanne giggled and a soft blush rose to her cheeks. If she could but see herself through his eyes at that moment, she would—for the first time in her life—indeed believe herself beautiful.

"Who are you here with this evening?" he asked, adoration ill-disguised.

"My brother and sis—" Jeanne froze with her hand outstretched toward the dancers. In the middle of the group, a solitary figure stood still as a statue, staring at them with such intensity, Jeanne felt its burn on her skin.

Henri whirled to follow her frightened gaze with a quick flick of his head. There she was, the woman from that night, her face ablaze with recognition. His hand reached out, grabbing Jeanne before she launched toward the woman.

"But Margaux, she knows. We must—"

"*Oui,* she most certainly does." Henri whirled her around, their backs to the woman, rushing from the room, Jeanne in tow. At the large, delectable-crammed table in the Mercury Drawing Room, he placed tiny pastries on a small porcelain and gold plate. "This is disastrous, *ma chère.* I never wished for you to become so involved in this nasty business."

I would see this nasty business done, and by my hand. Jeanne saw his worried brow and swallowed back the thought. Did she hurt him as well, cause him the pain of worry? She and her dreams were a selfish beast devoured all.

"I love our Queen," she said no more than the truth but it served a poor, vague explanation. She dared a quick glance over her shoulder but did not see Margaux in the tumult of milling courtiers.

Henri nodded, a proud, shy smile forming under his mustache.

"I know. But you must be wary. You must be in fear for your own safety now."

I will gladly forfeit mine, if I may take hers with it. Jean-Luc said in her head.

"Be not wor—"

"Daughter," her father's voice barked from behind; Jeanne jumped. As the master of her future demise stepped around to face her, she dropped into a curtsey.

"Père, pray may I introduce you to Monsieur Henri d'Aubigne."

Jeanne rose, gesturing from father to friend. "Monsieur d'Aubigne, my father, the Comte de Moreuil."

Henri bowed deeply while Gaston silently glared at the young man.

"*Enchanté,* monsieur." Henri greeted the elder courtier cordially. "I am so pleased to finally make your acquaintance."

Gaston ignored Henri's outstretched hand, choosing instead to take his daughter by the arm and lead her away without word, nod, or acknowledgment.

"I hope we may meet again," Henri called, smiling at their retreating forms.

Jeanne looked over her shoulder, impelled by her longing for the man she left behind. Catching his glance, his spirited wink gave birth to her smile.

* * *

Her father had lost his meager purse many hands ago and had left the room in a huff, but Jeanne sat still, her own piles of gold and silver coins growing larger and larger in front of her. She tried desperately not to gloat outwardly, but the satisfaction in besting these haughty, judgmental courtiers provided her with a fiendish vindication reaching far beyond the reward of money.

In the Mercury Salon, what used to be the State Apartments before the King's new, grander suite of rooms was completed, the rules of etiquette were much more relaxed. Here everyone was allowed to sit with no need to rise for every Prince and Princess of the Blood when they entered the room, or even if the King and Queen were to stroll by.

At the table with Jeanne, absorbed in their game of lansquent, were some of the best card players at court. The Marquis de Dangeau sat across from Jeanne, while by her side perched the boisterous Marquise de Soissons, who would shout with joy whenever she won a hand. On her other side sat Mademoiselle de Cavois and the Marquis d'Heudicourt, the latter of whom Jeanne found especially repugnant. This elderly man, with his ragged wig, wrinkled and age-spotted face, and heavily decorated attire spit over his shoulder at any given moment without a care or consideration for anyone who might be so unfortunate as to be passing behind him at the time.

The gambling took place at every table in the chamber, mostly over cards, sometimes over dice. The oaths and cursing of the losers and the startling banging on the tables of the winners overrode the music of the small group of musicians tucked in a corner. Large sums of money changed hands; the loud exclamations announced the appropriate joy or sorrow. At the gaming tables, good manners and dignity were not required; one of the few places where the courtiers' perfect masks of gentility melted away, replaced by their true miens; dramatics abounded, losers shrieked and howled and threw themselves to the ground, cheating was not only accepted but expected.

Throwing down her cards, rejecting the bad hand, Jeanne studied those closest to her. Turning to her immediate left, she watched the Princess de Soubise at the next table. The pretty redhead, rumored to have slept with the King, leaned dramatically over the table, making to whisper something to the man across from her, allowing her vast bosom to spill from her bodice, drawing the attention of all the men, and even some of the women, while from beneath the table, the woman's long, thin hands drew cards out from their hiding spot in the bottom of her bodice. Jeanne chuckled silently, amused by the princess's audacity and daring.

At the other end of the room, two older but still beautifully regal women entered. Walking beside Madame La Marechale de l'Hopital, renowned for her jewelry, including the heavy strand of marble-sized pearls she wore this evening, came Madame de Beauvais. Not only had this elderly woman been a waiting woman to Queen Anne of Austria, Louis XIII's wife, but many believed she had seduced the King, Louis XIV, when he was but a teenager, taking his virginity. She still lived in one of the best suites of rooms in the palace and was treated with marked consideration whenever in the King's company.

Jeanne watched the humanity swirling all around her like an eddying pool of dank and dirty water, feeling as if she sat invisible in the middle of the circus. These were the real people in her world, and their true personas frightened and disgusted her.

Hour after hour the game dragged on. Stifling a yawn behind her hand, Jeanne studied the piles of coins on the table before her. The amount hadn't changed in many a hand; she seemed to be neither winning nor losing and wanted no more than to be gone from this place.

"Ladies and gentlemen, pray forgive me, but sleep pulls at me and I must excuse myself." Jeanne stood, pushed her chair in, and curtseyed to the hardcore gamblers still left at the table.

"Please do not go, mamselle," the Marquis de Dangeau pleaded with his smooth voice. "We would so miss your beautiful face."

"*Oui, oui*," the others at the table, including the two women, piped in.

Jeanne smiled with a nod and another shallow curtsey, but she knew it was the money she would take from them they would truly miss. "Perhaps another time."

With great reluctance the other players reached into their pockets, handing over the large sums owed to Jeanne, all save for Mademoiselle de Cavois. The attractive, voluptuous blonde, just a few years older than Jeanne, was a renowned rude snob whose greatest claims in life were how well she played cards and how often she had sex.

"I will walk with you, mamselle." Cavois rose from her chair and twined her arm in Jeanne's, all smiles and prattling politeness until they left the room and entered the quiet hallway.

"I fear I do not have your money." The manipulative woman hung her head in abject shame and overdone dismay, informing Jeanne she was penniless when she owed her close to ten thousand livres.

Such a surprise, Jeanne thought.

"Indeed, Mademoiselle de Cavois?" Jeanne's own sugar-sweet voice sounded as insincere as Cavois'.

"No, indeed," the woman replied, looking up hopefully. "But I will sell you my position as one of Madame de Montespan's second ladies."

How ironic, Jeanne thought, and how happy it would make her father; how easy it would be for Cavois.

With a dainty curtsey, Jeanne shook her head.

"I could never deprive you of such a prestigious position, dear Beatrice," Jeanne said, spreading her voice like thick frosting. "Pay me when you can. I know our friendship is worthy of trusting a debt."

Mlle. de Cavois stood speechless; to object would be completely inappropriate, but to be in debt to someone most considered a great embarrassment.

"Of course, Mademoiselle du Bois," Cavois said, her smile as fake as her sentiment. "It shan't be long, I assure you." With the shallowest of curtseys, the blushing woman turned back the way they'd come, perhaps to try her hand once more at the card tables.

With a sigh of relief, Jeanne turned and made her way slowly down the corridor to the stairs outside the Diana Drawing Room. In the muffled silence of the late-night/early-morning stillness, all the worrisome thoughts in Jeanne's head, those festering silently in her mind through the long hours of card play, rushed back in. She dragged her feet, her head held low, barely watching where she walked, barely hearing the sound of her own steps on the hard floors.

The hand came out of a corner's dark shadow and clamped down on Jeanne's mouth with ferocious strength. A second of still, stunned shock—then Jeanne began to struggle, fiercely, with all the strength she possessed. Her own hands flew to the ones accosting her, pulling and scratching at them for release. She tried to turn her head to face her molester, but he held her tight.

It was a man; he grunted deep and low as he fought to restrain her. She felt cold, smooth leather at her back, smelled the unclean, heavy odor of an unwashed male. She pushed down with her feet, trying to plant herself in the floor, trying to prevent him from taking her further. Picking her up, the man's own body shook back and forth as Jeanne began to kick her feet in the air, anything to find release. Her head hummed with the blood surging in her veins, her breathing heavy and hard out her nose and against the hand that still held her mouth so tightly.

"You are a feisty one—they warned me you were." The sickening snicker came close to her ear, and Jeanne felt his damp, hot breath on her skin, smelled the onions he must have eaten earlier in the day.

Her stomach lurched. She thought she would vomit, almost wished for it; surely that would make him release her. Instead, she fought to open her mouth, managing to separate her lips a couple of inches. Closing her eyes, she bit down on the hand across her face, bit and held until the acid-thick flavor of blood flooded her mouth.

"*Râler*!" The man screamed in pain.

He released Jeanne with the injured hand only to push her hard against the wall, her face to the marble, pinning her there with the other. "You will pay for that, my dear. *Oui*, you surely will. I have not been compensated enough to cover such abuses."

He pressed his whole body against Jeanne's. Pain ignited as her pelvic bones ground into the wall, his bones and extremities pressed against her back. She flayed her arms and kicked her feet; she knew his intent and would rather die than allow it. Jeanne longed for the feel of her sword in her hand; how she would make him pay with the power of the cold steel.

Twice she pushed him off her, but she gained no more than a step or two away when he captured her again, forcing her upon the wall once more. She heard a jangle and rustle behind her, felt his hands down near her waist.

Flattening the palms of her hands against the wall near her shoulders, she pushed with all her might, raised a leg, braced a foot against the wall to use her greatest strength, pushing him off her and against the opposite wall.

She ran, screaming in pain as he yanked her hair, jerking her head back, ripping some of the floss from its roots.

"No more!" the vile man yelled. Using his grip on her hair, he shoved her head against the wall, banging it with all the strength he possessed.

Jeanne's vision blurred, eyes rolling in their sockets; her spirit left the fight in her befuddled mind. As if from a distance, she heard the rip of her petticoats from under the bunched-up long skirts, felt the cold air on her exposed skin. The pull of unconsciousness called to her, and she meant to ride it.

The pressure from behind vanished so quickly she fell against the open, unsupported air it left behind. Falling to the floor, she landed on her back. Half-conscious, she watched the action above her.

Henri battled the miscreant, his beautiful face twisted in possessive, cold fury; he screamed it with every attack he made. The surprised knave was no match for such brutal strength; it felled him quickly to his knees. Henri did not hesitate before plunging his sword into and through the man's chest, pulling it out before his dead opponent fell to the floor in a lifeless heap.

For a moment Henri stood over the body, heaving and gasping for breath, body pulsing with barely contained rage.

Jeanne tried to sit up and wavered, almost falling back down but catching herself with shaking limbs. Henri rushed to her side; he threw his arms about her, embracing her so tightly all air rushed from her lungs. Grabbing her shoulders, he shoved her from him, looking closely at her face, grimacing at the tear in her lip and the bruise already forming on the side of her face.

Jeanne stilled in the calm of his touch.

"I knew when I saw your face I would be saved." Unbidden tears mixed with the blood on her face. "I was almost ravaged, almost … killed, yet I knew it would not happen. I know with you I am safe."

Jean-Luc had fought well; Jeanne had been no match for it. Jeanne gave Henri his due, her trust.

Henri's sweet smile touched his lips. Holding her face gingerly between his two hands, he covered every inch of the tender countenance with soft, fluttery kisses. "For a moment, when I thought you would die, it felt as though I might lose a part of myself, my soul."

Jeanne surrendered to his lips, his words of comfort, letting their succor wash over and heal her.

Henri stood, pulling her slowly to her feet. "Let me take you—"

The sounds of footsteps and laughter echoed through the corridor, around the corner. Henri shoved Jeanne behind him while drawing out his blood-encrusted sword.

The King stepped into the corridor, still dressed in full court attire of red velvet, a shockingly young, wickedly curvaceous brunette on his arm. His intelligent study took in every detail of the scene.

"What has happened here?" Louis demanded.

"Mademoiselle was attacked by this creature on the way to her rooms, Sire," Henri reported with a small bow. "I have … taken care of the situation."

Louis nodded, satisfaction blossoming on a quirk of his lips, keen gaze scouring them, their proximity to each other.

"Your aunt wishes you would spend more time at court. As you can see, you are much desired here." Louis' low timbre barely contained his chuckle.

"My duties as a lieutenant in your Musketeers keeps me quite busy, Sire," Henri replied, ignoring the mention of his aunt.

"Hmm, yes. Well, you've done a good bit of work this evening. It will be nice to see you at my lever in the morning, d'Aubigne."

It was no invitation, but a command.

"Of course, Your Highness. It would be my honor."

Jeanne heard the false authenticity in Henri's reply but doubted the King did.

Looking down at the dead body, Louis sniffed imperiously.

"Have it removed immediately."

Turning away, the King and his companion left the scene without any more ado, his hand firmly on her derrière.

"Yes, Your Majesty," Henri assured his sovereign with another bow.

Alone again, Henri turned back to Jeanne, supporting her with his strong arm, bringing her to the stairs leading to her rooms.

"This cannot be allowed to happen again."

Jeanne knew not to whom Henri hissed such words of determined aggression, her or himself; he could not know he spoke to Jean-Luc.

"We must end this."

~Twenty-Four~

Henri arrived at the antechamber to the King's bedroom at precisely five minutes to eight the next morning. With him, hundreds of other men filled the room and the corridor beyond. He stood with his arms crossed over his blue jacket, alone in the midst of the mayhem, wondering why he felt compelled to be there, other than the wish to escape the ire of his aunt, whose power at court increased with each passing day. She would be the first to know if Henri ignored the King's order.

"D'Aubigne? Is that really you?"

Henri turned as the firm hand grasped his shoulder. Two men of his age stood before him. Frederick de Gabrielle and Armand du Plessis had changed little in the years since the three of them had attended school together. Their sallow skin an outward sign of their indoor lives; the high wigs on men so young a symbol of their all-consuming ambitions.

"We haven't seen you in ages." Armand took his hand, pumping it with great spirit. Henri greeted his old acquaintances with equal politeness.

"Why are you never at court?" the taller Frederick asked.

"I prefer the battlefield and the company of the King's Musketeers," Henri replied with little affectation.

"But your aunt could secure you a privileged position, could she not?" One dark eyebrow rose up on Armand's pale forehead.

Henri smiled with little amusement in it and a shake of his head. "I would not impose upon my aunt in such a way."

Henri's two old friends shared a look of confusion; to not take advantage of every connection at court was unfathomable behavior. Their look of bewilderment became one of disdain. Henri was no player and never would be; without the courtesy of a nod of adieu, they turned to each other and began to talk of yesterday's hunt. Henri felt no slight. He smiled inwardly, grateful to these two men, whose abhorrent behavior confirmed Henri's own choices.

The large mahogany clock in the far corner of the room chimed the hour and like slowly released smoke, the whispering slithered through the room, announcing the beginning of the day.

"It is time."

The King's *Premiere Valet de Chambre* rose from his pallet in the King's antechamber and entered Louis' private room. Through the doors left wide open, Henri watched as this elderly man drew the blinds and snuffed the candles, coming to a stop by the large, gilded, canopied bed on the public side of the balustrade.

"Sire, it is the hour," La Porte said, waking the King as he did every morning.

As if on cue, the outer doors of the antechamber opened and the next act in the stringently choreographed dance of the lever began. In the portal stood an elderly woman who shuffled across the threshold, her frail body indistinguishable beneath her hooded cloak and on her piled hair a coif of lawn such as the peasants wore. Many of the nobles she passed bent their knee in respect; Madame Hamelin, the King's old nurse, still claimed the privilege to be the first to speak to the King each morning.

With slow but sure steps, Mme. Hamelin stepped behind the golden railing, drew back the red embroidered curtains surrounding the King's bed, leaning over Louis, who pretended sleep. With a gaze of love in her milky old eyes, Mme. Hamelin placed a kiss upon the King's forehead.

"Did you sleep well, Your Highness?" The elderly nurse's voice warbled.

Through the brocade curtains, Henri glimpsed one of the most genuine smiles he had ever seen on the King's face.

"I did, *ma chère*, thank you." Louis cooed. Largely ignored by his own mother, this woman had given the young Louis some of the only tenderness he had known as a child.

Louis rose from his bed, taking a drink from the cup of sage tea at his bedside, then knelt to say some quick prayers, oblivious to the growing activity at the edges of his room.

Behind Mme. Hamelin, the morning's procession began. Three doctors, including the King's First Physician and his First Surgeon, entered, all three men elaborately dressed in their enveloping black robes, long wigs of white curls, and tall, peaked hats belonging only to those of their vocation. After a cursory examination by all three men, the parade of nobles began.

The First Entrance, led by the Princes of the Blood, was fairly short. With barely an open eye and no inhibitions whatsoever, Louis strode to the corner, lifted his nightshirt, and relieved himself in his *chaise percée*. Nowhere was the lack of privacy more evident.

The Kings of France lived under the constant eye of their people; even here in what should have been a person's most private moment. The young and old men bowed to their sovereign as the Grand Chamberlain handed over the dressing gown, the one presented by the First Lord of the Bedchamber, to the King. With dressing gown in place, Louis gracefully pulled on his own hose, only to have a couple of high dignitaries kneel and fasten his bejeweled garters for him. They stood, the signal for the Second Entrance to begin.

Today Jules de Bourbon, the son of the Prince de Condé, led this larger group of courtiers, traditionally preceded by the First Nobleman of the Realm, the highest-ranking man in attendance each day. Not far behind him, Henri entered the room. From over his shoulder, he glimpsed Gaston du Bois a few steps behind; perhaps it was the heat of the man's displeased glare which made him turn. No doubt du Bois would be not only peeved to walk behind Henri, he would be indignantly inquisitive as to why.

How long can I keep my truth from Jeanne? How will it change us?

Henri could chew no more upon such thoughts; the Duc de Beauvilliers presented the King with his shirt, then the First Lord of the Bedchamber attached the right cuff while the First Lord of the Wardrobe attached the left.

The Third Entrance began to make their way in, line after line of barons and peers, bowing and scraping and bumping one another in their thirst to be in front and perhaps be the one bestowed with the honor of handing the King his waistcoat. The Fourth Entrance, including the Secretaries of State, quickly followed.

Louvois strode in before Colbert, though the older man retained seniority by greater rank as well as age. The Secretary of Finances moved much slower these days; he appeared wan, the skin on his round face pale and sagging around his deeply dimpled chin.

Any visiting ambassadors filled the Fifth Entrance, while the Sixth was by far the most colorful, made up of red cardinals and purple bishops. All the day's lever participants now filled the room, close to one hundred men, and the final touches were put to the

King's outfit. The Master of the Wardrobe fastened the King's jabot, then the Lord of the Neckcloths adjusted it.

Completely dressed, Louis bowed to the vast assembly before him, noticing every face, making a mental note of those whose faces he failed to see.

"How is your daughter?" Louis asked, passing the Duc de Vandreuil.

The older man snapped to attention as if he still served in the King's army, thrilled to be one of the few the King chose to speak with this morning, a privilege Louis doled out sparingly.

"She has married a fool, Sire," Vandreuil said matter-of-factly, pleased at the laughter crackling around him, rewarded by a nod and a smile from his sovereign.

Having made his way to the far corner of the room and the grand table awaiting him, Louis ate his breakfast of meager broth while his watchmaker wound the timepiece Louis wished to adorn himself with that day. The group of lookers-on shuffled their attention as the activities in the room increased. The *Porte-chaise d'Affairs*, the black-clad, sword-brandishing man who emptied the royal *chaise percée*, completed his morning mission. As the chamber pot exited by one door, another gentleman, carrying a wig, entered by the door in the north wall, from the ridiculously small chamber—a mere closet-sized area between the Bedchamber and the Council chamber, devoted solely to rooming the King's wigs. Under the watchful eye of Benet, the King's hairdresser, the rows of faceless plaster heads held the King's hair behind protective glass cases.

Later today the King would be washed, combed, and shaved as he was every other day by his personal barber, yet another of the King's five hundred attendants who received free rooms at Versailles as well as a stipend. But for now the formalities of the morning were over, and Louis dismissed all but his most inner circle of friends, those who would gather with Louis in his private chamber.

Henri and Gaston made it out of the antechamber at the same time.

Henri felt relieved, longing for his uniform and the company of his Musketeers. Other thoughts, new feelings of yearning, followed, ones he'd never before experienced.

How would it feel to have a home to go to, one with a welcoming wife, a woman like Jeanne who awakens both my mind and my body?

Henri stopped in his tracks, causing a domino effect in the congestion behind him. Never in his almost twenty years had he had such a fantasy. An astonished broad smile spread across his face.

* * *

Gaston quit the King's bedchamber with clipped strides, burning with envy. Again he was not among the exalted chosen ones still in the room with Louis. The lofty group planned the activities of the day, as they did every morning, but what else were they saying? Was his name ever mentioned? He was sure they never worried about losing their position at court. Marching through the antechamber, Gaston bumped into Henri, seemingly frozen in place.

"*Bonjour*, Monsieur du Bois." Henri greeted the father of the woman who had abducted his thoughts.

"*Bonjour*," Gaston replied gruffly, with no answering gentility.

Who is he? Gaston wondered again, not hesitating a moment to stop and ask.

~Twenty-Five~

Jeanne slithered through the castle, around to turn every corner, watchful to walk down every long corridor, but it was not another attack she feared, but Henri. If he found out her destination, his anger would be a terrible thing indeed. With a brand-new, prettily dressed doll in her hands, Jeanne headed to the quarters of Athénaïs and her children.

Jean-Luc's blood pumped in her veins; 'they' dared to see the face of the evil Margaux at the moment she realized Jeanne still lived, Margaux's conspiracy foiled. It would not serve any other purpose than to feast upon some smug self-satisfaction, perhaps a small consolation for the painful, makeup-disguised bruises; a consolation nonetheless, though it could bring upon them all crescendoing calamity.

Mademoiselle de Desoeilets, one of Athénaïs's attendants and a conniving woman not unlike her mistress, quickly admitted Jeanne into the lavish suite of rooms.

Jeanne approached Athénaïs, seated at a cherry-wood writing table, and dropped into a deep curtsey.

"*Bonjour*, Madame. You look especially well today," Jeanne greeted Athénaïs, scanning the room peripherally, searching the vast room and the many women in it for the face of her would-be assassin.

"Do I? Ah, *oui*, I most probably do." The King's mistress put a hand to her high-piled blond hair, the color of angel hair, bringing it slowly down her long neck, her full bosom, and onto her lap draped in rich green satin. Athénaïs turned with almost bored contempt in her stunning blue eyes. "I am surprised to see you here today, mamselle."

Jeanne swallowed the lump of skepticism in her throat. A true warrior always listened to their gut. From her first visit and what she'd overheard, Jeanne's speculations had always included Athénaïs as part of the dastardly plan that had almost taken Jeanne's life. Margaux could be working alone, wanting her mistress to sit on the throne to better her own position. Such a notion did not sit well in Jean-Luc's gut.

"I do not see why, Madame," Jeanne said with the same nasty sweetness so many courtiers used. "It has been several weeks since my last visit."

Athénaïs gave no permission for her to sit, forcing Jeanne to remain standing. Pushing back her shoulders and jutting out her chin, Jeanne stretched herself to her tallest, an imposing height for a woman. If forced to stand she would make the most of it.

"True." Athénaïs was all business this morning. "But I did not think we were to become close friends. You have not married, as I advised, and from what I hear, that may no longer be an option for you."

Thousands of souls lived upon the Versailles estate, yet theirs were lives merely for the purpose to amuse others, those endowed with the power to watch everyone and everything they did. Those like Athénaïs.

"Nothing is ever truly what it appears to be, don't you agree, Madame?" Jeanne would rather cut out her tongue than discuss the Polignacs with this woman.

Athénaïs did smile then, an odious, biting grin. "You've learned the ways of court quickly."

"I have had no choice," Jeanne responded, clasping her hands, one still holding the doll, smartly before her.

Eyeing the toy, Athénaïs gave it a nod. "Is that for me?"

"Oh, no, Madame." Jeanne looked down in surprise, having forgotten it, her ruse for being there, in the jungle of innuendo-thick conversation. "I've brought it for Françoise-Marie. There seemed to be a problem with her old one."

"Very well. They are in the nursery, but I am not sure if you will find them alone."

Jeanne saw the beautiful woman's jaw twitch and her eyes narrow; she waited in patient silence. Athénaïs would spew her anger any moment; she was famous for flying quickly into angry outbursts, with the King himself most often the victim. Many a porcelain statue ended in pieces, hitting the wall behind Louis after Athénaïs launched it at him. Fits of weeping quickly followed her tirades and he would gather her to him and bestowed his forgiveness.

"If she is there, then the King may be as well." The words hissed out from between the perfectly arranged, small white teeth.

"She, Madame?" Jeanne feigned ignorance.

"Françoise, who else?" Athénaïs shot her a look filled with all the hatred festering in her soul. "She loves nothing more than to spend hours and hours with them. With children. How completely preposterous."

Jeanne said nothing; she herself would love to do nothing more, especially with children of her own. Athénaïs maintained no fondness for youngsters, even her own.

Athénaïs stared out the window, into the distance of the gardens. "You know what I find highly amusing? I brought that woman into this palace. I actually had to force her to become our governess when Auguste was first born. She didn't want the position, and Louis did not like her. I made him order her to do it. And now … now…"

Silk and satin rustled behind them; Athénaïs's attendants strained to hear the conversation of their mistress and her visitor. The rising, screeching pitch of the woman's agitation roused them from their doldrums. Jeanne knew only seconds remained.

"And now?" she prodded, using Athénaïs's own anger to loosen her tongue.

"Now he spends more time with them—her and the children—than he ever does with me." Athénaïs banged her open palm down on the table top; a sharp slapping sound echoed through the still room. "She is naught but an intellectual cold fish who could never satisfy the great lust of the Sun King."

"Madame, would you care for some tea?" Heloise rushed to her mistress's side, fairly pushing Jeanne out of the way as she saw the volcano of Athénaïs's anger about to erupt.

Her words broke the possessing tantrum of the King's mistress. Athénaïs shook her head, eyes rolling. She looked sharply around, seeing Jeanne and the worried faces of her women staring at her. Athénaïs sat higher in her gilded chair and turned back to her parchment and quill.

"Take Mademoiselle du Bois to see the children, Heloise, and then get me some refreshments."

"*Oui*, Madame." Heloise curtseyed and led Jeanne away, gently though authoritatively, by the arm.

"*Merci*, Madame," Jeanne called back, but the gorgeous woman spared her not a second glance.

Heloise took Jeanne to the single side door and opened it. As Jeanne stepped into its threshold, she heard the double main doors behind her open and glanced over her shoulder. Bonds of anger and fear squeezed around her heart. The black-haired Margaux rushed up to Athénaïs, screeching to a halt as she caught sight of Jeanne.

Biting down hard on her tongue to keep from yelling out, Jeanne could not contain her actions; Jean-Luc ruled them. She pulled her arm from Heloise's, turned back to the room and Margaux, offering her a deep curtsey. Raising herself back up, she smiled into the bloodless, face of Athénaïs's attendant, a smile of satisfied vengeance.

With a deep sigh of contentment, Jeanne turned back to the guidance of Heloise.

"Thank you, kind woman," Jeanne thanked Heloise once on the other side of the door, "but I can find my own way to the nursery. Why do you not get Athénaïs something to drink? She looks as if she needs a little sustenance."

"*Merci*, mademoiselle." Heloise gave a shallow curtsey. "I think you are quite correct."

Jeanne moved as if to continue to the nursery; as soon as the woman rushed out, she jumped back, putting her ear as close to the cracks of the door as possible. At first, she heard only murmurs, the rumbling of voices, a jumble of incoherent words. Jeanne pushed one ear directly against the cold wood frame and closed the other with a pressing hand.

"It is true, Madame." Jeanne felt sure Margaux spoke. "The Queen has taken ill."

Jeanne almost gasped, controlling herself at the last minute.

"How long?"

Jeanne heard Athénaïs ask.

"Just a day, but they say it is serious," Margaux answered.

"Well, well," Athénaïs said snidely; Jeanne could picture the audacious smile forming on the woman's lips. "Perhaps God will do what we seem unable to."

* * *

I must be mad, I must. The thought burned a path through his mind as he walked out of Versailles' side front gate and onto the Place d'Armes. Bowing to the porter who held it open, he kept his head down, sure he would recognize the other face behind the mustache. Though the wide brim of the felt hat cast a long shadow across determined features, Jean-Luc feared detection more than ever before, though he walked without thinking, swaggered naturally. To walk in full daylight beckoned recognition and apprehension with open arms, but to walk the streets alone as Jeanne was impossible.

He needed to tell Henri and the others about Athénaïs; he had no choice.

Though autumn fluttered in on every other breeze, the sun still burned hotly in the late September sky. As many people congested the streets as during high summer.

Zigzagging through the avenues around the chateau, sidestepping the scores of familiar noble families roaming through them, it took twice as long as usual to arrive at the Hôtel Treville only to find not a one of his friends in attendance.

Back out on the streets, he ran to the Café de l'Oiseau. Drenched in perspiration, frustration was all to be found in the dim but empty room. Accepting a moisture-laden mug of ale, Jean-Luc chugged it down in one gulp, tossed a coin at the serving wench, running back out into the blinding light of midday.

Where the deuce are they? Jean-Luc wracked his mind, walking a circle in the narrow cobbled street in front of the café. With a snap of gloved fingers, he knew, took off like a loosed arrow, running back in a northerly direction.

He heard them before he saw them; the shing and clang of swords, the grunt of men exerting themselves. Rounding the corner of the tall, old flagstone building of the Pré aux Clercs, the awe-inspiring sight panned out like a magnificent play.

At least ten pairs of duelists fought in the courtyard with the circular well in the center. Dressed in only fine lawn shirts and breeches, the men were intent upon each other, upon honing their craft. Since the day of Louis XIII, fencing had become an obsession for the men of France, and nowhere was it more evidently displayed.

The beautiful foils sparkled in the sun, sending out bright reflections bursting in the air like shooting stars as they clashed against each other. Espying Henri, Jean-Luc sidled right to get closer to him, to watch his manner and technique.

His was an aggressive style, determined to gain control at the onset and keep it. The words spoken in one of Moliere's plays defined it to perfection.

The whole art of fencing consists of just two things, to hit and not to be hit.

Henri commanded this skirmish. He lunged, flung back, beat, reposted. His feet moved so fast, they blurred, denying detection. With one more advance, a graceful lunge, Henri pinned his opponent to the ground; the beaten man dropped his sword and raised his arms in surrender.

Henri's lips spread in a wide smile and he reached down to help his defeated adversary to his feet.

"You will get me next time, Roussier." Henri clapped the man on his back, who merely nodded, rubbing his behind as he limped off the field.

"Well, look who has come to join us." Henri's eyes lit on Jean-Luc and he jogged over to where his friend stood against the wall of the convent. Breathing a little heavily, sweat pouring in rivulets down his face, Henri put his sword in its scabbard, and removed his shirt, using it to mop the perspiration off his face.

The sight of Henri's naked torso stole Jeanne's breath, her thoughts, her words. Tongue expanded to inhuman proportions; it felt like a wad of cotton in a suddenly dusty mouth. She tried to speak but nothing more than a few strangled grunts emerged. She knew she should blink but couldn't.

Jean-Luc gave Henri a graceful leg while Jeanne fought for composure.

"Pick a partner." Henri appeared oblivious to Jean-Luc's discomfort, drawing out a beckoning arm to the many men in the stone courtyard. "Any one of them would be honored to face such a fine blade as yourself."

Jeanne drank in the hard, golden flesh of Henri's chest, the tight, well-defined muscles, the moisture as it ran in caressing streams down his ribs, over the firm swells of his abdomen and down even farther, under his belt.

"*Merci*, monsieur, but I cannot stay." Jean-Luc pulled his hat down low, hoping Henri would not see the fire burning as Jeanne ravaged his body with her mind. He meant to tell him of what 'Jeanne' had learned, but it was impossible to stay, to be near him in this way. "Jeanne has sent me."

The name stilled Henri. "Is she well?"

"She is fine, but she needs to see you. She wonders if perhaps you could spare her some time today." Jean-Luc looked up, then quickly away.

"I would spare her a lifetime," Henri replied. "Tell her to meet me this evening at our place in the South Parterre at the onset of the *Couvert*. It is the best time for a private conversation."

Unseen with any gaze, 'Jeanne' smiled. *Our place*—Henri's words hummed like the most magnificent of songs.

"Ten o'clock in the South Parterre." Jean-Luc nodded. "I will tell her."

Henri grabbed for Jean-Luc's hand and pumped it. "Thank you, friend."

"My pleasure," Jean-Luc responded, though Henri had no idea just how much of a pleasure it was. With a tip of his hat and one last, longing glance to Henri's alluring torso, Jean-Luc hurried back to Versailles.

* * *

Her feet sprouted wings as she rushed from the north side vestibule exit, across the *Cour de Marbre* and back in at the vestibule to the Queen's Staircase. Instead of climbing, Jeanne opened a side ground-floor door and peered inside into the Dauphine's first antechamber. Finding it empty as usual, she tiptoed through the opulent sitting room and left the chateau once more through the garden door. The promise of a storm thickened night air; the distant rumblings foretold the coming of cold autumn air determined to take its rightful place over the stubborn, lingering summer heat. Dark clouds, full and ripe, hung overhead and a coppery odor dwelled below them. Running down the length of the palace's main building, she took a quick left at the corner and, with a few quick steps, came to the South Parterre.

Jeanne stopped, smoothing her skirts, tucking in a few wayward strands of hair. Placing a hand just below her breasts, her heart slamming against her ribs. She took a steadying deep breath, another, centering herself as her uncle had taught her to do when first gripped by the panic of battle. For she entered a fray, of this she was sure, but of a completely different nature.

Strolling into the Orangery, the pungent scent of the full trees overwhelmed and invigorated her, reminding Jeanne of the first time they were there, the first time they danced.

"Jeanne."

The flutter of a whisper hovered on the breeze. Her skin prickled merely at the sound of his voice, it flowed over her like cleansing, cool water. Turning to the right, she entered a slim, torch-lit avenue cut through the redolent trees. There he stood, just before the entrance to one of the gardener's outbuildings, his silhouette strong and broad against the light stone.

He saw her, moved toward her, his shoulders and hips moving with that distinctive manly, sensual grace. He wore naught more than shirt and breeches, and her eyes traced the outline of his muscles through the thin cloth.

In a few long strides, Henri stood before her. Without a word he took both of her hands and raised them to his lips. His kisses covered each knuckle, his golden eyes never leaving hers. Jeanne became a fluid being beneath his touch.

"You are most kind to meet me." She dared not speak louder than a whisper, for surely any loud sound would break the magic of this moment.

One corner of Henri's mouth rising higher than the other, the joy of his grin infesting his entire face. "I will meet with you any day, every day, whenever and wherever you say."

Jeanne blushed at his words, his gaze. A curl dropped from her coiffure, landing along her neck. Henri reached to it, the back of his hand brushing her skin as he stroked it for a moment, the pleasure rolled through Jeanne's body. With extreme gentleness, he put the plait back down. Jeanne reached up as if to fix it, but his hand stopped her.

"Leave it, please." His voice, so low and husky, sounded more than human.

Jeanne did not have the strength to bear her desire for him. She had never suffered such want, and she did not know what to do with it. She longed only to surrender to it and forget everything else, for nothing else mattered in comparison. But she must think clearly, for a few moments at least. She must tell him of Athénaïs.

"Athénaïs tries to kill the Queen, I am now completely sure of it," Jeanne blurt, sobering them both like the drench of a cold rain.

"Tell me."

She did, everything she had heard and seen in the chambers of the King's mistress. Henri walked a small circle of concentration. "The others must be told. We must put a watch upon the Queen, Athénaïs, as well as Margaux. But first..."

He mumbled. Did he talk to her or himself; she could not discern.

"But first, I want you away from here."

"What do you mean?" Jeanne stepped back, fearful of his rejection.

Henri reached for her, pulling her into his strong arms. "I could not bear to lose you, not now, not ever." He looked into her huge brown eyes. "They will come for you, they must. She is aware of your knowledge. She cannot allow you to live."

Jeanne turned her head from him, shaking it stubbornly. "I will not leave the Queen." Neither she nor Jean-Luc would relent. Looking back to him, all the strength went from her. "I cannot leave... you."

Henri ravaged her face with his gaze; with a gasp of breath, his lips devoured hers.

Jeanne gave sway to him, to the soft heat of his mouth, tender yet commanding. Never before had she relished being subservient to a man, but for this, she would gladly allow it. The attack of sensual pleasure hit her from every side: his mouth on hers, on her face, on her neck. His hands on her back, manipulating her flesh, pulling and squeezing it, as his own desire overwhelmed him. His body pressed against hers, his hard chest, his powerful thighs. She grabbed his head as it lowered to her chest, held on as if her life depended on its succor. She heard him moan, and her head fell back on her neck. Her hands flowed down his back, caressing the hardness just below the veil of soft shirt. His lips and tongue drew lines of fire across the tops of her breasts.

And then it stopped.

Jeanne panted into the empty air. Dumbstruck, she searched his face, finding him blighted.

"Have I ... do I displease?"

Henri laughed, a loud, manly guffaw.

"I have never felt so ... pleased," he assured her with words and once more with his mouth upon hers. "But it would not be honorable for us to continue."

Jeanne's brows furrowed, staring at his lips; they looked as red and raw as her own felt.

"Must we be honorable?"

Henri laughed again, pulling her hard against his chest. "You are a woman unlike any I have ever known. Yes, we must be honorable, for I am going to ask your father for your hand, and I will do so with true respect."

Jeanne pushed him away, shocked and incredulous.

"He will never agree."

"We will make him agree."

Toe to toe they stood, of almost equal height and assuredly of equal strength. Slowly a smile crept onto her face. Thunder roared above them in the starless sky, the sound closer than ever. Henri raised a hand to her.

"Come, my love, I will get you back before the rain comes."

~Twenty-Six~

Henri paced about the antechamber, the room empty save for the two Swiss Guards who stood at attention by the doors. He pulled absently on the cuffs of his best shirt, one trimmed with the finest Venetian lace. His royal blue, tailored jacket felt tight as if it squeezed the air from his lungs, he longed to unbutton the silver tongs from their silver braid bindings. The *lever* he attended yesterday had seemed long; today's seemed interminable.

Henri waited for Jeanne's father who was once again in attendance, determined to speak with him before the day aged beyond infancy, but he had no desire to attend the actual ceremony again. He wondered if this silent waiting was not more of a torture than the mundane absurdity of the function. It gave him too much time alone with his thoughts, rehearsing what he planned to say to Monsieur du Bois over and over again in his mind, words he had conceived and practiced since leaving Jeanne at her door the night before.

Henri felt the sweat break out on his scalp and doffed the blue felt hat from his head. He ran a hand through his long, golden hair, wreaking havoc upon his curls, and shoved his hat back down upon them. How bad would the comte's reaction be? Surely if the man's intention was to rid himself of his daughter through marriage, would he truly care to whom he gave her?

The doors burst open and a wave of men flowed from it with loud release. Henri jumped to the side, craning for a glimpse of the short man he sought.

"Monsieur du Bois?" he called, rising on tiptoe and waving an arm toward Gaston when he finally glimpsed him through the throng of men.

Gaston turned at the mention of his name, but at the sight of Henri, his already garrulous countenance scrunched in anger and he kept walking as if no one had called to him at all.

"Monsieur du Bois, I must speak with you." Henri refused to be daunted by the slight. Using his long legs to his advantage, he weaved his way through the lines of men leaving the King's bedchamber and arrived at the comte's side with just a few steps. A flick of the older man's eyes told Henri that Gaston knew he was there, but he didn't stop, didn't acknowledge his company.

"Please, monsieur, it is of the greatest importance." Henri stayed by Gaston's side, step for step as they quit the antechamber, heading through the guardroom, but still, a red-faced Gaston gave no acknowledgment.

Henri's patience ran thin; the rudeness of the man slapped like a hand to the face, one he found difficult to turn a cheek to. Instead, he raised his voice.

"I wish to ask permission to marry your daughter."

The boisterous declaration brought Gaston to a standstill, silencing many of the men around them as well.

"My daughter... will marry Percy de Polignac." The muscles of Gaston's splotchy face twitched, eyes narrowing to slits.

"She does not love him, monsieur," Henri replied softly.

"I do not care one whit," Gaston said with frigid coldness.

"Monsieur," Henri spoke kindly as he took Gaston gently by the upper arm and led him out of the path of the exiting courtiers, closer to the windows that looked down upon the *Cour de Marbre.*

"You wish your daughter gone from court and wed to a well-positioned family. I can make all that a reality for you."

Gaston looked at Henri with sheer contempt in his incredulous expression, removing his arm from Henri's hand with a flare of his nostrils and a curl of his lips.

"I do not even know who you are."

"I am—"

"Stifle yourself, young man." Gaston raised a hand to Henri's face. "I have no wish to hear another word out of your lying mouth."

"Upon my word, you insult me, sir," Henri snapped, all hopes of convivial discussion gone in the face of this difficult man's effrontery.

To be abrupt and rude was one matter; to call Henri's honor into question quite another. "Beware of what you say and to whom you say it," Henri warned with a grumbling whisper full of the promise of malice, leaning down toward the odious man.

"You are nothing," Gaston spat in his face, his anger beyond his control. "My daughter will marry whom I say...because...I...say...it"

"You obviously have a much higher opinion of yourself than does the court." Henri almost bit his tongue, ashamed at himself for stooping to Gaston's vile, knowing that, to men such as this, their position was all that mattered. The older man's hands curl into fists, rigid and trembling with anger. Would Gaston dare to strike him?

"I will ruin you, monsieur." Gaston's face burned livid.

Henri saw this man, truly saw him as he existed, a slave to his inner beast, a soul to whom hate was the blood keeping it alive. Henri would do anything not to become one of them.

"I have the undying love of one whom he loves." Henri had had enough of niceties, he menaced. "Who do you think our King will listen to?"

Gaston's black eyes stared into Henri's golden ones; for the flash of a moment, Henri saw them flinch with uncertainty. Without another word, Gaston turned on his high leather heels and strode away.

Henri stood alone at the window, watching the last few *lever* attendees depart the area, still stricken by the violence of the last few short minutes.

"That went well," he berated himself.

* * *

Jeanne needed something to occupy her; these plodding minutes of waiting and wondering were intolerable. Her thoughts bounced from what took place between Henri and her father to what she would tell the Queen when she paid her a visit this afternoon.

Marie-Thérèse still suffered a lingering malaise, and though her life did not seem to be in danger, she took little part in the court's activities, only receiving visitors for a few hours each afternoon. Jeanne needed to fill the hours until then with something distracting or she would surely lose what little sanity she still possessed.

Her mind jumped between the two crashing events in her life: who would she marry, and would she end up in the Bastille? Would Jean-Luc and Henri save the Queen or would evil reign? Each passing moment her body surged with adrenaline, knowing full well the smallest turn of events could change the rest of her life forever.

In search of relief, Jeanne went looking for her uncle hoping for another lesson, wishing to lose himself to the feel of the sword and the challenge of the duel, but he had taken the girls to Paris for a few days. Her mother and sister had left just a few moments ago for a walk in the gardens, and Jeanne decided to join them, thinking of nothing else to distract her, to relieve her of the gnawing anxiety writhing so deep in her gut.

She ran from her apartment, down the stairs, and along the north wall. Entering the Hall of Mirrors, intending to exit the chateau from the Peace Drawing Room, Jeanne skidded and slid. The line of people waiting to get in to see the King in his Council Chamber snaked the inner wall's entire length. Thursday, of course. Moving against the tide of the crowd, she offered a smile or a bob of her chin to those friends and acquaintances within the swarm.

Bodies swayed and shifted around her, all save one.

The Vicomte du Ludres, Olympe's husband, made no attempt to disguise his lascivious perusal of her with complete disregard that she was his wife's best friend. In his high white wig and his bright yellow embroidered jacket and breeches, he looked quite the dandy—his intent, no doubt. Jeanne made a curtsey to his leg and rushed out of the room, a new destination in mind. At the far back of the line, it would take the vicomte hours of waiting for his turn to see the King. Jeanne would not let the time go to waste.

Rushing out to the *Cour de Marbre*, the sun seemed far brighter after the gloom of the indoors. The heavy clouds that had brought last night's rain and this morning's cooler temperatures broke apart and separated in the deep azure sky. Through the cracks between them, the bright sun streamed down with visible distinction, as if God had sent the bright rays from his own hand, splaying them out in the sky like the veins of a fan.

"Monsieur, monsieur," Jeanne cried as she reached the end steps of the courtyard, waving one hand in the air, desperate to catch the attention of a chair driver, while shielding her blinking, watering eyes with the other.

One of the small, single-manned wheelchairs drew up to her quickly, and without the usual polite banalities, Jeanne jumped onto the unadorned, fabric-covered chair.

"To the Chateau du Ludres. Quickly, monsieur, *s'il vous plaît.*"

Most often used for leisurely transport to town and back, these vehicles were not for those in a hurry. Jeanne squirmed, growing frustrated with the driver's leisurely pace. She knew the vicomte would be occupied for some hours to come, yet the compulsion to hurry—an unknown, unnamed fear—nagged at her. She fairly threw the *louis* to the driver upon arrival at Olympe's home, rushing to the door to knock insistently upon it.

Agonizing minutes passed until the door inched open; in its cleft, the expressionless countenance of a silent and smug *maître d'hôtel,* who offered her no greeting of any kind.

"I am here to call upon the Vicomtesse du Ludres." Jeanne forced her way past the stony butler to stand in the foyer. "I am her dearest friend, Jeanne du Bois."

"I will see if Madame is available," the valet said with a disdainful, barely perceptible bow.

Left alone under the vestibule's cathedral ceiling, Jeanne ticked off the passing seconds with a tap of her foot, shoving her hands upon her hips, her arms out akimbo.

Why was this huge house so quiet? Surely Olympe had heard her voice, would be thrilled to see her. Above Jeanne's head, the picture of the centaurs molesting the maidens taunted her; she crossed her arms tightly against her chest as if to stave off their evil bearing. She could stand it no longer.

Without waiting for the butler to return, Jeanne ascended the winding stairs, taking them as fast as her heavy-skirted legs would allow. Scouring her mind for the memories of the chateau's arrangement from her one other visit, Jeanne slipped swiftly down to the end of the long, narrow hallway and thrust open the door she thought was Olympe's boudoir.

Her friend lay stretched out upon a settee, barely moving, a thin linen cloth veiling her face, awash in muted light oozing out from behind the drawn, heavy lavender curtains.

"Olympe?" Jeanne whispered, having no wish to disturb her if her friend slept.

"Huh? What?" Olympe jolted up, the cloth slipping from her face.

"*Mon Dieu!*" Jeanne cursed and rushed to Olympe. The woman's face, one of such astounding beauty, was but a ghost of itself; huge dark circles surrounded sunken eyes; pointy cheekbones jutted from hallowed, gaunt skin. Tears clogged Jeanne's throat as she threw herself on the divan by her friend's side.

"What?" Jeanne asked, not needing to ask whom. "What does he do to you? Why?"

Olympe shook her head feebly. "I'm not really sure."

Jeanne went to the sideboard, doused the cloth in a basin of cool water, and brought it back to her friend. Forcing Olympe to lie back down, Jeanne applied the damp material gently to her friend's forehead and studied her. Olympe's ravaged face appalled, scarred by fear and torture, her grooming nearly as shocking. She wore no dress, only a wrinkled dressing gown over corset and petticoats. She wore no makeup; her lustrous black hair hung in stringy tresses haphazardly about her head.

"Tell me." Jeanne waited, watched Olympe's face twist in anguish, the tears slide out from her closed lids.

"He likes it...sex...rough. It would seem he always has."

"When did it start?" Jeanne stroked her friend's face, love and mercy in each touch, yet in her heart...in his heart...there blazed violent anger. Jean-Luc had killed before; to do so again would be of no consequence.

The image came, sure and swift, Jean-Luc in his leathers, a bloodied sword grasped in a gloved hand, standing over the inert body of Olympe's husband.

For Jeanne, such thoughts—such actions—should not, could not be. For Jean-Luc, it would be but another honorable action, another act to protect a woman in need of it.

The two who resided in the one body took turns more and more of late.

"On my wedding night." Olympe lips quirked with bitter irony. "The night I had so longed for and dreamed about my whole life."

"Real life is never like our dreams," Jeanne consoled.

Olympe laughed, taking Jeanne's hand to still its motion. "You were right, you know. No position, no prestige, is worth ... this."

"You must leave him." Jeanne stared with deadly intent at her friend.

"Where would I go?" Olympe shrugged her shoulders helplessly.

Jeanne looked at Olympe and her helpless expression, remembering well the lost feeling of despair when she had contemplated running away. A thought possessed her, and a timid smile spread across her wide mouth.

"You will come live with me," she announced to Olympe, almost laughing in relief. "With me and my husband."

Olympe looked sideways at her friend with a tilt of one skeptical brow. "I do not think Percy de Polignac would have the backbone to protect me from Lothair when he comes looking for me, which I assure you he would."

Jeanne pursed her lips in distaste. "I am not marrying that fraud of a man. I intend to marry Henri, Henri d'Aubigne."

Olympe pulled the cloth away from her face, sunken eyes piercing the depths of the friend before her. One corner of her mouth twitched upward. "What have you been about?"

Jeanne smiled, pure and wide. "Lay back, *ma chère*, and I will tell you a story."

* * *

Wrapped tightly in their friendship, time slipped by unnoticed by as Jeanne's words spun her tale of adventure and love. They shared the moments greedily, holding them close between them, filling them with their laughter, their tears, their love. Jeanne lay down beside Olympe, hands clasped in shared conspiracy. Many a time Olympe gasped, covering her heart or her mouth in complete shock at Jeanne and Jean-Luc's experiences, yet in those vicarious moments, she forgot all about her own hideous destiny.

"Upon my word, you astonish me," Olympe cried as Jeanne's story carried them to this moment. "What will you do if your father denies the match?"

"That I do not know." Jeanne rose from the lounge, straightening her tangled skirts, and crossed the room to the window, pushing back the curtain to stare at the garden behind the house. "I suppose it will depend on Henri. I would be willing to gainsay my father's demands, but I am not sure if he would."

Olympe rose slowly, stepping behind her friend, putting her arms firmly around Jeanne's shoulders. "Oh, he will, *ma chère.* I have seen the way he looks at you. That kind of love knows no limitations."

Jeanne brought her hands up to Olympe's arms and smiled against them, willing their convictions to turn destiny in the proper direction. Olympe giggled softly in her ear.

"What is so funny?" Jeanne implored, grateful to hear the joyous sound from her tortured friend.

"I am happy," Olympe whispered, and in her laughter, tears mingled. "You will marry for love. One of us will live free."

~Twenty-Seven~

The rumble of so many voices echoed merrily within the stone enclosure of the Queen's Staircase, and the tang of fall flowers, the bright mums and tall sunflowers, replete in the air. Jeanne slowly wound her way through the stalls and stands, giving a cursory look at the goods displayed.

Jeanne wished to buy Olympe a gift, a silly token of the promise standing between them. Her life with Henri would be a reality, not only for the love she felt for him, and the not inconsiderable lust as well, but also to make a family, one to include Olympe. She would not suffer another such loss; it was inconceivable. She had not saved Lynette, she would Olympe. She would save Jean-Luc as well.

Passing a row of basket goods sellers, a particular face caught her attention; Jeanne slowed down to take a good look at the young woman. Jeanne had not seen the girl here before, but she knew the merchant from somewhere.

A hearty blare of raucous male laughter came from the small legion of men perusing the wares, and with the sound came Jeanne's recollection. The dark-haired young woman was one of the serving wenches at the Café de l'Oiseau.

"What is her name?" Jeanne muttered to herself. "Ah, yes, Philonade. Even her name is ill-suited to a lascivious place like that."

The young girl had made quite an impression on Jean-Luc, for unlike the other wenches, this girl shunned the bawdy attention of the male clientele. She wore more modest attire; of poor quality yet always clean, never skin-hugging tight or with a bodice so low her nipples peeked out of the top. Philonade possessed self-respect; Jeanne recognized it in her manner. It was a quality in short supply among women in this brazen, flamboyant, shock-oriented society. Even the men responded to her self-possession, treating her with courteous approbation instead of lustful coarseness. It would seem her firm self-worth was a tool she wielded with great success. Jeanne only wished other women of her world would comport themselves as did Philonade. Perhaps then all of her gender would garner the homage they deserved.

Jeanne watched the young, dark woman, admiring her for her courage and her demand for respect. At that moment, Philonade looked up and saw Jeanne staring at her. Jeanne offered her a shy smile, surprised when no like answer came.

She knows only Jean-Luc.

Jeanne turned, intent once more on her destination.

"Some flowers for the mademoiselle?" Philonade stood right next to her, holding out her basket, pushing it before Jeanne as her dark eyes flicked again and again over her shoulder.

"I will—"

Metal clanging against metal suddenly filled the vestibule, a contingent of Swiss Guards marching righteously in their direction; understanding came with them.

Philonade most probably held no license to be there, a privilege exceedingly difficult to gain these days unless one had enough money to bribe the proper officials. New but not ignorant, Philonade knew, as did Jeanne, that if she sold just one piece of her goods to a person of noble birth before being turfed out, a license would perforce be given a permanent license.

Jeanne knew the yearning to be something else…to be something more than what one had been born to; oh yes, she knew that hunger well. With great pleasure, Jeanne turned back to the needful woman and, with a quick wink of assurance, reached into the small pouch hanging from her belt. Moving quickly, Jeanne pulled out two *ecrues* and pressed them into Philonade's palm.

Philonade's dark eyes became large circles in her petite face, eyes that flicked from her hand to Jeanne's smiling face. She closed her fingers tightly over her prize, the knuckles whitening in her fierce grasp. With a smile of joyful relief, Philonade grabbed a small cache of herbs wrapped in embroidered linen and thrust them into Jeanne's waiting hand.

"For head pains, mademoiselle," Philonade said. Bending her knee, she offered Jeanne a small curtsey accompanied with pooling tears. "I thank you with all my heart."

"It is my greatest pleasure," Jeanne replied happily.

The metal clanging grew louder and louder, finally stopping with military precision. The Swiss Guards stood behind them, the white, flounced neck ruffs bright in the shadows of the portico. Leading them, a red-faced Monsieur Dremont, the official who made a fine living off the extortion he perpetrated upon those desperate to improve their lives by becoming a merchant of the court. From such penniless, comely women as Philonade, he received other, more fulfilling payments.

The man's fury shrouded him, radiating from a pox-marked face. He'd witnessed the whole exchange between Jeanne and Philonade. His outrage blistered from him; Jeanne's actions forced him to give this newcomer a license. There would be no payment, none of the monstrous sums he usually received, nor the affection of one so young and pretty.

"*Bonjour*, monsieur." Jeanne curtseyed with her brightest smile.

"Mademoiselle du Bois." M. Dremont tipped his head ever so slightly, the words slithering out from between clenched teeth.

Jeanne turned her back on the inflamed man and began the climb up the marble stairs leading to the Queen's suite of rooms.

"Come with me, young woman." M. Dremont's voice boomed against the stone walls of the foyer. "I will give you your papers."

Jeanne tried but couldn't help stealing a quick look over her shoulder and the marble balustrade. Philonade walked behind M. Dremont, her face glowing bright with triumph, nodding her head at the many merchants she passed who called out their congratulations.

Jeanne shared the triumph; not only had she changed Philonade's life irrevocably, but she had changed as well the direction of the lives of all of Philonade's descendants for decades to come. A good day's work indeed.

* * *

Two of Henri's friends stood guard in the corridor leading to the inner Guard Room of the Queen, soldiers never before posted there; Jeanne had no doubt they were there by Henri's instructions.

She entered the antechamber, and M. de Villemont rose quickly from his perch behind the paper-strewn desk in the corner and gave her a leg.

"Mademoiselle du Bois, how wonderful to see you again."

"And you, sir." Jeanne curtseyed. "How is our Queen doing? May I have a visit?"

M. de Villemont shook his head, his bushy gray brows knitting on his wrinkled forehead. "She still ails, I am afraid. She is taking visits, but only a few at a time. Right now the Duchesse de Lorraine and the Marquise de Villeroi are with her. Would you mind terribly to wait for them to depart?"

"Of course not," Jeanne replied ingenuously. "Is my mother in attendance at this hour?"

"No, mamselle, she will be here later in the day."

"Very well." She bowed her head to the dear, older man, always such a good friend to her Maman. "Go back to your work, good man. I will be patient."

Jeanne stood quietly before the high windows, looking out over the back of Versailles. Looking past the gardens, her gaze wandered to the plots of strawberry patches and pear trees all the way to the crops of wheat, making the earth shimmy like the ocean as the crème-colored stalks moved in graceful waves at the pull of the wind.

Will our gardens be as grand and plentiful? Jeanne wondered, thoughts always on Henri and the promise of the life she held on to, a talisman to keep her safe. *We must resolve this dilemma with the Queen, and then we will leave and never return,* she promised both her selves then turned quickly on her heels as the inner door opened and two grandly plumed elderly women made their way out of the Queen's bedchamber.

Jeanne dropped quickly into a deep curtsey and stayed so inclined until the noblewomen made their way out of the antechamber as well.

"Come, mademoiselle," Villemont called to her, holding open the door to Marie-Thérèse's private chamber.

"Thank you," Jeanne whispered and entered the darkened room.

Drawn curtains denied the light, most of it; only thin streams of muted sunshine sneaked their way past the heavy fabric. Dust motes swam in the rivers of light, undisturbed in the still room. In the far corner, two women sat quietly, embroidery in their hands as they took a stitch then glanced at their mistress. Jeanne smiled and bowed her head at the Marquise de Laigues and the Duchesse La Combalet, two of the Queen's other attendants, and tiptoed her way to the Queen's balustrade.

From behind the gilded rail, Marie-Thérèse sat propped up on a pile of plush pillows, looking smaller than ever in the large canopied bed with its layer after layer of comforters, quilts, and linens.

Seeing Jeanne peering at her over the balustrade, a faint smile blossomed upon the Queen's wan face. With a fluttering, limp hand, Marie-Thérèse beckoned for her young friend to enter the sacrosanct enclosure of her bed area. With a deep curtsey, Jeanne crossed the room to the far end where an opening in the rail offered her entry into the exclusive space. Jeanne approached the bed and curtseyed deeply once more.

"How lovely to see you." No more than a low whispered croak, the Queen's voice crackled and wheezed. "Please sit and visit for a few minutes."

Jeanne sat in the small gold-gilded bedside chair upholstered in fabric of crème and embroidered with pink, yellow, and blue flowers of varying shapes and sizes, the same fabric repeated on every piece of furniture and every wall of the room.

"Have the doctors been to see you today, Your Highness?" Jeanne frowned, studying the sickly countenance of her Queen.

"Oh, fey upon doctors." Marie-Thérèse shrugged her slim shoulders and turned away. "They come every day, and every day they do the same things, say the same things, and yet I get no better."

"I am sure they do their best," Jeanne assured her, taking the Queen's childlike hand in her own, rubbing the thin skin gently. "Is it your regular physicians who attend you?"

Marie-Thérèse turned back to Jeanne with a puzzled frown.

"But of course, *ma petite*, and the King's physicians come as well. As does Louis. He comes every day…now."

Jeanne faked a smile through the wave of sadness; that she should find such happiness that her philandering husband deigned to visit her sickbed every day was morose, pathetic. She listened quietly, trying to keep her expression blank as the Queen told her of the sympathetic attentions of the King. The Queen's eyes began to close, her eyelids drawing together with greater frequency, lingering upon each other longer and longer.

"It was wonderful to see you. You are most kind for visiting me," Marie-Thérèse mumbled, voice but a ghost of itself. "But I think I shall take a rest now."

"Of course, Your Highness." Jeanne rose but made no move to leave. Instead, she leaned over the bed, drawing her mouth close to Marie-Thérèse's ear. "Let no one in you do not know, Your Majesty. Accept no gift from any stranger."

The Queen's drowsy eyes flickered. "What nonsense do you speak, child?"

"Your life depends upon it, I swear to you. Please do as I say. If not for you, then for your son and your grandson."

Marie-Thérèse's gaze lay captive in Jeanne's.

Jeanne dared to take the Queen's face in both her hands, her gaze piercing. "I will not allow you to be hurt. I will lay down my life for you if needs be.

"You...you would..." Marie-Thérèse, Queen of France, daughter of a king, became no more than a confused woman.

"You will do as I say, yes?" Jeanne insisted, hands still upon the Queen.

The glooming in Marie-Thérèse's eyes cleared; she nodded her acquiescence.

"For my children, and for you, I will do as you say."

* * *

Jeanne returned to her family's quarters frustrated and emotionally exhausted: her time with Olympe, so dear yet so maddening; her moments with the Queen, so daring and bold; and through it all her worry for

Henri and his success with her father. She had spent an entire soirée in the company of some friends, the whole time searching everywhere for Henri and her father, but nowhere were they to be found, and their absence only heightened her anxiety.

Jeanne found herself in the empty suite, forgoing attendance at the King's *Coucher*, for she refused to wear the mask of congeniality any longer. Strangely, she hoped to find her father at home, to glean from his comportment what had transpired that day, but even in this, she was denied.

Disheartened, she threw herself down in one of the sitting room's cushioned chairs, dropping her arms dejectedly in her lap, flopping them upon her air-filled skirts, and looked around. In the grate a small fire burned merrily, the first of the season, she believed; it was the first night when the cool, crisp air of an autumn evening chilled the vast chateau. Otherwise, the room appeared as always, the two chairs and the small dark wood table between them. An open parchment lay on its shiny surface; paper filled with a short missive written in a firm, tight hand. The signature at the bottom jumped out at Jeanne.

Jolting up, she grabbed the paper, eyes flitting across the lines of script.

Dear Comte de Moreuil,

I am in receipt of your letter and am aware and understanding of your difficult situation. I recant my withdrawal of our agreement from yesterday's letter. As my son is so enamored of your daughter, though to be truthful I have little notion from whence this desire should spring, we are willing to accept your payment and conditions. Three days hence our family will meet yours in the Chapel Royale, where our children will be wed.

Most sincerely yours,
Baron l'Haire

The paper shook in Jeanne's hands; she dropped it into her lap as if it burned her fingers. She stared at the parchment; it couldn't be real…naught more than a figment from a nightmare. The Polignacs had denounced her, yet somehow her father had managed to convince them of her worth once more; a death sentence. Grabbing the page fiercely off her lap, she crumpled it into a ball and put it back upon the table where she had found it. In the oppressive silence she heard minute, arrhythmic tics as the paper uncrumpled.

Jeanne stared at the ball of parchment, amazed, jumping in her seat as, with one loud click, the wad of paper flinched, now a hairsbreadth more open than a moment before.

Was it alive? Would it unfurl itself completely to lay bare the words, the truths, she longed to bar from her sight? No. No, thankfully, the effects of inertia ceased, and the ball of paper was still just that, though of a slightly larger circumference then when first formed. Still, Jeanne glared at it. But its inaction was not good enough, not by half.

Jeanne's long right arm thrust out, snatching the paper off the table and throwing it into the heart of the fire with superb accuracy.

The small burst of flame testifying to its true death calmed her. Lowering her long, dark lashes, her chest rising and falling with a deep, cleansing breath, Jeanne lulled.

* * *

At first, Jeanne thought it part of her dream, the screaming voice came from her mind only and even though she turned and saw Bernadette asleep beside her, she too slept. The strange shadows in the room cast by a single, guttering candle intensified the surreal moment.

The door to her bedchamber burst open, crashing against the opposite wall with a crack of plaster. The bright light of candelabra and fire surged in, and Jeanne blinked against its harshness. A lone figure stood in the doorway, a dark, foreboding silhouette.

"You will not disobey me."

Jeanne immediately recognized her father's hate-filled growl; she jumped out of bed, grabbed her flimsy dressing gown, wrapping it protectively around her.

Her brown curls in complete sleep-wrecked disarray, eyes still swollen from sleep, Jeanne stood tall and righteous against him.

"Not this time, father. Not anymore."

"Do not speak so, Jeanne." An urgent whisper came from behind her.

Jeanne spun; a wide-awake Bernadette trembled in fear as she watched from the confines of the bed's covers.

"Go back to sleep, dear." Jeanne tossed the words over her shoulder, striding from the room. She shut the door quietly behind her, pushing past her father though she trembled in fear to draw near him.

Jeanne saw her mother sitting quietly in the salon, one elbow perched on the arm of the chair, head rested in the palm of her hand. Adelaide looked up at her daughter, studying the face, searching it. Slowly, a tender smile formed on her lips.

Jeanne took a deep breath, taking in all the support and love from that small smile. Pushing her shoulders back, she turned and faced her father.

"You will still get your wish, sir. I will be gone from your sight. You will never have to see me again if you so choose."

Gaston's anger hung in the air like dense fog on a cool morning.

"I have made an agreement, and you will stand by it." The short, stout man stood with his arms tightly entwined across his chest, a boulder that would not move.

"The baron broke the arrangement. You could have left it alone. Why did you not? Why could you not?" Jean-Luc's voice demanded.

Gaston flinched back at the sound, at his daughter's knowledge. It seemed only to entice his anger into rage.

"Because it was my order, and for once in your miserable life, you will do as you are told."

"I will find love and happiness with Henri, and you may pretend I never existed. Why will this not satisfy you?"

Gaston took two quick steps toward his daughter, his face just inches from her chin, glaring at her.

"What makes you think you deserve such happiness when your own life has brought me nothing but dismay?" Gaston poked an emphatic finger at his own chest.

Jeanne swallowed hard; in her father's lined face, rigid and trembling with anger, the truth of this man, that his dissatisfaction in her he perpetrated, not what she deserved. Jeanne saw her father clearly for the first time in her life.

"Your dismay, your unhappiness, is what you choose to see, what you choose to experience in your own life. It did not have to be like this."

Her heart broke at what could have been between them, but it was as if he didn't see her, didn't hear her. She knew now…he never had.

"You will marry Polignac in two days," Gaston spat, the hot spittle flicked against her skin.

"I will not." Once more Jean-Luc spoke, low and threatening.

Gaston reacted to the power of it, the threat of it, and roared against it, raising his tightly clenched fist to his ear, posed and aimed at Jeanne. "YOU WILL!"

"Gaston!"

Adelaide grabbed her husband's arm, halting the strike aimed at her daughter.

"Henri d'Aubigne is the nephew of François Scarron."

Time stopped. A void possessed them.

Gaston and Jeanne turned to Adelaide with the same confounded, gawking stare. The calm, self-possessed woman allowed the silence to linger, allowed the true import of her words to make their way into the fuming consciousness of these two combatants.

"He is the son of Madame Scarron's sister, the Baroness de Berry."

Being the son of a baron came with some prestige and power; being the nephew of the King's confidant, and perhaps his latest lover, rendered much, much more.

"He never told me," Jeanne whispered aloud without intention.

Adelaide smiled, reaching up to tenderly brush some curls off her daughter's comely face.

"Perhaps he wanted you to love him for who he is, not who he is related to." She smiled with small, wicked mischief, her golden eyes, so much like Henri's, twinkling at her child. "There are some people who have no care for the pompous ways of the court."

Jeanne snuffled at her mother's sarcasm, still confounded by the truth of Henri. Did it change how she felt about him? Yes, of course it did. She loved him more; she felt it burst within her heart. His refusal to use his position to wallow in the machinations of a nobleman, to foster a better position and drown himself in the simple, meaningless life of a courtier, proved him to be worthy of all her respect and devotion.

Like her, he wanted to be something other than what his birth demanded of him.

"I do not give a damn who he is. You will never marry him," Gaston barked, breaking the calm silence and Jeanne's contemplations.

Mother and daughter blanched, incredulous. The man's rage, his thirst for power and control, still possessed him wholly; sallow skin burned with red anger, black eyes narrowed to mere slits between wrinkled lids.

Adelaide set her jaw tight against his furor. "You know what is being said about Madame Scarron, Gaston," The hushed hissed came with fatal strength. "She is the voice of the King's conscience. One word against us by her tongue and we are finished."

"To hell with Scarron," Gaston screamed, fisted arms pulsing in the air about his face. His manic actions exploded from thoughts bereft of sanity. "I will ruin him even if it ruins me."

"You are spiting yourself, you silly man," Adelaide screamed back at him, freezing him, and Jeanne, with her own ferociousness. Never had they heard her speak thusly. Never before had she raised her voice at her husband; never had she questioned his authority in such an overt manner. "Do not let your vile maliciousness cloud your judgment. You will appear a fool at the feet of Louis."

Adelaide knew her husband, knew what it would take to make him see the consequences of his rash actions. To appear the fool before the King, to suffer his ignominy, would be to make Gaston's worst nightmare become a reality.

Gaston clamped his lips tightly together, all blood rushing from the pale, thin skin. In this fuming silence, he turned from his wife and daughter, heading for the door out of the apartments. Reaching for the handle, he turned back to them.

"Let it be, but let it be on your head." He gestured to his wife with a crooked finger as he opened the apartment's door.

"Gaston!" The harsh call came from the voice of Jean-Luc but it was Jeanne who strode toward her father. "If something should happen, if anything happens to my mother every again...," she stretched to full height, lowering her head to within inches of his, "...you will not live to see another day. I know...many who would gladly do the deed for me."

Gaston's head flinched back, face blanching. "What? What nonsense do you—"

"Not another hand upon her, father, not ever again," Jean-Luc thundered.

Slowly and backward, Gaston tried to escape the creature that was his daughter.

"Do you understand me?!" The being demanded, face as black as a storm.

They saw no one, nothing, but each other; their gaze at war.

Gaston stepped through the doorway, from the threshold he replied, "I understand." As if to show a power he did not possess, he slammed the door behind him.

In the tranquility left in his wake, the reality of Jeanne's fate entered the deep recesses of her brain, and the scorching emotions—happiness, freedom, relief—rushed through her. She threw her arms around her mother with such force, she almost brought them both to the ground.

"Ah, Maman, *merci, merci*," Jeanne laughed and cried, covering her mother's dear face with kisses and tears. "You have saved my life, Maman. How can I ever thank you?"

Adelaide chuckled and sobbed along with her daughter, allowing the dear child to smother her with her affections. "It was my life to give you as I did seventeen years ago. Live it in love and happiness. That is all I would ever ask."

"I will, Maman, I swear to you, I will." Jeanne refused to release her mother, pulling and pushing her into a dance of joyous relief.

Adelaide stilled her with her hands on Jeanne's shoulders, pushing her back to look closely at her daughter's shining face.

"Are you sure this is the man you want?"

Jeanne nodded, hair flying about her face with her exertions. "Oh, *oui*, Maman. He is more than I ever dreamed possible."

"Can you be ... can you live ... subservient to him?" Adelaide asked the hardest question of all.

"I will not have to," Jeanne spoke as if she prayed. "He loves me, and he accepts me as his equal and will treat me so, at least in private. This is all a woman of our time can ask for, is it not?"

Adelaide heaved a sigh of relief as her daughter threw her arms about her once more. "True, *ma chère*, too true."

~Twenty-Eight~

Jeanne attended chapel the next morning, sitting through an extra-long sermon from Bishop Bossuet, one of the most famous preachers in France. He had been the Dauphin's teacher until the heir grew to adulthood, at which time Louis had made Bossuet a bishop. His orations were beautiful sophistry but unbearably long, especially today.

With Bernadette by her side, Jeanne took part in the morning's promenade with Louis, taking a different route than before, one to highlight the fall vegetation. In the afternoon they browsed the aisles of the vestibule where so many courtiers flocked. Everywhere she went, everywhere she looked, Jeanne looked for Henri, but he was nowhere to be found. Jeanne felt as if she were trapped in a nightmare, the sort where she ran and dashed about, but the one thing she sought, the one thing she held most dear, was always kept an arm's length away.

"Perhaps he is on duty?" Bernadette finally offered gently later that evening. They'd finished their third walk through the four rooms hosting the evening's soirée, creating a cross pattern among the many groups, both large and small, of twittering courtiers, still with not a glimpse of the face burning in Jeanne's mind.

The need to find Henri, to tell him all that had transpired in the one day since they were last together, burned her. To tell him the idea of a life together was no more a dream but a reality spurred her on her manic search. But the other words, those she must, as duty demanded, share with him as well, scared her just as frantically. Jeanne was determined to tell Henri of her covert life as Jean-Luc; she knew now, without doubt, she was both Jeanne and Jean-Luc, it was no pretense.

She would not solidify their betrothal without the truth being revealed; her honor would not allow it. But the fear of what repercussions the truth would precipitate, the abject dread that he would shun her, turned Jeanne's stomach to the point of nausea.

"Perhaps," Jeanne answered distractedly. Straining her head and the high plumage of piled hair and fontange back and forth to no avail became too much. "But I can take this waiting no longer."

Without another word, Jeanne began to walk away from her sister.

Bernadette reached out and grabbed Jeanne by the arm, halting her exit.

"You cannot go by yourself," her younger sister beseeched her.

"You are right, *ma chère*, Jeanne cannot." Jeanne released her sister's grip, smiled, and rushed from the room.

* * *

Jean-Luc walked into the rowdy pub and searched the dark confines. Bodies filled the tavern to the brim tonight; Musketeers, merchants, peasants, every sort of everyday people took up every chair, and the many without a seat stood along the walls. The raucous voices, raised high in laughter, song, and jeers, rose to almost deafening heights, and Jean-Luc knew it would do no good to call out his name.

He walked a clockwise path through the crowds, the smells of roasting meat over the pit assaulting his senses as he answered with a small wave and a nod the calls from those growing familiar with Jean-Luc.

He turned breath stopping, heart pounding in his chest. There he was, with Antoine, at a small back table. Jean-Luc rushed to him, already smiling.

Reaching the scarred wood table, her buoyancy burst at Henri's appearance. His clothes hung messily upon his body, his hair mussed; he slouched at the table in a slovenly manner neither Jeanne nor Jean-Luc had never seen him adopt before, barely holding his head inches off the table with a bent arm. When his mournful gaze rose to him, he felt a moment of shared despair.

“Ah, Jean-Luc, come join us.” Henri’s foot kicked out from under the table, pushing a vacant chair toward his friend. “Come help me drown my sorrows.”

Jean-Luc heard the slurred enunciation of his words and wondered just how much drowning he had already done. If only he had found him sooner, how much sorrow could have been unfelt. There was no doubt Gaston’s denial distressed him so.

Jean-Luc took the chair and nodded to Antoine, who sat in silent support of his distraught friend.

“Monsieur.” Antoine filled an empty mug with wine and slid it across the table.

Jean-Luc caught it, allowing only a few drops to splash across the surface.

“I won’t drink with you, sir.” He inclined his head to Henri, finding it difficult to speak in her deep with the excitement frantic to burst forth. “But I will drink to you and your future wife.”

Henri began to nod in clueless agreement, stopped, and puckered his face. With eyes narrowed and brows furrowed, he stared at Jean-Luc, lifting his head off his hand, the muscles of his neck bulging.

“What do you say, sir?” The urgency in Henri’s voice would not be denied.

Jean-Luc raised a glass in salute. “I drink to you and your future wife, Jeanne du Bois.”

The dagger tip nipped at Jean-Luc’s throat before he realized what had happened. His mug flew out of his hand, spilling the rich, dark red liquid over the dirty floor. Henri held the weapon against his skin, its sharp point pressed harshly against tender skin into.

Antoine jumped from his chair, leaning forward and grabbing at Henri to try to stop him. Jean-Luc stared at the emotionally ravaged face now just an inch from his own.

"Do not toy with me, sir," Henri growled from deep in his throat. "I had thought my life completely over. Do not make me believe otherwise unless it is true. I could not bear it."

The scarcely contained sob crackled in his voice, the utter heartbreak darkened his bereft eyes, the body trembled with emotion; 'Jeanne' longed to throw her arms around him, console him with the heart belonging so completely to him.

"I would never hurt you so, Henri," Jean-Luc said, speaking for both her selves. "I have come from Jeanne herself with the news."

Henri's desperate gaze raked the face before him. With slow, hesitant movements, he lowered the knife, withdrawing his hands across the uneven surface of the table as he sat back in his chair.

"Tell me all," he demanded, unmoving in his chair, holding his breath as the fate of the rest of his life tottered in the balance. Antoine released him but did not retake his chair; instead, he stood behind Henri, keeping his hands firmly upon his friend's shoulders.

Jean-Luc sat forward, rubbing the skin where the dagger had nicked.

"Madame du Bois has … convinced her husband that Jeanne would have a wonderful life as your wife." To say the words aloud was to know a never known joy. "They are at your disposal to finalize the arrangements."

Jean-Luc watched as the words became truth in Henri's mind. He swallowed hard, swallowed again. He blinked back tears welling without shame. Leaning forward, he raised a hand to Jean-Luc.

Jean-Luc responded, lifting his own, and Henri pumped it. "Thank you," he whispered, and the smile spread across his mustached lips.

Henri jumped up, releasing a cry of delight whooping through the room, making heads swivel toward him in surprise and curiosity. He turned around to his other friend behind him.

"Did you hear, Antoine? She will be my wife!" Henri threw his brawny arms around his friend, forcing the quiet man to jump up and down, sharing Henri's delight.

"I did, I did." Antoine rolled his eyes at Jean-Luc; his elated smile told her the depth of his pleasure.

"I must go. I must see—"

"Henri! Antoine!" The loud, booming voice of Gerard ceased all other sound in the small café. The giant of a man hurled his way through the room, the patrons in his path jumping out of the way before they were crushed by his rushing, mammoth body.

"Ah, Jean-Luc, it is good you are here as well," Gerard said, reaching the table. "You must all come now. Laurent has just sent word from his post on the chateau's gate. Five, maybe six masked men have just slipped onto the castle grounds."

Jean-Luc jumped to her feet, all other thoughts save that of her Queen's life forgot. Evil moved on the Queen again.

Henri grabbed his jacket from its fallen place on the floor, completely sober in the face of danger, and the four warriors rushed from the café, overturning chairs, spilling revelers here and there in their haste to be gone.

Out on the street, the cool night air did nothing to douse their urgency; they ran.

Thoughts pulled on the mind in every direction; Jeanne—Jean-Luc—wanted nothing more than to get Henri alone, to tell him the truth of who they were, but the life of the Queen was at stake and both selves had sworn to protect it.

"We must try to take them alive," Gerard growled. The quick clacking of their boot heels on the cobble street sounded like the hooves of a galloping horse.

"We must save her life at all costs," Antoine remarked, rapid breath streaming from his nostrils, white, eerie vapors in the cold air.

"But alive," Henri agreed with Gerard. "All we need is for one to testify against the leader of this dastardly conspiracy and the threat will be thwarted for good."

Jean-Luc nodded, comprehending. To sever the legs of evil would be to slow it; to remove it once and for all, they needed to stop it at its core. Not only would it save the life of her Queen, it would vindicate Jean-Luc's existence; fulfill his purpose.

Reaching the side gate of Versailles, Laurent waited for them impatiently. The torches near the front gardens of the palace glowed but dimly; their sight carried no farther than the guard post.

"They went that way. Quickly," Laurent urged, an outstretched finger pointing toward the south wing. He could but watch anxiously as they ran from him, forced to remain at his post with a long night of duty still ahead.

Gerard took the lead, Antoine beside him; Henri and Jean-Luc close behind. Crouching down, using the shrubs and bushes as cover, the four stealthy soldiers made their way where Laurent had pointed. They exchanged no words, using only hand gestures to communicate.

Jean-Luc felt her heart beat to a flurried rhythm; eyes firm on Henri, taking instructions from his eyes and hands. Almost at the outer wall of the south wing, they had still seen nothing.

Gerard stopped, snapping a hand in the air, halting all movement. With his gloved hand, he pointed to the far corner of the building. A small, pale light appeared amid the stone; in its glow, shapes moved...human shapes.

The three other warriors nodded; they saw them. Antoine raised two fingers, pointed to himself and Gerard then to the left of the opening. The same two fingers pointed to Henri and Jean-Luc then to the right of the aperture.

Nods of understanding. They set off, silent on the balls of their feet, swords held still and quiet in their scabbards.

The position on the wall where the light emanated from revealed no door. Jean-Luc, armed with vast knowledge of the secret passages of the castle, knew what to look for.

He ran his gloved hand along the wall, looking for a slim line of demarcation.

The three men watched as Jean-Luc's probing stopped, fingertips disappearing into a crack. One hand traced the line of a rectangle, then pushed at the corner. The stone slab gave way but moved no more than an inch.

Gerard pulled Jean-Luc away. Pressing his brawny shoulder against the indented portion of the wall, Gerard pushed, a low grunt escaping from between his grinding teeth. His efforts created a thin opening, but one wide enough for each man, even Gerard, to slip through and into a passage.

Once inside, Gerard used his strength to close the egress behind them; they would use any barrier to stop the cutthroats to escape.

Before them lay a small, narrow passageway, dark and dank. Pale light shone from some unknown source up ahead. Little dirt grimed the stone floor, no cobwebs hung to capture them; a well-traveled path.

The Musketeers, and the one who wished to be one, bent at the waist; the ceiling so low not even Jean-Luc, the shortest of the group, could straighten. One behind the other they tiptoed, the corridor too narrow to move abreast.

They came upon an intersection; three possible directions lay before them.

"How do we know where—" Jean-Luc began.

"Shh," Antoine commanded, now leading the procession. "Listen."

Not a one moved, not a breath taken among them. Straining their ears, they heard it: the shuffling and stepping of boot-clad feet coming from the left corridor.

"We follow the sound." Antoine gave a dangerous smile, a flick of his brows, and led them away.

Jean-Luc had no idea where they were in the castle; the dark, winding tunnel disoriented him. The faint light from ahead gave birth to gnarled and twisted shadows behind them. The light glowed brighter, the sounds louder. The passageway expanded; they stood up.

"Behind you!" a voice screamed through the dark, cutting the silence like a cleaver.

From behind Antoine, the others rushed forward.

All four spilled into an open space, an empty chamber; six black-clad, masked men stood, stunned out of movement, one with a hand on the only door.

"Attack!" Gerard growled, face gnarled by militancy.

The shing of swords loosened rang out; the clang of steel upon steel replied.

Gerard engaged two, as did Antoine; their arms wheeling frantically, spinning, plying swords and daggers.

Henri and Jean-Luc took on one each.

Jean-Luc quivered with the power, the anger at these miscreants, surged through him, igniting strength. The pommel of the sword in hand seemed as if it grew skin, became a part of his being. Charging with an animal's growl, the lessons of Uncle Jules coming instinctively to mind. In the name of the Queen, no rules or codes of conduct adhered.

He flayed the sword overhead, all the passionate fury powering each thrust and slash. Mouth hung open with effort, saliva dripped from lips. Feinting, beating away, lunging back in terce; he had the opponent on the run, able only to defend himself and retreat and retreat.

The sound of the battle the only sounds. Grunting and growling, the criminals sought the death of their enemies and nothing less.

Bone hit bone as fists, elbows, and feet engaged in this violent brawl. Hiss. Swish. Swords cut the air savagely.

A moan of pain, feet slipping on stone. Jean-Luc knew that voice.

A quick look over a shoulder. Henri faltered, his opponent's sword at his throat.

Thrashing at the man before him, Jean-Luc roared, jumping closer, shocking him, using the jolt to push him away and against the wall. Two steps back now, kicking out behind him, hitting Henri's assailant in the back, evoking no injury, throwing him off guard and away from Henri.

Henri sprung up out of his crouch, attacking, gaining the upper hand once more.

Jean-Luc heaved relief, spinning back to his opponent.

The villain hung halfway down the wall, back pressed up against the stone, keeping him from slipping the rest of the way down. A dagger gleamed in his other hand.

Grabbing his hair, Jean-Luc yanked the man's head toward him then away, ramming his opponent's head against the stone.

His skull shattered with a grotesque crack.

Jean-Luc watched him slither to the floor. Was he dead or just unconscious?

Stepping toward him. Jean-Luc kicked the dagger, sending it flying away from the thug's hand. He turned back, turned to the sword hand, intending to do the same.

The hum attacked Jean-Luc's ears, embraced him, wiping all other sound from existence. The cold descended upon his body, a freezing breeze that never abated. Jean-Luc looked down...into the open eyes of her enemy.

Slowly, through shifting time, Jean-Luc turned from their evil sparkle, gaze floating around the chamber, barely recognizing where he was...why he was there. His head lowered, as though pushed by a force from above him.

The sword stuck out of his chest. He stared at it, studied it, having no idea what it was... what it meant.

Surely this is someone else's body, for I feel no pain.

Thoughts became disjointed, nonsensical. His mind said to reach for the weapon impaling him, to pull it out, but his arms would not answer the command.

Jean-Luc's legs gave way as if they mutated from flesh to fluid.

His skull hit the hard floor, bounced.

Somehow his gaze moved, watched his friends battle. The scarlet of blood splotched all around them, savagely bright against the shades of gray of both men and stone chamber. From within the tunnel of vision he watched as Henri triumphed over his foe; a strange peace came to dwell within.

He turned, allowing weary eyes to close as they so longed to do.

"Nooo!" The wretched scream echoed again and again.

Jean-Luc opened his eyes again, though the pain now coursed through him, enveloping and crushing all other senses. He felt a cold dampness on his stomach and reached out to it.

Raising the hand, finding it covered in thick, sticky blood.

Henri's face hovered above.

Who does he see? Which me does he see?

Awareness, remembrance of who he...she...was could not be grasped. Henri's frenzied, fear-ravaged features offered no clues. Bringing the blood-dripping hand to touch the face, fingers quailed about the mouth, found the mustache.

Ah, I am Jean-Luc. I must remember that.

But at that moment, all cognitive thought escaped.

* * *

Nausea bubbled up in his intestines. He lifted Jean-Luc's head, placing it gently in his lap. Sweat dripped off Henri's nose and onto the blood-covered face of his injured friend.

The sounds of the fight behind him faded away. Someone came to stand beside him and he looked up quickly, fearing an assailant, seeing Antoine studying their comrade's wound.

"Not him," Henri whispered as if in prayer. "He is so young. He fights so bravely."

"Feel for his heart." Antoine crouched down beside him.

Henry bit at one fingertip of his gloved hand, pulling off the gauntlet with his teeth. He pressed two fingers against Jean-Luc's neck, the blood from his face running onto Henri's hand.

"It is faint, but it is there." He brought his hand away. Reaching under his shirt, he pulled out his cravat and began wiping at Jean-Luc's face, despising how the fluid tainted the young man's countenance.

He wiped at the mouth.

His hand stilled, trembling an inch above the skin.

Had Jean-Luc's mustache…moved? Incredulous, he wiped again.

Life stopped; time hung suspended and motionless. The mustache was no longer on the face but on the cloth. Henri stared at features so familiar to him, recognizable as not one person in his life…but two.

"My God." Antoine gasped.

Eyes fluttered open. The unfocused gaze caught upon Henri's face, tears welling within them.

"Please, Henri," Jeanne whispered. "Please do not be angry with me, I beg you."

She coughed, and a small trickle of blood bubbled up and out of her lips. A depth of pain hit Henri like a sword shoved deep in his gut, churning. He blotted at the dark fluid with his cloth.

"Shh, do not speak," he said gently to her, to the only woman he had ever loved, to the young cavalier he respected, to the soldier who had saved his life more than once.

But Jeanne would not be stilled. She shook her head with small, agitated movements, her eyes never leaving his face.

"Do you remember what you asked me once?" A heartbreaking, sweet smile spread across her trembling lips. "You asked if I trained to be a Musketeer, and I told you it was my greatest desire."

Henri nodded, unable to speak.

"It was," Jeanne mumbled. "This was the only way. Please do not hate me for it."

Henri threw his arms around her, squeezing her with his agonizing emotions.

"I could never, would never. I love you," he told her his truth.

Tears trailed slowly down Jeanne's bloodstained face. "You have given me a love I never thought I would find. You have given me a life I thought could never be mine. I thank you."

Her tender words pushed him to the edge of despair.

"Stay with me, do not go," he implored her, pleading with her.

With a flick of his head, Henri motioned to Antoine. They spoke with no words; Antoine winced but nodded. With trembling hands, he yanked the sword from her gullet.

Jeanne moaned and thrashed as more blood gushed from her stomach. Pulling out his own scarf, Antoine knelt on the other side of Jeanne and pushed the cloth against her wound; the blood came too fast, the sticky fluid flooded every thread within seconds.

"Did we do it? Did we get them? Ish t' Queen safe?" Jeanne slurred, trying to lift her head, to scan the room.

"*Oui*, all is well. They will not harm her, ever," he assured her.

"Antoine? Gerard?" She called their names and cast her nearly vacant sight about, searching for their faces.

"Here," Antoine assured her.

"Beside you," Gerard growled from next to Antoine.

Pleasure meekly touched upon her features.

"One...for all..." The words slipped out of her trembling lips.

Henri dropped his head; Gerard shook his. But they would not deny her.

"And all for one," the three responded solemnly.

Her hand grasped, floundering at her side.

"What is it? What do you want?" Henri implored.

"My sword," she breathed. "Where my sword?"

Antoine turned behind him, grabbing the *colichemarde* and placing it into her grasping palm.

Jeanne smiled and heaved a shallow breath of relief; her eyes fluttered to a close.

"I felt it. I felt the power. It was … *magnifique*."

~Twenty-Nine~

A band of solemn Musketeers let the rope holding the casket slip slowly through their hands, lowering it into the earth where it would lay. The circles of attendants wound round and round about them, tears trickling down many a face, man and woman.

The bright stone that would mark the body's place shimmered against the deep green grass as dappling sun flickered through the dancing orange oak leaves overhead, their somnolent rustle a gentle song of lament.

"Into your hands, Lord," the dark robed priest concluded his service, "we commend Jeanne Yvette Dumas Dubois' spirit." With a silent sign of the cross, the holy man left the gravesite and the mourners gathered around it.

The final words spoken, the casket in its eternal place, the many grieving slowly stepped away, scattering like leaves upon the wind.

From Henri's side, Adelaide knelt down by the grave, her heavy gray silk skirts billowing around her. Reaching out, she traced the letters of her daughter's name carved into the white marble maker.

Henri stepped to the grave hole, staring into it with longing of all sorts.

"As you requested."

The words came from behind him. Turning he found Antoine, a mahogany box the size of a crate balanced upon his arms.

Henri dipped his head in thanks, accepting that which was offered and placed it on the ground before him. Like Adelaide, he traced the name etched upon it, a shorter name but one that symbolized no lesser a being.

The others came to him then; together the four men used the ropes and lowered this casket to sit upon the other. In it lay a hat, a fake mustache, even a pincushion.

"He is gone as well." The warbling voice of Jules Henri du Mas pronounced.

Henri stood, placing a hand on the older man's shoulder. "He is, good sir, but he will not be forgot." Reaching a hand out, knowing Laurent would be there with it, Henri took the slender sword and offered it to Jules.

With trembling hands, the man took back the *colichemarde.*

"They would both want you to have it," Henri whispered.

Jules could but nod, lips a fine, tight line as tears drew a track down his face.

"What is in that box?" Bernadette had come upon them unnoticed. "Why do you put it with my sister?"

Beside her stood Adelaide held by Raol; Gaston had retired to his country estate without attending his daughter's funeral service. He would not have been welcomed, not by those who knew his truth, not by the spirits that welcomed his daughter into their arms.

"Henri?" Adelaide stepped away from the cradle of her surviving children. "What are you about?"

Henri dropped his head, knuckling his brow. But when he looked up, a tender smile graced his lips.

Stepping to Adelaide's side, he offered her his arm; Raol relinquished his mother to the man with a nod.

"Would you like me to tell you of your daughter, Madame?" Henri cooed, a one full of love and pride stronger than his grief. "Would you like to know who she really was? Why her death is one she would have wished for?"

Adelaide slowly wrapped her arm around his, moist eyes as big as the sun intent upon his face.

"I believe I would, monsieur."

Together the small group walked from the grave. Above it, a pure white griffin soared.

~The End~

~Epilogue~

For the next year, Louis XIV continued his hedonistic, promiscuous lifestyle. During these months the Queen continued to suffer a growing debilitation. Louis spent hours by Marie-Thérèse's bedside, as did François Scarron, and they prayed together over the Queen's soul. The Sun King grew closer and closer to François as he slowly but inexorably turned away from Athénaïs.

On July 30, 1683, the Queen died. The true cause of her death was never determined, but many theories abound—including those suggesting that she was poisoned.

A few months later, Louis secretly married Françoise d'Aubigné Scarron, now the Marquise de Maintenon; his life changed completely and inexorably. It is theorized that Françoise turned him to more devout religious practices, while some say it was the fear of eternal damnation that changed the King, fearing, in middle age, that he would indeed pay for all his flamboyant, avaricious, and lascivious years in the burning hell of afterlife. Athénaïs remained at court for a few more years, her golden light flickering out as her desperate attempts to win back the King's heart failed miserably.

Louis became entirely devoted to Françoise and deeply religious. Though he still lived grandly, he began to use his own fortunes to support his military, melting down precious sculptures for their monetary value, selling paintings, masterpieces, to the highest bidders. King Louis the Great, for that is how history remembers him, lived until the ripe age of seventy-six, passing of gangrene on September 1, 1715. Louis had reigned for seventy-two years, longer than any other King who came before or after him. He outlived most of his contemporaries, including his brother and Athénaïs, his son, and two of his grandchildren, leaving his great-grandson the Crown when this child, Louis XV, was only five years old, a year older than Louis XIV had been when he succeeded to the throne. The Sun King's reign glows still in the annals of time as one of the grandest in all history. A period of time when France reigned as well, if a bit gaudily in its opulence, over the rest of the world.

The Musketeers continued to guard the Kings and Queens of France up until 1791 and the Revolution, where many of them lost their lives doing their unwavering duty. Their reputation has sustained the passing of years, and they are still considered to be the noblest and most renowned soldiers the world has ever known.

~Author's Note~

To assume women do not possess a warrior's heart has been just that, an assumption, a false illusion, for women have been fighting for thousands of years. They've fought to stay alive in a world where they were thought of as no more than chattel; they've fought for votes, the right to be employed, equal pay for equal work, against being used as merely amusements, for their children and families...and the right to do with our bodies as we see fit. The woman warrior was the inspiration for this book; she lives within me.

The imaginary lives of my fictional characters occur within the framework of historical events and customs, architecture and artwork, based, as much as possible, upon notable research aided by imagination and supposition. In some cases, liberties were taken as to when things transpired. For example, the descriptions of Versailles assume almost all the renovation was complete, when in truth, in 1682, there was still more than a decade of work yet to occur. The Feast of Saint Louis as described within actually took place a few years before the setting of this story.

And, while Captain d'Artagnan, and the man upon whom the iconic fictional character was based, did serve as the leader of the Musketeers for many years, he had, sadly, passed away nine years before the setting of this work. His impression on me, which began in 1973 when I first saw Michael York portray him in The Three Musketeers (originally released by Film Trust S.A.), demanded his inclusion in this piece.

~Acknowledgments~

It is a wondrous gift for any artist/creative to be given the opportunity to return to a previous work, improving and evolving it with aptitude gained over the many years and the many works that came since its first inception. *The Courtier of Versailles* is the retelling of my first book, *The Courtier's Secret.* My first book... the book that started my career, the book that brought me my first agent, my first publisher. Said publisher requested that I completely change the ending. So amazed and overwhelmed that dreams of becoming a published author were within my grasp, I agreed. And yet, as the years passed, I regretted doing so. That story was not the one my muse demanded I tell... *The Courtier of Versailles,* however, is. I will be forever grateful to Next Chapter for allowing me and my muse to tell the true tale that lived within.

No historical fiction is possible without great sources of information and the willingness of others to share their expertise. Researchers and nonfiction authors make the fact-based fancies of fiction authors possible. Particular works I'd like to acknowledge, and recommend to those with interest in these characters and their time period, are: The Sun King and His Loves (1982), by Lucy Norton; The Splendid Century (1957), by W. H. Lewis; The Story of Versailles (2005), by Francis Loring Payne; By the Sword: A History of Gladiators, Musketeers, Samurai, Swashbucklers, and Olympic Champions (2002), by Richard Cohen, and Europe in the Age of Louis XIV (1969), by Ragnhild Hatton.

I'd also like to acknowledge the help and guidance of The Research Center at the Chateau Versailles and the Rhode Island Fencing Academy. Innumerable Web sites provided invaluable material, including Royalty.nu, The World of Royalty (http://www.royalty.nu); Great Fencing Masters of History
(http://www.acfencers.com/fencingmasters.html); The Association for Renaissance Martial Arts (http://www.thearma.org/); and Internet Modern History Source Book
(http://www.fordham.edu/halsall/mod/modsbook.html).

And of course, to Monsieur Alexandre Dumas, I doff my ostrich feather–plumed hat.

With an interest in history, we pay homage to the lives that came before our own, giving purpose to them by learning and experiencing all that they did; by delighting in their achievements and grieving with their sorrows, we acknowledge the progress and evolution of Human Beings and their Spirits.

~A Reading Group Guide~

THE COURTIER OF VERSAILLES
Donna Russo Morin

ABOUT THIS GUIDE

The following questions are intended to enhance your group's reading of THE COURTIER OF VERSAILLES.

~DISCUSSION QUESTIONS~

1. How would you characterize Jeanne du Bois? What is it about her that makes her unique from other women of her era? How do these differences affect her life, both positively and negatively?

2. In Chapter One, Gaston du Bois pulls his daughter through the palace "like a dog on a leash." How is this similar to his manner of parenthood? What are the consequences of his behavior, not only immediate but long-term? How do his attitudes toward his three children differ, and why?

3. In Chapter One, Jeanne describes her frustrations at the limited choices in her life to her mother, saying, "I cannot bear a life where the most momentous decisions I have to make are what to wear and what to serve. It is too meaningless and trivial. I want to learn things, study, be a part of the world." Do you feel the women of today experience the same problems? In what way is it the same? How have things changed? How does Jeanne's attitude frame the entire story?

4. How do Jeanne and her friends Olympe and Lynette differ in their desires for their lives? How are they all representative of the women of their era? In what way do they all ultimately receive what they want?

5. What does Jeanne mean when she says, in Chapter Two, "How can my love of God be measured by how deeply I curtsey to the nuns?" What other events and statements reveal her inner feelings of religion, and how are they juxtaposed to her feelings about God?

6. Why do you think Jeanne's Uncle Jules helps her with her disguise, enabling and encouraging her to lead a double life?

7. Athénaïs, the Marquise de Montespan, was one of the few married women to become a King's mistress. What factors allowed it? What in her past ignites the fear of François Scarron in King Louis' life?

8. Is it just an advantageous match Gaston demands for his daughter or is there more to his insistence upon Jeanne marrying Percy de Polignac? What other advantages were there for arranged marriages? Could such a practice be possible in today's society?

9. How do the memories of the Fronde affect Louis and the manner in which he rules? Is his response reasonable? Why did his people continue to love him, both peasant and noble alike, regardless of his ill-treatment of them?

10. To what extent does the particular time in history in which the story is set influence the tone of the story?

11. Why does Henri d'Aubigne hide his family connections? What does he fear would happen if they became known? How does his behavior differ from most others of the age?

12. In Chapter Thirteen, Queen Marie-Thérèse d'Autriche utters the famous quote, "Let them eat cake." Which other Queen of France is most

often, and erroneously, credited for the divisive statement?

13. In Chapter Eighteen, Jeanne describes the frightened look of the deer it is hunted down. What does the deer symbolize for her, and in what ways?

14. As Henri escorts Jeanne's mother away from her grave, what does he mean when he asks, 'Why her (Jeanne's) death is one she would have wished for?'?

15. Stories of Musketeers have enjoyed popularity since the first, written by Alexandre Dumas in the mid-1800s. What is it about the tales of these men that is so enduring? Are there any similarities to another group of like-minded warriors in modern-day stories? How are they alike?

16. The truth of this story lies in the internal conflict raging within Jeanne. What is that conflict?

Dear reader,

We hope you enjoyed reading *The Courtier of Versailles.* Please take a moment to leave a review, even if it's a short one. Your opinion is important to us.

Discover more books by Donna Russo Morin at https://www.nextchapter.pub/authors/author-donna-russo-morin

Want to know when one of our books is free or discounted? Join the newsletter at http://eepurl.com/bqqB3H

Best regards,
Donna Russo Morin and the Next Chapter Team

The Courtier of Versailles
ISBN: 978-4-86745-042-0 (Mass Market)

Published by
Next Chapter
1-60-20 Minami-Otsuka
170-0005 Toshima-Ku, Tokyo
+818035793528
4th May 2021

Lightning Source UK Ltd.
Milton Keynes UK
UKHW040641270521
384468UK00001B/26